AUSTEN'S UNBECOMING CONJUNCTIONS

AUSTEN'S UNBECOMING CONJUNCTIONS

SUBVERSIVE LAUGHTER, EMBODIED HISTORY

Jillian Heydt-Stevenson

palgrave
macmillan

First published in hardcover in 2005 by
PALGRAVE MACMILLAN®
in the United States—a division of St. Martin's Press LLC,
175 Fifth Avenue, New York, NY 10010.

Where this book is distributed in the UK, Europe and the rest of the world,
this is by Palgrave Macmillan, a division of Macmillan Publishers Limited,
registered in England, company number 785998, of Houndmills,
Basingstoke, Hampshire RG21 6XS.

Palgrave Macmillan is the global academic imprint of the above companies
and has companies and representatives throughout the world.

Palgrave® and Macmillan® are registered trademarks in the United States,
the United Kingdom, Europe and other countries.

ISBN-13: 978–0–230–60248–9 paperback

Library of Congress Cataloging-in-Publication Data

Heydt-Stevenson, Jillian.
    Austen's Unbecoming Conjunctions : Subversive Laughter,
Embodied History
        p. cm.
    Includes bibliographical references and index.
    ISBN 1–4039–6410–6 (hardcover) 0–230–60248–7 (paperback)
        1. Austen, Jane, 1775–1817—Criticism and interpretation.
    2. Body, Human, in literature. 3. Humorous stories, English—History
And criticism. 4. Love stories, English—History and criticism. 5. Austen,
Jane, 1775–1817—Humor. 6. Sex in literature. I. Title.

PR4038.B17H49 2004
823'.7—dc22   2004044504

A catalogue record for this book is available from the British Library.

Design by Newgen Imaging Systems (P) Ltd., Chennai, India.

First PALGRAVE MACMILLAN paperback edition: September 2008.

10 9 8 7 6 5 4 3 2 1

Printed in the United States of America.

Transferred to Digital Printing in 2008

For John

CONTENTS

LIST OF ILLUSTRATIONS

ACKNOWLEDGMENTS

Parts of this book appeared first, and in different form, in several journals. For permission to reprint versions of these essays, thanks to *Nineteenth-Century Literature*, 55:3 (2000), © by the Regents of the University of California; by permission of the University of California Press; *The Lessons of Romanticism*, ed. Thomas Pfau and Robert Gleckner, 1998, Duke University Press; and *Eighteenth-Century Fiction*, 8.1 (1995). I want to acknowledge my appreciation as well to The Royal Collection, the V&A Picture Library, the Bildarchiv Foto Marburg, Ann Louise Luthi, Search Press, and the British Museum.

Many people helped make this book a reality. My first thanks go to Jeff Cox, who has been a wonderful colleague and friend. I deeply appreciate his insightful readings of multiple drafts and tireless support over the past six years. I want to extend many, many thanks to Marilyn Gaull for her valuable editorial suggestions and enthusiasm for this project. I am indebted to my colleagues at the University of Colorado. Anna Brickhouse's encouragement and advice helped me in more ways than I can easily say, and our years of Sunday morning writing sessions inspired me to finish this book. Many thanks go to Charlotte Sussman for her insightful responses to various drafts of the book, and for the pleasure of collaborating with her on several projects. I am also especially grateful to Bruce Holsinger for his advice and ready help about everything academic. For their help, I owe a large debt of gratitude to Chris Braider, Jane Garrity, and Paul Gordon, who each generously read drafts of different chapters, as well as to Katherine Eggert, Peter Knox, Tim Morton, Jeffrey Robinson, and Terry Robinson, who helped supply important references and suggested indispensable sources. Eric White provided much encouragement. I extend my deep appreciation, as well, to my colleagues from Texas who provided so much support, encouragement, and friendship: Mark Allen, Judy Fisher, and Jeanne Reesman, and to my teachers from graduate school, Alistair Duckworth, James Kincaid, and David Morris.

My distinguished colleagues in the wider world of Romantic Studies and beyond also thought Jane Austen was funny and that this project was worth pursuing. I thank them for their laughter and their intellectual inspiration: Rob Anderson, Alan Bewell, Joseph Bristow, Marshall Brown, David Clark, Angela Esterhammer, Joel Faflak, Mary Favret, Dino Felluga, Geraldine Friedman, Tim Fulford, Michael Gamer, Denise Gigante, Bruce Graver, Gary Harrison, Sonia Hofkosh, Claudia Johnson, Theresa Kelley, Greg Kucich, Beth Lau, Harriet Kramer Linkin, Mark Lussier, Laura Mandell, Daniel O'Quinn, Thomas Pfau, Alan Richardson, Jane Stabler, Nan Sweet, Katie Trumpener, Orrin Wang, and Paul Youngquist. My endless gratitude goes to Julie Carlson, William Galperin, Deidre Lynch, Anne Mellor, and Mary Ann O'Farrell.

Graduate students Terry Robinson, Courtney Wennerstrom, Elizabeth Franko, Dana Van Kooy, and Hannah Dunn helped me in the preparation of this book. To them I owe infinite thanks for their friendship and their dedication. The enthusiasm and excellent humor of my students at the University of Colorado influenced this book at every turn, and to them I am especially thankful.

I cannot adequately thank my parents, Richard Heydt and Mary Heydt. Though my mother died long before this book was even begun, my father helped make it possible: I hope he knows how much I appreciate his belief in my abilities, his intellectual support and shrewd observations about my ideas, and all the time he spent poring over press catalogues and searching in book stores for everything written on Jane Austen he could find. I am thankful for the encouragement my brother, Michael Heydt and sister-in-law, Susan Chetlin gave to me. My son, Will Heydt Minor, always inspired me to finish this book. I am also indebted to the wisdom and unique support of Mary Lou Acimovich and Jeffrey Dann. I thank Joy Lanzano, Mary Anne Lutz, and Heather Sellers for the gift of their friendship.

John Allen Stevenson's inspiration and intellect is on every page of this book. To him, I am most grateful for everything. I will always be thankful—and I can never thank him enough—for his conversation, brilliant wit, and indefatigable faith in me and in this book.

Introduction: Did Jane Austen Really Mean *That*?

Slipping into the Ha-Ha

In *Pride and Prejudice*, Lydia intimates that her virginity has already been lost when, on the eve of eloping with a scoundrel, she explains that "I shall send for my clothes when I get to Longbourn; but I wish you would tell Sally to mend a great slit in my worked muslin gown, before they are packed up" (291–292).[1] In *Northanger Abbey*, Thorpe congratulates himself on his masculine prowess by displacing it on to his carriage: "What do you think of my gig, Miss Morland? a neat one, is not it? Well hung; town built" (46). Mary Crawford urges her chaste friends to imagine "with what unwilling feelings the former belles of the house of Rushworth did many a time repair to this chapel? The young Mrs. Eleanors and Mrs. Bridgets—starched up into seeming piety, but with heads full of something very different—especially if the poor chaplain were not worth looking at . . ." (*Mansfield Park* 87). In *Sense and Sensibility*, Sir John exclaims to Marianne, "Aye, you will make conquests enough, I dare say, one way or other. Poor Brandon! he is quite smitten already, and he is very well worth setting your cap at, I can tell you, in spite of all this tumbling about and spraining of ancles [*sic*]" (45). To "tumble" meant to "lie down to a man"; and "tumble in"—that is, tumbling—referred to copulation (Partridge 915). Furthermore, according to Grose's *Dictionary of the Vulgar Tongue* (1811), "a girl who is got with child, is said to have sprained her ankle." Thus, Sir John's comment suggests that "in spite of all this tumbling about and spraining of ancles," Marianne is still marketable and "marriageable."

Spicy allusions such as these abound in Austen's novels: still, the myth persists that Austen's world was limited to the cerebral and refined, an elegant, ahistorical zone remote from her uncouth and politically turbulent era. *Austen's Unbecoming Conjunctions* is the first comprehensive investigation of the formative role that dissident comedy plays in Austen's writings, from her earliest, unpublished works to her last novel, *Persuasion*. I ask readers to rethink some ingrained assumptions: that Austen's novels exclude the sensual world of things, of stuff, of commodities; that there is no sex in them, and neither are there any bodies—although, to play off Catherine's speech in *Northanger Abbey*, some, "if hard pressed" (200), might yield a few notable exceptions, such as Lydia Bennet. I take a new turn in Austen studies by illuminating three, interlocking ideas that challenge those assumptions. First, focusing on sexuality in Romantic literary culture, I recover dimensions of Austen's work that academic critics and sentimental cultists have sometimes rendered unintelligible and inaccessible. Second, I argue that Austen emphasizes the physical life of her heroines and, as contemporary neuroscience did, acknowledges a close, even indissoluble, connection between mind and body. Third, I explore those English habits of female consumption that pervade Austen's fiction: popular literature and commonplace books; clothing, jewelry, and crafts; and travel and tourism. In her novels, such *things* delightfully further Austen's erotic comedy, but they also provide the raw elements for devastating critiques of courtship, and resonantly dramatize revolutions in politics, gender, and consumption.

Jane Austen lived from 1775 to 1817; her first writings stem from 1787, almost exactly the period that Charles Rzepka has argued represents

> a hot chronology and always will. In thirty years alone from the fall of the Bastille in 1789 to the Peterloo Massacre of parliamentary and labor reformers in 1819, the West experienced its first wholesale political revolution; its first total war on what was, for the European imagination of that time, a world scale; and the first boiling over in the modern nation-state of a long-simmering revolution in modes of production and consumption, living and working conditions, and class relations. ("The Feel" 1427–1428)

Amanda Gilroy and Wil Verhoevan, responding in part to Rzepka's statements, extol the way in which novels of the Romantic period "give us access to the history of the period: extraordinary in the variety and magnitude of events and processes it contains" (156). Working from this principle, I analyze Austen's focus on how both "high" historical events and "low" popular cultural productions are allied with the most important matters facing her heroines and readers— love, affection, courtship, marriage, and mourning—as well as betrayal, rape, prostitution, venereal disease, and money. Austen wakes her readers up with some unwholesome humor and finds symbolic weight in "trivial" and evanescent details.

In its aim to historicize Austen and to "brin[g] nonnormalizing . . . readings back into view" (Johnson, "Divine" 39), *Austen's Unbecoming Conjunctions* has clear affinities with recent criticism by Claudia Johnson, Deidre Lynch, William Galperin, Mary Ann O'Farrell, and Clara Tuite. Each of these scholars offers a sophisticated sense of Austen's relationship to the Romantic era, one that grants her a central position in the most important political and literary debates of her time,[2] a position on the radical edge of revolutionary thinking. William Galperin argues that Austen's contemporaries found her work unconventional; it was not until later that she became, because she was made, conservative (*Janeites* 90). In her Introduction to *Janeites*, Deidre Lynch points out that "Contemporary scholarship has demonstrated just how hard conservatives have had to work at their mythologizing in order to depict Austen's classic novels as . . . 'a world that seems to have been the same from everlasting to everlasting, . . . a kind of ideal centre of calm which was conceived, and for a time . . . actually realised by the eighteenth century' " (7). *Austen's Unbecoming Conjunctions* also draws upon, and at times reevaluates, theories of Austen's comedy. Feminist interpretations, such as those of Regina Barecca and Eileen Gillooly, acknowledge her wit's subversive qualities, though they tend to dissociate Austen, and women's humor in general, from what they consider to be male—that is, tendentious and aggressive—motives. Aggression, however, is not solely a masculine characteristic, and I argue that Austen's wit ranges through an expansive tonal register that includes both the empathetic and the hostile.[3]

Prostitution and pornography, sodomy and syphilis would seem to have little place in Jane Austen's literary world, if that world is defined only as one of genteel rural domesticity articulated in a cultivated linguistic style, and thoroughly detached from the libidinous. Even though critics have addressed the novelist's eroticism, her voice is often perceived as bearing no more than faint traces of the gritty world outside her cozy narrative domain.[4] Yet, her consistent and career-long investment in the literary pleasure of the body contradicts the view that she avoids sexual allusion and content. Consider *Emma*: near the beginning, as the heroine promotes the courtship between Harriet and Mr. Elton through a suggestive game of riddles and enigmas, Emma's father recalls a verse entitled "Kitty, a fair, but frozen maid" (78). Written by David Garrick and first published in 1771 as "A Riddle" in the sensational *New Foundling Hospital for Wit*, "Kitty" recounts the plight of a man infected with venereal disease: he "prays" for a cure, not to Cupid, but to a chimney sweep, thereby evoking the widespread medical practice of using heat and mercury as a treatment. He also alludes to the notorious masculine custom of seducing virgins, the folkloric claim that sex with the innocent would cure syphilis. The third stanza reads,

> To Kitty, Fanny now succeeds,
> . . . With care my appetite she feeds.
> Each day some willing victim bleeds
> To satisfy my strange desires. (11–15)

More than an offhand cultural allusion, Austen's interjection of this smutty riddle (and the narrator's pointed reference to its frequent recitation in the Woodhouse household) becomes a springboard for analyzing the sentimentalization of prostitution and revealing how the same ideology that produces the prostitute also engenders the courtship rules that the heroine must follow. The riddle's dangerous content couples the images of poor health in *Emma* to a larger social disease and helps the respectable novel speak the unspeakable.

"Flabbergasted." This is the students' response as they listen to the fictional but perspicacious Professor Morris Zapp when he argues that readers of Jane Austen

> should not be misled by the absence of overt reference to physical sexuality in her fiction into supposing that she was indifferent or hostile to it. . . . Mr. Elton was obviously implied to be impotent because there was no lead in the pencil that Harriet Smith took from him; and the moment in *Persuasion* when Captain Wentworth lifted the little brat Walter off Anne Elliot's shoulders . . . He snatched up the text and read with feeling: " '. . . she found herself in the state of being released from him . . . Before she realized that Captain Wentworth had done it . . . he was resolutely borne away . . . Her sensations on the discovery made her perfectly speechless. . . .' How about that?" he concluded reverently. "If that isn't an *orgasm*, what is it?" (Lodge 215)

Even if one is not flabbergasted, one must acknowledge that Austen's candid humor appears at odds with social expectations of the woman novelist of her time. Critics such as Audrey Bilger, Eileen Gillooly, and Maaja Stewart have demonstrated that in the eighteenth and early nineteenth centuries, laughter in general and female humor in particular were seen as a threat to the foundations of public order and social harmony, partly because sexual freedom was linked to—or even seen as a consequence of—the authority that a witty person commands. Lord Lyttelton, for example, writes in his "Advice to a Lady" (1731) that of those women who "claim" wit, "more than half have none, / And those who have it, are undone" (ll. 35–36). Without becoming "undone," Austen "claims wit" by including funny double entendres that announce her "knowingness." An episode from *Mansfield Park* and, in particular, Fanny Price's phrase "slipping into the ha-ha" from that novel, provide a metonymic expression of Austen's comic irreverence. In the visit to Sotherton, the characters amble through a landscape replete with sexual symbols: a locked iron gate, missing keys, and threatening spikes and a wilderness that is "laid out with too much regularity" (97–99, 91). In this scene, Austen has the future adulteress, Maria Bertram, sliding around an iron gate in order to escape from her sluggish fiancé and spend some quality time alone with the man she would rather marry. Her shy cousin, Fanny, intuiting that the danger to her dress foreshadows a threat to Maria's virtue, calls out, "You will hurt yourself, Miss Bertram, . . . you will certainly hurt yourself against those spikes— you will tear your gown—you will be in danger of slipping into the ha- ha" (99–100). Imperceptible from a distance, the ha-ha was a sunken fence that prevented livestock from crossing from the park into the garden but at the same time allowed the viewer to maintain the fiction that the grounds were seamlessly connected. The ha-ha was so named because viewers would react with both surprise and laughter when they realized this earthy *trompe l'oeil* had deceived them.[5] Austen's own bawdy "slip" into the ha-ha extends and expands the space normally allowed to a woman during this period. Although I am not drawing any comparison between Miss Bertram and the novelist, I am saying that Austen's bawdy humor ignores locked "gates," pushes beyond "spikes," and threatens to "tear" Austen's gown.

Whether or not Austen metaphorically tears her gown when she includes such subject matter depends, in some measure, on how one situates the novelist with regard to the demands of propriety forced upon women writers as attitudes toward gender and sexuality became codified in new and increasingly restrictive ways. Scholars are familiar with the shift in eighteenth- and nineteenth-century medical discourse from considering women as strongly sexual in nature to envisioning them as quiescent and erotically anesthetized. This later development, which separated pleasure from conception, arose in part from the discovery that women need not experience orgasm in order to conceive, knowledge that "opened up the possibility of female passivity and 'passionlessness' " (Laqueur 3). No one can know the degree to which this ideological shift changed behavior, leaving women sexually unresponsive and appalled by erotic literature and bawdy humor. Sir Walter Scott's often quoted anecdote suggests that this repressive discourse did have an impact: his great aunt was ashamed when, after rereading Aphra Behn in 1821, she was unable to fathom having ever heard such material "read aloud" among the "first and most creditable society in London" in the 1760s (Gallagher 1; Ballaster, *Seductive* 205). On the other hand, Austen's characters imply that although such a theory infiltrated the cultural imagination, its application was tenuous indeed. Juliet McMaster, analyzing Elizabeth Bennet's "sexual vitality" and the "exuberant quality" and "sexual piquancy" of *Pride and Prejudice* "find[s] it hard to credit that anyone . . . could subscribe to the view of Miss Austen as an old maid who wrote sexless novels" (*Novelist* 156). Thus, although it is common to argue that women metamorphosed from the sexually vigorous to the frosty, "such sweeping teleologies . . . and all-encompassing paradigms on repression and libertarianism" are problematic given the complexity of eighteenth-century society, as Julie Peakman has observed (10). For example, rather than reading the history of sexuality as a narrative moving toward inhibition, Randolph Trumbach argues that after 1750, the new emphasis on romance and domesticity encouraged sexual passion, a theory that Austen's novels reinforce. Also available to encourage wedded affection were texts such as *Aristotle's Master-Piece*, a longtime best-selling manual intended for couples on the verge of marriage, newlyweds, nurses, and midwives, and one which Austen no doubt knew since it went through "twenty editions in the eighteenth century and far more in the nineteenth" (Porter, "Secrets" 13, 2). If she did not have access to a copy, she would have encountered the book through Laurence Sterne's *Tristram Shandy*, a novel that draws on this work (Hitchcock 18). Although an edition from 1776 stipulates that sexual pleasure should be confined to marriage, "else it will become a curse to them instead of a blessing," it encourages "all those therefore of either sex . . . to enjoy the delights of mutual embraces of each other" (27). It explains that the clitoris, "the seat of the greatest pleasure in the act of copulation . . . and therefore called the sweetness of love and the fury of venery," functions by *Blowing the coals up of those amorous fires, / Which youth and beauty to be quenched requires* (24, 17).[6] This manual was free of the most common eighteenth-century gender prejudices, such as, in Roy Porter's words, the "double-standard," "gross misogyny," and portrayals of women "as nymphomaniacs, . . . hags, . . . sexless, passionless, delicate [or] liable to hysteria and neurasthenia"; in it, "women enjoy parity in sexual desire, and female desire is not viewed as grotesque or psychopathological . . ." ("Secrets" 14–15).

Codes of repression could be strict. Alexander Hamilton's *The Family Female Physician, or a Treatise on the Management of Female Complaints, and of Children in Early Infancy* (1793) offers no references to copulation, as opposed to John Mowbray's earlier work, from 1733, *The Female Physician, Containing all the Diseases incident to that Sex, in Virgins, Wives, and Widows; Together With their Causes and Symptoms, their Degrees of Danger, and respective Methods of Prevention and Cure*, which describes how the "*Conjunction* of both Sexes, is the *consummation* of Love, and the *Pinnacle* of the *Lover's* natural Felicity. It is the Sum and superlative Degree of their *terrene Happiness;* above which the *Lovers* cannot aspire, naturally speaking, in *Human Society*" (53).[7] And even the preface to the second edition of *A Classical Dictionary of the Vulgar Tongue* (1788) attempts to palliate the potential discomfort of its audience:

> some words and explanations in the former [first] edition having been pointed out as rather indecent or indelicate, though found in Le Roux, and other Glossaries of that kind, these have been either omitted, softened, or their explanations taken from books long sanctioned with general approbation, and admitted to the seminaries for the education of youth—such as Bailey's, Miege's, or Phillip's Dictionary; so that it is hoped this work will now be found as little offensive to delicacy as the nature of it would admit. (Grose iii)

Grose's concerns verify Tim Hitchcock's point in *English Sexualities 1700–1800* that a transition occurred toward the end of the eighteenth century away from men's and women's mutual enjoyment and widespread consumption of sexually explicit material in chapbooks, pamphlets, poetry, and midwifery manuals (ch. 2, passim). Within this context, Austen's bawdy/body humor does breach convention, challenging assumptions of propriety and arguing instead that some women of her era enjoyed steamy talk as much as men.[8] Her humor reveals her ability to evade those constraints that required women in general to conform to a "presence of indisputable virtue" and that "redefin[ed]" and "limited" women writers in particular by transforming them into the "signifier of moral purity and incorruptible truth" (Ballaster, *Seductive* 210).[9] This humor's very existence, however, also raises the question of how severe those constraints were.

TITTERING AND LAUGHING WOMEN

There were ways to skirt censorship: Mary Poovey argues that by writing, women authors necessarily confront orthodox gender expectations, and that their productions offer "readings of contemporary propriety that . . . often obliquely sought to reconcile desire and satisfaction, conventional manners and genuine self-expression" (41). My point, however, is that Austen often directly and *not* "always tactfully and with ladylike restraint . . . criticize[es] the way [ideology] shaped and deformed women's desires" (Poovey 47). Further, the kind of bawdy humor Austen employs pervaded mainstream culture. Shakespeare offers the richest source for her allusions. I argue that Austen uses some of Shakespeare's licentious allusions to critique conservative patriarchal attitudes. Her intertexuality had precedents: using the same technique, though for conservative purposes, George Ellis, publishing in the *Anti-Jacobin*, plucks some bawdy lines from Shakespeare. In the "ODE TO LORD M – – RA," criticizing Lord Moira, Ellis writes that

> New grace adorns your figure;
> More stiff your boots, more black your stock,
> Your hat assumes a prouder cock,
> Like Pistol's (if 'twere bigger). (ll. 9–12)

Here, he alludes to Pistol, Falstaff's companion, in Shakespeare's *Henry V*, II.i.53–54: "and Pistol's cock is up, / And flashing fire will follow."[10]

Functioning as code breakers for this kind of sexual cryptography, the editions of the plays from the 1780s and 1790s gloss at least some of Shakespeare's ribaldry. Emma quotes a line from *A Midsummer Night's Dream*—"The course of true love never did run smooth"— and explains that "A Hartfield edition of Shakespeare would have a long note on that passage" (*Emma* 75)—a comment that suggests that young women did study the footnotes in their household editions of the Bard. Many sexual allusions are clear without annotation, as in *Romeo and Juliet* when Mercutio describes Queen Mab (who makes a titular entrance in *Sense and Sensibility*) as the hag who "when maids lie on their backs, / . . . presses them and learns them first to bear, / Making them women of good carriage" (I.iv.92–94). Though the lines' meaning is obvious, Steevens's gloss offers bawdy erudition: "So in Gervaise of Tilbury, Dec.I. C. 17. *Vidimus quosdam daemones tanto zelo mulieres amare, quod ad inaudita rorumpunt ludibria, et cum ad concubitum earum accedunt, mirâ mole eas oprimunt, nec ab alliis videntur* " (43). This roughly means that "We have seen that some spirits love women with such fervor that they break out into outrages unheard of, and when they come to have intercourse with them, they overwhelm them with amazing power and are unseen by others."[11] Does the Latin remain untranslated so as to prevent young women from understanding it? Or would it spur curiosity?

What the editions choose to gloss would require a study in itself. Eighteenth-century editions of Shakespeare, however, reveal both a public discourse that attempted to suppress (or pretended to be blind to) bawdy references in the plays and a continuing (if grudging) acknowledgment of their presence. These issues have their own interest, but for my purposes, such commentaries point to the presence of bawdy annotation in standard eighteenth-century editions of Shakespeare, such as any educated household might contain. For example, Gordon Williams explains that in his 1793 edition of Shakespeare's plays, George Steevens "suggests that . . . where Falstaff has 'his poll clawed like a parrot' (*Henry IV, Part Two* II. iv. 281), [the reference] represents a recognized amatory caress . . ., probably borrowed from 'the French, to whom we were indebted for most of our artificial gratifications' " (Williams 153–154). In another instance, this from *Much Ado About Nothing*, Benedick teases Claudio, "do you play the flouting Jack; to tell us Cupid is a good hare-finder and Vulcan a rare carpenter?" (I.i.185–186). Steevens's 1766 edition has a long note glossing the Cupid reference, and he cites the explanations of several earlier editors. Samuel Johnson admits to some confusion, "I know not whether I conceive the jest here intended," though he thinks Benedick is saying something like, "Do you mean to tell us what we know already?" But Steevens also cites the poet William Collins, another editor of Shakespeare: "After such attempts at decent illustration, I am afraid that he who wishes to know why Cupid is a good *hare-finder*, must discover it by the assistance of many quibbling allusions of the same sort, about *hair* and *hoar*, in Mercutio's song in the second act of *Romeo and Juliet*" (273). Collins may not come right out and say that Cupid is a rare whore-catcher, but his drift is clear enough, and he does a naive reader the service of pointing him (or her) to a much racier passage in another play.

Erasmus Darwin's *The Loves of the Plants* (1789), Part II of *The Botanic Garden*, is a sustained masterpiece of erotic suggestion, as he describes botanical mating in the "Inchanted Garden." Delectably allusive, Darwin teaches his readers about the sensuous marriage rituals of the Lychnis:

> *Five* sister-nymphs to join Diana's train
> With thee, fair LYCHNIS! Vows,—but vow in vain;

Beneath one roof resides the virgin band,
Flies the fond swain, and scorns his offer'd hand,
But when soft hours on breezy pinions move,
And smiling May attunes her lute to love,
Each wanton beauty, trick'd in all her grace,
Shakes the bright dew-drops from her blushing face;
In gay undress displays her rival charms,
And calls her wondering lovers to her arms. (ll. 107–116)

Here, modest virgins, initially scornful of love, nevertheless respond to nature's amorous foreplay, finding May's soft hours and melodies irresistible. Meaning to woo the reader with poetic music and lubricious language (the young rose "Drinks the warm blushes of his bashful bride"), Darwin's poem offered a legitimate and available source for a host of readers, portraying reproduction as a naturally pleasurable amorous activity. In *Parodies of the Romantic Age*, Graeme Stones points out that "[f]ew poets would dare to versify the Sexual System (of botanical classification) of Linnaeus, with his promiscuous analogies and lingering descriptions of stems, stamens, receptacles and petioles. Anna Seward made an attempt, found the subject improper for a female pen, and suggested it to Darwin" (I, 161). Though unacceptable for the "female pen" and perhaps for the female reader, women did, nevertheless read Darwin's *The Botanic Garden*.

Women may also have read Mr. Higgins's "The Loves of the Triangles," which parodies *The Loves of the Plants;* originally published in *The Anti-Jacobin*, the spoof is as erotically charged as Darwin's text, and captures the fantastic potential of sensuous give and take, though this time in geometry, not plants. In Issue XXIII of the *Anti-Jacobin*, Higgins reveals some women's interest in Darwin's botanical descriptions, as he disingenuously contends that "the more rigid and unbending stiffness of a mathematical subject does not admit of the same appeals to the warmer passions, which naturally arise out of the *sexual* (or, as I have heard several worthy Gentlewomen of my acquaintance . . . who delight in [*The Loves of the Plants*] term it, by a slight misnomer no way difficult to be accounted for—the *sensual*) system of Linnaeus" (*Parodies* 166). The parody's potential as either licentious or effective in encouraging mathematical studies seems doubtful to the editors of *The Anti-Jacobin*, who

apprehend little danger to our Readers' morals, from laying before them Mr. Higgins's doctrine in its most fascinating shape. The Poem abounds, indeed, with beauties of the most striking kind, various and vivid imagery, bold and unsparing impersonifications; and similitudes and illustrations brought from the most ordinary and the most extraordinary occurrences of nature . . . appealing equally to the heart and to the understanding, and calculated to make the subject of . . . the Poem . . . rather amusing than intelligible. (*Parodies* 166–167)

Mr. Higgins's verse offers some zesty entertainment as it describes how for the sensuously deadened "sons of WAR and TRADE AND THE LEGION FIENDS OF CHURCH AND LAW" (l. 2),

> No DEFINITIONS touch *your* senseless mind;
> To *you*, no POSTULATES prefer their claim,
> Nor ardent AXIOMS *your* dull souls inflame;
> For *you* no TANGENTS touch, no ANGLES meet,
> Nor CIRCLES join in osculation sweet! (ll. 6–10)

The verse jokingly reprimands those oblivious to geometry's fecund call. Simultaneously, the notes gloss the last two words as the "kissing of Circles," and advise readers to "see Huygens . . . who has veiled this delicate and inflammatory subject in the decent obscurity of a learned language" (165).[12] In contrast, "wanton optics roll the melting eye" of the poet, as he gazes on

> The flaunting drapery, and the languid leer;
> Fair Sylphish forms—who, tall, erect, and slim,
> Dart the keen glance, and stretch the length of limb. (ll. 20–24)

Soon the "*Planes*, their substance with their motion grown, / Form the huge *Cube*, the *Cylinder*, the *Cone*" (ll. 43–44). And later we are directed to "behold" "the fair PARABOLA,"[13]

> Her timid arms, with virgin blush, unfold!
> Though, on one *focus* fix'd, her eyes betray
> A heart that glows with love's resistless sway,
> Though, climbing oft, she strive with bolder grace
> Round his tall neck to clasp her fond embrace,
> Still e'er she reach it, from his polish'd side
> Her trembling hands in devious *Tangents* glide. (ll. 107–114)

Higgins's poetry points out the physical luxuriousness of Darwin's language but he imitates it in ways that render the parody, if anything, more indecent than the original. The poem ultimately becomes a direct attack on Jacobinism and its supposedly libidinous undercurrents ("Alas! That partial Science should approve / The sly Rectangle's too licentious love" (Canto I, ll. 75–76). Sexual humor could, however, be appropriated to attack a conservative cause (and this is what I will be arguing that Austen does) as surely as *The Anti-Jacobin* could exploit it to critique a radical one. Whether for educational purposes or satire, both Darwin and his parodist provide extended examples of erotic material, which reputable publications made available to women readers.

James Boswell's *Life of Johnson* provides a famous and funny anecdote about how, despite patriarchal regulation of humor, men and women could laugh spontaneously at bawdiness, whatever repressive energies were otherwise in the air. Johnson,

> [t]alking of a very respectable author [Dr. John Campbell], told us a curious circumstance in his life, which was, that he had married a printer's devil. REYNOLDS. "A printer's devil, sir! Why, I thought a printer's devil was a creature with a black face and in rags." JOHNSON. "Yes, Sir. But I suppose, he had her face washed; and put clean clothes on her. (Then looking very serious, and very earnest.) And she did not disgrace him;—the woman had a bottom of good sense." The word *bottom* thus introduced, was so ludicrous when contrasted with his gravity, that most of us could not forbear tittering and laughing; though I recollect that the Bishop of Killaloe kept his countenance with perfect steadiness, while Miss Hannah More slyly hid her face behind a lady's back who sat on the same settee with her. His pride could not bear that any expression of his should excite ridicule, when he did not intend it; he therefore resolved to assume and exercise despotick power, glanced sternly around, and called out in a strong tone, "Where's the merriment?" Then collecting himself, and looking aweful, to make us feel how he could impose restraint, and as it were searching his mind for a still more ludicrous word, he slowly pronounced, "I say the *woman* was *fundamentally* sensible"; as if he had said, hear this now, and laugh if you dare. We all sat composed as at a funeral. (99)

Johnson, embarrassed, needs a scolding from Elizabeth Bennet, who finds that those who are "not to be laughed at" have "an uncommon advantage, . . . for it would be a great loss to *me* to have many such acquaintance. I dearly love a laugh" (57). Here, no possibility for the playful banter of *Pride and Prejudice* exists between Johnson and his audience. When Elizabeth challenges Darcy—"despise me if you dare"—he responds, "Indeed I do not dare" (52); Johnson's "dare," however, leads not to "gallantry" (52), as in the novel, but to a funeral silence. Boswell's readers, however, get to laugh both at Johnson's bawdy gaffe and at his pride. Relevant to my argument is the way that an unbecoming conjunction like this—his gravity joined to a ludicrous word—makes nearly everyone "titte[r] and laug[h]," especially Hannah More, the last person we would expect to be "slyly" hiding her face because she could not help laughing at a blue slip of the tongue.

Perhaps it should not be surprising, then, to discover sexually charged humor in an unlikely source, the era's decorous magazines aimed toward ladies. Bawdy wit in this kind of periodical makes it difficult to calibrate the degree of success that repressive ideologies actually enjoyed, and makes me wonder if a widespread incidence of sly jokes among women was more common than what a theory of unilateral censorship can account for. For example, in 1775, *The Lady's Magazine* included a column called "The Lady's Practitioner," which, in a "Receipt for changing Yellow Hair," advises that though the style for "agreeable black" hair has eclipsed that of the "golden," the writer maintains that women with red hair "have the finest skins, with azure veins, and generally become the best breeders of the nation" (VI, 316). *Women's Worlds: Ideology, Femininity and the Woman's Magazine* argues that such a comment was possible because the column itself, written by "Dr. Cook," "provided a means of indulging prurient sexual curiousity and a more vulgar brand of humour than the magazine commonly sanctioned" (70).

The Lady's Monthly Museum also authorizes strict morality, yet it published some tangy accounts, and not in a doctor's column or other such section that in itself might justify libidinous humor. The series called "Le Melange" records the "The Last News from Brighton": "As Miss Clementina Darnwell was yesterday taking the air on her donkey, accompanied by her groom, she was unfortunately thrown, and received a violent contusion on her right elbow, and a terrible splash on the left. All Barbican is disconsolate at the melancholy intelligence" (Le Melange V, Dec. 1806, 253). Jokes there also approach the sexually sadistic: "A gentleman having married a lady of the name of Lamb, who had very little beauty, but a very great fortune, was told by an acquaintance that he would not have taken the *lamb* had it not been for the *mint sauce*," and another entry "mentions that lately a Miss *Legg* gave her *hand* to a Mr. *Grasp*" (Le Melange IV, Nov. 1806, 218).[14] The tale describing an irate husband's discovery that another man "dyes" for his wife includes an ancient pun on orgasm:

A lady having sent a very costly silk gown to be dyed, the dyer very politely carried it home himself, that he might be certain of its being conveyed with care. It so happened that the lady's husband opened the door to him, and being a very proud man, vexed at having condescended to open the door to a *low tradesman*, asked very angrily what he had in his hand, and whom it was for? "Sir," replied the man, "it is a parcel for the lady of the house." "What, for my wife!" answered the gentleman, "what can you have for my wife?" "Sir," rejoined the man, trembling, "*I dye for your wife*." "My wife!" "Yes, Sir, I dye for your wife and her two sisters." "You impudent dog," exclaimed the gentleman, in a violent passion, "do you dare to tell me so to my face. Come, some of you, (calling his servants) and kick this presumptuous and ignorant blockhead out of the house." They were proceeding to put his commands in execution, when the lady luckily came down stairs, . . . and not only rescued her gown from the damage it might have sustained in the scuffle, but also the poor man, who for many years had actually *dyed for her whole family*. (Le Melange IV, Nov. 1806, 221)

This pun, which depends on the fairer sex recognizing the double entendre, encourages female solidarity by making fun of jealous, arrogant husbands who are ignorant about domestic matters, and it extends beyond heterosexual love in italicizing (literally) how the tradesman has "dyed" for the entire family. The italics send a visual signal even to the woman who would not have understood the allusion; by triggering curiosity and, perhaps, questions, the bawdy humor provides an avenue in a proper female publication for sexual pedagogy.

In *The Lady's Monthly Museum*, an essay in its recurring series, "The Old Woman," sarcastically describes a "good wife" as a "toll-gate continually exacting pay," a woman who "considers her husband only as an useful slave to her pleasures. . . . She speaks in bass all day, but changes to treble at night; and—'My dear!' and 'My love!' of the morning, is the 'Brute!' and 'monster!' of the day" (Feb. 1800, 89, 90). Although meant to show "'Vice her own feature,' in order that conscious Virtue may rejoice in its exemption from the deformity" (89), this description nevertheless describes the possibility of ecstatic, though selfish delight. It elicited an indignant response, entitled, "A Spirited Address to the Editor of the Museum, For having imprudently inserted a *Libel* upon the *Ladies*, under the sanction of an Old Woman": The letter writer, who signs her correspondence, "*A Champion for my Sex*," protests that

[a]s you profess to write for the entertainment of the Ladies, I think you might adopt a more agreeable method than that of *satirizing*, or rather *characterizing*, their foibles. . . . Be that as it may, Mr. Editor, it was not a proper kind of letter to appear, and is impertinent enough to ruin the future sale of the Work. As to the comparisons of the 'Toll-gate,' the 'Fury in adversity,' and the 'Enemy to domestic felicity,'— the first is *vulgar*,—the second *virulent*,—and the third *wicked*. (Mar. 1800, 177–178)

The admonition takes a feminist tone, when the writer asks if domestic unhappiness "alone proceed[s] from *Female Frailty*? Or have the *mighty lords* of the *creation* some *little* right to share the general blame?" The "Champion" goes on to blame marital infelicity on "Libertines," for whom "a Wife is the . . . last resource!—the sovereign antidote for all his cares! . . ." (179). In doing so, the writer reverses standard moral ideology that a woman could save a ruined man. Further, in repeating the double entendre of "toll-gate," which is described as "vulgar," the admonition, ironically, also permits a second opportunity for laughing at specific allusions to the female body and its desires.[15]

In July 1789, *The Lady's Magazine* included the comic entry "The Humours of the Card-Table; or, A Silent Game of Whist," in which the four players frankly gossip about the sexual goings-on of their circle: "Mr. Spruce's affairs with Mrs. Blackstone," which led to "an absolute necessity for their marriage"; the speculation that Mrs. Irish is carrying on with Tom Neatly, the shop man (353–354); and the bawdy jokes about a Miss Popple, who is unmarried and pregnant:

Mr. Tattle: "—has any of you seen Miss Popple lately?"
Omnes: "No—"
Tattle: "O then—probably you may see *double* soon" (*a laugh*)— "yes, yes, fine doings in the *Alley*—I thought it was not for nothing she preserved that situation. But, however, that is no business of ours—"
Mrs. G: "What! has she had a slip too?"
Tattle: "A slip! ay, a tumble too—They say in the neighbourhood, that she already waddles out of the *Alley*"—(*a laugh*). (354–355)

As I suggested earlier in this introduction and develop in chapter 1, Austen uses the word "tumbling," as this little play does, to denote sexual intercourse. This appears to have been a common use of the word. For example, it also shows up in another publication including sexual humor that would have been available to female readers. *The Spirit of the Public Journals. Being an Impartial Selection of the Most Exquisite Essays and Jeux D'Esprits, Principally Prose for 1797, That Appear in the Newspapers and Other Publications* (Higgins's "The Loves of the Triangles" was reprinted here as well) includes the "Epigrammata Bacchanalia" (1797), which plays with a conspicuous double entendre about Prime Minister William Pitt (1759–1806): "But sure our Billy well may grumble, / Fate views him with unequal eyes, / For Bacchus always makes him tumble, / And Venus never makes him rise" (Vol. I. 14.LXXXI).[16] In another poem, the type of which recurs often throughout these volumes, a woman who has vowed to be true to her lover, but is not, receives supernatural punishment. In "Giles Jollup the Knave, and Brown Sally Green," subtitled "A Romance" by its author, Matthew (Monk) Lewis, the hero complains to Sally that once he leaves for Jamaica, "You'll tumble in love with some smart city beau, / And with him share your shop in the strand" (319, ll. 9–10).

Austen's biting quips and bawdy comedy, far from being an isolated occurrence in British culture or women's reading matter, often resemble the off-key references in these various publications, in which funny epitaphs were popular and in which sexual allusions, though rare, do occur. The broad channels Austen deploys to make people laugh call for an acknowledgment of a wide range of human emotions: passion, sexuality, aggression, and grief. Austen's laughter, moreover, both in itself and in its frequent source in the body, thus complicates debates about late-eighteenth- and early-nineteenth-century assumptions regarding women's sexuality. Her success at finessing those restrictions that required women writers to represent elevated moral principles while becoming embodiments of chastity and modesty implies a freedom and an agency for women that some historians have not allowed.

"Two Inches Wide of Ivory"

When Austen limns her imaginative process as "work[ing]" with "so fine a Brush" on "the little bit (two Inches wide) of Ivory," she expands rather than limits her literary aesthetic when she likens her novels to miniature creations. This iconic—and ironic—phrase appears in a letter to her nephew, Edward Austen, himself a hopeful novelist:

> I am quite concerned for the loss your Mother mentions in her Letter; two Chapters & a half to be missing is monstrous! It is well that *I* have not been at Steventon lately, & therefore cannot be suspected of purloining them;—two strong twigs & a half towards a Nest of my own, would have been something.—I do not think however that any theft of that sort would be really very useful to me. What should I do with your strong, manly, spirited Sketches, full of Variety & Glow?—How could I possibly join them on to the little bit (two Inches wide) of Ivory on which I work with so fine a Brush, as produces little effect after much labour? (Le Faye 323)

Austen has ample riches and does not need to "purloin" anyone else's, especially "strong, manly, spirited Sketches." Her grotesque image

here, binding his unruly twigs, crude and stiff, with her finely delin-
eated, painted ivory surface serves (quite politely) to reduce his work
to nature and instinct and elevates her own to art and design. Austen's
metaphor of "two Inches wide of Ivory" resonates: the word "miniature" derives from "minium," red lead pigment; and miniature painting,
done by watercolor on ivory, developed from the art of manuscript
illumination. Austen thus self-consciously affiliates herself with the
famous miniaturists (many of them women) who flourished during
the Romantic period. And what a surprising cosmos these tiny articles
in the novels reveal, as their earthy and unsettling impulses emerge
from the glossy coat of Austen's prose. Her ivory surfaces depicting
miniature portraits, all contained inside elaborate fictional frames,
evoke worlds within worlds, thereby producing their own sublimity.
As Gaston Bachelard insists, the miniature is "a narrow gate that
opens up an entire world" (155).

Chapter 1, for example, examines how miniatures—such as crafts,
jewelry, seals, lockets, and portraits—destabilize the cool surface tone
of Austen's voice in *Sense and Sensibility* and draw attention to the
dangers of rape, ownership of the female body, and sexual usury.
Miniature paintings and hair tokens (such as the long lock Marianne
allows Willoughby to cut and the ring that Edward wears, which holds
Lucy's hair) play paradoxically with the conjunction between the
private and public. Such anamorphic objects, richly productive of
dense, complex ideas, often perform the roles actual characters desire
but cannot enact. Because hair jewelry and portraits prismatically alter
meaning given their placement and context in the novels, Austen
employs them to illuminate how closely courtship rituals resemble
consumer ventures. These possessions join bawdy words in this novel
in taking on a subjectivity, and in doing so, the objects reveal secrets
that would otherwise be occluded.

In projecting personal, even physical human attributes onto things,
Austen is not unique. Personifying things was popular during this era,
especially in the genre of poems to objects, wherein the inanimate
item often carries sexual or romantic connotations. Some examples
are "On a Pincushion" (1771), "The High-prized Pin-Box" (1680),
and "Sent in a Snuff Box, to Lady S– L–"[17]—the latter is a piece of
bawdy verse: "Think, and some useful lessons 'twill impart, / That
when you open it, you ope my heart; / Think, when you see this present from your lover, / Yourself's the *bottom*, and that I'm the *cover*"
(141). A tamer poem than the last three, though still associating an object with some erotic *frisson* is Samuel Johnson's "To
Miss_____, on her giving the Author a Gold and Silk Net-work

Purse of her weaving." *The Lady's Magazine* (1780) gives an "Account of a new Comedy, in three Acts" entitled *The Miniature Picture*, in which a tiny portrait becomes the means of uniting two couples (Vol. XI, 229–230). Another example, Mary Robinson's "Lesbia and her Lover" (1804), describes the way objects take on a life of their own and offer a substitute relationship when reality does not suffice:

> LESBIA upon her bosom wore   1
>   The semblance of her lover;
>   And oft with kisses she would cover
> The senseless idol, and adore
>   The dear enchanting rover.   5
>
> LESBIA would gaze upon his eyes
>   And think thy look'd so speaking
>   That oft her gentle heart was breaking;
> While glancing 'round, with frequent sighs,
>   She seem'd her lover seeking.   10
>
> One day says REASON, "Why embrace
>   A cold and senseless lover!
>   What charms can youthful eyes discover
> In such a varnish'd, painted face?
>   Pry'thee the task give over."   15
>
> Cried LESBIA, "REASON, wherefore blame?
>   Must you the cause be told?
>   My *breathing* lover I behold
> With features *painted* just the same,
>   As *senseless* and as cold.   20
>
> Then REASON, 'tis the better way
>   The harmless to commend:
>   My breathing lover soon would end
> My weary life, to grief a prey;
>   *This never can offend.*"   25

Robinson's speaker displaces her affection onto the "semblance of her lover," creating an alternate reality as she thinks his eyes "loo[k] so speaking" (2, 7), and yet she also enacts with that "painted face" the same relationship she would with the original insofar as both the miniature and the man are "cold and senseless lover[s]" (2, 7, 12). The miniature speaks truths about the lover, simultaneously allowing her to carry on a harmless affair that "never can offend" either by causing her to fall or to die of grief.

Like Robinson, Austen, in *Sense and Sensibility*, uses miniatures in complicated ways. For example, these semblances, such as cut hair and hair jewelry, allow Austen to make it transparent from the very beginning that Willoughby is a sexual threat to Marianne. Minor characters such as Mrs. Palmer and Mrs. Jennings serve as vehicles for Austen's discussion about attitudes toward the role of sexual humor in courtship. In miniature form, these two women spark thoughts about Austen's mingling of tragedy and comedy in even so serious an issue as the physical and emotional danger of men that prey on well-read young women. Austen's careful attention to these diminutive objects and particularized details unveils the potentially violent sexuality that lurks behind both sense and sensibility.

AUSTEN'S EMBODIMENTS

Austen's risqué humor in her double meanings, displaced forms of irreverence, literary allusions, and frankly unambiguous sexual references depends on how funny the body is, especially in eroticized situations. Although Austen does not show bodies in the same way that, say, Swift does (there are no enormous breasts or defecating "primitives"), her novels focus on how well one can decipher the individual through his or her physicality and on the degree to and method by which social rubrics should control the body, particularly the female body. Appearances and objects in Austen's novels question how confidently one can move from the external signifier to the underlying "truth" of the individual. Because the body manifests political and social constructions, and because diminishing corporeality at the expense of celebrating the mind is a feminist and political issue, examining the characters' physicality helps clarify Austen's response to the systems that govern her culture. Austen's humor consequently takes part in a larger enterprise, one that places the physical world's viscera at the center of her fictional universe. Thus I want to revise the common idea, one that has been well articulated by Carol Shields, that Austen "is unconcerned with the manifestations of human physicality. Her narrative intricacies and turns are propelled for the most part by incident or by reason and not by the needs or responses of the body. The brain . . . presides over the rest of the corporeal body which is treated with what? indifference? incuriosity? disregard? or perhaps a metaphorical shrug that all but erases" (132). According to this argument, Austen participates in that dichotomizing point of view that privileges mind over matter and renders the body, the lower entity, inferior.

Romantic-era scientific theories provide a historical basis for my argument that Austen accepts an organic connection between body and mind. Alan Richardson's influential research on Romantic-era neuroscience illuminates the many ways in which late-eighteenth- and early-nineteenth-century science tried to articulate an intimate and irreducible reciprocity between mind and body. As he writes of Austen's art, it "all speak[s] of a mind that has no location or meaning apart from the body" (112). I focus on how the novels acknowledge the physical dimension of consciousness and, in doing so, dislodge that hierarchical (and patriarchal) assumption that Austen "erases" the body. Elizabeth Grosz's terms "*embodied subjectivity*" and "*psychical corporeality*" (22, her emphasis) offer an opportunity to anatomize how Austen's characters physically respond in social spaces[18] and how the body registers social constructions that attempt to shape one's freedom for expression. Elizabeth exclaims, in an epiphany of new clarity, that "Till this moment, I never knew myself" (208). This statement from *Pride and Prejudice* has led to interpretations that maximize Elizabeth's intellectual growth at the expense of her physicality, a reading that, as Shields's does above, limits an understanding of somatic expression in the text. While allowing that the novel esteems rational capabilities, I shift attention to the narrative's kinetic energy and argue that it emphasizes how, once internalized, social expectations *feel.*

Northanger Abbey pays attention to fashions, both those kinds that bodies wear, such as sprigged muslin and turbans, and those that bodies perform, such as gender roles. This novel about meeting, flirting, and marriage that ends, albeit with irony, in a love match between the heroine and her suitor, provides a humorous, bawdy, and sober scrutiny of stylish ways to court. The characters' apprehension of chic identities, behaviors, and objects provides the runway for observing the impact of courtship's "natural" rituals on the body and sexual identity. A variety of comic and dangerous ways to "make" love unfold in the novel: so "feminized" that she is virtually in female drag, Mrs. Allen dreads leaving the house for fear that her clothes will be ravished; Isabella, the novel's preeminent coquette and fashionista, conflates personal disaster with the arrival of the spring fashions; Henry, alternating between snippy fop and gallant hero, verbally cross-dresses so as to woo and patronize women; Thorpe, playing the role of the hypermasculine man's man, relishes the exchange of horses between men and savors brutalizing his animals and the women they symbolize. And while the Tilney family's dramas and politics "undress" Catherine's gothic expectations, she herself becomes the exemplar of originality and freshness—the goal of the modern tourist who decries modernization. A woman who appears to have escaped all fashions except for the gothic, Catherine appeals to Henry in a world where the "beau monde" makes culture appear ever more culturally determined.

When Austen, the master prose stylist of the Romantic era, deploys sexual humor and elevates popular culture, she engages language in ways that complicate the public body of Jane Austen. This body, formed from a repetitive process over the last two centuries, has systematically removed her from the coarse and grotesque, the popular and the low. Among others, Mary Wollstonecraft exemplifies how the Enlightenment makes the body fundamentally incompatible with reason, the function of which is to purify and refine human matter. In that vein, Peter Stallybrass and Allon White argue that "eighteenth-century Augustan poetry . . . battled . . . to cleanse the cultural sphere of impure and messy semiotic matter, . . . [while] it also fed voraciously and incessantly from that very material. It nourished and replenished its refined formalism from the symbolic repertoire of the grotesque body *in the very name of exclusion*" (108). They analyze how, in English neoclassicism, "the civic body is *topographically* reformed by the unceremonious exportation and dumping of libido in the countryside and in the far colonies, where, at the end of the next century, it will be miraculously rediscovered and hailed as a new life-source" (89). Austen, I believe, does not perform this particular kind of colonizing exploit, but in fact joins the Romantics in "rediscovering" the physical as a "life source."

Plenty of instances exist in her letters and in every novel in which Austen incorporates the life force of the "low" for complex reasons that travel along a current between anarchic pleasure and stinging critique. Austen's letters often portray a world where one can laugh robustly and wickedly. In 1801, Austen writes to her sister Cassandra that a certain Admiral Stanhope "is a gentlemanlike Man, but then his legs are too short, & his tail too long"; during Austen's time, "tail" was a well-known phrase that signified the male genitalia; thus Austen, making her own careful observation of the male body, jokes about the Admiral's disproportionate form.[19] Having spent November 8, 1800 being driven about in the rain, Austen received a welcome invitation to Ash Park, "to dine tête à tête with Mr Holder, Mr Cauntlett & James Digweed. . . . I believe Mary found it dull, but I thought it very pleasant. To sit in idleness over a good fire in a well-proportioned room is a luxurious sensation.—sometimes we talked & sometimes we were quite silent; I said two or three amusing things, & Mr Holder made a few infamous puns" (Le Faye 56). In other words, a room, like a novel, can be well proportioned and yet replete with racy humor; the content of character can be gentlemanlike even as the physical apparatus remains asymmetrical.

In the Juvenilia, instances of double entendres spring forth, crisp and biting: the revolutionary, libidinous, and unforgiving humor comments sharply on Romantic culture. Austen cozily incorporates sexual witticisms in these unpublished works, which were written in part for her family's enjoyment, suggesting that the Austens were comfortable and familiar with a whole range of comedic situations. This fact coexists uneasily next to another one: that nineteenth-century propriety influenced the way that Austen's early biographers—all members of her family—addressed her irreverent wit and constructed her posthumous persona. For example, Henry Austen's biography insists on her "faultless" innocence, "placidity of temper," and her refusal to comment on any foible with "unkindness" ("Biographical Notice" 31). Early accounts of her life labored in particular to omit material that smelled of Regency coarseness: Roger Sales discloses how in an edition of her letters, her great nephew, Lord Brabourne, eliminated Austen's indelicate references to bad breath and pregnancy (*Jane* 9). Although few readers today see Austen through her family's timid eyes, even later biographers, Marilyn Butler has shown, "continue the practice of isolating, provincialising and domesticating this sophisticated writer" ("Simplicity" 6). Eve Kosofsky Sedgwick argues that her novels have been sexually "sanitized" as well: "most of the love story of *Sense and Sensibility* . . . has been rendered all but invisible to most readers, leaving a dryly static tableau of discrete, moralized portraits, poised antitheses, and exemplary, deplorable, or regrettably necessary punishments, in an ascetic heterosexualizing context" (*Solitary* 150). In turn, Sedgwick's paper, read at the Modern Language Association, was, in Claudia L. Johnson's words, "savagely attacked in the press for having violated the monumentally self-evident truth that Austen had the good fortune to predate such indecorous sexual irregularities as homo- and autoeroticism" (*Equivocal* 192). Such early bowdlerizing accounts of her life and the influence they have wielded contradict some of what the novels present. In working to understand her bawdy humor, I ask if her irreverence provides the "ha-ha" in the grand landscape of her prose, so notable for its judicious and balanced style?—a "ha-ha" that surprises any automatic assumption of her inviolable propriety when immodesty unsettles decorum's illusion. It will be part of my argument here to assert that although her style changed when she began publishing, she never stopped including the kind of humor that flavors the Juvenilia—whether for the fun of it or for an exegesis of women's lives in patriarchal culture.

For example, in *The History of England*, which Clara Tuite identifies as crossing "sexual plots" with historical plots (41), the young Austen, delighted with herself, makes reference to James I's homosexuality when she notes that one of the King's "favourites," Robert Carr, later Earl of Somerset, was James's "pet"—a pun she includes in her charade: "My first [a car] is what my second [pet] was to King James the 1st, and you tread on my whole" (148). David Nokes suggests that "Jane was bold enough to emphasize [James's homosexuality] with another *double-entendre*" (126) when she wrote that "His Majesty was of that amiable disposition which inclines to Freindship, & in such points was possessed of a keener penetration in Discovering Merit than many other people" (*History* 147). I think Nokes is correct here, though the pun no doubt extends even farther in the charade's third clue: "you tread on my whole," "hole" being a common vulgarism for anus from the fourteenth century (Partridge 397). Austen enforces that she wants her readers to "get" the sexual allusion: she gives the charade's answer before writing out the riddle and then stresses in italics that the charade itself "May afford my Readers some amusement to *find it out*" (148). Since she gives us the solution, the point is not to *find out* the answer to the riddle, but to discover *it*: that is, James's same-sex relationships.

The jokes about sodomy that appear in the Juvenilia return in the later novels. For example, in *Mansfield Park* when Miss Crawford describes how her home life acquainted her with a "circle of admirals," she jokes that of "*Rears* and *Vices*, I saw enough. Now, do not be suspecting me of a pun, I entreat" (60, Austen's emphasis). D. A. Miller says that one reaction to coming upon a double entendre such as this in Austen is to be "embarrassed and often arrested by the question, 'Could a character in Jane Austen ever mean *this*?' " (32 n.). Miller poses a good question. My answer is that, yes, despite her lady-like manners and spinster status, Austen can create characters who mean "that" and in meaning that, her (and their) sexual humor exposes and clarifies the consequences of patriarchal power. In "Cultural Feminism versus Post-Structuralism: The Identity Crisis in Feminist Theory," Linda Alcoff points out that men's behavior tends to be thought of as "underdetermined, free to construct its own future along the course of its rational choice" whereas women's own nature is said to determine her behavior, a nature which "limits . . . her intellectual endeavors . . . and the inevitabilities of her emotional journey through life" (96). Brian Southam repeats this argument that a woman's "nature" determines her behavior: he argues that Austen's publisher "Thomas Egerton . . . would never have permitted such an outrageous joke from Mary Crawford or anyone else. Sodomy was a taboo topic in mixed company and it is unthinkable that it should appear in respectable fiction, let alone in a novel by a lady" (*Navy* 185). To define it as "unthinkable" that a "lady" could make such a joke, not only essentializes Austen, but presents a monolithic view of culture and of how well British society at this time implemented its rules. As Roy Porter argues in "Sexual Advice before 1800," "censorship and repression work in subtle ways. . . . Carnal knowledge was evidently a complex thing, desired, dangerous, denied all at once. And readers surely enjoyed playing with fire" (137). If magazines for ladies and for a mixed readership could make sexual jokes, why couldn't Austen? Further, once Austen writes the pun and Mary verbalizes it, the joke's power extends beyond the censor's control since nothing, short of excising the joke from the novel, can stop or regulate the associations it generates.

Mary's joke carries its own punch, but it is also reasonable to interpret it as being purposively bawdy since it joins a network of images in *Mansfield Park* that highlight how virtually every character tries "to make" or "be made," a verb the novel exploits to signify the improvement of property, promotion, and marrying well, but which also takes on a sexual suggestion. Henry Crawford engages in altering Rushworth's Sotherton estate by reorienting the mansion's approach and redirecting his fiancée's eyes away from her future husband and toward him. Austen, engaging contemporary discussions of picturesque improvement, links national debates about land use to courtship as she focuses on nature's erotic associations and the characters' flirtations as they wander through Rushworth's grounds. Henry Crawford "makes"—the century's lingo for promoting—William Price's career in the Navy to secure or "buy" Fanny Price's favors and thereby "promote" her by making her his wife: in the process, he transforms both brother and sister into commodities.

The tendency to sanitize Austen parallels similar efforts at policing the novel as a genre during the Romantic period. Amanda Gilroy and Wil Verhoeven point out that with the "magisterial exception of [Katie] Trumpener," major examinations of the Romantic-era novel by critics such as William Hazlitt, J. M. S. Tompkins, Ian Watt, Michael McKeon, and Julian Moyahan "discount its existence, power, and significance" (149). "By and large," they argue, "the Romantic era novel, rather than constituting the first great age of the popular novel in English, which it was, came to be seen as 'problematic': post-Richardson and pre-Dickens, but otherwise a taxonomic challenge" (155). Such evaluations have emanated partly from the era's own reprobation of the novel as potentially corrupting, and the conservatives' call to reclaim the genre from radicalism and other licentious purposes: "the Jacobin novel had jumped the genre boundary of 'polite entertainment' and now it had to be disciplined and brought back in line, along with other types of inflaming fiction, such as the sentimental and the gothic novel" (Gilroy, Verhoeven 153). While scholars have recognized the Victorian expurgations, including elisions from the letters, that contributed to biographers' and editors' adjustments of Austen's character, I propose that censoring Austen and censoring the Romantic novel go hand in hand. Thus, to remain "in line," Austen's fiction, like Austen herself, has been "disinfected," so to speak, from the same sort of contaminating and defiling proclivity of the novel itself. Rather than seeing Austen's narratives as part of the movement to discipline and bring back in line the Jacobin novel, I am suggesting instead that Austen herself pushed those boundaries even while participating in what has come to be seen as the apex of genteel diversion. Katie Trumpener reads the romantic novel as "obsessed with the problem of culture: with historical and cultural alterity, with historical and cultural change, with comparative cultural analysis, and with the way traditional customs and values shape everyday life" (xiv). Drawing from Trumpener's interpretation, I argue that in each novel, Austen employs multiple historical narratives (the popular and the doctrinal) and polyandrous language systems (the cultivated and the colloquial) to take on "the problem of culture" and to examine how customs shape everyday life.

UNBECOMING CONJUNCTIONS

Austen chose the name Bennet from her parish register, naming the moralistic, younger daughter Mary after a promiscuous peasant girl who figured prominently in the local bastardy records (Nokes 113–114). In doing so, she blurs the line between "good" and "bad" girls and localizes one of the sources of promiscuous behavior in the tomes that Mary reads, books that reinforce double standards and whose moralizing tales aim at controlling female physicality. This example from *Pride and Prejudice* aptly deserves denomination as an "unbecoming conjunction," a term Austen uses to describe what happens when two ideas or images or people, set side by side, reveal unforeseen similarities "which reason will patronize in vain,—which taste cannot tolerate,—which ridicule will seize" (*Persuasion* 68). Austen's conjunctions allow for the simultaneous apprehension of paradoxical responses when she presents courtship as comic and moving, as erotic and ridiculous, as satisfying and disturbing. An elastic structure, the unbecoming conjunction shakes up conventions and emphasizes point of view and the process of judging over judgment itself. As Austen acknowledges in *Sanditon*, her last, unfinished, novel, human behavior can be "very striking—and very amusing—or very melancholy, just as satire or morality might prevail" (396).

These conjunctions provide a way to represent how both the tragic and the comic figure into matters of the flesh.[20] Austen's generally comedic handling of such a comingling differs from the treatment of the body, sexuality, and family relations in other novels of the period. For example, in Mary Brunton's *Self-Control*, Captain Hargrave propositions Laura, the heroine, at the point where she thinks he is proposing marriage; realizing the truth, she loses consciousness and when she awakes finds "blood gushing from her mouth and nostrils" (10), a shocking instance of how Brunton embodies the language of sexual violence in a hymenal trope. No droll wit or irony inflect the didactic mission of this passage. To take another example, Harriet Freke, from Maria Edgeworth's *Belinda*, bawdily decries ideology when, in response to Mr. Percival's celebration of the "decent drapery of life," she retorts that "Drapery, if you ask me my opinion, . . . whether wet or dry, is the most confoundedly indecent thing in the world," alluding here to the Romantic fashion for translucent garments. As another name for ideology, drapery *is* indecent, but this ribald remark is hardly funny because of the way that the novel anathematizes Mrs. Freke and a few lines later cordons off her attempt at humor when she stretches so violently that her "habiliments gave way" (230, 231). In comparison, Austen finds witty amusement in Louisa Musgrove's sexual escapades: In *Persuasion*, all the women in the company "were contented to pass quietly and carefully down the steep flight, excepting Louisa; she must be jumped down them by Captain Wentworth. In all their walks, he had had to jump her from the stiles; the sensation was delightful to her" (109). In contrast to Brunton and Edgeworth, Austen wryly invokes a bawdy pun and inspires knowing laughter at Louisa's expense; while acknowledging the character's failings, she also normalizes female heterosexual appetite. When the narrator of *Persuasion* describes the Musgroves's son, who has died while serving in the navy, as "nothing better than a thick-headed, unfeeling, unprofitable Dick Musgrove" (51), the novel suggests that not everyone deserves to be mourned, and when she describes his mother's sorrow for him as "tasteless," Austen transforms what is sacred—lamentation for those who are lost—into an aesthetic experience, and in doing so, points out the radical relativity of perception.

One of the most important jobs of feminist critics, according to Margaret R. Higonnet, is to "interrogate the problematic assumption

of a 'female' identity" ("Comparative" 157). Austen's use of such
unbecoming language questions the degree to which the bawdy can
or cannot constitute the notion of a "genderlect." Her low humor
suggests the inverse of what is usually acknowledged: that is, as
Higonnet, drawing from her studies of Deborah Cameron, has argued,
"women historically in most cultures have suffered from social
disadvantages that produce specific linguistic behaviors. Men have
controlled literacy and certain elite linguistic registers" (161). Here,
though, the question is, how does our understanding of Austen's novels benefit from including her in the male-dominated, but *"non-elite*
linguistic registers" of subversive humor? I believe that Austen is not
trying to "be one of the boys" in using shocking diction; rather, she
manipulates male "genderlect" for subversive feminist purposes.
Certainly, "encoded verbal practices can serve to shield and unite
groups in the face of repression by dominant political, racial, or sexual
cultures. These verbal strategies can be woven together in complex
forms of *metissage*" (Higonnet, "Comparative" 162).[21] Austen's
hybrid, code-switching language—a lexicon that combines high and
low, propriety and sexuality, direct and indirect erotic allusions, and
the uncoded and coded ways of understanding women's physicality in
the novels—allows her to acknowledge her heroines' bodies and their
sexuality in a manner distinctively unlike the focus on blind obedience
and uninformed innocence many conduct books endorsed.

Austen's Unbecoming Conjunctions: Subversive Laughter, Embodied
History shows how Austen's humor, her exploration of the body's
expression of social constructions, and her presentation of women's
histories through the everyday objects they handle all encourage a
reassessment of cultural expectations, Romantic-era assumptions, and
the history of the novel as it provides coordinates for a journey into
territory largely unexplored. Linda Alcoff points out that woman "is
always the Object, a conglomeration of attributes to be predicted and
controlled along with other natural phenomena" (97). An Austen
liberated from predictable attributes is an artist whose comedy opens
up interstices that prevailing assumptions about women (their humor,
their sexuality, their married or unmarried status) have sutured.
Austen examines the body's role in her novels, calling attention to the
incarnations of gender inequity by finding wit in male anatomy,
female sensibility, the eroticism and horror of death, the "nothingness"
of the everyday, and the inability to tolerate the emotions of those
who are aesthetically unappealing. As Cixous argues, if you "censor the
body . . . you censor breath and speech at the same time" ("Laugh"
311–312). In writing through her body, Austen uses language in a

way that "cuts through, gets beyond the ultimate reserve-discourse" ("Laugh" 315). *Did Jane Austen Really Mean That?* This book contends that she did. In often unbecoming conjunctions, these "unladylike" references foster erotic delight, critique patriarchal ideologies, and offer a reevaluation of Austen's literary achievements and the place of the woman writer in the Romantic era.

CHAPTER 1

BEJEWELING THE CLANDESTINE BODY/BAWDY: THE MINIATURE SPACES OF *SENSE AND SENSIBILITY*

Oh! What a snug little Island,
A right little, tight little Island.

> —Thomas Dibdin, "The Tight Little Island,"
> *The British Taft*, 1797

True wit is like the brilliant stone,
Dug from Golconda's mine;
Which boasts two various pow'rs in one,
To cut as well as shine.
Genius like that, if polish'd right,
With the same gifts abounds;
Appears at once both keen and bright.
And sparkles while it wounds.

> —"On Genuine Wit," *The Lady's Monthly Museum*, 1807[1]

THE CLANDESTINE OBJECT: EMBODIED IDENTITIES IN MINIATURE PORTRAITS, HAIR JEWELRY, AND TOY BASKETS

At the end of *Sense and Sensibility*, Willoughby apologizes for betraying and abandoning Marianne. Elinor, recounting his confession to her sister, miniaturizes his disclosure: she offers "the chief points [of] his apology . . . and was carefully minute in every particular of speech and look, where minuteness could be safely indulged" (347–348). In a hyper-vaulted juncture of the symbolic and the literal, Marianne, seizing each microbic sign of Willoughby that Elinor offers, "caught every syllable with panting eagerness" (348). Such a moment typifies this novel's attention to the minute—that is, both the detailed and the small. Austen's incorporation of the miniature occurs in a particular context: eighteenth-century Britain had seen the revival of art forms such as painting in miniature (figure 1.1), the exchange of hair as gifts, the preservation of hair in jewelry (figure 1.2), and the craft of filigree, also known as "quilling" (figure 1.3). Women, both amateurs and paid professionals, often worked these arts and materials, and such items were linked to ideologically coded feminine sensibilities because of their small size, intimacy, and intricacy.[2]

As I examine Austen's use of popular, commonplace objects, I argue several primary points: first, sentimentalized and sexualized miniature objects both insist on and diminish a stable sense of identity. For example, it is fitting that Austen would have John Dashwood "bespeak

Figure 1.1 Charles Hayter (left) "Portrait of an unknown woman and two of her children" (1800); "Unknown boy holding a miniature" (right) (1800). Courtesy: V&A Picture Library.

Figure 1.2 Hair Jewelry (from left to right) Earrings, braided hair, and gold rosettes (1810); Brooch, braided hair, and gold rosettes (1810); Ring, braided hair under glass, with inscription inside (1810); Brooch, hair under glass (ca. 1830). Courtesy: Bildarchiv Foto Marburg.

Fanny a seal" (222). Between 1790 and 1820 seals were fashionable and, worn as an accessory, combined sentiment and business because they were used to fasten and authenticate professional and personal letters (figure 1.4). An apt gift for his wife since she cannot separate family concerns from business, the seal's practicality masculinizes her and underscores how her voice dominates the family, especially its money matters.[3] In Fanny's case, this gift works as a character enforcer; miniature objects most often, however, draw attention to the character's *inability* to sustain authoritative conceptions of identity. As Ralph Rugoff says, "minute artworks involve us, sometimes quite literally, in acts of discovery. . . . If a skein of expansive possibilities erupts from the tiny object, it is not through any logical dialectic of opposites (of large and small), but in a destabilizing seduction that seems to turn our world upside down" (14–15). The objects challenge convictions of selfhood once they are worn since the person who places another's face around her neck or buries the memento within the folds of clothing takes her own identity in part from the one represented. Second, both offering and withholding information, the jewelry settings or picture frames and the sometimes-mysterious relation between the person who wears the miniature and the miniature's image, tease the viewer. This point follows from the fact that, during the Romantic period, hair tokens and miniature portraits were at their most detailed and naturalistic, prized for their resemblance to the sitter and for the genuine emotion they evinced. However, because miniatures also featured privacy, settings such as "heavily-faceted crystal fronts" (Bury 36), often disguised the content and compromised this naturalism. For example, miniatures that illustrated only one eye both confided and withheld clues about the subject's identity. Artists paint the eye in realistic particularity in these pieces; they add abstraction, though, when they isolate the eye from the face and thus

Figure 1.3   Princess Elizabeth, Fire Screen: Filigree work on a wooden frame (1787).
Courtesy: V&A Picture Library.

Figure 1.4 Topaz fob seal, mounted in gold, engraved with a view of the Battle of Trafalgar. Inscribed with "ENGLAND EXPECTS THAT EVERY MAN WILL DO HIS DUTY" (ca. 1815). Bequeathed by P. M. Sheward. Courtesy: V&A Picture Library.

Figure 1.5 Three Painted Eyes: (bottom) an eye in a frame of seed pearls; (top) the eye has a diamond "tear" (late eighteenth, early nineteenth century). Reproduced by kind permission of Ann Louise Luthi, *Sentimental Jewellery.* Photo by Alice Fowler.

from the larger context of identification, making the sitter almost impossible to recognize (figure 1.5).

Third, these objects embody the characters' subjectivity, often hypostatizing their personal desires and fears. In doing so, these material goods help make prominent and physical concerns such as the eroticized body, consumerism, and the paradox of authenticity. Simply put, they reveal secrets that would otherwise be occluded from the reader. By visualizing meanings in the novel that words evade or only imply, these ornaments provide an "inside-out" view, drawing attention to the liminal relationship between jewelry and the body. Finally, Austen weaves these tiny objects, replete with secret meanings, into her narrative in order to expose male entitlement in general and the way Brandon and Willoughby in particular manipulate sensibility's moral and sexual discourses.

Austen includes up-to-the-minute fashions in her novel when Willoughby cuts off one of Marianne's locks, Lucy gives her fiancé some of her hair, and Elinor believes that Edward preserves her tresses in a ring he wears. The exchange of hair as gifts and the preservation of hair in jewelry was a popular and conventional practice in Britain during the eighteenth and nineteenth centuries, and, after 1800, such gifts were prominent (Bury 36, 41). Leigh Hunt, for example, says in his opening essay, "Pocket Books and Keepsakes," for the *Keepsake* of 1828 that, to emphasize intimacy and cordiality, one should combine the literary memento with that "most precious of all keepsakes—hair. A braid of it may be used instead of ribbon to mark the page" (18). A good example of the sexual intensity associated with such exchanges occurs when William Hazlitt, left by his lover, Sarah, describes in *Liber Amoris* (1822) how he "tore the locket which contained her hair (and which I used to wear continually in my bosom as the precious token of her dear regard) from my neck and trampled it in pieces." Later, he "gathered up the fragments of the locket of her hair . . . which were strewed about the floor, kissed them, folded them up in a sheet of paper, and sent them to her, with these lines written in pencil on the outside—'*Pieces of a broken heart, to be kept in remembrance of the unhappy. Farewell*' " (141–142, 150).

In the instances just cited, as well as in *Sense and Sensibility*, a woman gives a lock to a man, rather than seeking a keepsake from him. Strict rules dictated hair exchange: for example, an unmarried woman could receive a hair token from a man if she were engaged to him (Bury 44); thus, a man could plead for or claim what the culture considered to be a symbol of a woman's essence, but a woman could do so only if she had already surrendered her rights by agreeing to marry. The episode in which Marianne gives Willoughby a lock of hair provides a moment of dramatic revelation for Elinor, highlighting as it does the intimacy and sexual intensity of such a gift. Margaret narrates the telling event:

> "Oh! Elinor," she cried, "I have such a secret to tell you about Marianne. I am sure she will be married to Mr. Willoughby very soon."
>
> "You have said so," replied Elinor, "almost every day since they first met on High-church Down; and they had not known each other a week, I believe, before you were certain that Marianne wore his picture round her neck; but it turned out to be only the miniature of our great uncle."
>
> "But indeed, this is quite another thing. I am sure they will be married very soon, for he has got a lock of her hair."
>
> "Take care, Margaret. It may be only the hair of some great uncle of *his*." (60)

The sisters' conversation situates Marianne's and Willoughby's relationship within the amphitheater of inequitable laws governing the distribution of inheritance. A likeness of her great uncle, the one who leaves the sisters only a thousand pounds each "as a mark of his affection" (4), circles around Marianne's neck. That she wears her uncle's miniature around her neck, and not Willoughby's, denotes how Marianne is in effect bound—or "strangled"—by having been "cut off" from a fortune that morally belongs to her and her mother and sisters, but instead is bequeathed to a four-year-old boy whose "cunning tricks" (4) wooed and won this dying patriarch. Here Austen plays with the pun between hair and heir (both symbols of immortality), a conceit appearing in Shakespeare's plays and sonnets.[4] What Erik Gray calls the "shadowy presence of the second word" (i.e., heir) depends upon a similar pronunciation of the two terms and capitalizes on the notion that both the hair and heir are reproductions of the self that offer a youthful and vigorous reflection even after death, and "provide some prospect of life even in death" (225, 227). As Marina Warner argues, "hair is organic, but less subject to corruption than all our organs; and like a fossil, like a shell, it lasts when parted from the living organism to which it once belonged" (7). Thus, Margaret's observation that Willoughby has "cut off a long lock" of Marianne's hair, which Elinor suggests is only the "hair of some great uncle of his," reinforces how the actual threat of being "cut off" from an inheritance leads Willoughby to desert Marianne. His betrayal, in effect, constitutes the patrimony she receives from the relationship, but what is the nature of that "inheritance"? Given that Willoughby abandons her, the boundaries between erotic and mourning jewelry disintegrate; further, the demarcation between the symbolic exchange of bodies and actual contact also dissolves since Willoughby leaves

Marianne to fight a duel with Brandon, whose sixteen-year-old ward (the younger Eliza) Willoughby had seduced and left pregnant. Thus, Willoughby's past actions force him to end his love affair with Marianne. The fact that his scheme was, as he later tells Elinor, to seduce her, taints his protestations of regard and makes a mockery of her hair as a symbol of love everlasting (320).

Marcia Pointon explains Emile Durkheim's theory that "feelings evoked by one thing spread contagiously from a thing to the representation associated with it and from this to the objects with which these representations become associated" ("Materializing" 43). In the novel, Marianne and Willoughby's passion "spreads" toward her hair, which in turn generates further associations with her sexuality, italicizing the amatory content of their courtship. A "sign of the animal in the human" as well as "the least fleshly production of the flesh," hair, "in its suspended corruptibility . . . seems to transcend the mortal condition, to be in full possession of the principle of vitality itself" (Warner 7). The exchange of hair between Willoughby and Marianne also doubles as physical colloquy between bodies. As I will explore throughout this book, Austen links sexual exploitation with financial avarice, a major theme in *Sense and Sensibility* and a point Austen communicates when she offers the manifest possibility that Marianne "inherits" the loss of love and of reputation. Marcia Pointon argues that "hair symbolically connects the body to nature" ("Materializing" 43), and psychoanalytic theory interprets hair on the head as a metonym for the genitals; hair—so palpably material—has always been associated with sensuality and the language of sexual usury. Pope's *Rape of the Lock* made that clear: "Oh, hadst thou, cruel! Been content to seize / Hairs less in sight, or any hairs than these!" (Canto 4, ll. 175–176). From the mid-eighteenth to the twentieth centuries, hair signified the "female sex" and referred to women who were "viewed sexually" (Partridge 366), and the word "lock" meant both "a place for storing stolen goods" as well as the "female pudenda" (489). Thus, combining "lock" and "hair" doubles these connotations. Margaret's description of the event punctuates the literal and symbolic hybridity of this erotic moment:

> But indeed, Elinor, it is Marianne's [hair]. I am almost sure it is, for I saw him cut it off. Last night after tea, when you and mama went out of the room, they were whispering and talking together as fast as could be, and he seemed to be begging something of her, and presently he took up her scissars [*sic*] and cut off a long lock of her hair, for it was all tumbled down her back; and he kissed it, and folded it up in a piece of white paper, and put it into his pocket-book. (60)

Austen's pointed and repeated use of the term "tumbled," slang for copulation (which I discuss in detail later in the chapter), alludes to the *Rape of the Lock* and enunciates how the dispossession of her "hair" foreshadows an injury to her reputation.[5] *The Spirit of the Public Journals'* inclusion of Matthew Lewis's "Giles Jollup the Knave, and Brown Sally Green," which I alluded to in the Introduction, indicates that this meaning was well known: the hero worries that his lover will "tumble in love with some smart city beau, / And with him share your shop in the Strand" (319, ll. 9–10). Austen has drawn some distinction between Marianne and the other two fallen women in the novel, since Willoughby's and Brandon's father inflict irreparable damage on them, while Marianne's marriage to Brandon "redeems" her. However, in her uses of and references to hair jewelry, to portrait miniatures, and to bawdy phrases such as tumbling—which all occur, I might add, in the first seventy pages—Austen extends the tragic implications that Pope's mock-epic elides and draws an intimate link between Marianne and the two fallen women.

Because hair mementoes imply irreproducibility but involve mechanical reproduction, they allow Austen to make concrete and ironize the flagrant reproducibility of Marianne's and Willoughby's supposedly unique and everlasting love. Cut hair stays fresh and youthful through time, so it can symbolize the immortality of romantic love or familial union. As a result, jewelers employed hair in both sentimental and mourning jewelry, but because small factories produced such keepsakes, often randomly substituting individual locks of hair in the manufacturing process, these mementoes italicize the factory-like seductions Willoughby effects in which one woman's hair hardly differs from another's in his march through town and country. Marianne's cut hair also links the couple's courtship to the relation between sensibility and the discourse of sexuality. Bestowing such a sentimental gift spotlights how sensibility, as a code for "openness," becomes another ideological illusion, one that Willoughby exploits to seduce Marianne. When passionate love is concerned, Marianne heroically posits herself against the machinery of social protocol.[6] In her famous manifesto defending sensibility, Marianne exclaims that "if there had been any real impropriety in [touring Allenham] I should have been sensible of it at the time, for we always know when we are acting wrong, and with such a conviction I could have had no pleasure" (68). This logic could also be used to justify sexual commerce before marriage since she uses it to rationalize touring Allenham without its current owner's permission: it is a close step from this episode's literal content to the allusive significance of their intimate and wild buggy ride to a house where the couple examines Willoughby's "possessions"—the estate he will inherit. Helen Sheumaker argues that hair mementos were associated with sensibility because they were "emphatically individual in . . . material and manufacture" (422); hair's authenticity "could assert a sincerity of character that transcended the hypocrisy that fashionableness often implied": yet, although "fundamentally unchangeable[,] hair work was in effect the self being twisted, turned, and tied into an acceptable, usable commodity" (430).[7] The cultural associations hair jewelry had with authenticity and sensibility divulge the ironic absence of the genuine in Willoughby's and Marianne's relationship.

Because hair jewelry links the natural (derived as it is from the body), folk art (since such fashioning could be done at home), and commerce (since one most often paid to have hair set), it engages ideas about fashion, money, and authenticity. In *Sense and Sensibility*, such keepsakes, by linking matrimony and consumerism, break down the illusion of Willoughby's love. One of the convictions about hair jewelry, that it was "valued not for the goldsmith's art which it displays, but for the few hairs clustering within," as Alexanna Speight asserted in 1871 (84), governs the fantasy that Marianne's worth, embodied in her one long curl, offsets her financial poverty. Willoughby's actions reveal the material economy governing them when he begs for a lock of Marianne's hair, kisses it, and then "fold[s] it up in a piece of white paper, and put[s] it into his pocket-book" (60). Here the word "pocket" reinforces Willoughby's schemes, since (according to Barclay's *Universal English Dictionary—1800*) it meant both "to pocket, but also to connive at; to do anything clandestinely." Willoughby never sends Marianne's hair to a jeweler to be set in an ornament, though he four times embeds it—in paper, in her letters, in his pocket book, and in his clothes. The first two receptacles suggest that paper mediates their "authentic" love: that it is novels that dictate that Marianne is required to "nouris[h] [her] grief" (83) when Willoughby first leaves (ironically, at a point when she genuinely believes he will return). Ideological expectations mediate their courtship, which they perform according to fiction's script for "real" love. Thus, placing her hair in his pocket book reiterates the novelistic character of their relation while reinforcing the idea that as he kisses her hair and places it in his pocket, he also commodifies her, since pocket books often doubled as notebooks and as wallets, which sometimes held bank notes (paper money).[8] Finally, his placement of her hair in the warm materials of his clothes reiterates the sexual connotations of their exchange and splices the miniature object's focus on the sequestered moment with the possibility of public scandal. In the guise of true affection, Willoughby fetishizes her body by subordinating it to a market culture.

This hair fetish functions in the novel as a substitute with personal and cultural significance: the fetish depends for its "meaning and value on a particular order of social relations, which it in turn reinforces" (Pietz, II 23). Since fetishes are material objects that function as signifiers of collective values, in kissing her hair, he not only metonymically kisses her body and body parts, but also, from the collective point of view, links her to the other women he has seduced, rendering his worship and her significance in relation to the larger grammar of sexual exploitation in the novel. Fetish and fetishism carry multiple meanings. As Anthony Shelton argues,

> notions of "fetishism" often imply ambiguity and disavowal . . . and are used in discourses that are either about power or project power or authority on to supposedly subordinate groups such as foreign subjects, women, "degenerates" and the insane. . . . In early theories of religion in psychiatry, and in the work of Freud and Lacan, "fetishism" comes to be associated with deficiency, loss and disavowal, while for others, including Marx, Bataille and Baudrillard, it signifies excess. Frequently deficiency and excess occur in the work of the same writer. (7)

Hair tokens in the novel function both ways: as the sign of "excess," the hair stands for more than just the hair and, as a substitute for an actual marriage proposal, Willoughby's cutting of Marianne's hair suggests deficiency and disavowal. According to Susan Stewart, the miniature (such as hair jewelry) presents a world "frozen, limited in space, particularized and generalized in time; particularized because the miniature concentrates upon a single instance; general in that instance comes to transcend, to stand for a spectrum of other instances" (48). Early on, then, Austen reduces Willoughby's "love" for Marianne—one that can be read as a fulfilling version of romance tragically nipped in the bud—to appetite and ambition.

After Willoughby returns her hair, Marianne represents to Elinor the moment she bequeathed it to him as one of unmistakable sexual intimacy: "This lock of hair, which now he can so readily give up, was begged of me with the most earnest supplication. Had you seen his look, his manner, had you heard his voice at that moment!" (189). The miniature's capacity to embody diverging scripts operates at its most evocative here: is this a metonymy of his design to seduce her or is the exchange of hair a metonymy of seduction that occurred but is stated indirectly? The gift's visceral nature, replete with concupiscent implications, reinforces the connection between their relationship and her ruin. Marianne has been "framed" and can only acknowledge that she has been "cruelly used; but not by Willoughby":

> all the world . . . [has] leagued together to ruin me in his opinion . . . Whatever he might have heard against me—ought he not to have suspended his belief? ought he not to have told me of it, to have given me the power of clearing myself? "The lock of hair, (repeating it from the letter,) which you so obligingly bestowed on me"—That is unpardonable. Willoughby, where was your heart, when you wrote those words? (189–190)

Desperate to justify his behavior, Marianne reveals that the conventional (for her) alarm that he has left her because she is "ruined" provides a glimpse into the secret intimacies they shared. From a psychoanalytic point of view, the "world" here comes to embody the feelings she fears Willoughby himself holds.

Unknown to Marianne when she exclaims, "where was your heart, when you wrote those words?" is the fact that Willoughby's fiancée, the former Miss Grey, penned them. In showing how Miss Grey forces her future husband to sign a letter she has written, Austen offers an ironic and unexpected reversal of gender roles, since Willoughby thereby joins the ranks of the women he seduced. In marrying for money, Willoughby loses his masculine sovereignty; like women who lose all financial and legal control when they wed, Willoughby must "cop[y] [his] wife's words and par[t] with [the] last relics of Marianne"—must part with his most intimate possessions:

> [Marianne's] three notes—unluckily they were all in my pocket-book. . . . And the lock of hair—that too I had always carried about me in the same pocket-book, which was now searched by Madam [Miss Grey] with the most ingratiating virulence,—the dear lock—all, every memento was torn from me. (329)

Now that Miss Grey possesses him and he has "fallen" in the eyes of his former friends, one of his prime concerns is *his* reputation: "hearing that your sister was dying—and dying too, believing me the greatest villain upon earth, scorning, hating me in her latest moments—for how could I tell what horrid projects might not have been imputed?" (330–331).[9] Humiliated, he has only one resource left—to charm; like a coquette, he needs to imprint himself upon his listener, so when he wants assurance from Elinor that "you *do* think something better of me than you did?"—he lets her hand "fall, and lean[s] against the mantle-piece as if forgetting he was to go" (331–332). Elinor gives him her hand, but the incident alludes to the last time Willoughby was leaning against the mantelpiece: when he was leaving Marianne, lying to her that he would return (75).

Jewelry made of hair complicates the construction of a secure and unique concept of self. One gives hair to a jeweler to be "redressed" in new materials—gold, other jewels, and fabric, altering its appearance. Whose is the hair?—Can others identify it? Can a person even identify her own? Is the hair even one's own? (This was a serious anxiety for those having such jewelry made.) As I have argued above, these tiny materials embody and propel phantasmagorical fictions. Often, then, the artifacts—whether hair jewelry or portraits—perform the roles or the identities that the characters' bodies desire but cannot enact or the actions that the words keep elusive. For Marianne, Willoughby's request for a lock of her hair substitutes for a marriage proposal, for the promise that he loved her, and that spontaneous affinity exists and will lead, for her, to a marriage of congruent tastes and large income. She affirms the potential of cut hair to work magic.[10] Likewise, Edward's hair ring fosters Elinor's covert reveries (figure 1.6).[11] When Marianne spies a ring on his finger with a "plait of hair in the centre," she cries,

> "I never saw you wear a ring before, Edward . . . . Is that Fanny's hair? I remember her promising to give you some. But I should have thought her hair had been darker." . . .
>
> He coloured very deeply, and giving a momentary glance at Elinor, replied, "Yes; it is my sister's hair. The setting always casts a different shade on it you know."
>
> Elinor had met his eye, and looked conscious likewise. That the hair was her own, she instantaneously felt as well satisfied as Marianne; the only difference in their conclusions was, that what Marianne considered as a free gift from her sister, Elinor was conscious must have been procured by some theft or contrivance unknown to herself. . . . [S]he internally resolved henceforward to catch every opportunity of eyeing the hair and of satisfying herself, beyond all doubt, that it was exactly the shade of her own. (98–99)

Surprisingly, Elinor, at times cynical yet committed to keeping up appearances, here takes them at face value; despite "internally resolving" to appease her skepticism about the plait, she in fact instantaneously accepts that it is hers and finds "flattering proof" of his affection in the ring "which he constantly wore around his finger" (102).

42

Figure 1.6 Ring made from enameled gold and woven hair under a rock crystal panel (1791). The inscription around the edge of the ring commemorates Gabriel Wirgman. Courtesy: V&A Picture Library.

Context, however, relativizes evidence, just as it makes truth contingent, which in turn compromises any guarantee of authenticity: disguising the *content* of the ring by changing its *context*, Edward says, "The setting always casts a different shade on it you know."[12] These tokens were intended as identifiable keepsakes for the bearer; Edward knows that he wears Lucy's hair. But to accentuate the relativity rather than the certainty of decoding appearances and to emphasize the obstacles inherent in knowing the self and others, Austen here exploits the often-justified paranoia that infiltrated the hair-jewelry industry: uncertain provenance. For example, there were suspicions that convents on the Continent provided Victorian hairworkers with their raw materials (Bury 41).[13] In the "Remarks" preceding his *Pattern Book of Souvenirs in Hair, and List of Prices* (London, 1851), Mr. George Dewdney

> Conscientiously promis[es] to return the Hair entrusted to him; for on no account does Hair leave his possession until worked, and returned in the form desired. As all articles are made on the premises, and no secrecy made of working the same, Ladies or Gentlemen can see their *Own Hair* made into any souvenir they may wish to have; and thus receive the most unquestionable proof of preserving the much-prized lock of Hair. Any article commanded will be promptly executed, if the Hair sent be accompanied by Post office Order, or reference in town. Hair can be safely transmitted by Post. For additional security, every article sent by post above 20s. value, is registered,—the charge for the same being 6d. (N.p.)

Indeed, first the hair belongs to Fanny Dashwood (his sister), then to Elinor, and finally to Lucy (Edward's secret fiancée), though ironically it only presents an interpretation of "truth," not the certainty. The ring simultaneously embodies Edward's deceit and his loyalty. When Elinor mistakes her own hair, she exposes that she—who deftly commands social situations—cannot read her own body, the actions of the man she loves, or the truth of her own experience (when and how would he have secured her hair?). She dramatizes her own susceptibility to sensibility, as a piece of sentimental jewelry liquefies her defenses.

Her ruminations, like Marianne's, associate cut hair with magical rites; what kind of enchantment did Edward use to procure her hair? Imagining a situation in which someone could touch and then cut one's hair without one's knowledge or a ploy by which the depressed and passive Edward could devise such a theft suggests incantation, or, respectively, a frightening disenfranchisement from the body or from knowledge of him. So even though Elinor later "smiles" at her mother since she "must always be carried away by her imagination on any interesting subject" (336), Elinor herself gets "carried away" when she projects onto Edward's ring her own secret fantasies. And what those fantasies involve become disturbing since her response knots two matters central to the novel—money and sex: although Marianne considers the hair a "free gift from her sister," Elinor knows it was "procured" (meaning that it was obtained through care, but also signifying in general ways buying and selling and in specific ways the purchase and vending of women's services during the eighteenth century). Elinor's further speculation that he procured the hair by "some theft or contrivance" connects the triumvirate of consumerism, sexuality, and exploitation. Her speculation starts looking like a fantasy of seduction, one that resembles Marianne's experiences in Willoughby's hands.

Lucy Steele uses several miniatures and a piece of hair jewelry to highlight her authentic claims to Edward: she offers Elinor proof of her engagement to him in the forms of a ring, a tiny portrait, and another charged semiotic system—letters. These objects, disassociated from their past context of Edward's youthful infatuation, become a collection Lucy uses to manipulate the present. Susan Stewart argues that "[t]he collection is a form of art as play" (151). Lucy's collection, reframed (in Elinor's words) as a "body of evidence" (139), artistically rearranges the past. Elinor errs in contending that Lucy's goods indicate genuine feeling—an "engagement of the heart"—since this collection regenerates a fresh "context of origin" (Stewart 152), one with a new use value: to exclude Elinor so as to keep Lucy's future economic life secure. Lucy "possesses" Edward while exhibiting his portrait, and is particularly confident when presenting her collection. In a miniature, the face is immense in proportion to the dimensions of the frame and "apprehending the face's image becomes a mode of possession" (Stewart 125). Thus, it follows that while talking to her rival, Lucy expresses concern that Edward lacks a miniature of her: "If he had but my picture, he says he should be easy. I gave him a lock of my hair set in a ring . . . and that was some comfort to him, he said, but not equal to a picture" (135). Since Lucy does not love Edward (she later marries his younger, wealthier brother on the spur of the moment), it makes sense that he might want proof of her devotion.

The miniature thus orders chaos while also creating "a tension or dialectic between inside and outside, between private and public property, between the space of the subject and the space of the social" (Stewart 68). Material conditions dominate Edward's desire for her portrait and her longing that he possess one, since Lucy undoubtedly cannot afford to sit for a picture, which might cost between three and ten guineas, but can only offer an anonymous and less expensive, craft-like gift of hair jewelry; as the Steeles's friends report, Lucy "had nothing at all" (272).[14] Linked to Lucy's desire for upward mobility is the fact that the middle-class population, especially those visiting pleasure resorts and inhabiting urban areas, coveted such miniatures. The provenance of her particular ring is impossible to determine: she may have worked the hair herself or turned it over to a goldsmith, since she may have been able to afford a simple setting. Bury explains that "in the late eighteenth and early nineteenth centuries a single curl cost under a shilling if plain, but the addition of gold details or the introduction of seed pearls increased the price to five shillings or more, according to the complexity of the design" (41).[15] Moreover, the secret within the covert space is that though he may profess to be uneasy without a miniature of her, in fact, because he loves Elinor, he does not want Lucy's portrait at all; the anonymous hair ring, therefore, functions as a lexicon for the liminal nature of their secret commitment.

These two rivals, Lucy and Elinor, work together to finish another kind of miniature object: a paper filigree basket for tiny, three-year-old Annamaria Middleton. Bachelard proposes that "values become condensed and enriched in miniature" (150), and here, their construction of the basket provides an opportunity to watch economic worlds collide. The filigree toy connotes handmade, nonmechanized labor since the women construct this gift in a form known as "quilling," a craft that developed in European religious orders in the sixteenth and early seventeenth centuries. In quilling, one rolls thin strips of paper into different shapes and then manipulates them to construct designs, the way thin metal wire is worked in conventional filigree (figure 1.7). By the late eighteenth century, filigree, which had also been a popular peasant craft, became fashionable with wealthy, leisured ladies or, in Lucy's case, with those who toiled for those who enjoyed such status. Thus, this "work," which was always decorative, but once linked to religious practice and to lower-class life, now is used to construct a present for a three-year old; the activity, however, mimics industrialized labor in its tedious monotony and in its exchange value. The material conditions that govern these characters and that run through the novel emerge in strong relief in the drawing room when Lady Middleton announces that she is "glad" that Lucy is "not going to finish poor little Annamaria's basket this evening; for I am sure it must hurt your eyes to work fillagree [*sic*] by candlelight." Lucy, taking the "hint," announces that "I should have been at my fillagree already. I would not disappoint the little angel for all the

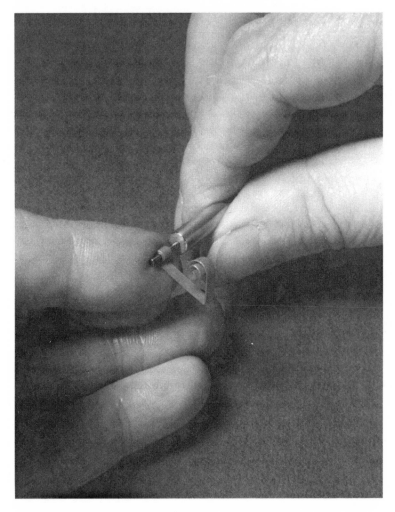

Figure 1.7 Quilling technique. Reproduced by the kind permission of Search Press.

world, and if you want me at the card-table now, I am resolved to finish the basket after supper" (144).

Women's work ensures material survival: here Lucy earns her keep, which Austen accents by repeating the word "work" six times in two pages: Lady Middleton orders "working candles," and Lucy draws her "work table" near her. Elinor, who wants to have a private conversation with Lucy, exploits this opportunity by announcing that she will "be of some use . . . in rolling her papers for her" and that she "should like the work exceedingly" (145).[16] Lady Middleton releases them from their other work—the social responsibility of playing cards—since Elinor, manipulating the situation so as to be alone with Lucy, claims that she "really likes the work of fillagree" (145). This scene calls to mind Mary Lamb's later disquisition, "On Needle-Work" (1815), in which she argues that the work women do in the home should be understood as *work*, that is, as a financial contribution to the family: by "calculat[ing] every evening how much money has been saved in needle-work done in the family, and compar[ing] the result with the daily portion of the yearly income" one could "for[m] a true notion and ge[t] at the exact worth of this species of home indus- try. . . ." (192–193). The worth of Lucy and Elinor's labor on this basket is precisely what the Middletons do not calculate. Mary Lamb acknowledges that although "Needle-work taken up as an amusement may not be altogether unamusing . . . let us not confuse the motives of economy with those of simple pastime" (193). What Lady Middleton posits as leisure activity is hard labor as they strain their eyes finishing intricate designs in a darkened room (figure 1.8). And what the young women posit as a partnership is competition as they, "with the utmost harmony[,] engag[e] in forwarding the same work" (145).[17]

Lucy professes love and affection for Edward while working filigree and manipulating Elinor; Austen thus exhibits how the companionate marriage, which evolves in lockstep with industrialization, is con- ceived under the aegis of capital. Because making this miniature basket stages the women's other labor—competitive procurement of a marriage partner—Lucy and Elinor's rivalry implies that the marriage market, even when weddings are made for love, resembles labor marked by reproduction, uniformity, and repetition. James Thompson observes that

> [t]he point to be made about this business or market or labor vocabu- lary is not that marriage had become more of an economic event, but rather that this economic vocabulary seems obtrusive and angry pre- cisely because marriage was coming to raise such different expectations. In other words, conflicts between love and money, romance and reality, had, if anything, become more exacerbated and more visible than they had been earlier in the century. The metaphor comparing marriage to business or to work suggests the degree to which marriage really was a form of labor, and so examination of this point should expose the nature of the antagonism between the economic reality of marriage and the romantic mythology that obscures it. (142)

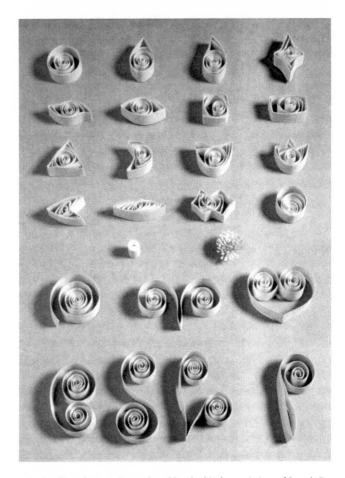

Figure 1.8 Quilling designs. Reproduced by the kind permission of Search Press.

Austen's doubling of their conversation with the toil of basket making highlights the paradox of the "love match" insofar as she coalesces the mercantile heart of matrimony and the commercial marrow of industrial labor. Even Elinor too "profit[s]" from her conversation with Lucy (145). The quilling scene italicizes how consumption and mechanized labor form the marriage market's core, most notably in that the hair in Edward's ring is unidentifiable and itself mirrors evidence in the novel that potential marriage partners are indistinguishable: it is as likely to Mrs. Palmer that she would have married Brandon as Mr. Palmer; even children themselves are indistinguishable: both Robert and Edward are at different points the "elder" son.

As Maaja Stewart argues, "Within the resemblances brought to the reader's awareness, . . . all stories threaten to become a single story, the model Ur-story. Colonel Brandon's attempt to unite Marianne's life with his cousin Eliza's and also with his ward Eliza's expresses the same impulse" (101). Gifts of hair ask the receiver to remember and forget the tension between the authentic and the mechanized object or person. Professing love, Lucy Steele grinds uphill practicing libidinal economy, while Marianne becomes a miniature of both Elizas, and in the way that Elinor's hair resembles Lucy's so do the women become portraits of the others.

And finally, although Austen usually avoids allegorical names (though as I have discussed, such names were considered funny in *The Lady's Monthly Museum*), that of Lucy Steele blatantly calls attention to her as a thief (of husbands and fortunes). As a character who is associated with jewelry, Lucy could also be linked to the early nineteenth-century fad for polished steel. Jewelry historian Clare Phillips explains that "all manner of jewellery was made from brightly polished steel in the decades around 1800—buckles, buttons, watch chains, necklaces, bracelets, tiaras, chatelaines, sword hilts, and the star badges for orders of chivalry" (64). Cut-steel jewelry was appropriate for those (like Lucy) who could afford only cheaper metals, but it also became popular among those who could, especially as an item of "Englishness" in France before the Revolution (Phillips 64). Associated with that other revolution—the industrial one—cut steel was manufactured by Matthew Boulton who "pioneered the use of steam power to drive the polishing machines and introduced an early system of mass production, described by the foreign visitor Lichtenberg in 1775, who wrote that 'each workman has only a limited range so that he does not need constantly to change his position and tools and by this means an incredible amount of time is saved" (Phillips 64). The name, Lucy ("light") Steele, also suggests just how bright cut steel was and recalls a caricature of 1777, which depicts how the light reflecting off of cut-steel buttons knocks a fashionable lady backward (figure 1.9). I do not know if Austen knew of this caricature, but she does replicate the action when Marianne reacts to Lucy's biggest joke, that is, tricking the Dashwood women into believing that she has become Mrs. Edward Ferrars. When she instructs the Dashwood servant to tell the family that " 'I suppose you know, ma'am, that Mr. Ferrars is married[,]' Marianne gave a violent start, fixed her eyes upon Elinor, saw her turning pale, and fell back in her chair in hysterics" (353). And when Elinor receives the truth that Lucy is, instead, "Mrs. Robert Ferrars," she is "in a state of such agitation as made her hardly know where she was" (360).

Figure 1.9 W. H. Humphrey, *Steel Buttons* (1777). © Copyright the Trustees of the British Museum.

The Clandestine Word: Encoded Bodies

Austen's use of such items as hair jewelry as well as her deployment of language that carries neutral and sexually evocative tones allows her to explore attitudes toward romantic love. Ribald puns encased in miniature portraits and lockets hold within themselves a latent world within a world that ambushes the reader with their surprising confidences. Because the novel emphasizes secrecy, Austen's use of sexual slang creates tensions between the revealed and unrevealed. Lucy's crude appetite for men and money, Miss Steele's obsession with "nasty" beaux, the electricity between Marianne and Willoughby, Marianne's physical aversion to Brandon, and the unmistakable connection between her and the two Elizas, whose sexual indiscretions have left one dead from disease and poverty and the other abandoned, shamed, and isolated, all intensify a truth that polite discourse might wish to suppress, the unmistakable current of sexuality animating courtship. And although Austen gives no absolute proof that Willoughby "ruins" Marianne, the novel everywhere intimates that he has in some way contaminated her; that the quieting of her sensuous vitality at the end of the novel announces a punitive consequence for some kind of excessive behavior (Leighton 65); that there is a secret within a secret that would reveal what the true nature of their relationship was; and that the clearer Austen makes these intratextual links between Marianne and the Elizas, the more enigmatic Marianne's "engagement" with Willoughby becomes. Thus, John Wiltshire argues that "if sexuality is at the heart of the book, it is a sexuality that is necessarily censored, or screened. It is plain that the energy that circulates in the novel is sexual, but also that explicit acknowledgment of this is avoided" (58). Angela Leighton persuasively reads *Sense and Sensibility* "as a palimpsest . . . where the surface text conceals and half reveals another, less obvious text, or where the narrative is deliberately complicated by secrets and enigmas, things unsaid and voices unheard" (54–55).

In *Sense and Sensibility* Austen reveals—in language now largely invisible to modern audiences—secrets that expose Willoughby as a threat from the moment he carries Marianne "down the hill" (42). Yet it must be acknowledged that the nature of the double entendre both veils and reveals subtexts in paradoxical open secrets; words in standard English, such as "tumbling," carry both neutral and charged signification. For example, Austen incorporates a suggestive cryptogram with the elder Miss Steele, a thirty-year old adolescent obsessed with male attention and the word "beau."

> "And had you a great many smart beaux there? I suppose you have not so many in this part of the world; for my part, I think they are a vast addition always."
>
> "But why should you think," said Lucy, looking ashamed of her sister, "that there are not as many genteel young men in Devonshire as Sussex?"
>
> "Nay, my dear, I'm sure I don't pretend to say that there an't. I'm sure there's a vast many smart beaux in Exeter; but you know, how could I tell what smart beaux there might be about Norland. . . . But perhaps you young ladies may not care about the beaux, and had as lief be without them as with them. For my part I think they are vastly agreeable, provided they dress smart and behave civil. But I can't bear to see them *dirty and nasty.* Now there's Mr. Rose at Exeter, a prodigious smart young man, quite a beau, . . . and yet if you do but meet him of a morning, he is not fit to be seen. I suppose your brother was quite a beau, Miss Dashwood, before he married, as he was so rich?"
>
> "Upon my word," replied Elinor, "I cannot tell you, for I do not perfectly comprehend the meaning of the word." (123–124, emphasis added)

This episode focuses on a word's multiple meanings. In this chapter of *Sense and Sensibility*, the word "beau" appears ten times, with Miss Anne Steele alone employing eight of those in three pages. To deflect attention from her sister, Lucy introduces another term—"genteel young men"—which at first functions as a synonym for beau, though later it sounds nothing short of euphemistic. Finally, Elinor calls attention to its definition when she replies that she does not "comprehend the meaning of the word." Indeed, what does Anne Steele mean? She uses "beau" to refer to an eligible—as opposed to a married—man, but the term also signified a male who gives particular or excessive attention to dress, mien or social etiquette: an exquisite, a fop, a dandy; John Wilmot, Earl of Rochester glosses it in his *Dictionary of Love* as a "common word to express a medley character of coxcomb and fop—one who makes dress his principal attention, under an utter impossibility of ever succeeding . . ." (10). *The Spectator* describes a beau's brain as smelling like "Essence of Orange-Flower Water" and consisting of "Ribbons, Lace and Embroidery" and "Billet Doux" (Vol. 275, qtd. in Mackie 66). Grose defines the term "beau nasty" as "a slovenly fop; one finely dressed, but dirty," and the word "beau-trap" ("one who is outwardly well dressed but of unclean linen, body, habits"—Grose, *Classical*) offers a word for what Miss Steele describes.

Austen does not use the vulgar word "beau-nasty," but she has Miss Steele give a definition of it when she exclaims that she "can't bear to see [beaux] *dirty and nasty.* Now there's Mr. Rose at Exeter, a prodigious smart young man, quite a beau, . . . and yet if you do but meet him of a morning, he is not fit to be seen." In making this allusion, she connects the sanitary world of Barton Park with the London demi-monde when she asks whether there are "a great many smart beaux" at Norland or in "this part of the world." Her comment divulges that such "beaux," like the Elizas in the novel, seem to be cropping up everywhere.[18] Miss Steele herself appears rather "nasty" when she exclaims that married men cannot be "beaux" because "they have something else to do." This statement humiliates Lucy, since it introduces the salacious question of what that "something else" might be, especially since, immediately following this, Mrs. Jennings and Sir John Middleton make "countless jokes" about the letter "f" (125).

Austen further parodies both sisters: for the man-hungry Miss Steele to be preoccupied with beaux is nonsensical since they were associated with effeminacy, and effeminacy with homosexuality.[19] Lucy ironically, though she believes triumphantly, propels herself into a marriage with a fop: her future husband, Robert Ferrars, is the beau who takes "a quarter of an hour" "examining and debating . . . over every toothpick-case in the shop" (220). Oblivious of everyone in the shop, he "seemed rather to demand than express admiration" (221). Austen's tone takes on a campy nuance in describing Robert's theatricality: ventriloquizing through his shopping that this is "the last day on which his existence could be continued without the possession of the toothpick-case" (221), "the puppyism of his manner" (221) impedes his ability to "decid[e] on all the different horrors of the different toothpick-cases presented to his inspection" (221). Partridge defines the word "puppyism" as "affectation or excessive care in costume or posture" (669). When he condescends to notice Elinor's and Marianne's features, he does so "impertinent[ly]" (221), asserting his masculine power over them while flashing effeminate traits, thereby trumping them as both a "man" and a "woman." His affected femininity and male assertion of privilege illustrate Robert Stoller's argument that "one cannot be a male transvestite without *knowing, loving,* and *magnificently expanding* the importance of one's own phallus" (188, qtd. in Garber 96). The eighteenth-century audience would have identified the transvestite as a sodomite, whether he was or not. In presenting Robert as a fop, and then marrying him to Lucy, Austen in no way backs off addressing same-sex love, but in fact makes a sly joke at the ambitious Lucy's expense, marrying her to a man who might be more interested in men than in "conjugal duties."

The period's own ambivalence about revealing the truth while it lauded frank and open behavior complicates a reading of its semiotic systems. Austen's own use of bawdy slang repeats the hide and seek patterns in the novel. *Sense and Sensibility* resolves one of its central uncertainties—are Marianne and Willoughby engaged? It leaves ambiguous, however, the other suspicion: did Willoughby sexually seduce Marianne.[20] For Austen to reveal Willoughby's motives in these erotically charged ciphers constitutes an open, yet covert way of communicating with her audience. Austen marbles the differentiation between secrecy and truth in the courtship between Marianne and Willoughby, who enact the cultural convention of love at first sight, a performance that is undermined by the fact that this kind of union is unequal, given his motives and the expectations of propriety for women.

In volume I, chapters VII–XIV, Austen uses bawdy humor to offer a relentless series of allusions to female ruin. What are the implications for our reading if Austen bares, rather than screens the text's sexual energy? Willoughby acknowledges at the end of the novel that he planned to seduce Marianne, to "endeavo[r], by every means in my power, to make myself pleasing to her, without any design of returning her affection" (320). Mary Poovey insists that "whenever Austen herself explicitly compares the two putative heroes—Colonel Brandon and Edward Ferrars—with the less moral, more passionate Willoughby, it is Willoughby who is appealing" (89). As I have shown, however, the miniatures, jewelry, and sexual slang in the novel illuminate Willoughby's seamy side early on, thereby making his later confession to Elinor less of a revelation than a mere confirmation for the knowing reader. It would be fruitless to argue that Willoughby literally "deflowers" Marianne; however, such an event would offer a compelling rationale for her marriage to Brandon, in that he (and apparently only he) can and is willing to "redeem" her. Further, the bawdy slang makes that actual contingency conceivable, adding an extra frisson of tension and suspense throughout a reading of the novel. Thus, although I agree with Edward Neill that "in her sublimated way [Marianne] gives herself to [Willoughby] completely," he overstates the case when he argues that "the full-blown seduction and betrayal" of Marianne exists only as one of the "text's silences," since "a novel engendered by 'Miss Austen' [could not] formally countenance" such an event (42).[21] Jocelyn Harris argues that although "Jane Austen does not permit her heroine to be actually ruined by Willoughby, . . . [events] make her look very much as if she has been" (*Art of Memory* 59). I add to that the point that Austen's sexual allusions also makes it *sound* as if she has.

Our first image of Willoughby as a violent threat—the picture of him as "a gentleman carrying a gun" (42)—limns the relationship less as a cynosure of romantic love than one that immediately places Marianne in a sexually compromised position. As Leighton argues, when Marianne seeks " 'the most distant parts of [the grounds at Cleveland], where there was something more of wildness than in the rest,' . . . the analogy to some more serious crime is totally suppressed in terms of plot, but still hinted at in the language" (60). In my opinion, these images and allusions alter our reading of the love affair between the couple in that they upset any complacent notions about the ideology of love-at-first-sight and marriage for love.[22] One could also argue that sexuality in the book, in general, is conceived of as dangerous and that "Willoughbys" are all too common. Thus, as Claudia Johnson asserts, "*Sense and Sensibility* . . . criticizes, not the unseemliness or the rebelliousness of Marianne's emotionality, but rather its horrifying conformity to the social context she lives within" (*Jane Austen* 69). I think Alison Sulloway is correct to observe that "By no means, as Austen's detractors have insisted, does she ignore the poignant spectacle of young people at their discreet sexual play. In her novels, there are dances, picnics, fireside confidences, gentle flirtatious teasing, [and] tense lovers' quarrels . . ." (84). However, *Sense and Sensibility*, in addition to flagging Willoughby's roué motives, renders male energies in general threatening, and intimates an undercurrent of pervasive and overdetermined danger: for example, Elinor, often touted as the sensible girl, projects what seems like excessive fear when, in anticipating an innocuous day's excursion to Whitwell, she is "prepared to be wet through, fatigued, and frightened" (63).

Any one instance of the bawdy language Austen uses could be dismissed; however, the context and multiplicity of these references provide a substantial body of evidence for its deliberate presence and significance. This language surpasses insinuation; it alters our reading of the plot. Further, Austen announces the reality of bawdy language and humor in upper-class domestic life by including characters like Sir John and Mrs. Jennings, who relish making such jokes and dramatize Jan Fergus's point that in Austen's novels, "publicity is not merely sanctioned in courtship but required" (67). Both the environment conducive to this sort of wordplay and the wordplay itself become clear in Willoughby's and Marianne's first meeting on the Devonshire Downs and then in Sir John's canvassing of that conclave. The vital Marianne, unable to "bear . . . confinement," finds consolation in resisting the wind "with laughing delight" and "running with all possible speed down the steep side of the hill" (41). As Sharlene Roeder points out, "Marianne does not fall to the bottom of the hill; rather, Willoughby 'took her up in his arms without further delay, and carried

her down the hill' (42), metaphorically deep[ening] Marianne's fall
from High-church Down. The name of the hill itself implies a fall
from grace—or, at the least, a fall from propriety" (60).[23] Once
Willoughby has "rescued" her, he defies her protests and takes "her
up in his arms without farther delay" (42); in doing so, he crosses,
without invitation, a series of private boundaries: those of her own
agency, her modesty (i.e., her body), the gate to the cottage (which
Margaret has left open), the front door, and even, once inside the
house, the entry into the parlor. Mrs. Dashwood and Elinor's reaction
resembles the stunned response of a family watching a romantic
fiction come to life in their little parlor, one they diegetically join, as
Willoughby's glamor lures them into the fantasy: they "admire" his
appearance, which gives "an interest" to the action (42). Marianne,
whose "confusion [had] crimsoned over her face, on his lifting her up,
had robbed her of the power of regarding him after their entering the
house. But she had *seen enough* of him" (43, emphasis added). As I
will discuss later in *Persuasion*, here the "secret" admiration of "manly
beauty" that Mrs. Dashwood and Elinor privately admit to themselves
reveals the novel's acknowledgment of mutual attraction between
men and women. As Richard Whately extolled in 1821, Austen's
heroines are "As liable to 'fall in love first,' as anxious to attract the
attention of agreeable men, as much taken with a striking manner, or
a handsome face, as unequally gifted with constancy and firmness, as
liable to have their affections biased by convenience or fashion, as we,
on our part, will admit men to be" (101).

Later, when Mrs. Dashwood asks the Middletons "what sort of
young man [he] is," Sir John's seemingly innocuous description
provides some specific—though not readily obvious—answers:
Willoughby is "as good a kind of fellow as ever lived, I assure you.
A very decent shot, and there is not a bolder rider in England" (43).
Partridge explains that a "rider" was low colloquial from the eighteenth
to the twentieth centuries for "an actively amorous man" (697), a
definition that follows from the fact that "to mount" was standard
English for copulation until 1780, a meaning it retained afterwards in
low colloquial. Edward Neill points out that "when Edward, himself
being duped by another scheming pretender to sensibility, slyly conjectures that 'Mr. Willoughby hunts' (100), he reminds us how 'hunting,' both by tradition and some contextual pressure here, may easily
be read as symbolizing predatory *sexuality*" (41). Significantly, Sir
John repeats the same phrase once again after he discovers
Willoughby has deceived and abandoned Marianne: "Sir John could
not have thought it possible. A man of whom he had always had such
reason to think well! Such a good-natured fellow! He did not believe

there was a bolder rider in England!" (214). The repetition of this phrase comically enforces Sir John's limited judgment, while also linking our now-confirmed knowledge of Willoughby as a serial seducer back to one of the first descriptions of him. Admonishing Sir John for his description of Willoughby as a "bold rider," Marianne exclaims, "And is *that* all you can say for him?. . . . [W]hat are his manners on more intimate acquaintance? What his pursuits, his talents and genius?" (43–44). He answers, "Upon my soul, . . . I do not know much about him as to all that. But he is a pleasant, good humoured fellow, and has got the nicest little black bitch of a pointer I ever saw. Was she out with him to-day?" (44). Though Willoughby and his pointers find prey for themselves, the comparison between the human pimp and the canine pointer in *The Sporting Magazine*, in an "Essay on the striking resemblance between some Men and some Dogs," potentially offers more clues about Willoughby's habits: the pimp, "who . . . draw[s] innocent girls from the paths of virtue, and put[s] them into his lordship's power, may be classed with the pointer, who hunts for that game his master wants to get into his possession . . ." (42).

The idea that Willoughby's "pursuits" and "genius" comprise the seduction of women, and that he victimizes Marianne, both become obvious when Sir John teases Elinor: "if I were you, I would not give him up to my younger sister in spite of all this tumbling down hills" (44). Moments later, he teases Marianne: "Aye, you will make conquests enough, I dare say, one way or other. Poor Brandon! he is quite smitten already, and he is very well worth setting your cap at, I can tell you, in spite of all this tumbling about and spraining of ancles [*sic*]" (45). To "do a tumble" meant to "lie down to a man"; and "tumble-in"—that is, tumbling—referred to the act of sexual intercourse (Partridge 915). Sir John says this twice, which reinforces the connotation. Yet, he suggests two different meanings in his repeated use of "in spite of." The sentence, "I would not give him up to my younger sister in spite of all this tumbling down hills" insinuates that Elinor should "set her cap at" Willoughby even if he has seduced her younger sister; while the line, "he is . . . worth setting your cap at . . . in spite of all this tumbling about and spraining of ancles" hints that Marianne is still marketable and "marriageable" in spite of having been seduced. Furthermore, another of his phrases—"spraining of ancles"—reinforces the previous allusions to sexual activity since, according to Grose's *Dictionary of the Vulgar Tongue* (1811), "a girl who is got with child, is said to have sprained her ankle."

This frank and often funny raillery in mixed company supports Jan Fergus's contention that "the constant awareness, the relentless dramatization [of sex in Austen]—is what makes her examination of it in social life so extensive and powerful" (67). The elegant Dashwood women evince a strong aversion to Sir John's (and later Mrs. Jennings's) "witticisms" such as "catching him" and "setting your cap." Marianne asserts that "I abhor every common-place phrase by which wit is intended; . . . Their tendency is gross and illiberal; and if their construction could ever be deemed clever, time has long ago destroyed all its ingenuity" (45). "Set your cap" was an innocent enough parlance meaning to "try, and keep trying, to gain a man's heart—or hand" (ca. 1770); because of that, her words "gross and illiberal" perhaps refer to his racier allusions, since the former meant "rude and uncultivated" and the latter meant "ill bred, ungentlemanly and vulgar" (*OED*). The tittering allusion to a sprained ankle, however, becomes a sober cipher of tragedy when Brandon compares Marianne to a ruined woman, projecting on her the "tender recollection of past regard" (57) he felt for a woman he loved, but who was exploited, robbed of her inheritance, seduced, and abandoned. Volume I, chapter XII continues this heady buildup of allusions and foregrounding when Willoughby offers Marianne a horse, cuts a lock of her hair (discussed in the first section of this chapter), and in the next chapters, takes her on a solitary ride in his curricle, giving her a private tour of his aunt's house.

Willoughby's desire to give Marianne a horse—named Queen Mab—provides a prime example of the risks she faces and the careful ways Austen uses Shakespeare to establish Willoughby's motives and complicate the seeming idyll of their short courtship. The Queen Mab allusion from *Romeo and Juliet* is well known: "she gallops night by night / Through lovers' brains, and then they dream of love" (I.iv.70–71). In this scene, Mercutio chides Romeo for thinking he is in love: "If thou art dun, we'll draw thee from the mire / Of this sir-reverence love, wherein thou stickest / Up to the ears" (I.iv.41–73) and concludes that Queen Mab has visited his sleeping friend. Queen Mab, a mischievous spirit that provides a dream of fulfillment of one's less noble longings—expensive fees, high tithes, successful lawsuits, and lustful desires—gallops over "ladies' lips, who straight on kisses dream" (I.iv.74). So, for Mercutio, rather like Willoughby, love has less to do with an intimate connection, a position both Romeo and Marianne share, than with the immediate fulfillment of "vain fantasy" (I.iv.98). Stephen Derry cites this allusion to indicate that "Marianne's hopes of future happiness with Willoughby will have all the substance of dreams, and that they will come to nothing" (37). Recalling Mercutio's admission that "dreamers often lie" (I.iv.51), Derry insists that "Dream-lovers like Willoughby . . . can lie" (37).

I agree with Derry that the reference accentuates Willoughby's deceit, but go further in noting the clear parallels established respectively between Willoughby and Mercutio and Romeo and Marianne. Further, the allusion implicates Willoughby's baser motives insofar as it insinuates that this midwife to the fairies, this "hag," will teach a class in sex education to Marianne, since she is the one who "when maids lie on their backs, / . . . presses them and learns them first to bear, / Making them women of good carriage" (I.iv.92–94). John Dussinger's idea that Elinor might have "associat[ed] Queen Mab and the gift horse with . . . the traumatic scene [in Fuseli's *The Nightmare*]," is tantalizing, but he does not develop the disturbing implications of such an association, only concluding that it leads Elinor "quite properly [to] believ[e] that Willoughby's sexual innuendoes must indicate a secret engagement to her sister" (88). If such a link could be forged, it would (contrary to Dussinger's argument) *diminish* the possibility of an engagement and amplify the potential for seduction and ruin; further, it incriminates Marianne, who, as possessor of the animal, plays Queen Mab; delighting in the fantasy of "a gallop on some of these downs" (58), Marianne metonymically becomes the seductress who incites Willoughby to dream of love as "she gallops night by night / Through lovers' brains." In giving her Queen Mab, Willoughby links Marianne with the seduced Eliza Williams, whom he describes as reproachable for her excess and lack: a woman of "violen[t] passions" and "wea[k] understanding" (322).

Again, a look at the slang is revealing. The name "Mab" was standard English for a "slattern, a loose-moral'd woman" and referred colloquially, verging on standard English, from the late seventeenth through the early nineteenth centuries to a woman who dressed carelessly (Partridge 502). This ideologically charged description of a "mab" describes quite well the two women in the novel whom men have, without a doubt, debauched: a mother and daughter, aptly both given the same name, Eliza; but it also alludes to Marianne, in that, when in London waiting for and then rejected by Willoughby, she is "wholly dispirited, careless of her appearance, and seeming equally indifferent whether she went or staid" (175).[24] Most modern readers would not consider these three women "loose-moral'd"; however, the men do: even though Brandon tells the narratives of both women with some compassion and moral outrage against their seducers, he still condemns the mother as having an infirm mind (208) and the daughter as having a mind "tormented by self-reproach, which must attend her through life" (210).[25] Though he has "ruined" her, Willoughby himself blames Eliza (the daughter), who becomes a kind of Queen Mab in his description of her strong passions and mental weakness. Here Willoughby and Brandon affirm the notion that if a woman is willing, she is inherently unchaste.[26] Unlike Eliza, Marianne declines the "horse," though Willoughby promises her that "[w]hen you leave Barton to form your own establishment in a more lasting home, Queen Mab shall receive you" (59). Is this the Queen Mab who, angry that the ladies' "breaths with sweetmeats tainted are," "blisters" their lips? (I.iv.75–76). Here, one bawdy novelist alludes to a bawdy playwright. As this discloses, Shakespeare's Queen Mab passage is quite vulgar, since "sweetmeat" referred to "the male member" and to "a mere girl who is a kept mistress."[27] Perhaps since Austen conjoins Marianne with Eliza and the mother, who becomes a prostitute, she suggests that the Queen Mab who "receives" Marianne would potentially also "blister" her lips—that is, see that she contracts venereal disease. The nexus of associations, erotic and ideological, surrounding both the Shakespearean and the colloquial "Mab," coalesce in this moment as Willoughby's covert marriage proposal doubles as a prophesy of her ruined terminus: like the first Eliza, dead from suffering and illness or like the second Eliza (or Maria in *Mansfield Park*, for that matter), who spins out her life isolated in a country cottage.

Austen's allusion to the scene from *Romeo and Juliet* still allows her to foreshadow the novel's conclusion, reinforce the ubiquity of such seductions, expose how vulnerable Marianne is to fantasies of erotic fulfillment, and establish the danger to Marianne's physical and emotional body. Finally, the fact that Shakespeare's Queen Mab is a miniature—"In shape no bigger than an agate-stone"—reinforces how in this novel Austen has "drawn . . . a team of little atomies" (I.iv.55, 57) that allow her to enact several roles at once. First, she is a kind of Queen Mab herself, fiction's "midwife," bringing dreams to life for her characters, and playing with cultural fantasies of true love. Her performance as Queen Mab thus undercuts her position as potential didact. Moreover, the high literary allusion (which in itself embeds a rich trove of indelicate images) and the low slang surrounding the word "mab" intimate that if Austen plays pedagogue here, her lesson plan devolves from the desire to alert her readers to the hazards of male seducers rather than, in Mary Poovey's words, to "correc[t] the dangerous excesses of female feeling" (98). I do not think that Austen concentrates on correcting rather than "liberating this anarchic energy" (Poovey 98). First of all, the multiple instances of bawdy humor do release unruly forces; and second, as the book dramatizes, when a woman cannot read the conventional signs of male sexual avarice, liberation such as that which Marianne strives for is impossible.

I want to stress that Austen promulgates an open and liberal (and so, ironic) "conduct book" of female sexuality: as Claudia Johnson argues, "Far from being a cautionary tale about the duty of fidelity, Eliza's story, like so much of the central matter in *Sense and Sensibility*, indicts the license to coercion, corruption, and avarice available to grasping patriarchs and their eldest sons . . . . In *Sense and Sensibility*, female modesty is no guarantee of female safety. It makes no difference whether one holds back with Elinor's modest caution or hurries forward with Marianne's dauntless ardor . . ." (*Jane Austen* 56, 60).

It is revealing, then, to historicize Marianne's situation within what Tim Hitchcock calls the "sexual revolution [of] the eighteenth century" (40), that is, "a change in behavior in favor of penetrative sex during and before courtship resulting in a rising population" (40). Drawing on the work of Adrian Wilson, Hitchcock suggests that "a London pattern of courting in which penetrative sex came before betrothal was gradually spreading to the rest of the country during the middle of the eighteenth century" (39), and that this "revolution," which "equat[ed] sex more firmly with activities that could lead to pregnancy," created a situation in which "a large proportion of women found themselves responsible for bastard children without even the meager supports offered by the nuclear family" (41). This recalls how the fashionable Willoughby, lately of London, has left young Eliza "in a situation of the utmost distress, with no creditable home, no help, no friends, ignorant of his address!" (209). Marianne unwittingly fore-shadows how immoderate Willoughby's "activities" are when she exclaims that "[w]hatever be his pursuits, his eagerness in them should know no moderation, and leave him no sense of fatigue" (45).

CLANDESTINE LAUGHTER: SEXUAL HUMOR AND THE BODY IN COURTSHIP AND MARRIAGE

In one intoxicating chapter (XII), Willoughby tries to give Marianne "Queen Mab," Marianne relinquishes a lock of her hair, and Mrs. Jennings and Sir John engage in a jesting riff at Elinor's expense. If Marianne catches "every syllable [about Willoughby] with panting eagerness" (348), Elinor's bantering relations gleefully launch another kind of miniature at her—the letter "F"—once Margaret reveals to Mrs. Jennings and Sir John that Elinor has a love interest and "his name begins with an F" (62). While the younger sister refers here to Edward Ferrars, the joking duo gets infinite pleasure out of the letter itself, which also begins that most famous of all bawdy words.

This joke indefatigably amuses mother and son-in-law before Edward arrives, and they are "not long in discovering that the name of Ferrars began with an F and this prepared a future mine of railery against the devoted Elinor . . ." (99). It becomes a recurring topic: "The letter F—had been likewise invariably brought forward, and found productive of such countless jokes, that its character as the wittiest letter in the alphabet had long been established with Elinor" (125). Since it is possible that they play on this letter's sexual associations, it explains why Lady Middleton had a "great dislike of all such inelegant subjects of raillery as delighted her husband and mother" (62). This miniature allows Austen to eroticize even Elinor and Edward's staid courtship as well as to explore the association between bawdy word play and conjugal procreation.

Mrs. Jennings is a "good-humored, merry, fat, elderly, woman, who talked a great deal, seemed very happy, and rather vulgar. She was full of jokes and laughter, and before dinner was over had said many witty things on the subject of lovers and husbands; hoped they had not left their hearts behind them in Sussex, and pretended to see them blush whether they did or not" (34). Her "common-place raillery" vexes Marianne, though the narrator asserts that in comparison to Lady Middleton's "cold insipidity," Mrs. Jenning's "boisterous mirth . . . was interesting" (34). Given Austen's own bawdy humor, one hesitates to dismiss Mrs. Jennings as easily as Marianne does. Instead, the elder lady complicates the division between the inhibited and private articulation of sexual matters associated with Austen and the earlier, frank and public expression of libido occurring roughly between 1700–1750.[28] This latter phenomenon, what Tim Hitchcock calls the "public cultures of sex" (9), was geared toward a conservative, heterosexual end: the happy and fertile union of married couples. It is helpful to recall here the swaggering Regency banter that Austen's relatives later excised from her correspondence.

The teleology of Mrs. Jenning's sportive fun allies her with the public culture of sexuality, in that "having lived to see" her two daughters "respectably married, . . . she had now . . . nothing to do but to marry all the rest of world. In the promotion of this object she was zealously active" (36). Her "endless jokes against [Marianne and Brandon]" (36) ultimately serve their cultural purpose, in that the two end up united. Marianne defines marriage as an erotic union and her physical aversion to the thought of wedding him arises from his age and "infirmity": "thirty-five has nothing to do with matrimony"; "he talked of flannel waistcoats" (37, 38). In this sense, Mrs. Jenning's bawdiness tries to perform the biological service such jokes were meant to fulfill, and that was to encourage erotic titillation and thus procreation. Further, the fact that the public culture of sexuality created works that were erotic rather than pornographic, and which reflected a "shared culture of sexual reference and humor in which genitals were funny" (Hitchcock 14) indicates one way of understanding the "countless jokes" (125) Mrs. Jennings and her son-in-law enjoy.

Mrs. Palmer, Mrs. Jennings's daughter, provides a miniature stage for exploring Austen's incorporation of that kind of humor she elsewhere terms "unbecoming conjunctions" (*Persuasion* 68). Charlotte Palmer has good qualities and is sentient; but her laughter avoids what Marie Swabey calls the "group of comprehensive regulations necessary to all systems, the basic logic of sanity and rationality" (17). Her unaccountable merriment renders her absurd but not necessarily funny, and the Dashwood women blink with surprise at how she stands outside the normal limits of behavior.[29] " 'Mr. Palmer does not hear me,' said she, laughing, 'he never does sometimes. It is so ridiculous!' " (107). Her sense of humor is droll, in that it is strange or quaint; in contrast, Mrs. Dashwood responds in a conventionally amusing way: "This was quite a new idea to Mrs. Dashwood, she had never been used to find wit in the inattention of any one, and could not help looking with surprise at them both" (107). But Mr. Palmer's "studied indifference, insolence, and discontent . . . gave [Charlotte] no pain: and when he scolded or abused her, she was highly diverted," merely remarking that "Mr. Palmer is so droll!" (112). Giggling and tittering when her husband ignores her renders *her* insensate reactions worrisome.

She may be just stupid, but I find a mystery in what she finds funny since her impenetrable humor excludes others from its origins and teleology: she laughs when her mother expresses concern for the health of her unborn baby; when Marianne tours Willoughby's aunt's house (108); when her husband has been asleep; when Elinor and Marianne say they will not be going to town (110); when her husband, contradicting everybody, is rude (112); when he abuses her mother; when she envisions that Mr. Palmer "cannot get rid of her"; when she thinks about her husband in Parliament (113); and when she enters a room (164). Merriment derived from such diverse and inexplicable topics puts pressure on the attempt to explain her character since she deconstructs the idea that laughter is shareable or predictable. Suddenly, rudeness is charming, a husband's inattention is almost an aphrodisiac, and the death of infant animals and parents who abandon their young provide "fresh sources of merriment" (303)—and for a new mother no less. Her astonishing laughter implies that she has reimagined the roles of wife, husband, lover, and mother outside of the confines of any cultural expectation.

The uncanny resemblance that sometimes emerges between Mrs. Palmer and Austen is disconcerting, for it is the novelist who laughs (and, I for one, laugh with her) when Marianne grieves for Willoughby after he has left Barton cottage; when Mrs. Dashwood plays friend rather than mother to Marianne; when Mrs. Jennings teases Elinor and Marianne, and when Austen describes how the John Dashwoods steal their impoverished sister's inheritance: in a *tour de force* of wicked dramatic irony that makes one laugh in spite of oneself, Austen has Mrs. John Dashwood exclaim that the women "will have no carriage, no horses, and hardly any servants; they will keep no company, and can have no expences [*sic*] of any kind! Only conceive how comfortable they will be!" (12). If her humor is transgressive, Charlotte could be seen to function as a miniature of a version of Austen. At the beginning of this chapter, the second epigraph, "On Genuine Wit," tells how nineteenth-century popular culture, sentimentalism aside, endorsed a wit that "boasts two various pow'rs in one, / To *cut* as well as *shine*." Certainly Austen's humor, in contrast to Mrs. Palmer's, constitutes "Genius": "polish'd right," it "Appears at once both keen and bright. / And sparkles while it wounds" (*The Lady's Monthly Museum*, 1807). As Mary Jane Humphrey argues, Mrs. Palmer maintains a lot of power by laughing and holds a certain authority over her husband: she gets him to respond to her—as if he were a small child—whether he wants to or not (13–15). Along these lines, both Austen and Mrs. Palmer's aggressive comedy displaces patriarchal control over women's lives. The irony and parody in her novels do reveal, as Karen Newman writes, "the romantic and materialist contradictions of which her plots and characters are made" (708). When Mrs. Palmer laughs, she exposes how ideological expectations are capricious and idiosyncratic, a fact her unstable relation to both art and nature makes palpable.

In her want of common sense, she appears irrational and elemental, yet paradoxically artificial since her reactions lack spontaneity. One cannot doubt her corporeal life force: she is healthy, attracted to her husband, active even while pregnant—traveling long and fast and "running" about the house (110); she is also psychically strong enough to withstand his verbal abuse, to assert equality with him, and perhaps power over him. Hobbes famously theorizes that humor is a sign of triumph and power: "The passion of laughter is nothing else but *sudden glory* arising from some sudden *conception* of some *eminency* in ourselves, by *comparison* with the *infirmity* of others or with our own formerly" (4:46). The Palmers' conversation about Willoughby's residence is exemplary: she states that he lives ten miles away; her husband that the distance is thirty miles away; she, that it is pretty; he, that it is vile; she concedes: "I must be wrong," but then later she "wins" by repeating again that it is a "sweet place" (116). Even his mother-in-law, Mrs. Jennings, controls this man, when she jokes that she has the "whip hand" (112) over him, an image that calls to mind human mastery over animals as well as humans, in that Mr. Palmer becomes the colonial subject who will never be free of her daughter, notwithstanding that he is an MP.

As I will discuss in chapters on *Emma* and *Mansfield Park*, humor (bawdy and otherwise) merges with tragedy in Austen's novels in disconcerting, though still comic ways. This pattern also occurs in her letters. Just before the publication of *Sense and Sensibility*, Austen responds in a letter to Cassandra about the casualties in the Duke of Wellington's troops: "How horrible it is to have so many people killed!—And what a blessing that one cares for none of them!" (Lefaye 191). In another epistle to Cassandra from London where Austen was correcting the proofs for *Sense and Sensibility*, she remarks, "I give you joy of our new nephew, & hope if he ever comes to be hanged, it will not be till we are too old to care about it" (182). In *Sense and Sensibility*, Charlotte's laughter provides an instance of similar, shockingly funny juxtapositions. Here, Mrs. Palmer responds to the death of her plants and infant animals:

> the rest of the morning was easily whiled away . . . in dawdling through the green-house, where the loss of her favourite plants, unwarily exposed, and nipped by the lingering frost, raised the laughter of Charlotte,—and in visiting her poultry-yard, where, in the disappointed hopes of her dairy-maid, by hens forsaking their nests, or being stolen by a fox, or in the rapid decease of a promising young brood, she found fresh sources of merriment. (303)

This episode performs the uncanny in the true sense of the word *heimlich*, which calls up the homey and the alien, in that it demonstrates Mrs. Palmer's unequivocal otherness while also bringing that strangeness "home"—and thereby making it canny. Her laughter, then, nonsensical at best and sadistic at worst, also provides an elegant miniature allegory of what has happened to the three women in the novel who have been betrayed by men they trust: the two Elizas and Marianne have all been "nipped" early, and at least one hen has been "stolen by a fox." Here Austen uses unconventional humor to reveal that Willoughby, like a fox, "steals" Mrs. Dashwood, the mother hen, by seducing her filial affections and threatening to cause a "rapid decrease of a promising young broo[d]" of innocent females (303). The novel elucidates how Mrs. Dashwood lives voyeuristically through Marianne's erotic adventure when the narrator says that "Indeed a man could not very well be in love with either of her daughters, without extending the passion to [Mrs. Dashwood]" (90). Mrs. Palmer's laughter suggests sheer unthinking silliness. The secret inside the satire of her merriment—an allusion to Willoughby's libertine behavior—however, yields further ironic humor in that she faces her own laughter's consequences when the "fox" enters *her* nest: Willoughby's harm to Marianne threatens (through her infectious, "putrid" fever) to harm the Palmers's heir and forces them to decamp from their own house (307). This is, after all, an "infection" that is spreading through the house, the county, and the country—rather like the multiplying Elizas. Thus Mary Lascelles's comment that keeping Eliza "out of sight" "is well judged in a novel of comic intention" (73) ignores the sheer amount of material that the narrative keeps directly in our sight. Austen's humor mingles with the tragic but also provides a kind of emollient. Charlotte may be "silly" but there is no doubt that she remains a vital member of Austen's team of "little atomies."

The novel suggests that the Palmers's marriage is less a farce about wedded bliss than it is a farce in the theatrical sense, a miniature performance of the mysteries inherent in every marriage, whose interiors are always unknowable. Thus, when Mrs. Palmer reveals that her husband "is just the kind of man I like" (117), does she assert an aggressive superiority over her husband's rude comments? Reveal the real tragedy at the heart of their marriage? Expose how in an unbearable situation she resembles Sophia, from *Love and Friendship*, who advises Laura to "run mad" laughing in a "frenzy" rather than "faint"?(122) Or does it signify that the couple has found a way to get along that suits them both? That they perform the roles of aggressor and imbecile would explain the emotional disassociation they both exhibit toward each other, and yet also comprehend the kindness they are able to feel later for Marianne. Their behavior suggests the result of something infinitely private—some secret, impenetrable world: how *could* he like her and how *could* she like him; Elinor "wonder[s]" at Charlotte's being so happy without a cause, at Mr. Palmer's acting so simply, with good abilities and at the strange unsuitableness which often existed between husband and wife . . ." (118). As Mary Waldron argues, the novel presents "a vision of the essentially anarchic nature of human relationships . . ." (83). When Elinor reveals that she could have "forgiven every thing [about Mrs. Palmer] but her laugh," perhaps what she cannot forgive is what she cannot understand (304).

Conclusion

Austen's novels themselves have been said to be about "miniaturized worlds" and that her "little bit (two Inches wide) of Ivory" (Le Faye 323) presents a world timeless and uncontaminated. The equation between smallness and inferiority is a chronic conviction: Henry James, fantasizing about Austen's work habits, wrote that "Sometimes, over her work basket, . . . she fell a musing and dropped stitches. . . . [T]hese precious moments were afterwards picked up as little touches of human truth, little glimpses, little master strokes" (63). James's "Jane" is the "Great Jane Austen of Mythology," the one Katie Trumpener sums up (and then deconstructs) as a "complacent, if witty, conservative," the kind of miniaturist who "liked everything to be tidy and pleasant and comfortable about her" ("Virago" 143).[30] Austen becomes the spokeswoman of the playwright Thomas Dibdin's "Oh! What a snug little Island, / A right little, tight little Island." Stewart argues that "the miniature, linked to nostalgic versions of childhood and history, presents a diminutive, and thereby manipulable version of experience, a version that is domesticated and protected from contamination" (Stewart, *On Longing* 69). *Sense and Sensibility* demonstrates that it is only while that "version of experience" stays stable that the interpretation is "protected from contamination." The novel, with its many secrets, both those in the plot and those embedded in its objects and language, demonstrates the chimerical nature of such stability. As Edward says, "the setting always casts a different shade on it you know" (98). Austen's use of the miniature highlights interpretation rather than truth, relativity rather than clear differentiation of terms such as sense and sensibility, and in providing so many possible accounts of any one ideological performance, the novel casts doubts on the ability to regulate point of view, an instability that may leave some readers tottering for the cozy.

CHAPTER 2

THE ANXIETIES AND "FELICITIES OF RAPID MOTION": ANIMATED IDEOLOGY IN *PRIDE AND PREJUDICE*

Pride and Prejudice's kinetic energy resists its evocation of an idyllic society at the height of a calm, country perfection; everyone in this novel is physically, and often extravagantly in motion: fleeing to London, scurrying to Brighton, flying from Pemberley or hastening toward it. Elizabeth remarks that "people themselves alter so much, that there is something new to be observed in them for ever" (43). Even so fundamental a fact as the population of local society fluctuates as the news about Bingley's number of guests varies wildly; and rumors speed through the town as it alters its opinions about Darcy (9–13). Motion propels marriage and generation. The subject of balls "always makes a lady energetic" (24): "to be fond of dancing was a certain step towards falling in love" (9). Bingley boasts that his "ideas flow so rapidly that [he has] not time to express them" (48). The brisk Mr. Collins means to find a bride during a visit of only one week—and he succeeds. Darcy's own restless evolutions drive him to change his mind in favor of Elizabeth just as he has decided against her (26), though a moment later he accuses Caroline of jumping to conclusions when he charges that "a lady's imagination is very rapid" in marching toward thoughts of matrimony (27). Elizabeth's own busy mind works dynamically, as when conjectures, "rapid and wild," about the reason why Darcy attended Lydia's wedding were "hurried into her brain" (320). Elizabeth's *immobility*—sitting out two dances without a partner—becomes a sign of rejection and casualty that offends

Darcy: he is in no mood "at present" to humor girls that other men reject (12); that "at present," though, suggests he will change his mind, and, indeed, he soon finds Elizabeth's animation magnetic: the "easy playfulness" of her manners, the "light and pleasing" quality of her figure, as well as "the brilliancy . . . [of] her complexion" (23, 33).

These examples speak to a consistent sense of "embodied subjectivity" (Grosz 22), that is, a synergetic relation between mind and body. A common reading of Austen in general and *Pride and Prejudice* in particular, however, discounts the physical, contending instead that the narrative bifurcates body and mind, accentuating mental constraint and repression over bodily excess. Tending to track the heroine's growth in terms of her mind and understanding, readers have often found the novels to be a classic *bildungsroman*. One consequence of such a perspective has been to insist that Austen's fiction lacks sex (Susan Morgan even titles one chapter "Why There is no Sex in Jane Austen"). The idea that elegance and maturity require Austen and her heroines to harness their feelings and curb their bodies traces its genealogy to Charlotte Bronte's extraordinary, but by this time shopworn, declaration that "The Passions are perfectly unknown to [Austen]. . . . [E]ven to the Feelings she vouchsafes no more than an occasional graceful but distant recognition; too frequent converse with them would ruffle the smooth elegance of her progress" (qtd. in Dennis Allen 425). Such a declaration occludes an investigation of the body's role in the novel—except for its criminal element (Mrs. Bennet and Lydia, for example)—by enforcing the idea that Austen advocates inhibition over expression. John Wiltshire claims, for example, that Mrs. Bennet's "unabashed sexuality is a demonstration of everything the novel assumes, but keeps otherwise implicit and under wraps," and wonders if her "baffled energies [are] a distorted, bizarre version of [Elizabeth's] transgressive high spirits—this daughter who runs everywhere?" ("Mrs. Bennet's" 185). Yet evidence indicates instead that all the characters unabashedly appraise sexual and physical appeal. Even a quick gathering of examples suggests that *Pride and Prejudice*'s world allows for more expansive expressions of physicality than just aberrant energy or the discipline of that excess. William Deresiewicz contends that "Austen transforms the process of courtship as she found it in her novelistic predecessors, making it both more conscious and more emotionally profound . . . . [Love], no longer an ecstasy antithetical or . . . unrelated to friendship, . . . becomes instead a form of friendship" (519). In general I agree, though this primary emphasis on dispassionate friendship discounts how these metamorphoses in self-knowledge sink in somatically. I want to highlight how the novel acknowledges the body's joyful effusions, its transgressions, the violations it endures and inflicts, and its function as an epistemic barometer. Instead of interpreting the body as a passive tool that mind fills up and out, or, in Locke's sense, of a possession or property that the mind controls, I argue that the narrative addresses the "bodily dimension of consciousness" (Grosz 22)—a dynamic, psychophysical process of expression—and dramatizes how the body materializes the ideologies it has absorbed.

KNOWING THROUGH THE BODY

Other considerations besides Jane's illness entice Elizabeth to walk six miles. Mary Poovey contends that "when [Elizabeth] bursts into Netherfield to see her sick sister . . . the mud on her skirts becomes completely irrelevant beside the healthiness of her unself-conscious concern for Jane" (195). I think, however, that the chance for action also lures her as she "cros[ses] field after field at a quick pace, jumping over stiles and springing over puddles with impatient activity, and finding herself at last within view of the house, with weary ancles, dirty stockings, and a face glowing with the warmth of exercise" (32). When Caroline sniffs a moment later that Elizabeth has "no stile" (35), her word reminds us that in catapulting styles as well as stiles, her physical flights *are* her mental flights. Darcy's famous appreciation of her brilliant complexion takes on greater significance when linked to medical discourse that associated exercise with a sharper and stronger intelligence, and also with a woman's ability to conceive: *Aristotle's Master-piece* warns that a "want of exercise and idleness are very great enemies to the work of generation, and indeed are enemies both to the soul and body. . . . A moderate exercise . . . opens the pores, quickens the spirits, stirs up the natural heat, strengthens the body, sense and spirits, comforts the limbs, and helps nature in all its exercises" (42). The synchronism between her body and mind suggests that although the heroine loves her sister, the pleasure of conversing and engaging in perhaps more than "moderate" exercise pulls her toward Netherfield. Once there, the drawing-room conversation launches her body out of her chair and away from the still perusal of a book: with a mind that races like her body, "Elizabeth was so much caught by what passed, as to leave her very little attention for her book; and soon laying it wholly aside, she drew near the card-table, and stationed herself between Mr. Bingley and his eldest sister, to observe the game" (38).

A psychical corporeality energizes Elizabeth and Darcy's conversations, which always exceed the merely cerebral. For example, when

Elizabeth rejects his proposal, Austen tabulates his reactions so as to suggest that the body–mind works together to articulate the physics of the moment: "[h]is complexion became pale with anger, and the disturbance of his mind was visible in every feature. He was struggling for the appearance of composure, and would not open his lips, till he believed himself to have attained it" (190). His color "heighten[s]," and he "walk[s] with quick steps across the room" when he exclaims, "And this . . . is your opinion of me!" (191–192). His proposal and the heated argument that follows exact a heavy physical toll: "[s]he knew not how to support herself, and from actual weakness sat down and cried for half an hour" (193). "Air and exercise" help her recover from her "indisposition" and only after physical release restores her strength can she comprehend the information from Darcy's letter (195):

> She read, with an eagerness which hardly left her power of comprehension, and from impatience of knowing what the next sentence might bring, was incapable of attending to the sense of the one before her eyes. . . . [W]hen she had gone through the whole letter, though scarcely knowing any thing of the last page or two, put it hastily away, protesting that she would not regard it, that she would never look in it again. . . . In this perturbed state of mind, with thoughts that could rest on nothing, she walked on; but it would not do; in half a minute the letter was unfolded again . . . . After wandering along the lane for two hours, giving way to every variety of thought [,] re-considering events, . . . fatigue . . . made her at length return home. (204–209)

Here, her mental revelation coincides with—even depends upon—physical movement: the truth about Wickham "unfolds" before her as she folds and unfolds the letter, and her eyes sprint so impatiently that their movement incapacitates cognition. Her "variety of thought" and "thoughts that could rest on nothing" convey the corporeal aspect of ideas. In contrast to her earlier walk to Netherfield, an act of jouissance that heightens her vitality, here Elizabeth walks her way to exhaustion and understanding at the same time.

Darcy and Elizabeth engage in what Peter Brooks has called "the project of knowing the body and knowing through the body, essentially by way of erotic experience, since eroticism makes the body most fully sentient and also most 'intellectual,' the most aware of what it is doing and what is being done to it" (Brooks 278). The characters cherish good figures and erotic magnetism with a nonchalance that allows, indeed expects, the reader to take sexual appeal for granted and to connect it with romance and romance with marriage. By treating erotic passion openly, and without embarrassment or alloy, the novel normalizes it, rendering it almost invisible. For example, Mrs. Bennet encourages Jane and then Elizabeth to join a group of young, mixed company for almost a week unchaperoned. If other novels of the period (Burney's *The Wanderer*, Edgeworth's *Belinda*, or Scott's *Waverley*, for example), are to be given any credit for verisimilitude about moral expectations, the Bennet sisters' freedom from adult supervision of their chastity is remarkable. Attentive to the allure of the flesh, "the gentlemen pronounc[e] [Darcy] to be a fine figure of a man" (10); Mrs. Bennet avows the sexual appeal of a red coat (29); Wickham has "all the best part of beauty," including "a good figure" (72).[1] Darcy's physical discomfort, registered in his unpolished manners—staring at Elizabeth, visiting her without speaking and so on—suggests that his attraction manifests itself in his very presence. Though the Bingley sisters are untrustworthy, they convey a sense of how Elizabeth joins Lydia in possessing "high animal spirits" (45).

> "She really looked almost wild."
> "She did indeed, Louisa. I could hardly keep my countenance. Very nonsensical to come at all! Why must she be scampering about the country because her sister had a cold? Her hair so untidy, so blowsy!"
> "Yes, and her petticoat; I hope you saw her petticoat, six inches deep in mud, I am absolutely certain; and the gown which had been let down to hide it, not doing its office." (35–36)

"Abusing" Elizabeth for her vitality, Caroline and Louisa associate that exhilaration with sexual drive, associating her with profligate women, such as gypsies and prostitutes, and thereby collapsing her body's motility with her mind's immoral migrations. Elizabeth's playful banter on the efficacy of poetry in driving away love gives the body priority over wit (though she does so in a witty way): "I have been used to consider poetry as the *food* of love," said Darcy. Elizabeth retorts: "Of a fine, stout, healthy love it may. Every thing nourishes what is strong already. But if it be only a slight, thin sort of inclination, I am convinced that one good sonnet will starve it entirely away" (44–45). The mere idea of love, given form but not a real body in a sonnet, offers nothing but starvation to a consumptive lover. For Elizabeth, no Platonist, the body is the ground of love, and ideas feed it, not the other way around.

Though usually roped off from interpretations of the novel or collapsed into the category of the kind of unbridled and unsuitable activity that Austen condemns are the "vulgar" pursuits of Elizabeth's aunt, Mrs. Philips: she watches the handsome Wickham through her front window for an hour "as he walked up and down the street" and

"Kitty and Lydia would certainly have continued the occupation, but unluckily no one passed the windows now" worth gazing at (74). This kind of voyeurism could be dismissed as the coarse behavior of the novel's marginalized, since it is Mrs. Philips and Lydia who are the flashy participants, but when Darcy acts in a similar fashion, his behavior underscores how the narrative affirms the power of knowing through physical appeal. Austen thus augments the list of those who enjoy the erotic gaze beyond men or those of lower rank or intelligence. Longing for Darcy's gaze and frustrated that he ignores her, Caroline moves from one physical "attitude" to another when she exclaims,

> "Miss Eliza Bennet, let me persuade you to follow my example, and take a turn about the room.—I assure you it is very refreshing after sitting so long in one attitude."
>
> Elizabeth was surprised, but agreed to it immediately. Miss Bingley succeeded no less in the real object of her civility; Mr. Darcy looked up. He was as much awake to the novelty of attention in that quarter as Elizabeth herself could be, and unconsciously closed his book. (56)

Austen may be satirizing Caroline by alluding here to the infamous originator of "the art of the attitude," Lady Emma Hamilton, who amused private audiences with a kind of pantomime in which scantily clad, she "shifted from one figure taken from classical myth to another, always freezing into a pose that recalled that of a famous statue" (Cox 171).[2] As if in on the joke of Caroline and Elizabeth as actors performing attitudes for his sake, Darcy reminds the women that they want him to admire their figures and that he is delighted to gratify their desire:

> He was directly invited to join their party, but he declined it, observing, that he could imagine but two motives for their chusing to walk up and down the room together, with either of which motives his joining them would interfere. . . . "You either chuse this method of passing the evening because you are in each other's confidence and have secret affairs to discuss, or because you are conscious that your figures appear to the greatest advantage in walking;—if the first, I should be completely in your way; and if the second, I can admire you much better as I sit by the fire." (56)

Caroline's remark—"Oh, shocking!"—spoken with mock horror, reveals how she basks in his plainspoken bawdy talk rather than registering it as an insult to her propriety. In this episode, Austen reiterates how well the characters understand their world's sexually charged atmosphere and how boisterously they participate in situations that the novel, at least, does not characterize either as *de trop* or as requiring censure.

VIOLATING THE BODY

It is unlikely that anyone reading Austen today would agree with Leslie Stephen's 1876 comment that her humor is "so excessively mild" (*Critical Heritage* 2, 174), or with J. I. M. Stewart, that her world is "drastically purged of almost everything alarming and mysterious in the human situation" (Southam, *Essays* 130), or with H. W. Garrod that she "describes everything in the youth of women which does not matter" (Southam, *Essays* 130). Instead, she invokes one of the "alarming and mysterious" aspects of the "human situation"—one of the aspects that "does . . . matter": the mistreatment of the body, an arena of experience that becomes visible in *Pride and Prejudice* once we acknowledge the novel's physicality. Erotic attraction, physical abuse, and institutional ideologies intersect throughout the novel, underscoring how the "body's history" partakes of "the history of bodily violation" (Lefkovitz 1). For example, Austen fuses these three matters when Lydia and Catherine recount their activities during the elder girls' absence: "Much had been done, and much had been said in the regiment since the preceding Wednesday; several of the officers had dined lately with their uncle, a private had been flogged, and it had actually been hinted that Colonel Forster was going to be married" (60). The disturbing nonchalance with which the younger sisters mention flogging here suggests that it was common: an anecdote from the *Entertaining Magazine* (1803) treats the subject as a joke (and with a stereotypical slighting of the Irish): "An Irish drummer being employed to flog a deserter, the sufferer, as is usual in such cases, cried out—'Strike higher! Strike higher!' The drummer, accordingly, to oblige the poor fellow, did as he was requested. But the man still continuing to roar out in agony—'Devil burn your bellowing!' cried Paddy; 'there is no pleasing of you, strike where one will!' " (135). Though not in the racist way that the anecdote does, Austen capitalizes on the comic potential of forming a discordant catalogue by inserting flogging between these social activities. Her flat equation of disparate matters calls attention to buried connections among these unlike phenomena: the reference to marriage has the effect of sexualizing both dining and flogging; and the reference to flogging conflates marriage with punishment.

The catalogue's elements, far from grating, correspond. That flogging was punishment for, among other "crimes," slaves who rebelled and men who chose men as sexual partners, reinforces a sense of the intrusion of patriarchal power into all areas of private life. In his discussion of humiliation, William Ian Miller points out that because "victimizers, according to our common notions, will tend to be male, and victims, if not female to the same extent as victimizers are male, will in many settings, be gendered female nonetheless. A male victim is a feminized male" (55). That women and slaves were equated needs no explanation; nor that flogging was common in early nineteenth-century life; nor that Austen would have been familiar with public whippings and graphic accounts in descriptions of colonial life, at the least from her reading of Thomas Clarkson's *History of the Abolition of the Slave Trade* (1808), which, as part of the antislavery campaign, utilized verbal and visual images of flogging to influence abolitionist legislation. As Mary Favret argues, "the white woman was repeatedly invited to view the representation of racial and sexual violence," asked "to fix [her] eyes on 'the strong marks of slavery' ": " 'Be not afraid,' wrote one tract, 'we do not ask you to do anything, to incite in anything unbecoming to your sex' " (Flogging 39, 40). The hope was that when women looked, they filtered out the pornographic gaze—cleansing the image with their own mercy. But those same images also offered women a chance "to participate vicariously in sexual excesses otherwise denied to proper gentlewomen" (Favret 41).

The uninflected clustering of these three activities—dining, flogging, and marrying—in one sentence (and a prominent sentence at that, since it closes a chapter) comments on how often women become "slaves" in courtship and marriage and how a coupling that promises to provide material security (the dining side of this triangle), can lacerate a woman's identity. In other words, Lydia and Catherine's story provides an example that dramatizes, at the most basic level, the negative impact that marriage can have on the body. The constellation of marriage and flogging provides a context for the full irony of Collins's reference to the "violence of [his] affection" (106) when he proposes to Elizabeth, and problematizes his comment when he anticipates that Lady Catherine will find Elizabeth's "wit and vivacity . . . acceptable . . ., especially when tempered with the silence and respect which her rank will inevitably excite" (106). By silencing her wit, such a marriage promises to demolish the cornerstone of Elizabeth's intelligence and life force. Favret, drawing on Shenstone's "The School Mistress" (1742), whose mission it was "to illustrate the secret connexion betwixt *Whipping and Rising* in the world," highlights how, in eighteenth-century education, "flogging" was linked with learning (26), and thus with social mobility. Extrapolating from this, it is appropriate that Austen would conjoin flogging and marriage, since matrimony was the only way for women to "rise" in this world.

As I discuss throughout this book, Austen's novels investigate how her heroines register through their bodies the experience of knowing and being known in courtship and marriage, and one important subset in that experience is sexual attraction. Mr. Collins illustrates Henri Bergson's point that the attitudes, gestures, and movements of the human body are laughable in proportion as the body acts like a machine (10). Collins's mental and physical inelasticity—his inability to hear Elizabeth's rejections of his proposals and his failure to use language in such a way that it correlates to the experience at hand— makes him funny. Needlessly worrying that this blockhead might lose momentum in his courtship of her, Charlotte plans her strategy for love: her

> object was nothing less, than to secure [Elizabeth] from any return of Mr. Collins's addresses, by engaging them towards herself. Such was Miss Lucas's scheme; and appearances were so favourable that when they parted at night, she would have felt almost sure of success if he had not been to leave Hertfordshire so very soon. But here, she did injustice to the fire and independence of his character, for it led him to escape out of Longbourn House with admirable slyness, and hasten to Lucas Lodge to throw himself at her feet. . . . Miss Lucas perceived him from an upper window as he walked towards the house, and instantly set out to meet him accidentally in the lane. But little had she dared to hope that so much love and eloquence awaited her there. (121)

Charlotte's spontaneous "scheme," the couple's "accidental" meeting in the lane, and Mr. Collins's "fire and independence" when he "throws" his body at her feet, amuse because they employ the mechanical gestures of beings programmed to enact the ideology of romantic love. They ape dynamic sexual energy here in a robotic way—hilarious in its brittleness, but pointing by contrast to the kind of knowledge that might be found in spontaneous physical attraction.

Charlotte's union with Collins is horrible to imagine not only because he is vengeful and mean, but also because she will have to endure a marriage suffused with physical aversion. In a displaced way, we get an insight into this aspect of their future when Elizabeth's dances with Collins produce what Austen describes as a sort of inverted orgasm: dancing with the clergyman brings nothing but "distress; they were dances of mortification. Mr. Collins, awkward and solemn, apologising instead of attending, and often moving wrong without being aware of it, gave her all the shame and misery which a disagreeable partner for a couple of dances can give. The moment of her release from him was exstasy" (90).[3] Charlotte thinks to herself that "the stupidity with which he was favoured by nature, must guard his courtship from any charm that could make a woman wish for its continuance" (122); her awareness of that fact ironically emphasizes that although she can control the length of courtship, she will have no such power in marriage, in which there will be no "ecstatic" release from his touch, from those "conjugal duties"[4] that Mr. Collins will expect to be fulfilled, given that his second reason for marrying is that it "will add very greatly to [his] happiness" (105). I thus disagree with Ruth Perry, who, arguing that "[s]exual disgust was an invention of the eighteenth century," claims that because Charlotte "is a vestigial character, left over from an era of pragmatic rather than romantic matches . . . the physical repugnance that we in the present century feel at the idea of sleeping with Mr. Collins is entirely absent in Jane Austen's treatment of the matter. . . . There is not the slightest whiff of sexual disgust about the matter; not from Charlotte, nor from Elizabeth, nor from the narrator" (121, 120).[5] The novel, however, delineates sexual attraction; and if that is identifiable, so too is physical revulsion, regardless of whether or not Charlotte is "vestigial" in her thinking.

Collins's bumbling body and insensitivity suggest that Charlotte does indeed experience disgust, insofar as her union with him disables her senses, shutting down at least three avenues of perception: touch, as I have suggested above; sound, since Charlotte "wisely did not hear" his shameful retorts (156); and sight, since to keep Collins out of her radius in her new house, Charlotte takes the inferior room:

> The room in which the ladies sat was backwards. Elizabeth at first had rather wondered that Charlotte should not prefer the dining parlour for common use; it was a better sized room, and had a pleasanter aspect; but she soon saw that her friend had an excellent reason for what she did, for Mr. Collins would undoubtedly have been much less in his own apartment, had they sat in one equally lively. (168)

Sitting "backwards" (i.e., in the back portion of the house) cuts her off from the "pleasanter aspect"—a wider view onto the road and the world outside—but this is the price that Charlotte accepts for avoiding her husband. Beyond these perspectival and sensory deprivations, however, marriage with him also obliterates that most significant element of consciousness, memory: to reduce his irritation on her nerves and brain, Charlotte lives in such a way that Mr. Collins is "often forgotten" (157). Elizabeth's parting thoughts about her friend's marriage spotlight how evanescent are the bewitching promises of marriage's material security, the comforts Lydia and Catherine's catalogue implied in its reference to "dining." Charlotte's "home and her housekeeping, her parish and her poultry, and all their dependent concerns, had not *yet* lost their charms" (216, emphasis added). The alliteration here, rare in Austen, reinforces the grim puns inherent in parish (perish) and poultry (paltry), all of it inadequate compensation for the loss of plastic and responsive mindfulness.[6] In order to "dine," Charlotte marries, only to face being flogged with corrosive stupidity every day of her life.

Elizabeth's marriage, by contrast, heralds the efflorescence of her senses, a process that begins with Darcy first making himself *known* to Elizabeth by wounding and marking her body—"he looked for a moment at Elizabeth, till catching her eye, he withdrew his own and coldly said, 'She is tolerable; but not handsome enough to tempt *me*; and I am in no humour at present to give consequence to young ladies who are slighted by other men' " (11–12). The "catching" of her eye suggests the sharp aim of the whipping words that follow, words that represent the collective male appraisal that rejects a woman "not handsome enough," a woman who is only "tolerable"—or just bearable. In objectifying her body he fragments her sense of self, but she fights back: as she later tells Darcy, "My courage always rises with every attempt to intimidate me" (174). Grosz argues that the body, "as well as being the site of knowledge-power . . . is thus also a site of resistance, for it exerts a recalcitrance, and always entails the possibility of a counterstrategic reinscription, for it is capable of being self-marked, self-represented in alternative ways" ("Inscriptions" 64–65). From the moment he insults her, Elizabeth reinscribes his attacks: she retells the "story . . . with great spirit among her friends; for she had a lively, playful disposition, which delighted in any thing ridiculous" (12). The problem, though, is that this counterstrategy fails since she remains irate through much of the novel, and that anger provides no effective way to resist Darcy's advances since he refuses to read her dislike as such. She may playfully protest that he is ridiculous, but her resentment reveals she is far from playfully amused.

Darcy's change of mind about Elizabeth's beauty and intellectual appeal is unmistakable; why then is Elizabeth, even though she dislikes him—the novel's famous and eponymous "prejudice"—unable to detect his crush on her? He tries to flirt with her by asking if she

"feel[s] a great inclination . . . to seize such an opportunity of dancing a reel?"

> She smiled, but made no answer. He repeated the question, with some surprise at her silence.
>
> "Oh!" said she, "I heard you before; but I could not immediately determine what to say in reply. You wanted me, I know, to say 'Yes,' that you might have the pleasure of despising my taste; but I always delight in overthrowing those kind of schemes, and cheating a person of their premeditated contempt. I have therefore made up my mind to tell you, that I do not want to dance a reel at all—and now despise me if you dare."
>
> "Indeed I do not dare."
>
> Elizabeth, having rather expected to affront him, was amazed at his gallantry; but there was a mixture of sweetness and archness in her manner which made it difficult for her to affront anybody; and Darcy had never been so bewitched by any woman as he was by her. (52)

She registers flirtation as another affront to her sexuality, since he implies that she has such a passion for dancing that she would "seize" any opportunity (even a country dance) to act like a "savage" (to quote his comment earlier that "every savage can dance") (25). She takes this insult to heart since it implies that her physicality coarsely embodies her "taste." When she declines in a manner that she expects will "affront him," her behavior instead enthralls him. Grosz explains that there is an "enormous investment in definitions of the female body in struggles between patriarchs and feminists: what is at stake is the activity and agency, the mobility and social space, accorded to women. Far from being an inert, passive, noncultural and ahistorical term, the body may be seen as the crucial term, the site of contestation, in a series of economic, political, sexual, and intellectual struggles" (*Volatile Bodies* 19). How can a woman know her own body or another's under the thumb of such a system?

Because of Darcy's confidence and the narrator's statement that "there was a mixture of sweetness and archness in her manner which made it difficult for her to affront anybody" (52), the novel makes it hard to see or to take her settled disapprobation for him seriously. The contradiction between Darcy's and Elizabeth's interpretation of her reactions to him provides an example of how her body becomes "the site of contestation" in the novel. She has expressed her aversion so well and to so many that when she decides to marry Darcy, she has trouble convincing her family that she loves him: Jane cries, "You are joking, Lizzy. This cannot be!—engaged to Mr. Darcy! No, no, you shall not deceive me. . . . I know how much you dislike him" (372); and her father reminds her, "have not you always hated him?" (376). In contrast, because he loves Elizabeth, Darcy misreads her choler, at least until his first proposal. Does he differ so much from Collins in construing Elizabeth through the ideological filter that says that women flirt, but they do not get angry? What feels to her like outrage sounds to him like delightful, coquettish wit. When Darcy says she "find[s] great enjoyment in occasionally professing opinions which in fact are not your own" (174), ironically, like Collins, he assumes that like a conduct book heroine, she dissimulates, and does so for his pleasure, engaging in that "sweet, reluctant amorous delay" that Milton assigns Eve in *Paradise Lost*. As I alluded to earlier, Darcy admits that because Elizabeth's and Caroline's "figures appear to the greatest advantage in walking, [he] can admire [them] much better as [he] sit[s] by the fire" (56). Miss Bingley wants to know how they shall "punish him for such a speech"? Elizabeth answers by instructing Caroline to " 'Teaze him—laugh at him.—Intimate as you are, you must know how it is to be done.' 'But upon my honour I do *not*. I do assure you that my intimacy has not yet taught me *that*' " (56). Elizabeth, the passage suggests, already has the secret for punishing— witty words that carry their own physical charge. Laughter embodies an aggressive purpose here, providing an outlet for both her hostility and perhaps her sexual attraction to him. Elizabeth says that if you want to punish, then, there is "Nothing, so easy, if you have but the inclination," and *she* is inclined to find release in such a way from the power Darcy holds over her sister and family. In this sense, her wit intends (as Regina Gagnier has argued feminist comedy aims to do) to be "metasemiotic, casting in doubt . . . cultural codes" (139). Darcy's attraction to her, however, nullifies her feminist gestures of revolt, since he interprets her remarks as appeals toward his body, toward a collapsing of subject and object; from Darcy's point of view, Elizabeth's laughter draws him closer.

In these varying responses—the fact that she "never knew" herself (208), that her mother and the Bingley sisters read her as "wild"; that her father and sister believe she "hates" Darcy; that the narrator discloses that she is, underneath it all, "sweet and arch"; that Darcy finds her "bewitching"; and that she herself believes that she articu- lates a transparent state of "immoveable dislike" (193)—a question emerges about her self-knowledge as well as the knowledge about her that others might have. The context of the *bildungsroman* provides an insufficient answer since the characters' diverging interpretations of Elizabeth expose the tension between her own agency and social pres- sures: the difficulty of reading identity outside of an ideological lens renders her growth curve more ineffable and labyrinthine than a movement from "a" to "b" ("until this moment I never knew myself"). As Katherine Canning emphasizes, "embodied practices are always contextual, inflected with class, ethnic, racial, gender, and generational locations" (87). Can Elizabeth read her own body, know her attraction to him—those signals that seem so clear in her playful wit— or do social constructions of gender preclude Darcy, and the narrator, from interpreting her humor as a real resistance to his attempt to mark her, markings so obvious, he believes, that she cannot be surprised that he proposes to her?

As if to reinforce the idea that a man's aggression is always pellucid, the novel renders Darcy's own truculence toward those he dislikes palpable. In the episode in which Caroline Bingley tries to make herself known to Darcy by flattering his epistolary style, he responds to her with the same hostility he had earlier directed toward Elizabeth. Miss Bingley irritates Darcy by complimenting him for writing to his sister, for writing "fast," and for writing "many" letters, including those of business, and for passing along from her a message to Georgiana in his letter (47). Unable to inspire a satisfactory response with her flattery, and incapable of grasping "the perfect unconcern with which her praises were received" (47), she shifts strategy and offers to be serviceable: "I am afraid you do not like your pen. Let me mend it for you. I mend pens remarkably well." Perhaps in desperation she here unconsciously tries to engage Darcy with a powerful metonymy of phallic power and feminine submission. Apparently recognizing the double entendre, whether she does or not, Darcy wittily invokes auto-eroticism when he answers, "Thank you—but I always mend my own" (47). A common pun, the pen as phallus occurs throughout literature written before the nineteenth century, especially in Shakespeare. For example, in *The Merchant of Venice* Gratiano says to his wife, Nerissa, "I'll mar the young clerk's pen" (V.i.237), when she threatens to tryst with the clerk.[7] And from Sir George Lyttelton's *A Collection of Poems*, comes this little poem, playing on the same idea: Epigram VIII, "On Mrs. Penelope," by Gilbert West. "The gentle Pen with look demure, / Awhile was thought a virgin pure; / But Pen as ancient poets say, / Undid the night of work by day" (2:230).

Whether Caroline understands the pun she has made or the one Darcy throws back at her, she does suggest one way women did serve men at the time, that is by making and repairing pens, and that historical context illuminates the power dynamics implicit in this exchange. John Savigny's *Instructions at Large for Making and Repairing Pens* (1786) relates that he has "instructed many young ladies, who at first entertained an idea of the difficulty of attainment, who, notwithstanding, are now capable of making pens for the most capital prize-writing . . ." (lviii). Savigny encourages young ladies to master this skill: "It cannot be imagined they can be capable of feeling a more exquisite degree of pleasure, than in finding the perfection of their faculties able to supply a remedy for the decay" of their parents' aging eyes. Savigny, devoted to his cause, wants all who write to "have it in their power to accommodate themselves with pens"; the treatise implies, however, that a woman's ability to make and repair these instruments might also be useful to the young gentleman, who a week after having "le[ft] the seminary, with the reputation of being a fine writer, . . . greatly disappoints his friends by his performance when he uses the pens he finds at home, or of such as may be purchased ready made" (lv). His strong moral tone in pleading for the handcrafted over the mechanically produced and consumed article of capitalist enterprise recalls the Romantic-era sentimentalization of objects explored earlier in my discussion of the production of hair jewelry. Savigny's morality also emerges in his sentimental picture of young female eyes helping deteriorating parental vision and in the anecdote he relates about a gentlewoman who "omitted sending her sister a letter for one whole month" because "her cousin, who used to make her pens, happened to be at Bath" (lx). The treatise reveals an unsteady union between its promise of empowerment for the women who gain this knowledge and the subordination of that skill to domestic duties: when one is "once rendered capable of making a fine pen, [one] will soon discover the proper means of suiting it to all the different hands now in use" (83). Though Savigny speaks literally here about the fit between a pen and an individual hand, he also implies that there are differences between the purposes a man or woman might put a pen to. Women should enable others to write.

This sense in the treatise that a woman should subordinate her initiative and knowledge to good service parallels Caroline's self-subjection, but it also reflexively recalls Austen's agency as a writer. Caroline wants to serve Darcy with her pen-making skill; Austen has a pen that fits her own hand quite well indeed, and she empowers her writing by her subversive pun on that word. The scene embodies female submission and male dominance; however, the fact that a woman has written this episode agitates that clear power balance. If it is impossible to believe that Austen knew she was making such a pun, perhaps she becomes, like Elizabeth, a site of contestation in which regardless of how legible her own anger may be (though couched in a witty double entendre), she must perforce be characterized as having a "sweetness and archness in her manner which made it difficult for her to affront anybody" (52). Lisa Merrill argues that "in feminist comedy, we are no longer cast as an omniscient audience laughing at a character 'unknowingly betraying' herself [;] rather, the context and the character interact in such a way as to stir our empathy as much as our amusement" (279). Feminist comedy, as Austen employs it, expands beyond Merrill's definition. In offering a bawdy witticism, the novelist expresses her hostility toward the kind of traditional female subordination that Caroline embodies here, and if she does empathize with Miss Bingley insofar as she exposes the social genetics that spawned such behavior—the kind of conduct-book discourse that permeates Savigny's treatise—Austen's empathy does not tenderize her hostility. Austen has "made" her own pen, and in doing so shows another way that feminist comedy might empower women. Darcy's aggressive humor, when directed toward Caroline, provides both him and Austen the opportunity to displace bellicose feelings with flogging double entendres that the public may or may not tolerate from a woman.

TRANSGRESSION

Lori Hope Lefkovitz argues that "as the body acquires new definition, what it means to transgress its boundaries changes accordingly" (1). The novel asks in a number of ways what it means when female bodies transgress the precincts apportioned to them, and those transgressions vary from Elizabeth's walk to Netherfield to Lydia's illicit days in Meryton and London. The novel's arresting reference to cross-dressing constitutes one fecund example of those transgressions: Lydia exclaims that

> we had such a good piece of fun the other day at Colonel Forster's. Kitty and me were to spend the day there, and Mrs. Forster promised to have a little dance in the evening; (by the bye, Mrs. Forster and me are *such* friends!) and so she asked the two Harringtons to come, but Harriet was ill, and so Pen was forced to come by herself; and then, what do you think we did? We dressed up Chamberlayne in woman's clothes, on purpose to pass for a lady,—only think what fun! Not a soul knew of it, but Col. and Mrs. Forster, and Kitty and me, except my aunt, for we were forced to borrow one of her gowns; and you cannot imagine how well he looked! When Denny, and Wickham, and Pratt, and two or three more of the men came in, they did not know him in the least. Lord! How I laughed! And so did Mrs. Forster. I thought I should have died. (221)

The women dress an officer up as a "lady," hoping, no doubt, to trick the unknowing men into a romantic advance; because of the context,

Austen's choice of names for Lydia's friend, Pen, perhaps short for Penelope, also suggests subversive gender play—with more "pens" in female hands, the cross-dressing now goes in the other direction. The narrator blandly explains that "with such kind of histories of their parties and good jokes, did Lydia, assisted by Kitty's hints and additions, endeavour to amuse her companions all the way to Longbourn. Elizabeth listened as little as she could, but there was no escaping the frequent mention of Wickham's name" (222). The narration here suggests that although she does not enjoy Lydia's stories, references to Wickham upset Elizabeth more than the "histories of their parties and good jokes." Dennis Allen argues that the incident hints that "romantic or sexual desire can ignore society's heterosexual imperative, leading to a homosexual eros which in effect obliterates the cultural distinction of male and female. . . . Lydia's trick suggests that desire has the potential to violate the logical foundations of her society, . . . [to] threate[n] a nihilistic dissolution of the social order that fully justifies Austen's fear of it" (438–439). I would argue, instead, as I will do in my analysis of *Northanger Abbey*, that Lydia's trick does not reveal Austen's "fear" of desire, but rather her recognition that people consciously act out many gender characteristics. The episode, for example, satirizes the gender status of the military, which supposedly embodies masculinity, and the male virtues of courage and volition. That certain members of the regiment and their wives enjoy cross-dressing as a form of recreation illustrates Wollstonecraft's link in the *Vindication* between idle women and a standing army—far from being purposeful, both are groups with nothing to do. Using comedy to raise insistent questions about gender constructions, the novel trumpets how the military uniform itself performs a role: both a disguise and a costume, it constitutes "another form of female attire" (Beerbohm, qtd. in Garber 55). In uniform, a soldier already dresses in drag. Marjorie Garber points out that "whatever the specific semiotic relationship between military uniforms and erotic fantasies of sartorial gender, the history of cross-dressing within the armed services attests to a complicated interplay of forces, including male bonding, acknowledged and unacknowledged homosexual identity, carnivalized power relations, [and] the erotics of same-sex communities . . ." (55–56). Mrs. Bennet, recalling "the time when I liked a red coat myself very well" (29), reinforces how military men wear, indeed in a sense *are*, costumes that provide a veritable fashion show for civilians.

This episode also introduces questions about the understanding and reception of homosexuality (as I have pointed out, the Romantic era collapsed the transvestite and the homosexual into one category), an issue also implied in the possible allusion to sodomy I analyzed above, with the flogging of the private. I discuss later in the book how male transvestism had become a "burlesque or grotesque" (Senelick 81). Here, Lydia's triumph—"you cannot imagine how well he looked!"—unveils how the afternoon's "fun" also provides a moment for Chamberlayne (itself a pointed act of naming; the chamberlain was the intimate servant of the bedchamber) to feel "at home" in his body and career, unrecognizable as a *man* to five or six of his peers. Many other Romantic novels include instances of cross-dressing, Scott's *Redgauntlet*, for example, but rarely do women attire men. This episode bears out Cixous and Clement's argument that "Laughter breaks up, breaks out, splashes over. . . . It is the moment at which the woman crosses a dangerous line, the cultural demarcation beyond which she will find herself excluded. . . . An entire fantastic world, made of bits and pieces, opens up beyond the limit, as soon as the line is crossed" (*Newly Born Woman* 33). In including transvestism, Austen undermines firm conceptions of gender identity and crosses a line that opens up the tranquilized perfection and so-called stability of gentry life.

Lydia experiences something like orgasmic delight in the titillating adventure of arraying a man in women's clothes, crossing physical boundaries as her hands move over his body, veiling his "real" identity under lavish female apparel: "—Lord! How I laughed! And so did Mrs. Forster. I thought I should have died" (221). She almost "dies" laughing again, and engages in a kind of cross-dressing herself, when she elopes with Wickham. In her goodbye letter to Mrs. Forster announcing her elopement, Lydia can "hardly write for laughing" (291). This image, almost defying representation—does Lydia double over with laughter? shake uncontrollably with the giggles? convulse with merriment?—evokes an instance of the physical almost overpowering the cognitive. If Lydia's laughter "breaks up, breaks out, splashes over," signaling "the moment at which [she] crosses a dangerous line," she significantly does not or cannot acknowledge the transgression she commits, and her apathy about consequences implies that she does not "find herself excluded" from "the cultural demarcation" she has crossed:

You will laugh when you know where I am gone, and I cannot help laughing myself at your surprise to-morrow morning, as soon as I am missed. I am going to Gretna Green, and if you cannot guess with who, I shall think you a simpleton, for there is but one man in the world I love, and he is an angel. I should never be happy without him, so think it no harm to be off. You need not send them word at Longbourn of my going, if you do not like it, for it will make the surprise the greater, when I write to them, and sign my name Lydia Wickham. What a good joke it will be! I can hardly write for laughing. Pray make my excuses to Pratt, for not keeping my engagement, and dancing with him to night. Tell him I hope he will excuse me when he knows all, and tell him I will dance with him at the next ball we meet, with great pleasure. I shall send for my clothes when I get to Longbourn; but I wish you would tell Sally to mend a great slit in my worked muslin gown, before they are packed up. Good bye. Give my love to Colonel Forster, I hope you will drink to our good journey. (291-292)

Like so many others in the novel, Lydia puts her body in motion; embracing her body's needs, she acts with a man's freedom. With a last lubricious request that they drink to her journey (not to her marriage)—that they imbibe her libidinous joy vicariously—she abandons all, and like nail clippings or strands of hair, leaves behind family, friends, dancing partners, and clothes, specifically one dress with a "great slit." Exultant, she uses the word "laughing" three times and calls her elopement a "good joke." Exclaiming that it would be fun if she were married, she sounds like characters from Austen's early "The first Act of a Comedy": When Chloe sings, "I shall be married to Strephon, / And that to me will be fun," a Chorus of ploughboys answer her with the refrain: "Be fun, be fun, be fun, / And that to me will be fun" (*Minor Works* 173).[8] Lydia's fun alludes to the sexual delight she anticipates with Wickham. The laughter that almost prevents her from writing her elopement letter, not to mention the great slit in her worked muslin gown, suggest that Lydia has already lost her virginity. The word "muslin" carried sexual connotations, as in the following definitions: "a bit of muslin" referred to "a woman, a girl"; "a bit of muslin on the sly" suggested illicit sexual relations (Partridge 545). In leaving this "wound" behind, her letter implies her conviction that elopement will repair the breach as neatly as Sally will mend her gown, and that she will return to her previous condition (hymenally sound), and that there will be no negative consequences to her actions—an assumption that proves largely correct. Rather than reading her conviction that anything can be restored as an indicator of her childlike sense of irresponsibility, I would suggest instead that like Cassandra ("The Beautifull Cassandra") and Eliza ("Henry and Eliza"), heroines from the Juvenilia, she has left her "dress" behind, literally and figuratively, and like a man, anticipates a sexual relationship without fear of repercussions for her respectability.

As the greatest transgressor in all of the novels, Lydia provides the deepest aporia in Austen's oeuvre, representing someone who, as cross-dresser and much else, both exists outside society's rigid gender expectations and embodies social constructions of sexuality. Nietzsche's aphorism in *Thus Spake Zarathustra*, "Not by wrath, but by laughter, do we slay" (41) helps explain why Lydia considers her elopement "a good joke." In a Hobbesian sense, she guffaws with the "sudden glory" her sense of triumph over her unmarried sisters affords her. If she has transgressed the culture's expectations for women, she has also fulfilled them, trumping her sisters (especially Elizabeth, whom Wickham rejected) by marrying first, and she does so without the fear or shame that the same culture inculcates in female minds. How she can neither grasp nor care about the possible repercussions of her behavior is mystifying, in large part because the novel so glaringly enunciates these consequences. Without Darcy's prestidigitation, chances are good that she would have become a working woman: that is, a prostitute. The slit in her dress and the reference in that letter to her "*worked* muslin gown" (emphasis added) foreshadows Lydia's possible future, since, as I pointed out, "muslin" was a common metonymy for "a girl"; the phrase that results, "worked girl," combines sex and labor. As I discuss in relation to *Northanger Abbey* and *Mansfield Park*, Austen is alive to the sexual double entendres attached to torn gowns. In making a joke about a "great slit in [Lydia's] muslin gown," Austen uses humor to suggest possible tragic outcomes and, in doing so, she also reveals the complex historical pressures propelling Lydia, the degree of Lydia's own volition in her behavior, and the vulnerability of young women in her culture in general.

The novel sets the precedent for reading her letter as a hint of future disaster, since the neighborhood itself expects—in fact, anticipates with pleasure—the denouement of her ruin; as Austen ironically puts it: "To be sure it would have been more for the advantage of conversation, had Miss Lydia Bennet come upon the town; or, as the happiest alternative, have been secluded from the world, in some distant farm house" (309). "Coming upon the town" means a life of prostitution, and "seclusion from the world in some distant farm house" refers to the practice of sequestering pregnant unmarried young women. Roger Sales, suggesting that Lydia resembles the famous courtesan, Harriette Wilson (whose story Austen knew), claims that the "world of organized prostitution is not very far away" from the world of *Pride and Prejudice* (*Janeites* 200). Other allusions to Lydia's alternative career abound: while in London, she and Wickham find lodgings with the help of Mrs. Younge, Wickham's intimate friend and the governess who betrayed Georgiana Darcy by trying to procure her for Wickham. Elizabeth's aunt, Mrs. Gardiner, explains in a letter to her niece that this panderer had a "large house in Edward-street and maintained herself by letting lodgings" (209). If "letting lodgings" is a euphemism for whoremongering, the house address somewhat corroborates the seedy associations: between 1770 and 1779, St. Ann's Parish, Soho contained 21 bawdy houses (by comparison, St. Martin's had 149, Covent Garden had 51, Marylebone had 2 and Bloomsbury had 1) (Trumbach 122).[9]

I have several times now drawn connections between Lydia and various transgressive characters in Austen's earliest writings. These genealogies merit close attention. Parallels emerge, for example, between Cassandra ("The Beautifull Cassandra") (1787–1790) and Lydia Bennet: both run away from home, have an adventure in London, cannot pay for food they order, dress up a man, are met by their respective mothers with love and transport when they return home from committing their crimes, and define "a day well spent" ("Cassandra" 47), as one spent in consumption and dissipation. Both also abuse their bonnets: Lydia exclaims,

> "Look here, I have bought this bonnet. I do not think it is very pretty; but I thought I might as well buy it as not. I shall pull it to pieces as soon as I get home, and see if I can make it up any better."
> And when her sisters abused it as ugly, she added, with perfect unconcern, "Oh! but there were two or three much uglier in the shop; and when I have bought some prettier-coloured satin to trim it with fresh, I think it will be very tolerable. Besides, it will not much signify what one wears this summer, after the – – – shire have left Meryton, and they are going in a fortnight." (219)

Lydia consumes for the sake of consuming when she purchases a bonnet she dislikes. Her plan to "trim it fresh" was a common activity at the time. Austen writes to Cassandra in December 1798 that "I took the liberty a few days ago of asking your Black velvet Bonnet to lend me its cawl, which it very readily did, & by which I have been enabled to give a considerable improvement of dignity to my Cap, which was before too *nidgetty* to please me" (Le Faye 25). Lydia's plan to retrim the bonnet with yet another purchase, "prettier-coloured satin," mimics how she transforms herself into a commodity for the militia. Her ferocious words, that she "will pull it to pieces," seem overdetermined. In its emphasis on violent refashioning, her remaking of the bonnet is linked to the radical capacity for remaking the self, which itself exists in paradoxical relationship to early-nineteenth-century women's fashions, which were predicated on "the effect of deliberate display . . ., supported by the effect of deliberate trouble taken for the purpose—elaborate headwear, difficult footwear, cosmetics, extraneous adornments and accessories, constriction and extension" (*Sex and Suits* 9). Lydia's fashionable redressing of her bonnet strikingly contrasts to the male ideal of fashion during the Romantic period, in which "decorative elements are integrated with the overall scheme, so that nothing sticks out, slides off, twists around, gets bruised, goes limp or catches on anything" (9). Men's clothing, in short, "reflects the modern esthetic principles that were conceived out of Neo-classic aspirations . . ., just like modern democratic impulses" (*Sex and Suits* 9).

Her mutilation of the bonnet / self to make it "tolerable" thus reveals less her democratic than her capitalist spirit, one in which she is both the product and the consumer. Lydia always sees herself being seen; she is a "visual transaction [that] is always ideologically organized" (Kaja Silverman 187). Retrimming the bonnet parallels the ambitious way she puts herself forward in the world but also reveals how ideological imprints always compromise (no doubt because they propel) her transgressive acts. As usual, she objectifies herself since whatever she does to the bonnet does not signify given that she (and it) will not have an audience now that the militia will soon leave Meryton for Brighton.

Lydia's rage against the bonnet is foreshadowed in "The Beautifull Cassandra," in which Cassandra "fall[s] in love with an elegant Bonnet," but later uses it to assault the coach driver she cannot pay by "putting [it] on his head and r[unning] away" (45, 6). The impulses generating Cassandra's adventures and perhaps Lydia's stem from terrible constraints on women suggested in the short work's dedication to another Cassandra, Miss Cassandra Austen:

> Madam, You are a Phoenix, Your taste is refined, your Sentiments are noble, & your Virtues innumerable. Your Person is lovely, your Figure, elegant, & your Form, majestic. Your Manners are polished, your Conversation is rational & your appearance singular. If therefore the following Tale will afford one moment's amusement to you, every wish will be gratified of Your most obedient humble servant The Author. (44)

That a story of feminine delinquency would offer "one moment's amusement" to this paragon of womanhood could be ironic, but it could also be apposite, insofar as the "Tale" offers psychic and physical release from the coercive demands placed on women. If Cassandra Austen is a "phoenix," perhaps it is from the ashes of those expectations that she so energetically reemerges as "the Beautifull Cassandra." Austen's listing of these absurd expectations in her dedication parodies the literature found in various lady's magazines, in which just these kinds of catalogues occur and aim to be taken seriously. Though the following poem, published in 1806 in the *Lady's Monthly Museum*, was written after Austen had composed "The Beautiful Cassandra," it offers a clear example of the kind of feminine ideal that Austen wants to satirize and does, through Elizabeth Bennet's voice in *Pride and Prejudice* (1813).

A GOOD WOMAN'S HEART.

Her price is far above rubies;
In her eye is the lustre of heaven:
The law of kindness dwelleth on her tongue;
Her whole exterior is stamped with the virtues of her life
Her manners delineate her heart,
And her heart embraces every ingredient of true worth;
   Virtue and Truth;
   Simplicity and Piety;
   Charity and Benevolence;
   Love and Modesty;
   Dignity, Elegance, and Delicacy;
   Prudence and Economy;
   Affability and Politeness;
   Humanity and Justice;
   Constancy, Chastity, and Honor;
   Humility and Good nature;
   Sincerity and Friendship;
   Compassion and Meekness,
   Gentleness and Fidelity;
   Industry and Contentment;
   Tenderness and Gratitude;
   Purity and Patience;
   Magnanimity and Mercy.
Happy woman! bless'd with these,
Her's, future hope and present ease;
Happier he whose wife she is,
The richest thing on earth is his. (220–221)

Elizabeth wonders that Caroline and Darcy could know "*any*" such women when they describe the "accomplished" lady as possessing "a thorough knowledge of music, singing, drawing, dancing, and the modern languages, to deserve the word; . . . a certain something in her air and manner of walking, the tone of her voice, her address and expressions, . . . and to all this she must yet add something more substantial, in the improvement of her mind by extensive reading" (27). Caroline and Darcy's language mirrors the lexicon Austen uses in her "Dedication" to her sister.

Toward the end of the beautiful Cassandra's day, during which she has wandered "thro' many a street" (a phrase that compromises her chastity), the narrative juxtaposes her extensive liberty with the financial, rational, and imaginative deprivation represented by "her freind [*sic*] the Widow, who squeezing out her little Head thro' her less window, asked her how she did?" (46). The widow's "less window"—her narrow point of view and even smaller prospects—exacerbates or perhaps explains the tiny intelligence suggested by her "little Head." This woman's "smallness" portrays an accurate picture of most women's lives, a reality in vivid contrast to Cassandra's. When the heroine feminizes the coachman by placing her bonnet on his head because she cannot pay him, she gestures toward the dis-gendering of male authority and to a different kind of female power than that promised by the acquisition of "accomplishments." Playing "man," she takes freedoms denied to women, especially those who must be paragons of "Virtue and Truth; Simplicity and Piety; Charity and Benevolence; Love and Modesty; Dignity, Elegance, and Delicacy"; and so forth. One could argue that Cassandra and Lydia both "turn round" and "trasvestie" themselves (to borrow Hazlitt's phrase about Byron)[10] insofar as they act out of keeping for their gender and refuse to place any more emphasis on their chastity than a typical man of their age would.

In "Jack and Alice," another story from the Juvenilia, Austen recasts roles assigned to specific genders in order to savor the absurdity of what the age deemed "natural" behavior for women. Lucy, Charles Adams's female admirer, takes the role of the male suitor when she writes a "very kind letter, offering him with great tenderness my hand & heart. To this I received an angry & peremptory refusal, but thinking it might be rather the effect of his modesty than any thing else, I pressed him again on the subject" (*Minor Works* 21). And when he departs, she writes him again "informing him that I should shortly do myself the honour of waiting on him at Pammydiddle, to which I received no answer; therefore choosing to take, Silence for Consent, I left Wales, unknown to my Aunt, & arrived here after a tedious Journey this Morning" (22). Here Lucy, performing the role Mr. Collins will later enact, interprets Charles in terms of social expectations for women—that they dissimulate under the mask of demure reticence: "no" means "yes," but so does silence. This transvestite activity, however, renders Lucy immobile when she falls into a trap set up for poachers and breaks her leg, circumstances anticipating Maria Edgeworth's *Belinda* (1801), in which Harriet Freke disables her leg in a mantrap. A similar breakdown of gender roles occurs in Harriette

Wilson's *Memoirs* (1825), in which she takes on the masculine role and solicits a man's "hand"; she sends no less a figure than the Prince of Wales what amounts to an ironic version of a proposal, wanting to know if he "would like to see" her and that he should write her back, if he believes he could make her love him (7).

LYDIA'S SEXUALITIES

The novel knows that sexual pleasure will not sustain Lydia's happiness with Wickham, but assessing her courtship story in such terms hardly exhausts this character's meaning; one can speculate, for instance, that some readers might find a point for identification, even a release in Lydia's riotous insistence on her freedom and physical self-fulfillment.[11] In the Juvenilia, characters such as Cassandra, who resemble Lydia, command respect and create a thrill of anarchic delight. Many readers of *Pride and Prejudice* find instead that the novel inhibits their identification with Lydia Bennet, and that the narrative, in encouraging a judgment against her based on patriarchal demands of women, disables vicarious enjoyment of her pleasure. Her joys simply do not titillate or inspire any desire for imitation: "even the notoriously 'fast' Lydia," Joseph Litvak remarks, "is stuck in a one-joke role" (*Strange* 23). As Johanna M. Smith argues, "why . . . does the novel chastise Lydia for wanting the same happy ending the heroines achieve?" (71). By contrast, Harriette Wilson (to return again to the famous courtesan) presents her sexual conquests and a rationale for her "elopement" in a way that fosters sympathy.[12] At the beginning of her *Memoirs* (which caused a near riot when they were first issued, the demand was so great), she explains that one of the inducements for running away from home to become the mistress of the Earl of Craven when she was fifteen years old, was her father's "severity," and that the "very idea of a father put [her] in a tremble" (5, 8).

A psychological reading might suggest that Lydia repulses because she does not risk any real feeling. From this context, Lydia, though an obvious gambler in the game of love and reputation, in truth hazards nothing in her "communications," a phenomenon that, in Bataille's words, takes place "*between two people who risk themselves,* each lacerated and suspended, perched atop a common nothingness" (*On Nietzsche* 21). Unlike Elizabeth and Darcy, pulled centrifugally from their settled positions, Lydia's orientation remains wholly centripetal. In other words, her narcissism prevents her from reaching outward to connect to others (Kristeva, *Powers* 14). Because Lydia does not see or hear anything of "which she chose to be insensible" (205), her remorselessness places her out of the rubric of controlling systems; she is immune to any attempt to break down her fiction of corporeal wholeness. In being unable to suffer, Lydia, in Elaine Scarry's sense, remains outside the "fundamental cultural activity of making a world, of creating artifacts and fictions" (164). Because her decisions lie outside the realm of behavior that could mitigate her actions—she does not run away from a cruel family; she is not a seduced innocent; she does not strive to make a political statement about the double standard—Lydia instantiates instead the abject "leavings" of her culture. She is a force of disorder in the system, an excess which threatens the sparkling, the tidy, and the wholesome, an object lesson in the voracious nature of female sexuality, a force that must be contained. Along those lines, one could argue that Austen reforms the "civic body" of the novel by jettisoning its libido onto Lydia Bennet and then transporting her and her vim to the north of England.

Reading Lydia as a homily, however, does not interest me. I am intrigued by the way in which she, though a rule-breaker, fulfills polymorphic cultural constructions of female sexuality. Inspired by her "high animal spirits," Lydia could be interpreted as acting from female instincts *if* those same recklessly carnal impulses did not also embody her mother's desperation to get her married. Though wild, Lydia, like Charlotte (her unlikely double), epitomizes the panic induced when a society thinks unwed women are worthless. As Fay Weldon points out, Mrs. Bennet is the only character "with the slightest notion of the sheer desperation of the world" (76)—and perhaps Lydia should be included with her mother in intuiting that truth. Her decisions thus arise from multiple and often conflicting impulses, a point that is less psychological than it is historical. How does history illuminate Lydia? First, how is she related to—how might she dramatize—the shift from an understanding of women as inordinately sexual to the belief that they were fundamentally passionless?

As I discuss throughout this study, Austen explores in subtle terms such a turn in medical discourse throughout her work. Her writings draw from ideologies that span the continuum of the mid-eighteenth to early nineteenth centuries, and in *Pride and Prejudice* competing discourses are at play—as, no doubt, they were at play throughout her lifetime. For example, Wickham tries to seduce two adolescent girls, both fifteen. One of them, Georgiana Darcy—the innocent, shy, reserved victim of his ambitious, heartless machinations—best resembles the later demure ideal of intrinsic innocence, while Lydia, erotically charged, partakes of the earlier prototype of woman, assumed to be sexual and responsive to amatory texts. The cross-dressing episode provides evidence that Lydia warms to sexually stimulating material.[13] As I discussed in chapter 1, earlier eighteenth-century courting was characterized by heavy petting, but no intercourse, for fear of pregnancy; while later in the century, the "London" style was to get pregnant, and then married. By any eighteenth- or nineteenth-century standards, Lydia transgresses the rules. The particular ways she embodies various expectations and prohibitions concerning the female body's agency and mobility, however, complicate any secure definition of what her transgression is. She could be seen as simultaneously embodying the earlier model of the young woman encouraged to be sexual in order to win a husband and thereby conceive *after* marriage and the later, fashionable trend of using pregnancy as a courtship strategy to get married, a plan that her words to Darcy imply: "She was sure [she and Wickham] should be married some time or other, and it did not much signify when" (323). Trumbach argues that "the new male heterosexuality encouraged men to seduce young women whom they had no intention of marrying, and that the young women usually consented in the belief that sexual intimacy was a prelude to marriage" (230)— a calamitous recipe for women who played this high stakes game and lost.

Lydia's pleasure always takes precedence over self-interest, but again, there is more to understand about her character than this fact. Shrewd enough to know that the only way to keep Wickham is to remain in his orbit and that to return home without him would be to have failed at the grand goal of marriage, Lydia "absolutely resolve[s] on remaining where she [is]" (322). Here, embodying the reluctance of a massive object to change its motion, she fulfills Newton's third law. Because Lydia is "untamed, unabashed, wild, noisy, and fearless" (315), the force acting upon her must be stronger than society's censorship, and given Lydia's limited intellect and self-knowledge, that force could only be another kind of censorship—the shame of being unmarried—or another kind of encouragement.

When Lydia refuses to leave Wickham, it is possible to see the impact of an alternate ideological imperative, one advanced by the discourse of sensibility—that it was "natural" to remain with a man she loves. Much has been written about Marianne Dashwood as a parody of sensibility; Lydia, though, functions as a parody of the Enlightenment's assumption that nature had so designed human nature as "to follow pleasure, that sex was pleasurable, and it was natural to follow one's sexual urges" (Porter, "Mixed Feelings" 4). In this sense, Lydia, like Sophia and Laura in Austen's *Love and Friendship*, iterates a one-pronged aspect of sensibility insofar as she isolates from the movement only its sexual discourse. That she is one of those "soft, plump, tender melting, wishing, nay, willing Girls," to quote Colonel Britton from Susanna Centlivre's *The Wonder* (6), a play the young Austens performed (Nokes 94),[14] suggests that Lydia follows advice from the popular *Aristotle's Master-piece*, a text that did not "stain sex . . . with stigmas of sin, decadence, libertinism, enslavement to passion, or psychological disturbance" nor decree that it should be "sublimated, suppressed, or sentimentalized. Rather it was viewed as an agency of nature" (Porter 15–16). *Aristotle's Master-piece* explains that "Tho' the great Architect of the world has been pleased to frame us of different sexes, and for the propagation and continuation of mankind, has indulged us in the mutual embraces of each other, the desire whereof, by a powerful and secret instinct, is become natural to us . . ." (26). The matter-of-fact way in which Lydia guiltlessly pursues her pleasure suggests this text's influence—or at least of those cultural forces reflected in it; as her elopement letter explains, "I should never be happy without [Wickham], so think it no harm to be off" (291). Lydia recalls "Aristotle's" demystifying explanation that "to some[,] nature has given greater desires after enjoyment than to others"; the author follows this statement with an account that both exonerates a woman who technically may not be a virgin although offering a kind of primer (though he qualifies it) for those women seeking pleasure: "tho' they abstain from enjoyment, yet so great is their lust and desire after it, that it may break the *Hymen* or *Claustrum Virginale*" (35–36).[15]

To sum up, Lydia could be fulfilling any number of roles: as the stereotype of the sexually voracious woman—a kind of Wife of Bath— a type recognizably alive at least in the earlier eighteenth century, when Pope said that every woman was at heart a rake; as the cipher of her mother's view that a woman signifies nothing without a husband; as a devoted follower of the fad for pregnancy as the inducement for marriage; as the avid consumer of the epistemology that sexuality, the guarantor of generation, is the agency of nature; as a believer in the sexual imperative at the heart of some theories of sensibility, one that liberates her native libido. In that last role, like Fanny Hill, Lydia is aware of "how powerful are the instincts of nature, and how little is there wanting to set them in action" (Cleland 98). All of these possible readings have their force. I want to emphasize, though, the way in which Austen breaks down the idea that Lydia's behavior is "natural" or that she deserves to be rebuked. In the fantasy world of pornography, Fanny Hill may be "guided by nature only" (25), but Lydia's "shamelessness"— a strikingly immovable force in this novel of mobility—arises from multiple causes and reveals that she crystallizes various and competing ideas about the female body. Lydia may lack an inner moral barometer, but she also labors under the burden of ideologies that pose as moral ideas.

Lydia allows Austen to examine one of the most popular, indeed ubiquitous, and charged subjects of her day: the fallen woman. Markman Ellis, analyzing the period's many narratives of redeemed prostitutes and unwed mothers, points out that these texts "have a distinct moral and political purpose: an ideologically correct reformulation of the seduction convention giving it, through repentance, a happy ending" (178). Austen treats this subject in other ways: with the exception of *Sense and Sensibility*'s Marianne, who marries happily (though that is debatable), the author provides sorrowful endings for these disgraced women, but not because she takes an unforgiving stance. Claire Lamont argues that when the married Maria Bertram elopes with her lover, she "offends against her creator's view of how responsible autonomy in a woman might manifest itself. Jane Austen may have 'a good eye at an Adulteress,' but it was not [Austen's] purpose to make a heroine of one" (79).[16] Austen obviously does not make Lydia and Maria heroines, but she reserves her scorn for those who castigate the fallen. She satirizes Collins's egregious response to Lydia's folly, a reaction that is, in the words of *Clueless*'s Cher, "Way harsh": the clergyman contends that Lydia's death "would have been a blessing in comparison"; that her "licentiousness" is the family's fault, and yet, on the other hand, that her disposition is "naturally bad"; that this "false step" will keep the other daughters unmarried; all of which make him relieved that he did not marry into the family (297). Through such a satire of his "solemn, specious nonsense" (Le Faye 203),[17] Austen shows how ideology dehumanizes women, denying them the independence to think for themselves, all the while expecting that they will nonetheless embody virtue.

Like many writers of the Romantic era, Austen "identif[ies] the social factors that drove women to their destruction" (Ellis 164), but she does not do so in any way that leads her to sentimentalize the fallen woman. She topples the contention that a disgraced woman's reclamation in a marriage such as Lydia Bennet's was better than nothing and that an empty ritual that could guarantee neither happiness nor fortune is better than scandal, than prostitution, than destitution. Further, the novels endorse Mary Wollstonecraft's point that "many innocent girls become the dupes of a sincere, affectionate heart, and still more are, as it may emphatically be termed, *ruined* before they know the difference between virtue and vice:—and thus prepared by their education for infamy, they become infamous. Asylums and Magdalenes are not the proper remedies for these abuses. It is justice, not charity, that is wanting in the world!" (71). Characters from their respective novels admit that an inadequate education has led to Maria and Lydia's ignominy. In *Mansfield Park*, the cosmopolitan

Mary Crawford lacks Wollstonecraft's philosophical eclat; however, she offers here an alternative to exiling the ruined: a social solution based on group effort that in spirit, if not in particulars, resembles what occurs in *Pride and Prejudice*: she suggests that once Henry has been persuaded to marry Maria Bertram, the adulteress, and once ". . . properly supported by her own family . . . she may recover her footing in society to a certain degree. In some circles, we know, she would never be admitted, but with good dinners, and large parties, there will always be those who will be glad of her acquaintance; and there is, undoubtedly, more liberality and candour on those points than formerly" (*Mansfield Park* 456–457). Mrs. Bennet requests and wants for Lydia, her disgraced child, the same kind of institutional markers that Mary Crawford does for Maria, the material foundations that will provide the "body" of a respectable marriage (201). To this purpose, in contrast to the neighborhood's fantasies of disciplining Lydia, the mother conjures up happy endings for her daughter about "elegant nuptials, fine muslins, new carriages, and servants"; she rejects possible houses because the "drawing-room" is too small or the "attics are dreadful"; and, believing that without wedding clothes, Lydia's marriage will be invalid, she expects Mr. Bennet to offer his daughter money for such finery, which he refuses to do.

Whether Lydia deserves her trousseau, however, is inconsequential; what is significant is that because Mrs. Bennet has no say over the family finances, she must depend on her husband for his good will, just as she had to do at the novel's beginning when he taunts her by refusing to visit the new and eligible bachelor, Bingley. Mrs. Bennet's lack of financial and decision-making power and her subsequent displacement of her ensuing frustration into nervous fits, angry sulks, and her emphasis on "frivolous" items such as clothing, constitute more typical and trivial ways of rebelling against female constraints than Lydia's elopement; but they also reveal ironically how the more effectively women embody those regulations—and Mrs. Bennet's name leads all the rest—the more they lead to self-destructive behavior. The novels satirize the culture's obsession with controlling the female body: by using humor to show how such constraints lead to rebellion and pathology, Austen can both canvass the wild girl/woman and critique the ideology that leads to her destructive behavior.

UNBECOMING DOUBLES

In this novel and the others, Austen breaks down the binary opposition between the good and the bad woman, the champion of ideology and the rebel against it. She accomplishes this by establishing links between the women characters and by showing the ways in which, for all their variations, they duplicate each other. Doubling Lydia to Elizabeth, Charlotte to Elizabeth, and Lydia to Charlotte enables Austen to concentrate on how ideology affects women, rather than on making moral judgments or on establishing an inflexible hierarchy among the characters.[18] Because the doubled characters differ, however, Austen can accentuate individual divergences and thereby allow the possibility for some agency, while also revealing the common denominators that govern their behavior.[19] As Paul Gordon argues in *The Critical Double*, "to be double is to be different and the same . . . to be therefore *both* one and two" (19). Lydia, then, is more than just a "wild animal" and Elizabeth is liberated from the narrow definition of having only a "quiet [autonomy that] invites the conventional female reader to identify with unconventional energies but commits her to nothing more" (Newton 79–80). Austen demonstrates the variety of ways expectations can crystallize in individual lives while revealing the power of those expectations by analyzing their influence in characters as diverse as Elizabeth and Lydia—the princess and the prostitute.[20] As Katherine Canning argues, "subjects . . . are not simply the imposed results of alien, coercive forces; the body is internally lived, experienced and acted upon by the subject and the social collectivity" (88).

My argument, I believe, counters the claim that *Pride and Prejudice* exploits the focus on an individual woman and her marriage because Austen has an interest in denying potentially disruptive female bonds, and that the happy ending's emphasis on the fate of an individual such as Elizabeth, combined with its rendering of the pleasures of marriage, means that the novel endorses patriarchal values, including a denial of real alliances among women.[21] For example, Judith Lowder Newton, addressing the novel's conservatism, claims that "if there is any punch . . . in Elizabeth's resistance to Darcy's traditional assumptions of control, it is certainly diminished by our continuing awareness that the rebellion itself works in the interests of tradition" (79). In other words, Elizabeth acquiesces to custom, and if she does resist, she does so within conventional parameters: by flirtatiously resisting Darcy, an act that leads to marriage, she fulfills the fantasy (and demand) for romantic closure.

I argue, instead, that doubling illuminates how ideology, like transference, manifests itself in infinite ways, although stemming from the same roots. Thus, as I pointed out above, a culturally determined desperation to compete for and win a husband drives both Lydia and Charlotte to self-destructive choices. No one could doubt that

Elizabeth and Charlotte inhabit different universes, a fact that has led to conclusions such as Judith Lowder Newton's that Charlotte Lucas's marriage functions to show "on the one hand, the perverting force of women's economic lot," while it "prevent[s] us, on the other, from feeling that force as a reality in the universe of Elizabeth Bennet" (72). But instead of polarizing these characters, I would suggest that recognizing their doubleness reveals how their converging worlds allow Austen to critique "women's economic lot" in subtle ways.

Elizabeth acknowledges her link to Lydia when she admits that they share similar sentiments about Wickham's fleeting interest in the heiress, Mary King: Lydia asserts " 'I will answer for it he never cared three straws about her. Who *could* about such a nasty little freckled thing?' Elizabeth was shocked to think that, however incapable of such coarseness of *expression* herself, the coarseness of the *sentiment* was little other than her own breast had formerly harboured and fancied liberal!" (220). Elizabeth here locates her sentiments in her body—her breast—reinforcing the novel's emphasis on the corporeal intellect, as she acknowledges the way the need for a husband shapes both herself and her sister. Their expressions of joy also link them. Lydia can hardly "write for laughing" as she euphorically prepares to elope. Elizabeth, on the verge of marriage, exclaims that, "I am the happiest creature in the world. Perhaps other people have said so before, but not one with such justice. I am happier even than Jane; she only smiles, I laugh" (382–383). William Deresiewicz analyzes Elizabeth's happiness as revealing an emphasis on pure mind, as he argues that "bliss belongs to Jane; to Elizabeth belongs the blessing of awakened consciousness" (529). Indeed, she experiences an awakened consciousness, but the singing out of joy and triumph that is Elizabeth's laugh arises from an aroused body–mind rather than a disembodied intellect. Jane's smile activates only the muscles of her face, and bespeaks a certain restraint; Elizabeth's laugh, like Lydia's, animates her whole system. A transporting mental and physical bliss belong to the heroine; her "psychical corporeality" (Grosz 22) unhinges the need to declare the superiority of reason at the expense of the flesh. In another instance of doubling, occurring at varying times in the novel, the daughters's transgressions lead Mrs. Bennet to hector Elizabeth and Mr. Bennet to bully Lydia with threats of expulsion from the family. Elizabeth hears her mother say, "*I* shall not be able to keep you—and so I warn you.—I have done with you from this very day" (113). Mr. Bennet echoes these words, when he says of Lydia and Wickham, "Into *one* house in this neighborhood, they shall never have admittance" (310). That neither young woman faces final exile does not obviate the threat; rather, sending the same warning to contrasting sisters reinforces the reality of such punishment in the culture, and its possibility undercuts the idea that Elizabeth inhabits a fantasy world quarantined from systems that pressure and tattoo women sexually and economically.

If the sisters are thus intertwined, how can whatever is abject in Elizabeth be purified?—that "wild manner" in which she is "suffered to" "run on . . . at home" (42); her "blowsy! hair" and "petticoat, six inches deep in mud" (36); the woman who will "pollut[e]" "the shades of Pemberley" (357); the firebrand of a radical who accuses Caroline of conflating Wickham's "guilt and his descent" (95). One solution is to expel Lydia. But that symbolic purification, that kind of ritual separation of the abjected from the good one who remains, serves only to underscore their deep connection. Unlike Maria Bertram in *Mansfield Park*, Lydia remains in play till the novel's ending, a fact that works to project her presence in its afterlife: when Lydia asks for money, Elizabeth "endeavoured . . . to put an end to every intreaty and expectation of the kind. Such relief, however, as it was in her power to afford, by the practice of what might be called economy in her own private expences, she frequently sent them" (386–387). "Defilement," as Kristeva, following Mary Douglas, argues, "is what is jettisoned from the '*symbolic system*' " (*Powers* 65). Though Darcy jettisons Lydia, she leaves her mark on the symbolic system through Elizabeth, who secretly contests her husband's will (the embodiment of the system) by helping to support her sister and brother-in-law.[22] Because Lydia embosses her signature on the Darcy family, because Elizabeth rebels privately by acknowledging that imprint, and because she can only help her sister in secret, I disagree with Mary Poovey's argument that *Pride and Prejudice*'s ending "disguise[s] the inescapable system of economic and political domination" (237). Closer to the mark is Karen Newman's point that in Austen's endings "we find an ironic self-consciousness that emphasizes the contradiction between the sentimentality of Austen's comic conclusions and the realism of her view of marriage and of women's plight" (704). Lydia, though earlier snubbing "social rationality, that logical order on which a social aggregate is based" (Kristeva, *Powers* 65), now makes use of it while also flaunting its rules: in a sentence that suggests that she disregards her wedding vows while also exploiting the safety they promise, the novel explains that Lydia, "in spite of her youth and her manners, . . . retained all the *claims* to reputation that her marriage had given her" (387, emphasis added). Austen laughs both at and with women who break rules governing gender and sexual behavior.

CONCLUSION

Few readers would agree with Austen's famous remark that *Pride and Prejudice* sparkles too lightly and brightly, since that "too" suggests something amiss, and most readers of the novel love it precisely because it is so deliciously high-spirited:

> Your letter was truely welcome & I am much obliged to you all for your praise; it came at a right time, for I had had some fits of disgust;—our 2d evening's reading to Miss Benn had not pleased me so well, but I believe something must be attributed to my Mother's too rapid way of getting on—& tho' she perfectly understands the Characters herself, she cannot speak as they ought.—Upon the whole however I am quite vain enough & well satisfied enough.—The work is rather too light & bright & sparkling; it wants shade;—it wants to be stretched out here & there with a long Chapter—of sense, if it could be had, if not of solemn specious nonsense—about something unconnected with the story; an Essay on Writing, a critique on Walter Scott, or the history of Buonaparte—or anything that would form a contrast & bring the reader with increased delight to the playfulness and Epigrammatism of the general stile. I doubt your quite agreeing with me here—I know your starched Notions. (Le Faye 203)

This passage is a mock depreciation, and Jane Austen hardly reveals dissatisfaction with her work here, since her comic examples (a history of Buonaparte added to *Pride and Prejudice* or any of Austen's novels is, indeed, nonsense)[23] are, themselves—in being witty, pointed quips—playful and epigrammatic. Instead, she takes pleasure in her creation, so much so that her mother's misreading gives her "fits of disgust."[24] Austen is right: not that the novel "wants shade," but that what might be called the "shady" material unravels in as much sparkle as the light. The same rapier style that fleetingly solidifies the glittering princess fantasy also describes such turbid matter as seduction, flogging, prostitution, and marriage for hire, events that in a hierarchical cosmos would constitute the novel's underworld—its umbra. Instead, they appear in just as rococo a style as the beguiling occurrences: the "playfulness and Epigrammatism of the general stile" diminishes bold contrasts between shadow and light, and these opposing events and characters, far from remaining safely cordoned off, remain always deeply linked.

CHAPTER 3

FASHIONING THE BODY: CROSS-DRESSING, DRESSING, UNDRESSING, AND DRESSAGE IN *NORTHANGER ABBEY*

Every fashion is to some extent a bitter satire on love; in every fashion, perversities are suggested by the most ruthless means. Every fashion stands in opposition to the organic. Every fashion couples the living body to the inorganic world. . . . The fetishism that succumbs to the sex appeal of the inorganic is its vital nerve.

—Walter Benjamin, *The Arcades Project* 79, B9, 1

Every Austen novel has its share of fakes, frauds, and humbugs: from the various texts, Wickham, Willoughby, Lucy Steele, Henry Crawford, Mrs. Elton, and Sir Walter Elliot and his heir glitter with pretense. And *Northanger Abbey's* own Henry Tilney, Isabella, Mrs. Allen, and John Thorpe emanate inauthenticity as each, in their own fashion, acts in manipulative, hypocritical—and in a couple of cases—imbecilic ways. Their flimflammery provides comic relief; however, they also dramatize how ideologies compromise what might be thought of as the genuine in courtship rituals. For instance, posited against Isabella's jaded maneuverings, Catherine's intellectual inelasticity appears charming. I will argue, instead, that the novel breaks down an opposition such as this one by exposing the difficulties that all the characters have in negotiating their society's conventions: while Catherine flounders because she is uninstructed in anagogical or psychoanalytic interpretation, the Thorpes themselves fail because they call attention to the artificiality of conventions by embodying them so exhaustively. An example from Leigh Hunt's *Feast of the Poets* helps explain this: in his critique of Erasmus Darwin's poetry, Hunt revealed how Darwin, "whose notion of poetical music, in common with that of Goldsmith and others, was of the school of Pope, though his taste was otherwise different, was perhaps the first, who by carrying it to its extreme pitch of sameness, and ringing it affectedly in one's ears, gave the public at large a suspicion that there was something wrong in its nature" (*Feast* 34). A similar pattern emerges in Austen's novel: Isabella's flirtatious machinations just do too good of a job of exposing marriage as a financial exchange, and John's extravagant masculine pose reveals manliness as created, as opposed to inherent. Austen unmasks how society depends upon distinguishing between "male" and "female," a requirement that essentializes behavior while fabricating instructions on how to behave. By acknowledging how these roles contradict themselves, she rejects a " 'natural' sexuality," insofar as she scrutinizes its "typical markers" during this era, that is "sexually differentiated male and female bodies" (Parker 4).

I will examine the fruitful ways Austen employs contemporary fashions as well as the metaphor of dress in order to analyze how the characters execute conventional expectations. The original definition of the word "dress" was to arrange, align or make straight; it also carried the slang connotation of a thrashing, a "dressing down" (*OED*). These various meanings provide a useful structure first for inquiring how the novel demystifies the ideology of the "natural," and second for exposing how every fashion—whether of jewelry, fabric choice, or action—"couples . . . the living body to the inorganic world. . . . The fetishism that succumbs to the sex appeal of the inorganic is its vital nerve" (Benjamin, *The Arcades Project* 79, B9, 1).

DRESSING

Readers censure Henry when he bullies Catherine, though they often excuse his manipulation of Mrs. Allen on the grounds that she deserves it; that is, because she defines herself in terms of dress, she is easily pegged as vain and superficial. Can there be any doubt about that? If anatomized, would Mrs. Allen's inner world resemble those *The Tatler* satirizes: "Were the Minds of the [female] sex laid open, we should find the chief Idea in one to be a Tippet, in another a Muff, in a third a Fan, and in a fourth a Fardingal" (151)? Here Austen perhaps alludes to *The Tatler* since Mrs. Allen's idea of conversation is to ask

James Morland to "guess the price and weigh the merits of a new muff and tippet" (51). Her emotions rise only when her fears about the dressmaker's delay are "incapable" of being soothed (51). And clothing offers her a self-pleasuring that inhibits her from enjoying the activities for which she has ostensibly been attiring herself: they arrive at the ballroom late since she "was so long in dressing" (20). Functioning as personal gods through which she maintains power and influences her environment, Mrs. Allen's clothes surpass her affection for her protégée, and her primary concern is to "preserv[e] her gown from injury" (22). Like the author of the "Ode to Fashion" in *The Lady's Monthly Museum* for March 1800, she "adore[s]" fashion and requires that it "Bless" her "with thy vary'd store; / Quick each sudden change impart / To my ever-restless heart" (1–3, 177).

Indispensable fetishes, Mrs. Allen's clothes are "the locus of [her] . . . psychic investment" (Pietz, II 23). The larger culture galvanizes her obsession with them; though, as with any fetish, her compulsion poses as a marker of her own individuality. Her fascination is "a kind of external controlling organ directed by powers outside [her] . . . [which] represents a subversion of the ideal of the autonomously determined self" (Pietz, II 23). Alexandra Warwick and Dani Cavallaro argue that "the unfixable character of dress as both a personal and a communal phenomenon is largely due to its ability to quiz conventional understandings of the relationship between surface and depth"; thus, an analysis of dress offers the chance to examine how "surfaces [can be] regarded as yielding no less crucial clues of the fashioning of subjectivity than the depths treasured by more traditional questions and methodologies" (xxii–xxiii). I would disagree, then, with Ann Bermingham, who claims that in Austen's novels an "over-concern with fashion . . . is a sign of superficiality and vulgar materialism. Authenticity is signalled by a lack of preoccupation with one's appearance . . . if not an outright indifference to fashion" ("The Picturesque" 95).[1] My point, instead, is that for Austen, authenticity is an unstable category rather than a fixed, inelastic marker of value: in the heroine's world, no simple equation exists between concern with dress and incontrovertible sincerity.

Mrs. Allen's paralyzing infatuation with her gowns does turn her into "a picture of intellectual poverty" (79), and her fetish renders her an easy object for parody and homiletics; however, I want to suggest that rather than interpreting Mrs. Allen's vapidity—a spot-on imitation of expectations for women—as a moral failing, it helps to look instead at how her character approaches the simulacra, a realm that "implies great dimensions, depths, and distances which the observer cannot dominate" (Deleuze 49). As a burlesque of feminine interests that patriarchal culture institutionalizes, Mrs. Allen dramatizes Alicia Solomon's argument that "femininity is *always* drag" (145). In other words, woman is already a copy—a construction of some form of femininity. Thus in the satirist's hands, Mrs. Allen's character exaggerates even "normal" female preoccupations; she functions, in short, as Austen's own reproduction of a social construction, and when Henry imitates her in his discourse on muslin, he plays a copy of a copy of a copy—that is, he plays a man's version of Mrs. Allen, who is Austen's version of a female stereotype, which is, in itself, already a misogynistic construction of a "real" woman. Henry claims to understand muslins "[p]articularly well" and finds amusement in what Mrs. Allen takes as his "genius": "I always buy my own cravats, and am allowed to be an excellent judge; and my sister has often trusted me in the choice of a gown. I bought one for her the other day, and it was pronounced to be a prodigious bargain by every lady who saw it. I gave but five shillings a yard for it, and a true Indian muslin" (28). He recreates this part quite well; as in actual cross-dressing, how fully he can "wear" woman determines Henry's "authority"; in "wearing" her, his expertise on the price, longevity, and grade of muslin both burlesques and nullifies her, and in doing so he replaces her. Like the actual cross-dresser, he renders woman's "actual presence unnecessary" (Phelan 161).

James Thompson argues that because it is impossible for the characters to "be above such concerns" as wanting and needing clothing, Austen "undercuts the obvious moral, as so often happens to obvious morals in Austen's fiction" (31). In her characterization of Mrs. Allen, however, Austen extends her critique farther than "undercut[ting] the obvious moral" in that she explores the desperation that these constructions of gender breed. Gratified by Henry's attention to her clothes, she regrets that "Men commonly take so little notice of those things . . .: I can never get Mr. Allen to know one of my gowns from another. You must be a great comfort to your sister, sir" (28). In another section in the novel, Austen suggests (albeit in an ironic passage) that a woman should not expect men to notice fashion, but to dress "for her own satisfaction alone" (74).[2] Yet, Mrs. Allen's passion for dress also represents her husband's income and her own commodification. On the one hand, according to such strict gender binaries, if Mr. Allen did distinguish her dress, he could not be defined as "man"; yet, because her dress hypostatizes and glorifies his cash flow, she renders him distinguishable.

The title of Blaise Cendrars' poem, "On Her Dress She Wears a Body," suggests how clothing renders dubious a clear demarcation between self and nonself and offers insight into Mrs. Allen's confession that she "can never get Mr. Allen to *know* one of my gowns from another" (emphasis added), an avowal that expresses the desire of all the women in the novel to be seen and their conviction that clothes are the medium through which they will be recognized.[3] As Elizabeth Wilson argues, "clothing marks an unclear boundary ambiguously, and unclear boundaries disturb us. . . . It is at the margins between one thing and another that pollution may leak out. . . . Dress is the frontier between the self and the non-self" (2–3). In *Pride and Prejudice*, I analyzed how the slang definition for "muslin" gave extra capital to Lydia's elopement letter. Here, too, that meaning of "a woman, a girl," and "a bit of muslin on the sly" enriches our understanding of *Northanger Abbey*. That Mr. Allen "takes so little notice" of his wife may suggest that he is a rational man, but it may also imply that her physicality, of which the clothes are a metonym, goes unnoticed and unknown as well; her husband, though, admires other women's beauty: Catherine assures James that Mr. Allen has noticed Isabella, whom he considers "the prettiest girl in Bath" (51). As Bermingham argues, though not in terms of Mrs. Allen, "Women's empathetic relation to the commodities of fashion must be seen within the context of their own commodification. Within the discursive space of the marriage market women continually had to discriminate between the tasteful and vulgar consumption of goods, cultural events and novelties. For how a woman consumed . . . would determine how, in turn, she was consumed" ("The Picturesque" 98). Perhaps Mrs. Allen's consumption is vulgar since consuming consumes her. Regardless, she has been taught that her safety depends upon fashion, although the novel makes it clear that fashion provides no such guarantee and in fact furthers her isolation.

Because she believes that style will ensure her security, her relation to her apparel, as I suggested above, is inseparable from her attitudes toward her body. Grosz points out that "the effects of subjectivity . . . can be as adequately explained using the subject's corporeality as a framework as it would be using consciousness or the unconscious. All the effects of depth and interiority can be explained in terms of the inscriptions and transformations of the subject's corporeal surface" (vii). This ligature between surfaces and interiority recalls Lydia's instructions to "Sally to mend a great slit in my worked muslin gown, before they are packed up" (291–292). One does not fear for the loss of Mrs. Allen's virginity or the preservation of her virtue. The actual and foreboding assaults on her clothes/body, however, place her person in a state of perpetual, global peril in scenes as banal as a ballroom, underscoring the infirmity of women's economic and legal grounding. Mrs. Allen, unnoticed and perhaps untouched, has an "amorous" relationship with her dresses and accouterments, a liaison that Bernard Rudofsky suggests is a general principle among those who clothe themselves: the embrace and rejection of garments "are the perfect analogy to the phases of courtship: craving for the love object, and its rejection after wish fulfilment. . . . Each new dress becomes something like an accomplice with whom we enter a most intimate, if brief, relationship. The first stirrings of timid desire for the adoption of a fad; the intense devotion to it while it lasts; the sudden boredom and physical revulsion for an outlived vogue . . ." (13). She does indeed appear to be fantasizing her own ravishing through the fears she expresses about the ripping of her clothes. In a popular song of the day, "The Coy Lass dress'd up in her best Commode and Top-knot," which links mauling clothes to mauling the body, the female narrator tells her suitor not to "rumple my Top-knot, / I'll not be kiss'd to Day; / I'll not be hawl'd and pull'd about, / Thus on a Holy-day" (*Wit and Mirth* VI 55). Mrs. Allen's trepidations for her dress indicate an urgent fear for the safety of her corpus. Everyday journeys include fielding dangerous threats to her apparel. She worries that a pin "has torn a hole" in her sleeve (28); she is thrilled when the "frightful great rent in my best Mechlin" is "so charmingly mended" and that her "silk gloves wear very well" (238). "Open carriages are nasty things" because "[y]ou are splashed getting in and getting out; and the wind takes your hair and your bonnet in every direction" (104). And given the danger Catherine finds in an open carriage with the lying Thorpe, a man who brutalizes his horses, Mrs. Allen's fears of being "splashed" and blown about take on a new urgency. *The Lady's Monthly Museum* (Mar. 1800) confirms the delicate and dangerous liaison between fashion and ruin: "Changes in French Fashions," translated from the French of M. Pouce (1789), warns that "when, by a happy hazard, a woman has nearly reached perfection at her toilet, that is to say, in what most becomes her, she ought to be very careful not to adopt new modes.—In so frivolous an age, an infidelity may be the consequence of their placing the hat from left to right. When a sentiment is founded on a trifle, a trifle may easily destroy it" (308).[4] As Henri Focillon argues, "Fashion thus invents an artificial humanity which is not the passive decoration of a formal environment, but that very environment itself" (qtd. in *The Arcades Project* 80, B9a, 2). In M. Pouce's hylozoistic doctrine, life is inseparable from matter, and clothing intimately shows—not disguises—unconscious desires and ideological constructions, which could very well be the same thing.

Early in the novel, when Mrs. Allen and Catherine attend the assembly rooms for the first time, the heroine must "lin[k] her arm . . . firmly within her friend's to [avoid] be[ing] torn asunder by any common effort of a struggling assembly" (21). Safe from "being continually pressed against by people" (21–22),

> Mrs. Allen congratulated herself, as soon as they were seated, on having preserved her gown from injury. "It would have been very shocking to have it torn, . . . would not it?—It is such a delicate muslin.—For my part I have not seen any thing I like so well in the whole room, I assure you. . . . But I think we had better sit still, for one gets so tumbled in such a crowd! How is my head, my dear?—Somebody gave me a push that has hurt it I am afraid." (22)

What function does such revolutionary imagery, embedded here in everyday conversation, serve? Peter Brooks argues for the " 'bodiliness' of revolutionary language and representation" insofar as "[o]ne can . . . see in the revolutionary moment the origins of what we might call an aesthetics of embodiment, where the most important meanings have to be inscribed on and with the body" ("Melodrama" 17). In the 1790s, the revolution abroad, and in England the trials for treason, gag orders, famine, and the subsequent uprisings protesting starvation and repressive measures made such physical imagery ubiquitous. Mrs. Allen and Catherine, for example, traverse a crowd described in terms of a revolutionary "mob" (20). As E. P. Thompson pointed out in "The Moral Economy of the English Crowd in the Eighteenth Century," the gentry referred to crowds as mobs to justify their power and dismiss the protesters' entreaties. Charles Pigott's alternate, ironic *A Political Dictionary: Explaining the True Meaning of Words* (1796) defined a mob as "a species of regular militia, kept in pay by the ministry, for the protection of property against Levellers and Republicans" (93). Both meanings highlight, in their own way, Mrs. Allen's aristocratic-like disregard for anyone but herself. The ways that the ballroom "mob" rises up against her recall some of the reasons for English political instability and the French populace's justified celebration of sovereignty during the 1790s. Here the head—that venerable seat of reason—signifies the headdress, which is in danger from a ballroom mob scene of "imprisonment" with "fellow captives" who "press" up against them (22).

Diction such as the push to her "head"—is this a comic allusion to the guillotine?—and the "dangers of [their] late passage" (21) through the company sound similar to Henry's description of what he assumes is Eleanor's mental image of a London riot:

> And you, Miss Morland—my stupid sister has mistaken all your clearest expressions. You talked of expected horrors in London—and instead of instantly conceiving, as any rational creature would have done, that such words could relate only to a circulating library, she immediately pictured to herself a mob of three thousand men assembling in St George's Fields; the Bank attacked, the Tower threatened, the streets of London flowing with blood, a detachment of the 12th Light Dragoons, (the hopes of the nation,) called up from Northampton to quell the insurgents, and the gallant Capt. Frederick Tilney, in the moment of charging at the head of his troop, knocked off his horse by a brickbat from an upper window. (113)

In the assembly rooms, Mrs. Allen labors to keep from being "torn" or having her "head hurt"; in Henry's depiction, Captain Tilney's own head is in danger from revolutionary civil forces, a "mob" that rises up against another "mob"—that is, the "regular militia" who "were very serviceable at Birmingham, and Manchester" (Pigott 93). Henry sneers at his sister's panic, but as Gary Kelly asserts, just such an uprising "was . . . what many people did fear, . . . and troops of dragoons were raised, ostensibly to resist French invasion but actually to suppress a popular uprising of the kind imagined here" ("Religion" 157). Warren Roberts' research on Austen's relation to the French Revolution demonstrates that Eleanor's "stupid" terror alludes to multiple events, including the Gordon Riots, uprisings in London in 1792 (one Eliza de Feuillide witnessed), and a radical gathering in 1795 which Henry's account describes in precise ways (22–27). "Given the political ambience of British fiction during the 1790s," Claudia Johnson argues, "it is not surprising that of all Austen's novels, *Northanger Abbey*, arguably her earliest, should be the most densely packed with topical details of political character . . ." (*Jane Austen* 41). I suggest that Mrs. Allen's near panic about her clothes recalls problems as serious as those Eleanor visualizes.

Austen unites the simple-minded Mrs. Allen and the complexities of fashion to larger historical events. Fulfilling social expectations while also experiencing the illusion of agency by consuming fashion, Mrs. Allen performs the Revolution, expressing her independence through the styles she chooses. The novel's revolutionary imagery recalls the manifesto of *The Lady's Monthly Museum*, inaugurated in 1798, the year Austen began *Northanger Abbey*. In its "Cabinet of Fashion"

> our Fair Readers are here presented with Two Figures, representing the London Fashionable Dresses for the present month. In this particular

department, it shall be our study, as much as the limits of our plan will admit, rather to excel than be considered inferior to any familiar production. The present sample of the intention of the Proprietors, it is hoped, will not disgrace them; but, in their future Publications, the *Revolutions of Fashion* may furnish what may be deemed more picturesque. (60, emphasis added)

Here, *The Lady's Monthly Museum*, like the *Gallery of Fashion* (1794), declares the English superiority over French fashion, uniting stylish dress with national loyalty. A column from the October 1789 *Lady's Magazine* also links the political upheaval to new styles; under the title "New Fashions in Paris. For October," the writer announces that "there could not be a doubt but a revolution, such as happened in France, would furnish several ideas of expressing it in the ton of fashion—one of which has just taken place among the Ladies" (Vol. XX, 511). The article then describes how the cap is "made to express the re-union, or rather confusion, of the orders, Nobles, Clergy, and Tiers;—though certainly it might be better done in the whole garment than in a simple cap" (511). This paradoxical statement announces that if ladies are interested in politics, it must be in regard to how those convulsions affect trends; nevertheless it also analyzes what those trends symbolize and even offers an amendment on how the idea could better be expressed "in the whole garment than in a simple cap" (511). As Bermingham points out, "fashion provided a comforting model of history, one that demanded, in an almost subliminal way, that 'revolution' be understood as both rupture—the myth of progress—and as continuity—the myth of historical repetition" ("The Picturesque" 100). The periodicals affirm that idea; when Mrs. Allen, however, enacts this relationship with revolutionary events in the ballroom, fashion does not provide a "comforting model of history."

Mrs. Allen's attire, instead, becomes the external signifier of the body's danger in a world of commodification and revolution, of the precarious links between the private and the public, and an anchor through which female characters try to control chaos and mediate romance. As Henry intimates in the discussion of Catherine's alleged journal, how will a woman recollect her life—lived through the "various dresses to be remembered,"—if she fails to record what she wore (27)? Clothes mnemonically revive events. Mrs. Allen's gloves conjure her first visit to the Lower Rooms; and Isabella's yellow gown and her friend's "puce-coloured sarsenet" (118) resuscitate for her the day she met James. The delicacy of Mrs. Allen's muslins refers both to the material's transparency, popular as a signifier of the "natural" during this era, and to women's fragile social status. Lynn Hunt points out that in 1793, 6,000 French women protested the demands made by a few female "Jacobines" that all women should wear a revolutionary uniform of "pantaloons and red liberty caps"; responding to the crowd's remonstrations that no one had the right to compromise a female's gender by forcing her to dress like a man, the Convention simultaneously declared "freedom of dress and the suppression of women's political organizations" (227). By linking Eleanor's panic about a possible riot to Mrs. Allen's alarms about her dress/body, the novel validates rather than dismisses her observations and suggests that a woman's only way to protest, assert individuality, and express her "inherent" gender essence—that is, through fashion—also constituted the way society rendered her most vulnerable.

CROSS-DRESSING

Critics writing on Austen once proclaimed Henry Tilney as a wise teacher and Austen's mouthpiece; recently, a compelling interpretation among feminist critics finds him instead to be a version of his father, a pedagogical bully, too often sarcastic, but not always right.[5] Joseph Litvak describes him as "the practitioner of a more systematically euphemized, more suavely generalized, and thus more conveniently misrecognizable male sadism than that directed against Catherine by his rather too anxiously and ineptly malevolent parent" (*Strange* 36). Austen agitates ideology's magnetic pull by revealing how Henry both critiques and reinforces female constructions as he participates in the creation of women as copies of male fantasy: Henry declares to Catherine,

> "Shall I tell you what you ought to say?"
> "If you please."
> "I danced with a very agreeable young man, introduced by Mr. King; had a great deal of conversation with him—seems a most extraordinary genius—hope I may know more of him. That, madam, is what I wish you to say."
> "But, perhaps, I keep no journal."
> "Perhaps you are not sitting in this room, and I am not sitting by you. These are points in which a doubt is equally possible." (26–27)

Here he enjoys seeing Catherine as a blueprint of what one expects from a woman (of course she keeps a journal), copying that blueprint in his imitations of her, and engaging in that construction of femininity: "shall I tell you what you ought to say?" In this conversation, Henry articulates the notion that gender expectations are so certain that if she does not enact these fashions, she quizzes the nature of material reality and the reality of *both* of their identities: "perhaps we are not sitting in this room, and I am not sitting by you." Peggy Phelan's theories of cross-dressing illuminate Henry's attitudes when she argues that in portrayals of the female, the " 'real' (of) woman cannot be represented precisely because her function is to represent man" ("Crisscrossing" 162). The "real" Catherine eludes him because she does not keep a journal and because the mirror in which he expects to see her reflection projects instead his own being and, in particular, his own male anxieties. Henry's cramped definition of Catherine represents his own grasping for self-identity: if women's style of letter writing opposes men's by its "general deficiency of subject, a total inattention to stops, and a very frequent ignorance of grammar" (27), Henry reinforces men's style as the antithesis and ratifies the patriarchal binary; in parodying constructions of femininity, Tilney validates male authority—men know better how to write, read and converse; they are even better shoppers.

I agree that Henry remains culpable for his intimidating ways; however, he also illustrates how gender roles are performances when he takes on, through a kind of verbal cross-dressing, the female affect and partakes in "feminine" topics of conversation. By calling himself an "extraordinary genius," Henry both mocks his own egotism while calling attention to his superiority; on the other hand, in describing himself as such, he provides a counter way of reading his character as one that is feminized and marginalized since "male genius came to be perceived" as having such gendered associations; in discussing the links between sexuality and genius, Andrew Elfenbein argues that "While a man with feminine characteristics might desire a woman, . . . there was always the lurking suspicion that the sublime excessiveness of genius might lead to less conventional sexual possibilities. . . . [T]reatises suggested that the greatest geniuses were so excessive and unbounded that they possessed feminine qualities . . ." (32).[6] Henry includes a word that subverts his portrayal of a conventional role since "genius" was linked to "*a creation of something not before existing*" (Jackson 196); "the introduction of a new element into the intellectual universe" (Wordsworth 48).[7] Henry's female "excesses" provide a gloss on ideological assumptions and thereby introduce a dialectical tension between "inherent" and "contrived" definitions of gender.

He performs and parodies the feminine role when he discusses with Mrs. Allen the cost of muslin by the yard, his frequent choice of a gown for his sister, the fabric of Catherine's dress, which he "gravely" predicts will not "wash well," and the recycling of extra muslin to worthy purposes such as "handkerchief[s], . . . cap[s], or . . . cloaks" (28). In his first conversation with Catherine, Henry plays the role of "woman":

> forming his features into a set smile, and affectedly softening his voice, he added, with a simpering air, "Have you been long in Bath, madam?"
> "About a week, sir," replied Catherine, trying not to laugh.
> "Really!" [he answered] with affected astonishment. (26)

His artificial smile, his faux female voice, his smirking air, and his mannered reactions imitate and exaggerate women's culturally determined, but supposedly genuine behavior. They also show him "playing" the role of a fop. As Christopher Breward shows, "after 1720 the fop's effeminacy had come to be identified in the popular imagination with the effeminacy of the exclusive adult sodomite, the molly or queen. . . . Extreme bodily gestures, affected mannerisms in speech and contrived magnificence in costume had come to indicate sexual preference" (139). My point here is that Henry's verbal cross-dressing makes him a less stable version of the patriarchal police than most critics contend.

In impersonating woman and fop, he exposes these roles as roles and engages as well in self-parody, becoming in Marjorie Garber's words, "the figure that disrupts" (70), the figure that unsettles expectations of gender conventions.[8] Catherine, "laughing," exclaims, " 'How can you . . . be so—' she had almost said, strange" (28). He indulges in caprice as he invents what Catherine will write in her journal:

> "I see what you think of me," said he gravely—"I shall make but a poor figure in your journal to-morrow." . . .
> "Yes, I know exactly what you will say: Friday, went to the Lower Rooms; wore my sprigged muslin robe with blue trimmings—plain black shoes—appeared to much advantage; but was strangely harassed by a queer, half-witted man, who would make me dance with him, and distressed me by his nonsense."
> "Indeed I shall say no such thing." (26)

Henry posits himself as appearing in her prose as a comic "figure," a "queer, half-witted man," and, in doing so, underscores his role playing, which he emphasizes in his use of the word "queer," which could mean "counterfeit" in eighteenth-century slang (Partridge 677). This teasing and self-parody suggest that he avoids mistaking performance for essence; in doing so, he provides a vehicle for Austen's observations on the artificiality of gender roles. In consciously playing the soubrette, he exposes female constructions and other frames of interpretation as mummery themselves and satirizes them as such. Though he satirizes gender constructions, Austen satirizes the power he enjoys as a man; his brandishing of the patriarchal club represents her criticism of how he exploits his knowledge.[9] Alisa Solomon points out that "gender-bending" can "explor[e] the relationship between narrative and social conformity, between the yoked constraints of naturalism and naturalized notions of gender . . ." (144).[10] Henry's verbal cross-dressing spotlights the consequences of making fabricated behavior natural: when he parodies the female persona, he reveals its constricted scope and excessive desires. His demonstrable pleasure in "women's" interests (clothes and novels) further complicates his appropriation of feminine concerns—he really does like muslin.[11]

In discussing the "writing" of the homosexual into existence, Lee Edelman argues for a distinction between two kinds of homographesis: a first one that puts into writing "the essentializing metaphors of identity" and another that deconstructs such sameness by neither reducing sexuality to a fixed identity nor silencing it. This second, deconstructive, hermeneutic refuses to make "male heterosexual identity as the exemplary figure for the autonomy and coherence of the subject . . . that homographesis, in its first sense, is intended to secure" (12). In portraying multiple sexual identities—woman, male patriarch, and fop—Henry's mimicry "puts into writing" the "essentializing metaphors of identity," but because he is not the "exemplary figure" that makes "male heterosexual identity . . . autonom[ous] and coheren[t]" (12), his simulations question the ability to determine identity based on social definitions of gender and sexuality. Thus in the same way that Austen interrogates authenticity, she cross-examines the coherent heterosexual self as the marker of normalcy by refusing to write into existence a "benchmark man" (Brook 97).[12] If Henry's masculinity is "strip[ped] . . . of its privileged status as the self-authenticating paradigm of the natural or the self-evident itself" (Edelman 12), so are the paradigms he endorses and makes legible.

J. C. Flügel coined the phrase "The Great Masculine Renunciation" to describe the historical point, "at the end of the eighteenth century," when "men gave up their right to all the brighter, gayer, more elaborate, and more varied forms of ornamentation, leaving these entirely to the use of women, and thereby making their own tailoring the most austere and ascetic of the arts" (110–111). This divesting of adornment led to defining men as the "unmarked gender" and the feminine as the "marked sexuality" (Vinken 37). Vested in female interests, "simper[ing] and smirk[ing]," speaking "nonsense," posing as an "extraordinary genius" and as a "queer, half-witted man," Henry "marks" himself as other than masculine by taking on the female role; here he provides the stereotypical contrast to Thorpe. In this sense, Henry plays the role of the "Pretty Fellow" that appears in *The Tatler* and *The Spectator*, in which "blind submission to fashion is emphatically the nonsensical, though passionate foible of women and of silly and, in an often complex sense, feminized men" (Mackie 193).

The failure to "renunciate" renders Henry comic. Laurence Senelick argues that

> by 1700, convincing female impersonation was no longer allowed to be sexually viable. . . . [T]he *adult* male in woman's clothing remained what he had customarily been—a figure of fun, invariably burlesque or grotesque, the travesty Medea or Polly Peachum[.] . . . This tradition was maintained because, as a nineteenth-century observer noted, "a man in female garb is apt to appear awkward and ungainly" and, in a word, "unsexed." (81)

Comically transgressing both masculine behavior and the rules of class, codes that reinforce each other, ironically leads to intimacy in Henry's and Catherine's conversation. In chapter 2, I argued that *Pride and Prejudice* offers a sense of this particular consequence of drag when Lydia and other military wives, as well as her own aunt, "dres[s] up Chamberlayne in woman's clothes, on purpose to pass for a lady,—only think what fun! . . . [A]nd you cannot imagine how well he looked! When Denny, and Wickham, and Pratt, and two or three more of the men came in, they did not know him in the least" (221). Colonel Forster's presence and awareness of this "fun" re-gendering of a soldier to amuse other officers and their ladies unmasks how drag disintegrates boundaries of profession, gender, rank, and age as this sixteen-year-old girl plays dress-up with the militia. In *Northanger Abbey*, Henry's "strangeness" disguises his own social and financial superiority. His posings and ability to engage in female conversation break down barriers, encouraging a teasing familiarity as when Henry remarks that Catherine's muslin "will not wear well," a comment complicated by the slang meaning of the word "muslin" (a girl) and the theoretical question of how to establish where the dress begins and the body ends. In fact, as he stays "on the subject of muslins till the dancing recommenced," Catherine worries about his parody of female excess, and feels "that he indulged himself a little too much with the foibles of others—" (29). Her silence leads him to wonder what she is "thinking of so earnestly" (29). Catherine's reply that she "was not thinking of any thing" steers them into a deeper acquaintance, since he claims that now "I am authorized to tease you on this subject whenever we meet, and nothing in the world advances intimacy so much" (29). Advertising the way verbal and actual cross-dressing create familiarity, Henry's teasing—like humor itself—emphasizes the instability of social formations.

DRESSAGE

In all her novels, Austen humorously mines the sexual nuances of all things equestrian, as men, women, and horses form multiple patterns of erotic synergy. John Thorpe's libidinal fascination with four-legged beasts of the hunt, however, suggests comic, but also deranged behavior. Of all the characters in the novel, he is the most criminal—a slanderer, kidnapper, animal abuser, liar, and con-artist. His bombastic masculinity, spliced with his fascination with exchanges between men, his reluctant interest in women, and his obvious misogyny, suggest that Austen casts her net wider to examine unconventional portrayals of sexual roles. Thus, with Mrs. Allen and Isabella, she addresses the traditional ways society represents women and with John Thorpe the hackneyed ways it portrays the sodomite. The novel satirizes Thorpe's misogyny by dramatizing it in terms of tired stereotypes: for example, Rictor Norton points out that "one of the most common terms for a gay man in the eighteenth century was 'woman hater,' " which suggests a public perception of homosexuals as men without an orientation toward women, not as sodomites (126).[13] Thorpe aches to embody ultimate masculinity: he claims to win the most races, shoot the most birds, and, like Willoughby, ride the most boldly (a charged phrase, as I analyzed earlier); he brags that he has led "others into difficulties" that "had broken the necks of many" (66). His unconvincing acting and his insincere interest in Catherine make Thorpe's identity appear posed and calculated; perhaps this is his attempt to defend himself against any accusation that he could slide from effeminacy to what Fielding in *Amelia* (describing a sodomite just imprisoned) called "certain odious unmanlike Practices" (33). I am *not* saying that the eighteenth-century male homosexual automatically disguised himself in a masculine pose or hated women or was interested in animals, only that Austen exposes these eighteenth-century clichés as conventions rather than as transgressions against "natural" behavior. Thorpe, though doing his best to appear anything but a "molly," encapsulates a series of signifiers used in the eighteenth century to label sodomites, since as Andrew Elfenbein points out, "[w]hile 'effeminate' and 'sodomite' never become perfect synonyms, [St.] Paul's text guaranteed that suspicions of sodomy might cluster around any given use of 'effeminacy' " (21).[14] From this point of view, Thorpe's appreciation for *The Monk*, for example, implies a queer interest rather than a heterosexual pornographic one since seventeenth- and eighteenth-century antisodomitical literature yoked male preference for men to Catholicism, assuming that its vows of celibacy encouraged unnatural behavior. *The Monk* includes Spanish foreignness (exoticism being another British association with sodomy), a celibate, perverted Catholic priest, and vicious attacks on women: matricide, incest, and rape. In a discussion of "The Tryal and Condemnation of Mervin, Lord Audley of Castlehaven at Westminster. April the 5th 1631," Todd C. Parker notes that the terms sodomy and Catholicism are "inseparable" in the attorney general's arguments against Castlehaven (15). *Satan's Harvest Home* (1729), a vicious diatribe linking Catholicism, celibacy, foreignness, and homosexuality, argues that Italy is the "*Mother and Nurse of Sodomy*" and in France the "*Contagion* is diversif'd, and the Ladies (in the *Nunneries*) are criminally *amorous* of each other, in a *Method* too gross for Expression" (51).

The homoerotic charge that occurs when men trade animals excites Thorpe: having elicited Catherine's promise to dance with him, he keeps her waiting without contrition while he talks "of the horses and dogs of a friend whom he had just left, and of a proposed exchange of terriers between them" (55). This adverts to the eighteenth-century association between sodomy and bestiality. Ed Cohen has written that before the nineteenth century, "sexual practices between men were almost universally understood as 'sodomy'—a category deriving from canon law that referred exclusively to a particular kind of sexual act whether 'committed with mankind or beast.' Since sodomy was never conceived of as the antithesis of any normative sexual standard, it was perceived to be a ubiquitous, nonprocreative possibility resulting from the inherent sinfulness of human nature" (171). Such a vinculum between "mankind and beast" emerges when Thorpe, seeing Tilney for the first time, asks if he "want[s] a horse":

> "Tilney," he repeated, "Hum—I do not know him. A good figure of a man; well put together.—Does he want a horse? Here is a friend of mine, Sam Fletcher, has got one to sell that would suit any body. A famous clever animal for the road—only forty guineas. I had fifty minds to buy it myself, for it is one of my maxims always to buy a good horse when I meet with one; but it would not answer my purpose, it would

not do for the field. I would give any money for a real good hunter. I have three now, the best that ever were back'd. I would not take eight hundred guineas for them. Fletcher and I mean to get a house in Leicestershire, against the next season. It is so d——— uncomfortable, living at an inn." (76)

Thorpe's immediate response to seeing Henry is to canvas his body, as if he were an animal, and to triangulate an "exchange" between Henry and Sam Fletcher, with whom Thorpe plans to live. In his references to prices and numbers in general—"fifty" minds and then "forty" and later "eight hundred guineas"—he is so obsessed with hyperbole, that he has to top his own already overinflated statements. In these numbers, he reveals his preoccupation with the financial worth of animals and women. Owning hunters for pleasure but requiring laborers (a field horse or wealthy wife) for economic support recalls Charles Churchill's paranoia in his poem, *The Times*, that sodomy has led to women being kept "for nothing but the breed; / For pleasure we must have a GANYMEDE, / A fine, fresh HYLAS, a delicious boy, / To serve our purposes of beastly joy" (ll. 331–334). Here, Thorpe's attraction to male and animal bodies might suggest, in itself, that his inflated masculinity disguises other desires, since the eighteenth century conflated effeminacy and male homosexuality, which becomes obvious in this comment from *Satan's Harvest Home* that describes homosexual men as "appear[ing] as soft as possible to each other, any Thing of *Manliness* being diametrically opposite to such unnatural Practices" (50).

Thorpe conflates his own sexuality with the horse's and sexualizes brutality when he denies James Morland's statement that his horse (after allegedly running twenty three miles in three and a half hours) "*does* look very hot to be sure." Thorpe cries,

> Hot! he had not turned a hair till we came to Walcot Church: but look at his forehead; look at his loins; only see how he moves; that horse *cannot* go less than ten miles an hour: tie his legs and he will get on. What do you think of my gig, Miss Morland? a neat one, is not it? Well hung; town built. . . . It was built for a Christchurch man, a friend of mine, a very good sort of fellow; he ran it a few weeks, till, I believe, it was convenient to have done with it. (46)

Here, Austen's bawdy comedy directs our gaze from the phallic object to its metonym for the male organs as our eyes slide from the horse's hot "loins" to Thorpe's "well-hung" "town-built" gig. His preening absorption in his horses, their vigor, and the "merits of his own equipage" (64) alludes to his narcissistic preoccupation with his own body. Horses and carriages, like companions or wives, emerge in this series of associations as useful until they are "convenient to have done" with. "Gig" also carried the slang connotation of "a wanton or a flighty girl" (Partridge 327), which comically undercuts his self-proclaimed prowess. Thus, the gig reinforces the dangerous erotics of carriage riding, confirms how he blurs the distinction between possessing women and objects, and exposes his underhanded intentions, all of which corroborate Catherine's uneasiness about the impropriety of riding alone with him.

Thorpe's sadistic fantasies recall the actual behavior of the Austen family's neighbor and a former pupil of Mr. Austen's, Lord Portsmouth, who tortured both animals and servants. Claire Tomalin narrates how he would "visit slaughterhouses in order to strike the animals awaiting death with a stick or an axe, saying as he did so, 'Serve you right.' . . . He also enjoyed having his servants and animals beaten, and once, when his coachman was lying in his room recovering from a broken leg which had been set by a surgeon, the Earl . . . re-broke his leg" (88). Tomalin links the Earl to General Tilney, arguing that "The Portsmouth saga makes Catherine's dark suspicions of an ill-used and murdered wife in *Northanger Abbey* seem mild stuff" (90). Her general point about Catherine's suspicions is apt, but I think that the Earl's behavior more closely resembles Thorpe's bizarre fantasies, as when he later assures Catherine that she should "not be frightened . . . if my horse should dance about a little at first . . .; but he will soon know his master" (62). That Thorpe would brutalize his horses is alarming, but that he misconstrues the "playful" nature of his horse and its tendency to "plunge or . . . caper" confirms his rupture from objective reality, since in this circumstance he is in no actual danger of having to control the animals. Thus, while Thorpe pictures his own gothic drama of wild horses careening out of control, the carriage in fact went "in the quietest manner imaginable" (62).

Austen plays with the border between the absurdly comic and its disturbing undertow. Thorpe's desire to have the horse "know his master" is unsettling since he blurs the line between the possession and treatment of horses and women. From the seventeenth through the twentieth centuries, one colloquial definition of "horse" (as a verb) meant "to possess a woman" (Partridge 406). Ample evidence of his misogyny materializes when he observes that both of his sisters "looked very ugly" (49), when he objectifies women by offering "a short decisive sentence of praise or condemnation on the face of every woman they met" (48), when he uses force to manipulate Catherine, and when he lies about her prospects to General Tilney, first to pump himself up and later to exact revenge. In the episode in which Thorpe ignores Catherine's pleas to let her leave his carriage and join the Tilneys, he brandishes his feral nature and his potential for violence. In this scene, which recalls Hargrave's kidnapping of Harriet in *Sir Charles Grandison*, Catherine cries,

> "*Stop, stop*, Mr. Thorpe, she impatiently cried, it is Miss Tilney; . . . *Stop, stop*, I will get out this moment and go to them." But to what purpose did she speak?—Thorpe only lashed his horse into a brisker trot; . . . and in another moment she was herself whisked into the Market-place. Still, however, and during the length of another street, she intreated him to *stop*. "Pray, pray *stop*, Mr. Thorpe.—I cannot go on.—I will not go on.—I must go back to Miss Tilney." But Mr Thorpe only laughed, smacked his whip, encouraged his horse, made odd noises, and drove on; and Catherine, angry and vexed as she was, having no power of getting away, was obliged to give up the point and submit. (87, emphasis added)

Here, where the word "stop" appears six times, Austen makes it impossible to read this kidnapping as anything other than a symbolic double of rape. She also links marriage for alliance to marital rape, insofar as Catherine is "whisked into the Market-place" and "obliged to give up the point and submit." Attempted rape was a frequent comic plot device in the eighteenth century; Susan Staves points out that in *Joseph Andrews* alone, Fanny is threatened by rape five times ("Comedy" 91). Thorpe violates Catherine's will, though not her body; however, if his laughing pleasure at her distress could be considered comic, it would be a grotesque, macabre, and bellicose humor, indeed. Thus, I am not able, like Mary Waldron, to see this episode only as a parody of a scene of abduction, like Delamere's of Emmeline (27) because although such a reading highlights its perverse comedy, it ignores Thorpe's discomforting sadism. Actual rape is the subject for tragedies, not comedies, and though Austen dramatizes sexual assault only emblematically, she highlights women's physical vulnerability by heralding the ease with which Thorpe accomplishes the violence he does commit.

Austen—unlike Fielding, who thought that "Female beauty . . . evoked male desire, as by some fundamental law of nature" (Staves, "Comedy" 90)—undermines any notion that Catherine's "charms" incite Thorpe's aggression; instead, her distress and his power excite him. Most of the sounds in this passage—Catherine's crying and Thorpe's lashing and smacking—are recognizable and distressing. His nonlinguistic discharges—his unspecified "odd noises" (are they grunts, grinding teeth, whistles?) are repulsive, though readers often nervously laugh at them. His nebulous emissions suggest the "unnarratab[ility]" of rape (Staves, "Comedy" 105) and in turn open the way for a reading of the episode as a scene of primal violence where noises become defamiliarized.

I have titled this section "Dressage," partly as a way to pun on dressing and partly to make a serious point. In England, dressage existed as an art form since the late seventeenth century. A. Crossley explains in *Dressage: The Seat, Aids and Exercises*, that International Rules for Dressage state that "the horse gives the impression of doing of his own accord what is required of him" (Crossley ii). A harmonious relationship between the rider and the horse precludes a rough or excessively forceful treatment of the animal. Thorpe's cruelty excludes him from any association with this art of riding; Henry, however, fulfills its injunctions: he drives both horses and women effortlessly. Catherine draws a comparison between men as "drivers," and the novel makes clear in her juxtaposition that more than just "driving" is at stake here, as her observations also implicate the two suitors as potential lovers: "Henry drove so well,—so quietly—without making any disturbance, without parading to her, or swearing at [the horses]; so different from the only gentleman-coachman whom it was in her power to compare him with! . . . To be driven by him, next to being dancing with him, was certainly the greatest happiness in the world" (157). Whether Thorpe prefers men or only treats women rudely, the novel italicizes the potential physical and erotic misery that would follow a marriage to him, especially when a woman has no choice but to "give up the point and submit" (87). Here, as when Elizabeth dances miserably with Collins, Austen expresses a patent interest in celebrating and protecting her heroine's body in marriage, reassuring us that Henry not only makes no "odd noises," but that he arouses Catherine, as she contemplates how "his hat sat so well, and the innumerable capes of his great coat looked so becomingly important!" (157).

Nevertheless, as I discuss in the next section, "Undressing," Henry's brilliant practice of "dressage" (again, speaking metaphorically) applies fittingly to the power he exerts over Catherine, when she follows his instructions for gothic detection without at first knowing or later understanding that she acts on an initiative he kindled. In other words, Henry has the ability to derive from Catherine "the impression of doing of [her] own accord what is required of [her]"

(Crossley ii). As Stephen Budiansky argues, dressage is not "natural": "these collected gaits are not ones that a freely moving horse . . . will ever select on its own—unless it is highly emotionally aroused" (qtd. in Landry 52). Henry's subtle—and sometimes blatant—movements create responses from Catherine that feel organic.

Edelman argues in *Homographesis* that "interpretative access to the code that renders homosexuality legible may thus carry with it the stigma of too intimate a relation to the code and the machinery of its production" (7). It is possible that Austen's attempt to deconstruct sexual identities cannot "disentangle itself from the regulatory homographesis against which it would gain some leverage" (22), but in the irony she brings to Thorpe's characterization, I think she calls attention to the impact of such regulatory constructions that tend either to "silenc[e]" sexuality or "inscrib[e] [it] as essential" (23). In Austen's characterization of Thorpe, I believe that she successfully walks a tightrope between employing the codes that make his sexuality visible and explicating the ideology that has produced such codes. That is, Austen associates Thorpe with "a universa[l] . . . set of actions or behaviors" that become "a defining characteristic of the actor, the subject" (8) in order to critique those descriptors as constructions in and of themselves. As a writer invested in playing various ideas against each other, Austen deconstructs both the way that "homosexuality historically is construed . . . [as] the reduction of 'différance' to a question of determinate difference" and the way that "dominant culture . . . names homosexuality as a secondary, sterile, and parasitic form of social representation" (Edelman 9). The novel introduces ideas about identity that differ from the constructions of gender one finds in texts such as Churchill's *The Times* or in conduct books for women.

Austen uses comedy to critique the misogynist and the terms that typify the sodomite; in doing so, she reveals the noxious effect of patriarchal expectations of gender as they are created, embodied, and performed in the everyday rituals of courtship. Austen "writes" Thorpe's homosexuality into existence by representing him in terms of sodomitical stereotypes. In doing so, she dramatizes the way that social roles and rules control behavior: that is, if he does prefer the company of men, his attempt to form a coherent self through a heterosexual disguise pushes him toward a disjunction from physical factuality (he cannot even tell whether the horse is hot). If he does prefer the company of women, his extravagant identification with ideologies of masculinity suggests what can happen when adherence to convention without variety or awareness becomes a form of psychosis.

His is a "dressage" gone mad. In the ballroom, Catherine is saved from Thorpe only when he is "born off by the resistless pressure of a long string of passing ladies" (76). The phrase suggests that regardless of his own sexual orientation, he cannot resist the pressures of romance conventions, since financial exigency forces him to propose marriage to Catherine, a woman he neither desires nor respects; but it also implies that the women—reduced from individuality to a "long string"—are themselves "resistless" to reject a man they would not find, in Catherine's words, "altogether completely agreeable" (66).

UNDRESSING

Fashion literalizes courtship conventions, denaturing the body in the most "natural" of acts. In a letter that Catherine interprets as "shallow artifice," a letter that (to quote Benjamin again) dramatizes how "every fashion is at war with the organic," Isabella juxtaposes her "fervent" love for James with a hint of the spring fashions:

> Your kind offices will set all right:—he is the only man I ever did or could love, and I trust you will convince him of it. The spring fashions are partly down; and the hats the most frightful you can imagine. . . . Anne Mitchell had tried to put on a turban like mine, as I wore it the week before at the Concert, but made wretched work of it—it happened to become my odd face I believe, at least Tilney told me so at the time, and said every eye was upon me; but he is the last man whose word I would take. I wear nothing but purple now: I know I look hideous in it, but no matter—it is your dear brother's favourite colour. (216–218)

J. C. Flügel argues that, through clothes, we "tr[y] to satisfy two contradictory tendencies" and that we "regard clothes from two incompatible points of view—on the one hand, as a means of displaying our attractions, on the other hand, as a means of hiding our shame" (20). Isabella's focus on fashion in the letter renders her unlikable because she seems not to feel shame. Her displacement of attention from her body's actions to her body's attire, however, reveals both her desire to "cover up" her behavior and to fulfill her need for exhibitionism; as Flügel suggests, "clothes resemble a perpetual blush on the surface of humanity" (21).[15]

This letter, then, is interesting in how it replays her mental and physical disorientation. She derives power from her fashionable beauty's ability to inspire worship, and this passage exposes how the loss of that power expunges her identity: as clothes and men are inseparable as commodities to her, it makes sense that she interchanges them promiscuously. Unhinged by Tilney's capricious rejection, Isabella draws on the topic of clothing to invoke magical powers and reestablish her mastery. Ideological expectations mediate her relations to both James and Tilney; and fashion—frightful hats, turbans, and James's favorite color—elucidates the mechanistic quality of romantic rituals and how Isabella functions as a feminine type who mirrors men in order to control them.

Her ambition creates the necessary conditions for affirming male identity—one day a turban, the next, purple gowns.[16] As if by magic talisman, purple will draw James back, suggesting that "the body is an optical effect accomplished by clothing" (Warwick and Cavallaro xxii). Though once an erotic amulet for Frederick and Isabella, the turban now represents the inorganic, artificial conventions of romance, a point Gillray highlights in his caricatures of headdresses in general and turbans in particular. Figure 3.1, for example, shows a woman creating her own turban out of yards and yards of material, a process that requires two assistants. According to *An Elegant Art: Fashion and Fantasy in the Eighteenth Century*, the turban was a "headdress resembling the oriental turban, elaborately trimmed" (237).

Figure 3.1   James Gillray, published by Hannah Humphrey, "A Lady putting on her cap" (June 30, 1795). Hand-colored etching. Courtesy: National Portrait Gallery, London.

Reflecting the cosmopolitan styles of the eighteenth century, the turban became fashionable in the 1760s and remained popular for many years running. For example, the *Lady's Monthly Museum* showed five turbans between 1798 and 1799, and the upscale *Gallery of Fashion* illustrated thirty-six turbans between 1794 and 1803, the period in which Austen was composing and revising *Northanger Abbey*, or *Susan*, as it was first titled.

Isabella's choice of headdress reflects how recent travel to and trade with Turkey had associated Turkish artifacts with exotic "pleasure, . . . amusement . . . [and] fancy" (Pointon, "Hanging the Head" 146). She envisions marrying splendidly and the turban encapsulates her fantasies of voluptuous leisure. The power she exerts over Captain Tilney and the other young women of Bath ("Anne Mitchell had tried to put on a turban like mine . . . but made wretched work of it") enables her to play the role of colonial victor over the military man and her social set. In turn, Captain Tilney finds Isabella's turban appealing because it evokes a sexualized and conquered nation: such "Turkish-style clothing" as Marcia Pointon argues, was "circulated in the west as an emblem of masculine power over female subjects and superiority of west over east" ("Hanging the Head" 151).

If the margin between the body and fashion is indistinguishable, the phrase in her letter, "the spring fashions are partly down; and the hats the most frightful you can imagine," functions as a metonymy of Isabella's "frightful" economic and moral fall. From this context, the slang definitions for "down," which include "alarm," "discovery," "depression," and the sexual connotation of "to prepare a woman for the act," all add an extra punch to the letter's connotations (Partridge 238). What does Isabella refer to when she reports that the hats are "frightful"? *The Gallery of Fashion* shows one turban cap in April 1798 and a Black Minerva bonnet with one green curled feather crossing the crown, and another placed on the right side near the front (fig. CLXXIV [174]). In May 1798, a month later than the letter, dress *à la Militaire* appears: a Dunstable casque bonnet with a military white feather across the crown. Perhaps the fashions in April 1799 are frightful since the *Lady's Monthly Museum* shows no turbans, but instead features headdresses worn close to the head and one with lilac bands and bows (fig. CCXIV [214]), which might make her feel out of vogue. In May 1799, the caps are again close to the head; one with a white satin "riband" under the chin, that also looks quite martial (fig. CCXVIII [218]). Could it be that the military tone uncomfortably recalls Captain Tilney? Does the accelerated changeability of hat couture remind her that she cannot keep up financially with the *bon ton*?

Or does fashion's flightiness resemble too closely Tilney's mercurial love making? In this letter, the turban appears as a "bitter satire of love" (Benjamin 79, B9, 1), its orientalism grafted on British fashion as artificially as Isabella has affixed herself to James and Tilney and they onto her. "The sex appeal of the inorganic, which is something generated by fashion" (Benjamin 79, B9, 2) filters James's attraction to Isabella and Isabella's to Tilney.

Fashion, as Kaja Silverman writes, "make[s] the human body culturally visible" (189); Warwick and Cavallaro, in turn, argue that there is no "obvious way of demarcating the body's boundaries. . . . Central to [examining the body in relation to dress] is the idea that the body is both a *boundary* and *not a boundary*" (xv), a point dramatized when Isabella indulges in some sexy talk with Frederick Tilney in front of her future sister-in-law. Enjoying his mastery over an engaged woman, Tilney teases Isabella:

> "I wish your heart were independent. That would be enough for me."
> "My heart, indeed! What can you have to do with hearts? You men have none of you any hearts."
> "If we have not hearts, we have eyes; and they give us torment enough."
> "Do they? I am sorry for it. I am sorry they find any thing so disagreeable in me. I will look another way. I hope this pleases you, (turning her back on him,) I hope your eyes are not tormented now."
> "Never more so; for the edge of a blooming cheek is still in view—at once too much and too little." (147)

Frederick's voyeuristic undressing of Isabella's cheek stages a performance of Henry's statement that nothing "advances intimacy so much" as teasing (29). Here, as with clothing, the body's "erotic lure" is the fascination of "the fragment, the slice, the cut, the seam" (Cavallaro xxii). His sense of the tantalizing presence of an absence summons up Rousseau's celebration of Sophy in *Emile*, whose dress, "simple as it seems, was only put in its proper order to be taken to pieces by the imagination" (qtd. in Wollstonecraft 88).[17] In retrospect, their conversation is poignant since after Isabella's gambles on Frederick Tilney fail, he and the society that endorse marrying well, "undress" her, exposing her as an interloping coquette rather than an authentic participant, a humiliation that would not have occurred had the Captain chosen to marry her—such a brilliant match would have exonerated her behavior.

As Captain Tilney embellishes Isabella's fantasies, so does Henry "dress" Catherine's imagination, only to divest her of the expectations he encourages. Žižek points out that "fantasy does not simply realize a desire in a hallucinatory way: rather . . . a fantasy constitutes our desire, provides its co-ordinates; that is, it literally 'teaches us how to desire' " (*Plague* 7). Henry teaches Catherine how to desire him through gothic fantasies. An emphatic example of this occurs during their coach ride from Bath to Northanger Abbey when Henry plays a game with Catherine (as Tilney did with Isabella), exciting her anticipation and ardor by fantasizing threats to her body. In a kind of verbal foreplay, he teases her with delicious warnings that she will be "lodged apart from the rest of the family . . . conducted . . . along many gloomy passages . . . in[to] [a] gloomy chamber . . . [with a] bed [of] . . . funereal appearance" and a "ponderous chest which no efforts can open"; her door will have no lock and will connect with subterranean passages into rooms where she will find daggers, blood and "the remains of some instrument of torture" (158–160). Following this scene, in her search (significantly while only partly dressed) through the old chest, she enacts the racy *frisson* of danger he has excited: "At length, however, having slipped one arm into her gown, . . . she sprang forward. . . . Her resolute effort threw back the lid" (164). Her expectation of signs of coercion—she imagines that the tarnished silver lock was "broken perhaps prematurely by some strange violence" (163)—complicates the erotic nature of her investigations, which her state of dishabille and "trembling hands" (164) punctuates. In *Seeing through Clothes*, Anne Hollander points out that "in the eighteenth century, . . . the idea of sartorial dishevelment for *women* achieved an even higher degree of sexual charge as an expression of submission" (210), a fact that underscores Catherine's surrender to Henry's fantasies. Later that night, when looking through the ebony cabinet, she finds it a "remarkable coincidence" when she discovers that the furniture Henry has described is, in fact, in her room: she cannot "sleep till she had examined it," she feels "breathless wonder," and in finding "a roll of paper, . . . her feelings at that moment were indescribable. Her heart fluttered, her knees trembled, and her cheeks grew pale" (168–169). Experiencing "what Henry had foretold" astonishes her: the "manuscript [is] so wonderfully found, [and] so wonderfully accomplish[es] the morning's prediction" (169–170).

Her searching yields disappointment, and although she can admit that her anticipation and actions were "in a great measure [Henry's] own doing," she feels the bulk of the shame (173). In the old chest she discovers something placid and modest, something neutered: "a white cotton counterpane, properly folded, reposing at one end of the chest in undisputed possession!" (164). The bedspread's virgin snowiness, so decently turned inward—"reposing" and either possessed by the chest, or possessing the chest—scolds her for her torrid expectations as she "gaze[s] on it with the first blush of surprise" (165). Instead of seeing the subjective presence of Henry and their intimacy embodied in the gothic, she finds objects that she believes rebuke the titillating fantasies he inspired and that she took seriously. Unlike Catherine, this counterpane is owned (an allusion to marriage and property) or in itself "owns" property (i.e., its dwelling). It "repos[es]" rather than searches (165). The passage introduces a gap between animate and inanimate, a gap that the object's anthropomorphic power reinforces— has it just "reposed" its self?

Henry's chastening rather than erotic presence gives her a dressing down: he duped her and she feels "shame" for her "absurd expectations," for having been "caught in so idle a search" (165), and then for having suspected the General (197–198); the "detestable" bills become "hateful evidences of her folly"; "unpleasant reflections" taint the room, and she fears that "her weakness" will be "suspected" (173–174). Her humiliated reactions seem excessive and thus overdetermined, arising more from the deprivation of the erotic "tortures" Henry promised than from having expected and lost the chance for a gothic experience. Joseph Adamson and Hilary Clark, writing on shame theory, argue that shame "*instantaneously* reduce[s] interest in the object[,] . . . temporarily discourage[s] any further attempts at communion[,] . . . [and] is particularly instrumental as a protective mechanism regulating human beings in their eagerness for communal life, in their expressiveness, perception, and interaction with others and with their environment" (14). Indeed, Catherine's embarrassment reveals, albeit unconsciously, that she wanted a connection with Henry based on the erotic titillation that he had promised, and her shame exists in direct proportion to the "eagerness for communal life" she had felt he was encouraging on their drive. Helen Lewis observes that "Fascination with the other and sensitivity to the other's treatment of the self render the self more vulnerable in shame" (108), a point that heralds how Catherine's inflation and distortion of erotic and emotional expectations embarrass her more than any cognizance that the gothic is a poor frame of reference for everyday life. She dreads she will be "caught"— that "Henry Tilney should ever know her folly!" (165, 173). And in fact, she has been "caught" violating the strict boundaries that establish what Barbara Brook calls the "transgressiveness and agency available to women performing explicitly and knowingly to a male gaze" (112).

Other reasons propel her shame, best examined by looking at her discovery of a "manuscript" that turns out to be an inventory of bills, one that offers images of a basal physicality linked to domestic economies.

> Her greedy eye glanced rapidly over a page. She started at its import. Could it be possible, or did not her senses play her false?—An inventory of linen, in coarse and modern characters, seemed all that was before her! If the evidence of sight might be trusted, she held a washing-bill in her hand. She seized another sheet, and saw the same articles with little variation; a third, a fourth, and a fifth, presented nothing new. Shirts, stockings, cravats and waistcoats *faced her* in each. Two others, penned by the same hand, marked an expenditure scarcely more interesting, in letters, hair-powders, shoe-string and breeches ball. And the larger sheet, which had enclosed the rest, seemed by its first cramp line, "To poultice chestnut mare,"—a farrier's bill! Such was the collection of papers, (left perhaps, as she could then suppose, by the negligence of a servant in the place whence she had taken them,) which had filled her with expectation and alarm, and robbed her of half her night's rest! She felt humbled to the dust. (172–173, emphasis added)

This mortifying inventory gazes at her. It may be permissible to spy on the sensational, but the passage exposes how it is forbidden to look voyeuristically at the mundane, especially when it includes references to the private parts of the male body, which the language here personifies: like an accusing eye, "Shirts, stockings, cravats, and waistcoats, *faced her* in each. Two others, penned by the same hand, marked an expenditure scarcely more interesting, in letters, hair-powders, shoe-string, and breeches ball" (172, emphasis added). Catherine, the tourist who searches for the aura of authenticity, finds instead the worrisome presence of the retrieved everyday object, one that brims over with discomforting links among clothing, consumption, and courtship. Within the context of the novel, the subjects of these financial accounts—clothes, letters, and horses—carry a thematic and psychosexual significance in that they replicate in miniature the topics of conversation and plot throughout the narrative. These are matters that in themselves carry a real, though subtle threat: Mrs. Allen too distracted with her clothes to be a fit guardian; John Thorpe mistreating his horses and whisking Catherine away against her will; letters arriving with news of Isabella's betrayal. Further, that she finds bills and not some other writing reinforces how Catherine, like the servant, has been instructed to keep an inventory of what she spends. Written in coarse and modern characters, the inventory of linen turns out to be the Viscount's invoices—that is, the man responsible for her ultimate marriage into the family: once he can pay his bills, so to speak, by inheriting a fortune and a title (which in turn sanctions his marriage to Eleanor), Catherine herself may marry without having to pay as many bills as her father-in-law would have preferred. The life of things are in "undisputed possession" of other things (164).[18]

The linen inventory both resists the essence of Catherine's "original"—a manuscript detailing the horrors of Matilda's sufferings, horrors based on fiction—but also (as a statement of accounts) replicates them in foreshadowing how money will threaten Catherine's happiness. Here in these financial reckonings is the symbolic currency of marital prostitution. The inventory redresses the gothic through divergent economies of signification and measure. Catherine's searches for an "authentic" tradition do reveal authenticity: that is, the authoritative tradition of bartering women for money, a custom motivating General Tilney and the villain from Catherine's beloved *Mysteries of Udolpho*, Captain Montoni. Thus, when the heroine chides herself for failing to find "what had filled her with expectation and alarm," little does she realize that she has found the source of gothic terror.

REDRESSING

As the novel's virtuoso in matters of courtship, Isabella's erotic knowledge far exceeds Miss Morland's, who "was not experienced enough in the finesse of love" (36), and whose innocence prevents her from finding Isabella's sighs and blushes legible and from seeing the electricity between amorous couples. Isabella, instead, has been initiated in the semaphore of courtship—she "could discover a flirtation between any gentleman and lady who only smiled on each other" (33); and perhaps even into the cabal of male sexual fantasies that women are indistinguishable, so need not be treated as individuals: she determines to be "dressed exactly" like Catherine, since "The men take notice of *that* sometimes you know" (42, Austen's emphasis). Indeed, she sounds positively Elizabethan when, wanting to see Henry Tilney, she cries "where is [Eleanor's] all-conquering brother? . . . Point him out to me this instant . . . I die to see him" (57).

Austen reveals through Isabella what happens when a female character cannot read courtship codes effectively or as effectively as she might think she does. Isabella performs the role of "young, available woman" who proffers herself for public consumption. Judith Butler's argument that "gender is . . . manufactured through a sustained set of acts, posited through the gendered stylization of the body," acts that when repeated enough times come to seem "utterly natural" (xv) helps explain why Isabella's immediate circle reads her rendition, for a while at least, as "authentic." Like Catherine searching chests and bedrooms for signs of erotic fulfillment, Isabella transgresses the boundary allowed to women who (to quote again) perform "explicitly and knowingly to a male gaze" (Brook 112) as she chases random young men down Milsomstreet, exchanges suitors according to their income, and in particular pursues Frederick Tilney, rehearsing spicy talk with him as he "undresses"—that is, interprets—her reasons for blushing.

In other words, both Isabella and Catherine have mastered certain signs, but not others. Thus, instead of positing Isabella's hypocrisy in opposition to Catherine's genuine freshness, I envision them first as entities existing along a continuum of code-breaking efficiency and second as interdependent, in that Catherine's "authenticity" makes sense only in relationship to Isabella's inauthenticity.[19] Juxtaposed to Isabella's jaded husband hunting, Catherine's "undressed" naiveté becomes appealing, whereas in another novel, such as *Pride and Prejudice*, it would be insufferable. In Jonathan Culler's semiotic terms, the point is that "[t]he paradox . . . of authenticity is that to be experienced as authentic it must be marked as authentic, but when it is marked as authentic it is mediated, a sign of itself, and hence lacks the authenticity of what is truly unspoiled" (164). Isabella's hypocrisy, her ability to decipher some sexual codes, her fortune hunting, and her sexual knowing throws into even stronger relief Catherine's "candid, artless" mind (206), marking her as authentic. Catherine may be more likeable, but that does not render her more "genuine" than Isabella.

Catherine's simplicity arises partly from her conviction that signs are transparent. This conviction finds its most thorough and comically devastating manifestation in her role as a traveler. At a structural level, the eighteenth-century fashion for touring provides the plot's foundation as Catherine travels circularly from Fullerton to Bath to Northanger Abbey and then home again. The crisis of authenticity permeates the entire novel, and thus at an exegetical level, tourism is a fitting heuristic device for analyzing the longing for the genuine and for understanding how Henry Tilney redresses the unsophisticated, yet charming Catherine into the "authentic" heroine. In multiple ways she masters the tourist's archetypal role insofar as she believes in the authentic and trusts that it exists in unmediated form; her ingenuous faith in such certainty has the effect of making her seem genuine. Her gothic journey orbits in conjunction with her search for romance, and both goals repeat a familiar ideology: whether in tourism or courtship, the desire for fulfillment without mediation relies on the same preeminent hermeneutic conundrum: "how can [she] come to terms with that which is Other without reducing it to the terms of [her] own understanding?" (Frow 130). The heroine reveals how foreign such a stance of negative capability is to her when Henry analyzes her thinking process: "With [Catherine], it is not, How is such a one likely to be influenced? What is the inducement most likely to act upon such a person's feelings, age, situation, and probable habits of life considered?—but, how should *I* be influenced, what would be *my* inducement in acting so and so?" Catherine simply replies, "I do not understand you" (132).

Throughout most of the novel, Miss Morland expects a transparent relation between sign and referent, which leads to an almost aphasic relation to experience because she often cannot read figuratively. For example, when General Tilney plans to take Catherine to Woodston Parsonage he assures his son that "You are not to put yourself at all out of your way. Whatever you may happen to have in the house will be enough. I think I can answer for the young ladies making allowance for a bachelor's table" (210). Catherine discovers, however, that he actually means that Henry should spend four days preparing for the family's visit (210), that "any thing would do" means preparing an abundant dinner and "frightening [his] old housekeeper out of her wits" (211). Oblivious to the General's obsession with food and table, which she has experienced daily at Northanger Abbey, and having had no experience in hypocrisy, double meanings or wit, but only having grown up around "plain, matter-of-fact-people," Catherine exclaims in amazement, "how were people, at that rate, to be understood" (211). Here she attempts to read experience "as a simple self-equality of any notional determination—red is red, winter is winter" (Žižek 130); or, in her case, all abbeys are in ruin and people always say what they mean.

The fashion for the gothic, which Catherine dons, offers her the opportunity to interact socially; by providing an immediate connection to Isabella and a deeper bond with Henry, gothic tourism makes her visible to them and them to her, supplying, as it does, conversational topics, opportunities for flirtation, and emotional crises. But as I analyzed in the episode where she explores the chest while partially dressed, her wardrobe of information and understanding is spare indeed. In Catherine's first approach to Northanger Abbey, her "tourist essenc[e]" (Frow 125) and her "romance essence," have both preceded her, as she "expected with solemn awe" "every bend in the road . . . to afford a glimpse of its massy walls of grey stone, rising amidst a grove of ancient oaks, with the last beams of the sun playing in beautiful splendor on its high Gothic windows" (161). She finds instead modern buildings and clear panes of glass, the difference of which "was very distressing" (162). Because she reads through the frame of "painted glass, dirt and cobwebs" (162) and because this frame defines for her what constitutes the authentic, she is *unable* to read the architecture and modern improvements as the embodiment of the general's financial and technological ambition, which in turn prevents her from penetrating his hypocritical statements about marriage for love. Catherine reconstructs and invents Tilney family history in terms of her Gothic and romantic expectations; she also invents Henry's love for her: the narrator "confesses"

> that his affection originated in nothing better than gratitude, or, in other words, that a persuasion of her partiality for him had been the only cause of giving her a serious thought. It is a new circumstance in romance, I acknowledge, and dreadfully derogatory of an heroine's dignity; but if it be as new in common life, the credit of a wild imagination will at least be all my own. (243)

Through her narrator, Austen links Catherine's failed search for authenticity with the novel's presentation of romantic love as ideology: Northanger's furniture is new, and so, too, is this a "new circumstance in romance." Since it is only too common that marriages arise out of many kinds of circumstances—a man's narcissistic gratitude for being loved, rather than loving another, being one of these—Austen's "wild imagination" provides a clear view of constructions of love and of experience in general.

In being invited to the abbey as a guest (rather than a paying tourist), Catherine experiences the traveler's coveted perspective, one that allegedly offers access to the authentic, what theorists Erving Goffman and later Dean MacCannell analyze as the "*front* and *back regions*" (MacCannell 92), the "back" presumably constituting an intimate and genuine point of view. Entrée to such a region allows Catherine to search for "narrower passage[s], more numerous openings, and symptoms of a winding stair-case," apertures that lead her to "believ[e] herself at last within the reach of something worth her notice" (*Northanger Abbey* 185). One could argue that, by breaking the fourth wall of her narrative when she speaks to readers directly, an action that splinters the illusion of realism, Austen could be said to be giving us the "back" view of courtship. Travelers often expect that the site they see will replicate the representation they are familiar with (an engraving, a guidebook description, an ideological notion of what a heroine is and what constitutes "true love"). But Northanger fails to correspond to itself (i.e., to what Catherine supposed it to be), and neither do the portrayals of gender and love correspond to what one might expect to find in this novel. As MacCannell argues, however, "It is always possible that what is taken to be entry into a back region is really entry into a front region that has been totally set up in advance for touristic visitation" (101). Likewise, it is fruitless to assume that in giving a reader the "inside of things," Austen offers an authentic view of courtship or "heroineness." In closing with a question, "I leave it to be settled by whomsoever it may concern, whether the tendency of this work be altogether to recommend parental tyranny, or reward filial disobedience" (252), Austen's back regions resemble a *trompe l'oeil* rather than a pellucid vision of the truth.

Catherine mediates her touristic experience of places through the gothic novel, and though her experiences foil her ultimate goal—unmediated experience—the text takes a playful turn when she herself comes to symbolize and embody what the tourist searches for. During the late eighteenth and early nineteenth century (as it often is today), travelers tended to seek that which modernization had not tainted. Thus, Catherine's devotion to a past that feels sacred to her—the touristic energy for things old and therefore "authentic"—operates in opposition to the General's obsessions with new-fangled possessions and innovative technologies. Her search for what John Frow refers to in tourism as the "charm of displays of preindustrial implements and artifacts in old houses" (130) and what Susan Stewart calls the quest for "the primitive, the folk, the peasant, and the working class" who "speak without self-consciousness" (16) malfunctions. Instead, she comes to represent these values. Understanding Catherine through the ideology of authenticity, Henry finds the "real" in her, finds that she represents the naive, primitive original. Unaccountably charmed by her nescience, Henry reads her distance from ideological codes as freshness and originality. His new bride offers him the genuineness that his father and brother lack. In Henry's eyes, Catherine is "Open, candid, artless, guileless, with affections strong but simple, forming no pretensions, and knowing no disguise"—descriptors he uses ironically to refer to Isabella, but which he associates with Catherine, since Eleanor replies "with a smile," that "Such a sister-in-law, Henry, I should delight in" (206). He reinforces our notion of Catherine as the uncorrupted and unmediated (she knows *no* disguise?) that is made real only in relation to Isabella's sexual knowing and marital ambition. If Catherine represents unalloyed simplicity in contrast to Isabella's tarnished sophistication, Isabella herself is a naïf in contrast to the cosmopolitan code-playing man, Frederick Tilney, whose manipulations throw her own art and guile into pathetic relief.

CONCLUSION

We should "all delight in" being and knowing those who are "open, candid, artless, guileless, with affections strong but simple, forming no pretensions, and knowing no disguise" (206). In a world of fashion and in a fashionable world, what would it look like to "kno[w] no disguise"? What is supposedly "false"—that is, fashion—makes what is "true"—that is, the human body—visible. Ideology made concrete, fashion reveals how a controlling point of view makes it possible to "see" but considerably limits interpretation. Austen embraces the paradox of the authentic and inauthentic without resolving it. Whether cross-dressed, undressed, or dressed, the novel's characters reveal how the fashions of their culture—whether of turbans or tourism—link their bodies to the mediated liturgies of human relations. Austen supports the notion of gender identity as constructed since the characters unconsciously parody expectations of male and female behavior. It is most convenient to call the Thorpes and Mrs. Allen con-artists or shallow artificers, but I would suggest that aversion to these characters arises from the fact that they denature "natural" deportment in courting rituals, revealing the seamy underside of patriarchal expectations. Mrs. Allen, Isabella, and John represent the paradox of the individual whose unsociability arises from being too socialized into cultural patternings. They offer (to quote Sydney Owenson) "servile copies, sketched by the finger of art, and finished off by the polished touch of fashion" (65), yet they leave me unable to shake off the feeling that their fraudulence, hypocrisy, and fakery is as organic as it gets.

CHAPTER 4

MAKING AND IMPROVING:
FALLEN WOMEN, MASQUERADES,
AND EROTIC HUMOR
IN *MANSFIELD PARK*

MAKING BAWDY TALK

Austen found the process of writing *Mansfield Park* immensely funny: a niece claimed that the novelist "would sit quietly working beside the fire in the library, saying nothing for a good while, and then would suddenly burst out laughing, jump up and run across the room to a table where pens and paper were lying, write something down, and then come back to the fire and go on quietly working as before" (Hill 202). Neglecting her "work," Austen runs off to write down her laughter, laughter that became *Mansfield Park*. What was she laughing at? Of all the novels, this seems like the least funny and the most morally earnest work, a text in which self-discipline, restraint, and self-denial triumph.

It seems likely to me that she was laughing at the novel's comic treatment of courtship and erotic material, something an emphasis on its apparent morality and endorsement of sacrifice has obscured. No one could argue that much of *Mansfield Park*'s content is indisputably risqué: the characters openly canvas Fanny's developing body, descriptions eroticize the landscape at Sotherton, and the narrator offers a worldly and unfazed account of adultery—one in stark contrast to her heroine's scandalized description of the crime. Fanny's sense of the wickedness of theater may amuse many readers, but some of the language in *Lovers' Vows* is quite steamy: Agatha lasciviously describes her attraction to the Baron who had seduced and abandoned her: "Oh! oh! My son! I was intoxicated by the fervent caresses of a young, inexperienced, capricious man, and did not recover from the delirium till it was too late" (I.i, 338). Indeed, *Mansfield Park* contains as much ribaldry as it does piety, and the morality that exists there is lodged in and complicit with the novel's unruly witticisms.

Miss Crawford's language, reminiscent of that in the Juvenilia and the Letters, propels an eroticism throughout the novel that shocks Edmund and Fanny. For example, when Mary jokes about the "vices" of admirals and the secret erotic life of the "belles" of the House of Rushworth, she speaks comically and yet shrewdly hits the mark. In the chapel at Sotherton, Mary, in a moment of what could be called materialist rigor, points out the hypocrisy in forcing the servants into compulsory prayer and chapel attendance while the family "invent[s] excuses themselves for staying away" (87). Her sentiments for working-class manumission slide into sympathy for sexual liberation as well when she says that the only way these "poor housemaids" and "former belles" could wile away the time during such services was by engaging in sexual fantasies: "Cannot you imagine with what unwilling feelings the former belles of the house of Rushworth did many a time repair to this chapel? The young Mrs. Eleanors and Mrs. Bridgets—starched up into seeming piety, but with heads full of something very different— especially if the poor chaplain were not worth looking at . . ." (87).

As I discussed in the introduction to this book, Austen's taste for bawdy humor first emerges in the Juvenilia, as when the young Austen candidly quips about James I's homosexuality in "The History of England." The author's jokes about the King bring into sharp relief Mary's comment in *Mansfield Park* about Naval officers, which I alluded to in the Introduction. She describes how her life at "home at my uncle's [made me] acquainted with a circle of admirals," and then jokes that "of *Rears* and *Vices*, I saw enough. Now, do not be suspecting me of a pun, I entreat" (60). Here, she refers to more than her boredom with the "bickerings and jealousies" of naval politics and ambition; that would not involve a *double entendre*, and her pun, as her false demurral emphasizes, establishes her point. That pun points directly to sodomy in the navy. Her bantering causes Edmund to feel "grave" (50), and later, when he and Fanny canvas Mary's statements, he both exonerates and censures Miss Crawford in such a way as to uncover the probability that the cousins "get the joke": "The right of a lively mind, Fanny, seizing whatever may contribute to its own amusement or that of others [is] perfectly allowable, when untinctured by ill humour or roughness; and there is not a shadow of either in the countenance or manner of Miss Crawford, nothing sharp, or loud, or coarse. She is perfectly feminine, *except* in the instances we have been speaking of. *There* she cannot be justified" (64, first emphasis added).[1] Mary's jest, framed in terms of Austen's own witticisms in her Juvenilia and other novels, makes Edmund look more priggish than justifiably offended; Austen emerges as Mary's ally, at the expense of the hero.

John Skinner suggests that the double entendre about rears and vices "invites us to reconsider Mary's evaluation of Edmund as 'no more than Mr John or Mr Thomas' " (211), insofar as "John Thomas" meant both a "flunkey" and the male member. Skinner argues compellingly for a "*diegetic space*" in the novel that "appears in a kind of narrative freedom, exemplified by . . . a certain linguistic licence evinced by some of the more outspoken voices within the text" (126). And while it seems unlikely that even Mary would refer at that point in the novel to the man she loves as just another penis, she is explicit when she exclaims that to persuade her brother to marry would require the "address of a Frenchwoman. All that English abilities can do, has been tried already. I have three very particular friends who have been all dying for him in their turn; and the pains which they, their mothers, . . . as well as my dear aunt and myself, have taken to reason, coax, or trick him into marrying, is inconceivable" (42–43). Mary's Elizabethan reference to "dying . . . in their turn" as well as the implication that one of the "tricks" might involve real or faux pregnancies expose her sexual knowledge and ready fluency in bawdy talk, a language supposed foreign to early-nineteenth-century women.[2]

Missing these unladylike allusions or feeling confused about their presence arises from the tendency, in Patricia Meyer Spacks's words, to link laughter in this novel with "moral weakness" and "ethical ambiguity" (76, 77). Such an argument, which assumes that the funniest personalities are the most "warped"—and therefore too dangerous to be laughed with or at—necessarily polarizes characters, especially Mary and Fanny (witty, amoral femme fatale and conversely, dour, moral, and modest paragon). Demonizing Miss Crawford and reflexively touting the narrator as Fanny's champion obscures the evidence that the narrative voice more closely resembles Mary's than Fanny's, a point both Eileen Gillooly (101–102) and Pam Perkins have convincingly argued. For example, when the narrator employs the comic double entendres that horses and riding provide to poke fun at Fanny, she does so in jokes that are reminiscent of Mary's and that also reinforce Mary's erotically charged energies. As I have pointed out in previous chapters, riding carries fleshly overtones. A contemporary helps illustrate the point: "A London rider returning home from a long journey, very much fatigued, went to sleep at night without performing some duties which his wife thought it natural for him to go through. The next morning, on going into the kitchen, he saw his boots burning upon the fire, and his spurs broke; upon enquiring into the cause, his wife replied, 'Why my dear, what occasion have you for boots and spurs, when you know you have left off *riding*' " (*Garrick's Jests* 62). In *Mansfield Park*, Fanny and Mary displace their attraction for Edmund onto an affinity for riding his horse; but in doing so, both women become the punch lines to bawdy jokes that situate them libidinously in terms of riding: Austen maneuvers the unwitting Edmund into making fun of his cousin when he remarks to Miss Crawford that "every sort of exercise fatigues [Fanny] so soon . . . except riding" (95); and the narrator gets frank when she says that Miss Crawford has so "very much surpass[ed] her sex in general by her early progress" in learning to ride that she is "unwilling to dismount" from Edmund's horse (67).[3]

Additionally, Mary sounds not only like the narrator, but also like Austen. When Miss Crawford exclaims with a stunning, but self-conscious, narcissism, "To say the truth, . . . I am something like the famous Doge at the court of Lewis XIV; and may declare that I see no wonder in this shrubbery equal to seeing myself in it" (209–210), she recalls Austen's wisecrack in a letter to Cassandra: "I am sorry for the Beaches' loss of their little girl, especially as it is the one so much like me" (Le Faye 2). In the introduction to this book, I pointed out that this kind of joking also resembles popular humor in women's magazines: a quip from "The Last News from Dublin" reports that "Yesterday Miss Georgina O'Griskin fell from a jaunting car, and broke her neck, but happily received no other damage" (*Lady's Monthly Museum* Dec. 1806, vol. 253). Mary's suggestive humor counterbalances the Austen family's insistence on sanitizing the author's reputation and on severing the Juvenilia's wild energies from the later novels, as when her niece, Caroline, "thought it remarkable that the early workings of Jane's mind should have been in burlesque, and comic exaggeration, setting at nought all rules of probable or possible—when of all her finished and later writings, the exact contrary is the characteristic" (*Family Record* 276). Whether one forges an antithesis between the Austen of the Juvenilia and that of the mature novels, or between

Mary's saucy back talk and Fanny's quiet compliance, the effect is similar: the earlier Austen and Miss Crawford become associated with mutinous energies, an act that discounts the rawer humor from the novels as a whole or specifically from *Mansfield Park*. Such anarchic and playful humor liberates what would otherwise be a somber novel, but I want to underscore that although Austen's bawdy allusions are often both witty and very funny, she also employs bawdy wit that is not necessarily funny, and that contributes to the narrative's gravity. *Lady Susan* draws such a distinction between delightful and "honest flirtation which satisfies most people" as well as that which "aspires to the more delicious gratification of making a whole family miserable" (248). The novel's concupiscent allusions serve a variety of narrative demands: though comic, they also expose much in Austen's world that is hardly laughable.

MAKING A CAREER

The unsettling trope of "making"—courtship's alarming double—lies at the heart of the humor and pathos in the novel, which rigorously links prostitution to courtship and courtship to corruption in the culture at large. Crawford announces to Fanny that through the Admiral's influence, "He is made. Your brother is a Lieutenant." Austen uses the same phrase when her brother is "raised to the Rank of Commander"— "Frank is made" (Le Faye 32); however, in *Mansfield Park*, "making" has exceeded mere promotion, since the terms of Henry's favor are sexual, "abounding in the *deepest interest*, in *twofold motives*, in *views and wishes more than could be told*" (298, 300, Austen's emphasis). Edward Neil observes that William Price "has in fact to *get made*" in order to get any interest from the Portsmouth girls, who "turn up their noses at any body who has not a commission" (*Mansfield Park* 249).[4] Unable to get promoted and therefore to draw the interest of women, William cries that "one might as well be nothing as a midshipman. One *is* nothing indeed" (249). This emphasis on nothing suggests that Price sees himself as a man transformed into a portionless woman. Apparently not an unusual double entendre, this conceit appeared in Peter Puzzlewell's polite eighteenth-century collection of riddles: "More tawdry than the dress of beaux, / More fickle than the gale that blows, / More constant than the turtle dove, / More beauteous than the girl I love; / What brave Byng did to save Mahone, / What, ladies, you may call your own" (Puzzlewell 34–35). The answer is "Nothing."

The novel renders the polymorphic eroticism of Henry's gift conspicuous: to procure Fanny, Henry has first to "make" her brother, a circumstance the text wryly anticipates when, discovering that William wants to hunt, Crawford finds that he "could mount him without the slightest inconvenience to himself" (237).[5] Ultimately, though, he cannot "mount" William's career, without his own uncle's collusion, which in turn is realized through a series of homosocial interventions—in other words, a series of intimate, companionable, yet ostensibly unerotic gestures that nevertheless prove loaded with sexual innuendo in Austen's rendition of them.[6] Fanny reads about the maneuvers to promote William in letters:

> one from the Secretary of the First Lord to a friend, whom the Admiral had set to work on the business, the other from that friend to himself, by which it appeared that his Lordship had the very great happiness of attending the recommendation of Sir Charles, that Sir Charles was much delighted in having such an opportunity of proving his regard for Admiral Crawford, and that the circumstances of Mr William Price's commission as second Lieutenant of H. M. sloop Thrush, being *made* out, was spreading general joy through a wide circle of great people. (298–299, emphasis added)

This description is funny because of the disparity between the task—advancing the picayune William Price—and the hyperbolic "great happiness" they receive from "making" someone whose accomplishments and character are irrelevant to them. Linked with Mary's earlier pun on rears and vices, this passage detailing William's advancement creates a continuum among promotion, corruption, and sodomy. Austen here explains the way in which the patriarchal system objectifies both men and women. The navy's brutal treatment of shipboard sodomy and Mary's need for Henry to marry Fanny in order to avoid "grow[ing] like the Admiral in word or deed" (296) imply that such bonding between men requires the regulative mechanism of homophobia, lest male friends become lovers. Homosociality in the navy devolves into both homophobia and misogyny since both William and Fanny become negotiable commodities available, after all, for a certain price. Promotion in the navy, like making a good match, becomes a series of commercial-sexual dealings legitimized by an ideology of patronage and alliance.

Austen makes this kind of patronage even more ironic in that the Secretary to the First Lord mentioned above was John Barrow, an editor of Lord Macartney's journeys and well known for celebrating Macartney's diplomatic triumph in China when he refused to be manipulated by the Emperor, in short to "kow-tow" to his demands (Knox-Shaw 212).[7] Austen's humor, based on hyperbole and disjunction, declares how the glorious British resistance to Oriental pressure abroad becomes at home an all too easy acquiescence to the pressures and leverage that a well-established power structure can bring to bear. Further, promotions of this kind were under special scrutiny as a result of the extensively publicized Mary Anne Clarke scandal, which was canvassed during 1809 in ballads, caricatures, pamphlets, and newspapers. The Duke of York (son of George III and Commander in Chief of the army) and Mrs. Clarke, his mistress, were accused of selling promotions to officers and ecclesiastics. She was paid in cash and both sold and received sexual favors.[8] "A Soldier's Wife," a humorous anecdote published at least as early as 1795 in *The Sporting Magazine* and then reprinted in 1803 in the widely read *Entertaining Magazine* uses the Duke of York to link employment and the military to illicit activities.[9]

> The Duchess of York having desired her Housekeeper to seek out for a new Laundress, a decent looking woman was recommended to the situation. "But," said the Housekeeper, "I am afraid she will not suit your Royal Highness; as she is a *Soldier's Wife*, and these people are generally *loose characters!*"—"What is it you say?" said the Duke—who had just entered the room—"*a Soldier's Wife!* Pray, Madam, *what is your Mistress?* I desire, that the woman may be immediately engaged." (135)

The Duke of York, as Commander in Chief of the Army, is a soldier, though one primarily famous for incompetence. Making a joke at the expense of the Duchess, this "select scrap" takes even greater liberties with the Duke, since the story implies that, despite his pompous dignity about soldiers and their wives, he has procured a "loose" woman not only in his wife, but also from 1803, the "loose" Mary Anne Clarke.

The scandal illuminates *Mansfield Park* in pointing out how thoroughly the granting of promotions had been sexualized in early nineteenth-century culture. By eroticizing William's promotion, Austen draws parallels between his advancement and scandal, in that these high-ranking officers, like Mrs. Clarke and the Duke, function as a cabal whose only goal is self-promotion. Further, the conditions of the trade Crawford expects when he "makes" William Price are akin to the giving and receiving of sexual favors: he "pays" to have Price promoted in exchange for Fanny Price's body, which he expects will be the reward for his labors. Bawdy humor, here again, provides a tool for probing urgent social controversies.

"MAKING A SMALL HOLE IN
FANNY PRICE'S HEART"

Henry proffers a barter: William's promotion for Fanny's hand. This exchange and others throughout the novel make it clear that the characters regard Fanny herself as little more than a fetishistic commodity, essentially bought and sold by members of her family, encouraged to sell herself for rank and wealth, and doubly deserted by both her immediate and adopted relatives. Her very name signifies prostitution: the price of the body, a fact that seems to link her etymologically to the infamous Fanny Hill, heroine of John Cleland's *Memoirs of a Woman of Pleasure* (1749), familiarly referred to as *Fanny Hill*, the narrative that helped codify the name Fanny as slang for female genitalia (Partridge 267). I am not suggesting that by including the name Fanny, a common enough appellation, Austen alludes to the *Memoirs*.[10] But in light of her knowledge of *Emma*'s riddle about two prostitutes named Kitty and Fanny (discussed in detail in the next chapter), I am proposing that she knew the slang associations of "Fanny," a knowledge that necessarily enriches the name's significance, especially in a novel so closely preceding *Emma*. Interpreting Fanny Price's name in the context of the riddle collapses the boundaries between prostitution and courtship.

Austen also associates courtship with prostitution through the significant intertextual relations between this heroine's story and Samuel Johnson's two essays, numbers 170 and 171, from *The Rambler*, "The History of Misella Debauched by her Relation" and "Misella's Description of the Life of a Prostitute," a sentimental narrative of a poor young woman seduced by her cousin/guardian. The remarkable parallels between these two narratives—connections that critics have not previously noted—suggest that Austen was working both with and against Johnson's (apparently) nonfictional account: the little girls' backgrounds and age at adoption are similar; their respective parents turn them over to other relatives with a "natural" ease; and both occupy a borderline space below the family but above the servants. The parallels begin to diverge when Misella's cousin seduces her, but even the early stages of this process resemble Fanny's chronicle. The prelude to Misella's sexual downfall, like Fanny's near-ruin, occurs when Misella's cousin, as does Sir Thomas, "bid[s] her 'assume' a more equal place in the family" ("Misella" 138). Vanity prompts both men to exploit the children they raise. Misella's protest that such betrayers "defeat no rivals, but attack only those who cannot resist" (139), recalls not only Sir Thomas, but Henry Crawford, who declares that he "cannot be satisfied without Fanny Price, without

making a small hole in Fanny Price's heart," a phrase that itself
suggests defloration (229).

MAKING MATCHES

When she lends Fanny a gold necklace on which to hang the amber
cross that William has given his sister, Mary thereby "make[s] over to
[Fanny] all the duty of remembering the original giver" (259)—her
own brother, Henry. This small moment affords a chance to watch
Austen deploy, as I analyzed in *Sense and Sensibility* and *Northanger
Abbey*, a material object in order to expose the subterranean layers
beneath a complex courtship scene. Miss Crawford's suggestive
language in this exchange further grounds the episode in the physical.
Although her words do not quite make a "whole family miserable" (to
quote *Lady Susan* again), they do hurt Fanny, and their sly violence
reveals that she labors to help Henry manipulate Fanny Price into
loving him. Here she tries to account for why it embarrasses Fanny to
receive a gift that had originally come from Henry:

> Miss Crawford thought she had never seen a prettier consciousness.
> "My dear child," said she laughing, "what are you afraid of? Do you
> think Henry will claim the necklace as mine, and fancy you did not
> come honestly by it?—or are you imagining he would be too much flat-
> tered by seeing round your lovely throat an ornament which his money
> purchased three years ago, before he knew there was such a throat in
> the world?—or perhaps—looking archly—you suspect a confederacy
> between us, and that what I am now doing is with his knowledge and
> at his desire?" (259)

In framing her reassurances with the infantilizing "my dear child,"
Mary might here be seen as a kind of witty Mrs. Jennings, using
laughter and bawdy innuendo to reconcile a virgin to sexual attraction.
She speculates that Fanny fears Henry will think her a thief, that Miss
Price dreads appearing physically appealing to Crawford, or that
Fanny suspects that the brother and sister unite to break down
Fanny's defenses. By imagining that Fanny thinks she will be thought
a thief, Mary reduces her not only to an untrustworthy servant but
also to a fortune hunter, and in doing so, pictures her as exerting
agency and resistance to her own exploitation. She also diminishes
Fanny by assuming she is uncomfortable with her attractiveness, but
in doing so, Mary objectifies her sexually by lopping her down to one
body part: referring not just once but twice to Fanny as a "lovely
throat." In emphasizing that "his money purchased" this chain,

Mary's unvarnished language overtly connects the necklace and Fanny as equivalently purchasable items; not only was the necklace not inherited, *he* did not even buy it; his *money* did. The phrasing distances the customer from the transaction, whether he is a groom, a consumer, or a procurer of prostitutes. Fanny as ornament recalls her earlier speech in the novel when she remarks on how "pretty" the shrubbery is, and notes that "three years ago, this was nothing but a rough hedgerow . . . never thought of as any thing, or capable of becoming any thing; and now it is converted into a walk, and it would be difficult to say whether most valuable as a convenience or an ornament" (208). In this "ode" to the hedgerow, Fanny unconsciously analyzes her own liminal situation: is she more valuable as a convenience or an ornament? Here in the elision between her and the necklace, the two values merge insofar as both families find it convenient for Fanny to be Henry's ornament.

In the revelation that Mary and Henry team together for his pursuit of Fanny, Mary casts herself as a bawd and minimizes Fanny into a sexual pawn. Here Mary's willingness to fulfill Henry's "desire" (259) recalls the failed plot in *Clarissa*, in which Lovelace tries to engineer one of Mrs. Sinclair's whores, Miss Partington, into bed with the heroine, or in *Pamela*, in which Mrs. Jewkes sleeps with the heroine in order to help Mr. B. enter Pamela's bed. Thus, Austen links the Henry/Maria/Fanny triangle with earlier novelistic treatments of women betraying women for male desire(s) and reinforces Henry's rakish character. Indeed, he resembles the character in *Sanditon*, Lord Denham, a self-proclaimed Lovelace who feels compelled to seduce an innocent heroine (405–406). Henry's chain thus becomes a painfully obvious signifier of entrapment. Further, the gift may ostensibly be for her but in reality it feeds Henry's own gratification. Later, when Edmund pleads with Fanny to wear Henry's chain, he too panders her in order to fulfill his own desires, since he covets Miss Crawford's favor: he wants Fanny to wear the chain "For one night, . . . for only one night, if it *be* a sacrifice—I am sure you will, upon consideration, make that sacrifice rather than give pain to [Mary], who has been so studious of your comfort. . . . I would not have the shadow of a coolness arise . . . between the two dearest objects I have on earth" (263–264).

Fanny, however, does not make any such "sacrifice" since Crawford's gold necklace "would by no means go through" Fanny's amber cross; it was "too large for the purpose," though Edmund's fits perfectly (276). She emphasizes that Henry's chain is "not handsomer, not at all handsomer in its way, and for my purpose not half so fit" as is Edmund's (263). Austen's emphasis on the right "fit" between a couple here recalls Catherine's delight with Henry Tilney's driving in contrast to Thorpe's; however, this amusing sexual allusion takes on a more significant ramification insofar as it demonstrates how Fanny, only through chance, really, can please herself and wear Edmund's simple chain around her neck.

I have been emphasizing throughout that Austen uses things to highlight phenomenological concerns and to supplement and complicate an understanding of courtship. William's gift of an amber cross once again demonstrates how an object's use and design shape perception, thought, and the dissemination of ideas throughout the novels. It is well known that her brother, Charles, delighted Austen by sending her and Cassandra "Gold chains & Topaze Crosses" (Le Faye 91). Austen does not use topaz in her fictional account of this true story, but amber in the shape of a cross that William has brought back from Sicily.[11] This translucent fossil resin has particular sensuous qualities that make it an apt vehicle for Austen's discussion of the amatory charge both the chain and the cross carry. All amber, for example, feels warm to the touch, but Sicilian amber was also prismatic with color, often exotically deposited with orange, red, blue, and green. It was known in the late eighteenth century that this fluorescent gem conducted electricity; in 1794, Sullivan in the *View Nat.* explains that "when rubbed, [it] was observed to attract bits of straw, down, and other light bodies" (II.27).[12] In his *Natural History*, Pliny had described how rubbing amber produces static electricity (xxxvii, ch. xi). It was once thought to attract lovers when in the form of an amulet because of its associations with fertility, scientists having been confused about whether it was a "gum that distills from trees," or instead was " 'made from Whales' . . . Sperm or Seed which being consolidated and harden'd by the Sea [was] cast upon the Shore" (*OED*).[13]

As a symbol of courtship's appeal and danger, amber's sexual connotations illuminate much of the unspoken content of this novel—and especially at this particular moment in *Mansfield Park*, a point when family and friends are pressuring Fanny into marrying Henry. In his *History of Life and Death* (1658) Francis Bacon connects amber to death when he observes that "we see spiders, flies, or ants, entombed and preserved for ever in amber, a more than royal tomb, although they are tender substances and easily dissipate."[14] "More than royal tomb," this amber cross—potentially suspended by Henry's chain—throws this suitor's earlier words into sharper relief: he plans to spend two weeks seducing Fanny, and claims that if "a fortnight can kill her, she must have a constitution which nothing could save" (231). Amber functions heuristically here to impart the aversion Fanny has to wearing "Henry" around her "lovely throat" (259) and to having his gold thread through her amber cross; at the same time, the thought of Edmund's necklace serving the same purpose electrifies her. She makes this clear when she "burst[s] forth" with the exclamation that William's necklace and Edmund's chain "must and shall be worn together" (262).[15]

MAKING IMPROVEMENTS—LAND HUSBANDRY AND BODY MANAGEMENT

In weaving together seduction, landscape improvement, and marriage for alliance, Austen draws on an ancient tradition of eroticizing nature that in the eighteenth century became an integral conceit in travel journals, descriptions of rural settings, and eco-critical landscape design. When the party arrives at Sotherton, both the estate's prospect and Maria Bertram are about to get "made" as Henry Crawford connives to "improve" Sotherton by altering it beyond recognition and by seducing its future mistress. Austen assigns various erogenous zones to the landscape as a mirroring backdrop for the characters' flirtations as they wander through the grounds of Rushworth's estate. In a narrative style dependent on a transparently symbolic lexicon, one that genders nature and inanimate objects, Austen highlights sexual attraction and foreshadows Maria's scandalous elopement as well as Mary and Edmund's aborted engagement. In dramatizing Maria's and Henry's flirtation in the outdoors, Austen follows in the tradition of picturesque writers, mostly male, in eroticizing the landscape: Uvedale Price writes that picturesque nature "*by a partial and uncertain concealment, excites and nourishes curiosity*" (*Essays* I.22) and

> curiosity, while it prompts us to scale every rocky promontory, to explore every new recess, by its active agency, keeps the fibres to their full tone. . . . [The picturesque] is the coquetry of nature; . . . by its variety, its intricacy, its partial concealments, it excites that active curiosity which gives play to the mind, loosening those iron bonds. . . . (*Essays* I.88–89)

Significantly, in this novel, Austen, while employing equivalent sensual terms to describe landscape scenery, thoroughly dismantles any sense of actual passion in order to tie together the commodification of nature (through aesthetic improvement) and of sexuality (through misplaced physical attractions and advantageous matches). Resembling a too "regular" wilderness, Henry and Maria's flirtations seem phatic, carried out mechanically like the estate that is "made by contract in London, and then sent down in pieces, and put together on the spot" (Price I. 242n.). Even if we liken Henry to a picturesque viewer hunting after sensual conquests, he lacks the spontaneous and almost child-like joy William Gilpin describes when he explains how, in viewing scenery,

> [e]very distant horizon promises something new; and with this pleasing expectation we follow nature through all her walks. We pursue her from hill to dale; and hunt after those various beauties, with which she every where abounds. . . . And shall we suppose it a greater pleasure to the sportsman to pursue a trivial animal, than it is to the man of taste to pursue the beauties of nature? To follow her through all her recesses? To obtain a sudden glance, as she flits past him in some airy shape? To trace her through the mazes of the cover? To wind after her along the vale? Or along the reaches of the river? (*Three Essays* 48)

The garden does allow Austen to explore courtship's more physical aspect when she makes use of "iron palissades" (90); an unlocked door leading to a wilderness, ironically laid out with "too much regularity" (91); side gates and locked gates (103, 98); and a ha-ha, designed to create the illusion of unbroken space while also serving the functional role of separating roaming animals from social spaces.

Austen mercilessly dramatizes Rushworth's impotence when he forgets the "key" to the ha-ha gate, "posting away as if upon life and death" (101) to retrieve it from the house, only to find that his fiancée and friend have no need of his key and have slipped around the gate to explore the "knoll." When Fanny replies that "it is a pity that he should have so much trouble for nothing" (101), the text alludes, as it does in William Price's speech, to his lack of sexual power. As surely as she "unmans" Rushworth, Austen exposes Henry's sexual ease and success when he helps Maria "with little difficulty pass round the edge of the gate . . . and to be more at large" (99).

As I discussed in the introduction to this book, Miss Bertram complies willingly when she slips around the iron gate, jeopardizing her dress, and foretelling her adulterous affair with Henry. Fanny, experiencing a terrible conflict in emotion as she watches Maria enact what she represses, calls out, "You will hurt yourself, Miss Bertram, . . . you will certainly hurt yourself against those spikes—you will tear your gown—you will be in danger of slipping into the ha-ha" (99–100). Anticipating her imprisonment as Mrs. Rushworth, Maria laments, "I cannot get out, as the starling said" (99). Maria here refers to Laurence Sterne's *A Sentimental Journey* (1768), in which Yorick realizes he cannot free a captive starling without "pulling the cage to pieces" (71). Austen's humor in this section, functioning as a heterodox activity that contests patriarchal expectations of female behavior, threatens to pull "the cage to pieces"—in other words, to undermine those ideological foundations that disguise and romanticize oppression. Using a complex intertextuality, Austen provides a chiasmus between landscape improvement and sexual conquest, since both Sotherton and Maria (like the stream running through Rushworth's property) "might be *made* a good deal of" (56, emphasis added).

Mansfield Park makes two connections clear: aesthetically managing the landscape directly echoes the treatment of and expectations for women, and land improvement alludes to the nation's conduct in its colonized territories. Austen explicitly invokes these nineteenth-century debates for the ironic counterpoint they provide. In this novel, she satirizes landscape architect Humphry Repton, who functions as the acknowledged authority for "making" and "improving" on a grand, and even titanic, scale. When the dinner guests at Mansfield Park discuss the improvement of Sotherton's seven hundred acres, Maria, Mrs. Norris, and Rushworth all agree that Repton would be Rushworth's "best friend upon such an occasion" (53). "Improving" in this conversation means altering to the degree that the estate and the grounds are virtually unrecognizable after the fact. Speaking of his friend's estate, Rushworth exclaims, "I never saw a place so altered in my life. I told Smith I did not know where I was" (53). Both Rushworth and Crawford strive to imitate Repton's designs, having gleaned from him that an estate that is "nothing" can become "something" primarily by taking "down" existing but now out-moded features like old trees, which obstruct views. Rushworth has begun the makeover that will render the estate more fashionable, opening "the prospect amazingly" by having had "two or three fine old trees cut down that grew too near the house" (55). Sotherton's "old avenue," a relic of the passé imitation of seventeenth-century imperialistic French designs, must also come down, a plan that brings forth Fanny's famous protest: "Cut down an avenue! What a pity! Does not it make you think of Cowper: 'Ye fallen avenues, once more I mourn your fate unmerited' " (56).[16] As Rushworth points out, "Repton, or anybody of that sort, would certainly have the avenue at Sotherton down" (55), an oak avenue that measures "half-a-mile" long (83). The same emphasis Fanny places on preservation over fashion also occurs in *Emma*, when the heroine, gazing on Donwell Abbey, admires "its suitable, becoming, characteristic situation, low and sheltered—its ample gardens stretching down to meadows washed by a stream, of which the Abbey, with all the old neglect of prospect, had scarcely a sight—and its abundance of timber in rows and avenues, which neither fashion nor extravagance had rooted up" (358). As both novels make clear, Austen understands the complicated contexts of picturesque landscape architecture and states her preference for a less improved, though obviously constructed landscape.

In an early ecological appeal, Uvedale Price and Richard Payne Knight—Repton's opponents—argued against sacrificing nature for what they considered fads. The English mind, they contended, may associate the avenue with absolutist government, but destroying so many magnificent trees because liberty is "in fashion" constitutes itself an act of absolutism. As Price writes, "[t]he destruction of so many of these venerable approaches, is a fatal consequence of the present excessive horror of strait lines" (*Essays* I.249). He goes on, "Even the old avenue, whose branches had intertwined with each other for ages, must undergo this fashionable metamorphosis" (256), and shows his deep contempt for Capability Brown in a footnote: "At a gentleman's place in Cheshire, there is an avenue of oaks . . .; Mr. Brown absolutely condemned it; but it now stands, a noble monument of the triumph of the natural feelings of the owner, over the narrow and systematic ideas of a professed improver" (249–250n.). Price and Knight distinguished themselves as advocates of the picturesque while calling Repton an improver, and argued that his stylish innovations, which included rules against groupings of trees and which insisted on isolating a house from its surrounding landscape to display its grandeur, atomized the natural world.

Scholars of the picturesque have analyzed how these debates about land management were in fact political and national debates in which the discussion of the life, placement, and destruction of trees becomes a broad metaphor for the role of the individual in British civil society. Marilyn Butler, for example, argues that Capability Brown and his followers (most famously among them, Repton) tended to see nature as a place where one finds "greater opportunities for sober usefulness" while the followers of Price and Knight (whom she calls progressive) are "liable to see [the country] as a place for the individual to expand in freedom, cultivating the self" (97).[17] To be sure, Price and Knight's politically charged language sounds radical: as Price argues, the improver resembles a French monarch and it seems as if he were saying, " '[y]ou shall never wander from my walks; never exercise your own taste and judgment, never form your own compositions; neither your eyes nor your feet shall be allowed to stray from the boundaries I have traced': a species of thraldom [*sic*] unfit for a free country" (*Essays* I.338).

Austen blatantly satirizes Repton's school of landscape improvement; in so doing she aligns herself with his rivals, Price and Payne Knight.

In finding Repton—and not picturesque aesthetics as a whole—the common problem,[18] Austen does not gaze with satiric disdain upon debates circulating in popular culture, but enters into them with passionate interest.[19] She incorporates the idea that the "making" of the landscape and the "improving of human beings" are ideas that share the same philosophy, one that fragments the garden as well as society. For example, Sir Thomas strives to improve Fanny and then later the neighborhood by cutting his niece and then his daughter off from connection when they disobey him: forbidden to "exercise [their] own taste and judgment," neither Fanny nor Maria is allowed to "wander from [his] walks" (*Essays* I.338). Sir Thomas practices a kind of human horticulture that alters the social "landscape," and Mrs. Norris draws parallels between improving the Sotherton estate by amending the landscape and by introducing a new bride. Fanny's eviction, when she refuses to accord to her uncle's prescribed model for marrying to advantage, and Maria's expulsion, when she fails to follow anybody's idea of matrimony, function to throw down the gauntlet in front of Sir Thomas. As a result, he cuts and prunes the human population of his estate in a way that resembles something very like the improvers' landscape designs that sacrificed nature's imperfections for greater social habitability. Ecological concerns and social debates about liberty infuse these landscape controversies that Austen draws on. According to Uvedale Price, Repton treated nature despotically: trees are "cleared round, . . . and even many of those outside trees which belong to the groups themselves, and to which they owe, not only their beauty, but their security against wind and frost, are cut down without pity, if they will not range according to a prescribed model . . ." (*Essays* I.256). Fanny resists her guardian's injunction to marry; Sir Thomas responds by cutting her down without pity, banishing her from Mansfield Park. When Austen incorporates aesthetic theories in relation to discussions of marriage and colonialism, she suggests that not only the placement of trees, but also the management of women and of other nations will affect the health and future of Britain. In thus taking up a national debate, Austen criticizes both matrimonial improvement and environmental decisions that ignore rather than venerate *feelings* for nature, and political preferences that unduly impose control and constraint over freedom and personal choice.

MAKING THINGS SAFE

Austen carefully sets the context for the news about Maria and Crawford's scandalous affair and elopement. Sitting in the parlor of

her parent's house in Portsmouth, Fanny, "deep in . . . musing,"
dwells on the filthy room, offering a magnified image that could have
been the fruit of any number of nineteenth-century optical devices,
such as the microscope or magnifying glass:

> Here [sun-shine] was only a glare, a stifling, sickly glare, serving but to
> bring forward stains and dirt that might otherwise have slept. . . . She
> sat in a blaze of oppressive heat, in a cloud of moving dust; and her eyes
> could only wander from the walls marked by her father's head, to the
> table cut and knotched by her brothers, where stood the tea-board
> never thoroughly cleaned, the cups and saucers wiped in streaks, the
> milk a mixture of motes floating in thin blue, and the bread and butter
> growing every minute more greasy than even Rebecca's hands had first
> produced it. (439)

Mr. Price interrupts her musings when he passes the newspaper
over to his daughter, in which Fanny reads that "the beautiful
Mrs. R[ushworth], whose name had not long been enrolled in the
lists of hymen, . . . having quitted her husband's roof in company with
the well known and captivating Mr. C. . . . and it was not
known . . . whither they were gone" (440). Mary Douglas has famously
argued in *Purity and Danger* that pollution is not intrinsic to an
object, but related to its setting; something is taboo when it is "matter out of place" (35). What this implies is "a set of ordered relations
and a contravention of that order. Dirt, then, is never a unique, isolated event. Where there is dirt, there is system. Dirt is the by-product
of a systematic ordering and classification of matter, in so far as ordering
involves rejecting inappropriate elements" (35).

Like the soiled marks on the wall from Mr. Price's greasy hair, so
Maria's crime arises because she is literally out of place—she has
slipped over the ha-ha and assumed an agency over her body that her
husband no longer controls. That Austen uses this grimy parlor
setting as a physical displacement of the adulteress' body seems clear
enough (dirty rooms and dirty women, systems breaking down everywhere), but she does so not to announce Maria's moral turpitude
(which would align Austen with Fanny), but instead and ironically to
create a bridge between the two families. She thus undermines rather
than reinforces the clear contrariety between Portsmouth and
Mansfield Park that Fanny, striving so desperately to create system and
order, needs to maintain: Fanny could think of "nothing but
Mansfield, its beloved inmates, its happy ways. Every thing where she
now was was in full contrast to it. The elegance, propriety, regularity,
harmony—and perhaps, above all, the peace and tranquillity of

Mansfield, were brought to her remembrance every hour of the day, by the prevalence of every thing opposite to them *here*" (391, Austen's emphasis).[20]

Sounding thoroughly like a plantation overseer, Mr. Price's disturbing, brutal comment, that he would "give" any adulterous daughter of his "the rope's end as long as I could stand over her" aims to brand the lawless daughter so as to mark her body with the crime and thereby restore his power over her in this sadistic and incestuous act. This image joins other colonial references in the novel, and like *Pride and Prejudice*, connects flogging to a constellation of subjects: education, sexuality, and violence. As I discussed earlier, Favret points out that "women readers were repeatedly asked to fix their eyes on 'the strong marks of slavery' thus violently engraved on the female slave's body" ("Flogging" 39–40). Mr. Price's graphic picture forces Fanny to gaze on her own, as well as on Maria's bloody "stripes." Maria's crime, her refusal to abdicate strong sexual passions, and, in her elopement, her rejection of the culture's conviction that one can achieve tolerable marital happiness by marrying for money, all become the mirror of what most seriously threatens the society, the pollution that must be hidden: if the woman's body is out of place the entire society will suffer. As Mrs. Percival exclaims to Kitty in *Catharine, or the Bower* (1792), when she catches her niece being kissed, "the welfare of every Nation depends upon the virtue of it's individuals, and any one who offends in so gross a manner against decorum & propriety is certainly hastening it's ruin" (*Catharine* 232–233). Appositely, Sir Thomas fears that Maria will contaminate the neighborhood with her presence. Most specifically though, Maria has insulted her father, something Fanny feels will destroy him: "Sir Thomas's parental solicitude, and high sense of honour and decorum . . . made her think it scarcely possible for [him] to support life and reason under such disgrace" (442). Cixous's comment that "to break up, to touch the masculine integrity of the body image, is to return to a stage that is scarcely constituted in human development; it is to return to the disordered Imaginary of before the mirror stage, of the rigid and defensive constitution of subjective armour" (*Newly Born Woman* 33) seems apropos to the impact Fanny imagines Maria's crime will have on the Mansfield men. When Sir Thomas casts his daughter out as ruthlessly as he had banished his niece when Fanny did not comply with his wishes, Austen once again shatters polarities by revealing the inevitably metonymic slippage between the two fathers' cruelty and the crimes of the daughter and daughter-in-law to be.

Sir Thomas and Lady Bertram argue the point that pollution cannot be disinfected when they see Maria's behavior "only in one light, as comprehending the loss of a daughter, and a disgrace never to be wiped off" (449). They reinforce the idea Wollstonecraft critiques when she protests how "a woman who has lost her honour, imagines that she cannot fall lower, and as for recovering her former station, it is impossible; no exertion can wash this stain away" (*Vindication* 72). But in the fact that they sterilize their home and neighborhood by displacing the contaminant out of view, the novel suggests that "life and reason" *can* be "support[ed]" (442) if the adulteration is out of sight. When Fanny's younger sister, Susan, anticipating her visit to the Park, dwells on "Visions of good and ill breeding, of old vulgarisms and new gentilities[,] . . . meditating much upon silver forks, napkins, and finger glasses" (446), the sparkling Mansfield cutlery, linen, and crystal must be seen in relation rather than opposition to the greasy butter stains and "cups and saucers wiped in streaks" at Portsmouth. The finger glass (or finger bowl) was instituted in England about 1780 and was "often omitted entirely" by 1880 (Beeton 1241). A dual sign of hygiene and contamination, these glasses were used both for washing hands and for rinsing out one's mouth at the table, a custom that by 1834 was deemed "filthy" (Áywyós 23).[21]

The finger glass functions as a dramatic sign here of the paradox of the clean: in a *Journal of a tour and residence in Great Britain during the years 1810 and 1811*, Louis Simond explains that "Towards the end of dinner . . ., bowls of coloured glass full of water are placed before each person. All (women as well as men) stoop over it, sucking up some of the water, and returning it, and, with a spitting and washing sort of noise, quite charming,—the operation frequently assisted by a finger elegantly thrust into the mouth! This done, and the hands dipped also, the napkins, and sometimes the table-cloth, are used to wipe hand and mouth" (48). In 1784, La Rochefoucauld had described this custom as "extremely unfortunate. The more fashionable do not rinse out their mouths but that seems to me even worse; for, if you use the water to wash your hands, it becomes dirty and quite disgusting" (29). Such washing only serves to illuminate dirt more conspicuously (and, in fact, scientists routinely use a "finger glass" as a container that aids in magnification). As an optical device and metaphor, the "glass" parallels the narrator's observation that the sun shining in the Portsmouth parlor served "but to bring forward stains and dirt that might have slept" (439); unseen spoilation still exists— the crucial point that Fanny cannot recognize about Mansfield Park. Apparently clean or egregiously dirty, both fathers' hands are guilty of "flogging" their daughters, and though servants offer Sir Thomas a finger glass and napkin to sanitize his hands and Mr. Price uses a pros- thetic to flog his hypothetical daughter, the blood secreted from her will leave visible "marks" and "notches"—like the ones on the walls and tea table. The Mansfield Park household avoids pollution, rather than exterminating it, by putting impurity in its "place" when Sir Thomas banishes Maria to "another country—remote and private" (465). Though significantly Fanny thinks that extinction either of Maria or the entire family (the passage is ambiguous) would be the best solution: "it appeared to [Fanny], that as far as this world alone was concerned, the greatest blessing to everyone of kindred with Mrs. Rushworth would be instant annihilation" (442). Thus, when our narrator proclaims, "Let other pens dwell on guilt and misery," she provides one way of addressing the ubiquitous fallenness in the novel: by simply averting her eyes to another set of characters.

MAKING DISGUISES

Austen destabilizes the boundary between prostitution and courtship, the clean and the unclean, Portsmouth and Mansfield; in doing so, she breaks down just those foundational binaries that sustain patriarchal ideology rather than affirm it. No one stays untainted in this novel, including Fanny: Johnson asserts that Fanny is "in some not fully definable way a very bad [girl]" ("What Became" 68); if not "very bad," she most certainly is not the paragon of virtue so often maintained. As Pam Perkins contends, Austen's "treatment of Fanny mocks and undermines rather than upholds [moral] conventions" (19). One of Austen's most unsettling and comic inversions makes Fanny, our presumed moral representative, the most brilliant actress in the novel. Fanny exclaims, "I could not act any thing if you were to give me the world" (145), but she transparently can and does. "Full of jealousy and agitation" (159), she disguises her love for Edmund. At the end of the novel, the narrator ruthlessly—and comically— exposes Fanny's pretended sympathy for Edmund's "disappointment and regret" over Mary: Fanny "was sorry; but it was with a sorrow so founded on satisfaction, so tending to ease, and so much in harmony with every dearest sensation, that there are few who might not have been glad to exchange their greatest gaiety for it" (461). Such examples demonstrate how spectacularly successful Fanny is at hiding the breach between her feelings and the social self she projects.

Through a series of substitutions, Fanny becomes the "masked" woman, a role that simultaneously empowers and debilitates her. When Crawford asks, "Is she queer?—" (230), the word's earlier meaning of "to counterfeit" takes on an added resonance (Partridge, *Slang* 677). Her doubleness—her repressed desires, smoldering jealousy, and passionate love contrasted to her sycophantic and virginal demeanor—resembles the doubleness of parts acted at a masquerade in which nuns, milkmaids, shepherdesses, and Quakers proved to be the opposite of their chaste exteriors. Tradition coupled prostitutes and actresses on the grounds that their careers are based on fiction: according to *The Whore's Rhetorick* (1683), the prostitute's "behavior, like her language, . . . must be wholly illusory" (46). Further, the prostitute's mask bespeaks her procurability; similarly Fanny's own masking of her love for Edmund registers her availability to Crawford, while her apparent prudishness—also a mask for her sexual desires—excites his craving. The fear that acting compromises young women is borne out in Fanny's case, but in a wholly transposed way: her real-life acting makes her susceptible to the machinations of Crawford, that refined libertine. While Ruth Bernard Yeazell may be correct that "few risks can attend Fanny in the role of the Cottager's wife" (151), ironically, the same risks *The Lady's Magazine* describes *do* imperil Fanny: the "modest miss" who, in home theater, "personates the coquette" renders herself vulnerable to the "polite *double entendres* of the refined libertine" (397, 398 qtd. in Yeazell 150). Thus, theater is not the fount of inequity, but a metaphor for the ideology that forces women to mask their true selves. Like Johnson's Misella, Fanny must repress "resentment," "continue [her] importance by little services and active officiousness, and . . . stud[y] to please rather than to shine" ("Misella" 137). In this sense Austen condemns conduct book advice to feign what one knows and feels, which, ironically, again strongly resembles the *Whore's Rhetorick*, which claims that the whore's "whole life must be one continued act of dissimulation" (46). Paradoxically, though, the mask also offers Fanny the liberty to "decide for [her]self"—and in this sense, her performance procures her sovereignty. Disguise for her, as for women at an actual masquerade, vouchsafed them, in Terry Castle's words, "the essential masculine privilege of erotic object-choice" (93). Edmund ultimately chooses Fanny, but until that happens, her acting allows her to protect the object choice she has made.

CONCLUSION

The novel explores the comic irreverence of seeing Fanny Price, in the words of the *New Monthly Review* (1852), as a "bewitching 'little body' " (Southam I. 138). One might suspect, then, that Austen would recognize the self-reflexive irony inherent in the narrator's reference to Miss Price as "my Fanny" (461). *Mansfield Park* provides the opportunity to perforate oppositions between respectable women and their deviant sisters, insofar as courtship and marriage negotiate their bodies as agents of exchange. Austen's irreverent humor leads her to conjoin her seemingly purest, most evangelical heroine to the overdetermined figure of the masked woman. By exploring the range of associations of Fanny's name and by linking her to Misella and the prostitute-actress, that same humor enables Austen to critique the ideology that divides women into either the pure or the fallen and suggests instead that in such a society, all women are fallen: and this includes both the Fanny Hills, who are prostitutes, and the Fanny Prices, who are expected to prostitute themselves in the marriage market. Fanny obviously is not a prostitute and she does not end up the victim of her guardian's machinations, but instead marries the man she loves and lives in proximity to her now devoted surrogate parents. Mansfield Park inverts certain expectations: the outcast little cousin becomes the heiress to the Park while it exiles the legitimate daughter from home, family, neighborhood, county, and country. In one sense, her new role provides an example of exactly what the masquerade effected: that is, a situation that was, in Joseph Addison's words, "top-side turvy, Women changed into Men, and Men into Women, Children in Leading-strings seven Foot high, [and] Courtiers transformed into Clowns" (502).

In another sense, while such an transposition may seem like an example of "Nature turned top-side turvy," at the larger systemic level it is not: Fanny's triumph depends upon the same order that exiles Maria—the acknowledged fallen woman—who has "lost" because she has acted out her desires openly. Fanny has "won" because she has dissembled—she has performed the role patriarchal rules dictate women should play. As the text says, "Fanny was indeed the daughter that [Sir Thomas] wanted" (472). Like her brother, William, Fanny has been "made" or promoted by the powers that be because it suits them to do so. It just so happens that their promotions also suit William and Fanny. In expanding the notion of what constitutes "fallenness," Austen suggests a far more radical attitude toward prostitution and courtship than was generally found in late eighteenth and early nineteenth-century England, in which, as Felicity A. Nussbaum argues, prostitutes were "conceptualized . . . as a species set apart from women" (21).[22] The adulteress, Maria Bertram, may have been banned from Mansfield Park, but Austen's final joke is that one of the fallen women is in the parsonage.

CHAPTER 5

"Praying to Cupid for a Cure": Venereal Disease, Prostitution, and the Marriage Market in *Emma*

"I'll Kiss you if you Guess": Courtship in *Emma*

Mary Wollstonecraft, with that discomfort toward the physical that marks *The Vindication,*

> object[s] to many females being shut up together in nurseries, schools, or convents. I cannot recollect without indignation, the jokes and hoiden tricks which knots of young women indulge themselves in, when in my youth accident threw me, an awkward rustic, in their way. They were almost on a par with the double meanings, which shake the convivial table when the glass has circulated freely. (128)

In *Emma*,[1] however, flirtation depends on just such "double meanings," which, combined with sexual secrets, drive the narrative. Trying to conjoin her poor, illegitimate companion, Harriet, with the ambitious vicar, Elton, Emma invites him "to contribute any really good enigmas, charades, or conundrums that he might recollect" (70). Deciphering such riddles becomes a form of sexual play, for the riddles, which carry an erotic valence, function as a kind of cupid, or mediator, for romance. Ironically, Emma's father, the impotent Mr. Woodhouse, figures prominently in this game: "So many clever riddles as there used to be when he was young—he wondered he could not remember them! but he hoped he should in time" (70). But the only riddle he can remember, and then only the opening lines, is "Kitty, a fair, but frozen maid."

A RIDDLE

Kitty, a fair, but frozen maid,   1
    Kindled a flame I still deplore;
The hood-wink'd boy I call'd in aid,
Much of his near approach afraid,
    So fatal to my suit before.   5

At length, propitious to my pray'r,
    The little urchin came;
At once he fought the midway air,
And soon he clear'd, with dextrous care,
    The bitter relicks of my flame.   10

To Kitty, Fanny now succeeds,
    She kindles slow, but lasting fires:
With care my appetite she feeds;
Each day some willing victim bleeds,
    To satisfy my strange desires.   15

Say, by what title, or what name,
    Must I this youth address?
Cupid and he are not the same,
Tho' both can raise, or quench a flame—
    I'll kiss you, if you guess.[2]   20

Written by David Garrick, the verse was first printed in 1771 in *The New Foundling Hospital for Wit*, a miscellany of verse and prose that was, in Donald Nichol's words, an "outrageous publicatio[n]," one that "reflected the political turbulence of the time" (14).[3] The contributors included members of Sir Francis Dashwood's Hell-Fire Club, a notorious fraternity predicated on debauchery. And though there are poems in it honoring Shakespeare's birthday and Johnson's *Dictionary*, most of the miscellany's verse contains salacious material; "Kitty's" sexual violence is especially disturbing. The riddle circulated throughout the culture, and a poem about another fickle Kitty appeared in *The Lady's Monthly Museum* (Jan. 1807): "Depriv'd, alas! Of hope and pity, / My breaking heart has bid farewell / To happiness, to love, and Kitty" (47).[4] The critical responses to Austen's use of Garrick's riddle vary: Nicola Watson acknowledges that it is "smutty," but rather than explore it as an expression of Austen's bawdy humor or as a critique of patriarchal ideology, she ties the riddle to Austen's "broadly conservative political agenda" (94–96); Alistair Duckworth mentions that Mr. Woodhouse's interest in this riddle is "simply childish" ("Spillikins" 293); and Alice Chandler observes that "[p]recisely what kind of game Jane Austen is playing with Mr. Woodhouse and her readers is hard to tell" (92).[5]

I will be analyzing what sort of game Austen plays and exploring how she integrates "Kitty, a fair but frozen maid" into the narrative as a whole. The riddle addresses the plight of a man (the narrator) who has been infected with venereal disease ("a flame I still deplore") and who "prays" to Cupid, "the hood-wink'd boy," for a cure. The riddle's solution (ll. 16–19) is that the youth who raises and quenches such flames is a chimney sweep, and the prize for guessing—the kiss—is slang for sexual intercourse.[6] The first two lines offer multiple interpretations about how the speaker has been infected. For example, did he contract it from Kitty, the "fair, but frozen maid," or from another woman? Moreover, why is Kitty frozen? Because she is dead (presumably from disease)? Because she was a virgin? Or is it that because propriety dictated that "pure" women should be sexless, his desire for Kitty drives him to a prostitute who infects him? His allusion in the third stanza to the bleeding victim adumbrates the sodomitical violence to which the narrator resorts, since for a time sodomy was thought to be a way to avoid infection (Trumbach 211).[7]

The next two verse paragraphs describe two possible remedies. Lines 11–14 reveal the narrator invoking a remarkable species of magical thinking since he believes (according to the folklore of the time which was still in circulation as late as 1857) that sex with a virgin (male or female) would cure him of the disease: hence, "each day some willing victim bleeds."[8] *Mansfield Park* also alludes to this myth in the romantic plot between Crawford and Fanny: the dissolute Henry believes that the virgin, Fanny—albeit through marriage—will "sav[e]" him from the "contagion" he caught from his uncle, the Admiral (295). Such a "cure" is as specious as eighteenth- and early nineteenth-century speculations about the origins of venereal disease. According to Mary Spongberg, medical discourse feminized venereal disease by theorizing that women themselves were the source of contagion (34). Spongberg documents how writers hypothesized from 1761 through at least the 1830s, that because "discharge was essential for the transmission of venereal poison," "venereal disease came to be seen . . . as a natural consequence of [female] reproductive systems." Moreover, "some went so far as to suggest that secretions of an uninfected woman could produce a spontaneous dose of syphilis in a man.

Sex during menstruation, too much sex, too little sex, sex with a woman after too much alcohol . . ., all were said to cause gonorrhea in men, while leaving the woman unaffected" (26, 32, 34).

The other cure that the riddle alludes to involved applying mercury—a metaphoric chimney sweep—to the body in such a way that one turned oneself into something that looked rather like a chimney. In order to be cured, the patient would stand before a fire, rub mercurial ointment into the lower extremities, and then cover them with flannel; this procedure would continue until the entire body was shrouded and the patient expelled pints of saliva. Sometimes when the patient would not salivate, physicians prescribed an extreme process—fumigation by cinnabar, a mixture of mercury and sulfur. Here, as Philip Wilson (drawing on contemporary accounts) describes it, treatment transformed the body into a literal chimney as the patient was placed on a

> seat that was "perforated" somewhat "like the close Stool." A blanket was wrapped around the patient, entirely "enclosing" his body and head, and was secured to a hook in the ceiling. Cinnabar was "sprinkled on" a hot iron placed below the seat, and the fumes ascended through the chair, guided by an inverted funnel so that they would flow "all round the Diseased Parts." (75)

Thus, the youthful chimney sweep in the riddle "can raise, or quench a flame" because he can kindle desire and cure venereal disease: that is, he "fought the midway air, / And soon he clear'd, with dextrous care, / The bitter relicks of my flame" (ll. 8–10).

Austen interweaves into her novel the same topics that the riddle introduces, such as prostitution, venereal disease, and the double standard; and she incorporates similar images, including a marked emphasis on heat and cold and on figures of cupids and chimneys. This vicious riddle exists both inside and outside *Emma*: Austen transcribes only one verse, but a contemporary audience with a better memory than Mr. Woodhouse's would have known it as well. Further, the young women have written it out entirely on their "second page," having copied it from the *Elegant Extracts* (79), another joke on Austen's part, given that the *Extracts* were a most conservative publication (the rest of its title gives the flavor: "Being a Copious Selection of Instructive, Moral, and Entertaining Passages, from the Most Eminent Prose Writers").[9] Given that they are in the habit of perusing improper charades, Emma's and Harriet's possession and reading of "Kitty" is not anomalous: Emma "could perceive" that Elton was "most earnestly careful that nothing ungallant, nothing that did not breathe a compliment to the sex should pass his lips. They owed to him their two or three *politest* puzzles" (70, emphasis added). Emma implies here that Elton may have heard ungallant puzzles when the convivial glass was passed round, but she and Harriet, like Wollstonecraft's females "shut up together," have collected material that is less polite than what the clergyman is willing to offer. That such riddles existed and were circulated is substantiated by one publication, which tries to redeem the genre's reputation. *Riddles, Charades, and Conundrums, the greater part of which have never been published. With a preface on the antiquity of riddles* exclaims that

> Enough has certainly been said to defend this species of writing from contempt, which, notwithstanding the laugh that may be raised against it, is still cherished by the lively and the young. None can dispute that riddles are at least an innocent amusement; and, when tolerably well chosen, they prove an exercise of ingenuity, and must have a tendency to teach the mind to compare and judge. It has perhaps been owing to the trash commonly disseminated under the name of enigmas, that they have fallen into disrepute. An attempt has been made in the following selection, to rescue them from the reproach of barbarism and puerility. (v–vi)

Because the riddle in *Emma* exists on a vulnerable border between the acceptable and the illicit, it highlights the novel's subversive content and also collapses the gulf between the sexual underworld of Austen's time and Highbury's respectable world.

Parallels between *Emma*'s characters and the riddle's narrator dramatize such a collapse. Austen raises the ludicrous and hilarious possibility through a series of covert associations that the asexual Mr. Woodhouse might have been a libertine in his youth and now suffers from tertiary syphilis. For example, this hypochondriac cannot bear to be cold and so prefers a fire, even in midsummer; the riddle's narrator, ill with venereal disease, also longs for "fire" to cure him. Both Mr. Woodhouse and the narrator despise marriage and want to surround themselves with young virgins, who will keep them "well." Further, it is also deliciously, though seditiously, funny that one of the reputed "cures" for venereal disease was a light diet, mostly consisting of a thin gruel, Mr. Woodhouse's favorite meal and the only one he can with "self-approbation recommend" (54). In *Domestic Medicine: Or, a Treatise on the Prevention and Cure of Diseases by Regimen and Simple Medicines*, William Buchan includes an entire section on "Of the Venereal Disease"; there he explains that

> when a person has reason to suspect that he has caught the venereal infection, he ought most strictly to observe a cooling regimen [in diet],

to avoid every thing of a heating nature, as wines, spirituous liquors, rich sauces, spiced, salted, high-seasoned and smoke-dried provisions, &c. as also all aromatic and stimulating vegetables as onions, garlic, shallot, nutmeg, mustard, cinnamon, mace, ginger, and such like. His food ought chiefly to consist of mild vegetables, milk, broths, light puddings, panado, gruels, &c. . . . Violent exercise of all kinds, especially riding on horseback, and venereal pleasures, are to be avoided. The patient must beware of cold, and when the inflammation is violent, he ought to keep his bed. (492–493)

Mr. Woodhouse also worries about asparagus, a vegetable thought to stimulate conditions ripe for infection (Spongeberg 34); he frets that it had not been "quite boiled enough," and so he "sent it all out again," a decision that "rather disappointed" Mrs. and Miss Bates (329).[10] Such remedies and preventatives were well known to the general population, and Austen would have been cognizant of them since these were common subjects advertised in eighteenth-century periodicals (Stone 379). Buchan, in fact, complains that the topic of venereal disease was "omitted" from the first edition of his book, and argues that these symptoms should be well known, so as to benefit "the patient from an early knowledge of his case, and an attention to a plan of regimen, which, if it does not cure the disease, will be sure to render it more mild, and less hurtful to the constitution" (489).

Surveying the whole novel, it becomes clear that "Kitty" implicates other characters besides Mr. Woodhouse. When Emma remarks that Miss Fairfax "is a riddle, quite a riddle!" (285), Jane's servitude takes on an even grimmer inflection. Emma is a matchmaker and, like the Cupid in the riddle, one whose pairings have devastating results: both she and the narrator, having kindled "flame[s] [they] still deplore," seek to "quench" them: she is on the receiving end of Elton's deplorable proposal and the riddle's antihero catches venereal disease. The logic of the riddle suggests that cures for disease derive from a balance of hot and cold: that is, the frozen virgin heals the hot syphilitic. In turn, Austen deploys a dense matrix of ice and heat throughout *Emma*. Mr. Woodhouse is most prominent in his need for heat, but he is not alone: John Knightley also reacts with alarm to a bit of Christmas snow—perhaps for a good joke on Austen's part since, as his father-in-law remarks, John's wife Isabella "was very near being christened Catherine," so "the name [in the riddle] makes me think of poor Isabella" (79). The healthy Knightley, in contrast, escapes to the cool confines of Donwell Abbey, so "that he might not be irritated into an absolute fever, by the fire which Mr. Woodhouse's tender habits required" (351), and Frank gets an overdose of "medication" when, agitated by the heat of his ride to the strawberry-picking party, he finds the elderly man's fire "intolerable": "the heat was excessive; he had never suffered anything like it— . . . nothing killed him like heat" (364, 363). Spurned by Elton, Harriet tries to recover her emotional health by burning the mementos she gathered during their abortive courtship. As I said above, the solution to the riddle is that the "Cupid"—the youth he addresses—is a chimney sweep, and, like the "kiss" at the end of the riddle, "chimney-sweeping" was also eighteenth-century slang for sexual intercourse.[11] Thus, when Harriet throws her mementos, metonymies for Elton himself, into the fireplace, she engages in mock sexual relations with him, sex that she also hopes will cure her.

Farmer and Henley list "to get . . . one's chimney swept out" as slang for sexual intercourse, used "of women only" (III. 208). Given this, Miss Bates's statement that "Patty came to say she thought the kitchen chimney wanted sweeping" comes at a fitting point in the text, just before Emma arrives to see the new pianoforté Frank has secretly sent to Jane. Miss Bates's response, "Oh! . . . Patty do not come with your bad news to me" (236), certainly does underscore, on a literal level, the family's poverty, since her speech lists all of her expenses and needs: how little Jane eats, perhaps because she tries to help conserve food; Miss Bates's gratitude to Knightley for his apples (they only had six left), and to the Wallis's, who have generously baked and delivered the fruit, presumably without charging her, and to Frank for repairing Mrs. Bates's only pair of spectacles, since otherwise she would have had to send them "over to John Saunders" and (presumably) pay to have them fixed (236).

Appearing at this point, however, Patty's reference to chimney sweeping adds another sexual innuendo to an already sexually charged situation, one so laden that Miss Bates herself senses it. For example, after hearing Miss Bates glide from topic to topic—Jane's cold, wanting Emma's opinion of the piano, Mrs. Bates's spectacles, the chimney, the apples and how they should be prepared—Emma wonders "on what, of all the medley she would fix": the older lady lights on Frank's determination to repair her mother's spectacles,

[w]hich you know shewed him to be so very. . . . Indeed I must say that, much as I had heard of him before and much as I had expected, he very far exceeds any thing. . . . I do congratulate you, Mrs. Weston, most warmly. He seems every thing the fondest parent could. . . . "Oh!" said he, "I can fasten the rivet. I like a job of that sort excessively." . . . And when I brought out the baked apples from the

closet, and hoped our friends would be so very obliging as to take some, "Oh!" said he directly, "there is nothing in the way of fruit half so good, and these are the finest looking home-baked apples I ever saw in my life." That, you know, was so very. . . . (237–8)

Miss Bates does not often use ellipses, and in this context, they intimate that her quick mind has come up against something unutterable—that she intuits affection between Jane and Frank, affection that would be more obvious when being played without Emma present and in Jane's private family circle. In this scene, however, in the Bates's "little sitting-room" (240), Frank devises a double-pronged enigma, flirting with and humiliating two women simultaneously: Emma and Frank coquettishly gossip in front of Jane about her supposed passion for Mr. Dixon; at the same time, Frank sends coded love messages to Jane, who reveals "with all the deep blush of consciousness, . . . a smile of secret delight" (243). Meanwhile, Jane sends erotic cryptograms back when she plays *Robin Adair* on the piano; its lyrics describe a woman's love for a man who has wooed and coldly abandoned her and is a ditty that, if one knows the words and knows of Frank and Jane's secret engagement, has private significance for them. Singing it, Jane can simultaneously commemorate their courtship in Weymouth, make an open secret of their stealth, and express her fear of abandonment. An old Irish tune called "Eileen Aroon," *Robin Adair* became popular in Scotland around 1715; in the 1750s, Lady Caroline Keppel, in love with a man of the same name, wrote the words: in the first stanza, the singer laments,

> What's this dull town to me?
> Robin's not near.
> What was't I wished to see?
> What wished to hear?
> Where's all the joy and mirth
> Made this town heav'n on earth?
> Oh! They're all fled with thee,
> Robin Adair.

The next two stanzas bemoan how he made "th'assembly shine" but "now thou'rt cold to me, / Robin Adair."[12] From Emma's point of view, the "amiable, upright, perfect Jane Fairfax was apparently cherishing very reprehensible feelings" (243)—the illicit love in *Robin Adair*, she doubtless imagines, refers to Mr. Dixon. Emma's illicit projections aptly suit a conversation that began with what could be a bawdy reference to "getting one's chimney swept out." By adding that the "kitchen chimney wanted sweeping" to an already innuendo-charged episode, Austen amplifies her multiple representations of sexuality, but also adds a level of pathos. Only if Jane marries well (her engagement with Frank is unforeseen at this point), will she get the chance to have a sexual union in marriage that will heal her—she who is subject to collective hysteria that she will catch cold, with Emma declaring the only solution, for one in her delicate health, is "Good fires" (217)—and only then will Miss Bates be able to give over agonizing about how to pay for sweeping out her chimneys.

Mr. Elton himself, "spruce [and] black" (114), hot with passion and overheated from drink, functions as a trope of a "chimney," a word that was itself slang for "clergyman" (Partridge 147). In his essay, "The Praise of Chimney Sweepers," for example, Charles Lamb refers to them as "young Africans of our own growth—these almost clergy imps, who sport their cloth without assumption; and from their little pulpits (the tops of chimneys), in the nipping air of a December morning, preach a lesson of patience to mankind" (249–250). When Elton, Austen's "clergy imp," proposes to Emma in the nipping air of a snowy December night, his heat and ferocity are palpable: "scarcely had they passed the sweep-gate and joined the other carriage, than she found her subject cut up—her hand seized—her attention demanded, and Mr. Elton actually making violent love to her" (129). Elton, an ambitious social climber, engages in a fantasy of upward mobility: in proposing to Emma, the wealthiest woman in his world, he imitates the actual chimney sweeps on May day. As William Hone describes this, "their great festival," in *The Everyday Book* for May 1, two sweeps were chosen as the lord and lady of the celebration, which was a kind of fertility pageant in which one of the sweeps is encased in a "Moving hillock of evergreens" (583).[13]

In the riddle, Cupid works as a pimp who conjoins Kitty and the narrator; in the novel, Emma turns Harriet into both a shopper and an irresistible purchase. She argues with Knightley that "a girl, with such loveliness, . . . has a certainty of being admired and sought after, of having the power of choosing from among many . . . [P]ray let her have time to look about her" (63, 64).When Emma pushes Harriet toward Elton and then Frank Churchill, when she teaches her vanity and class prejudice, and when she stimulates her romantic imagination, Emma's actions all enact various strands in the public discourse about the causes of prostitution. In his analysis of these theories, Markman Ellis lists the potentially dangerous behaviors: "pretension and ambition, over-education . . . hopes of marriage above one's station in life, [and] . . . an over-excited imagination or stimulated passion for romantic love, [which] lead to the weakening of the prophylactic power of innocence" (164). Emma thus becomes the kind of "novelist" whom many writers felt would threaten "female chastity by educating young women into an impossibly ideal view of love" (Ellis 165). When he reviewed *Emma*, Sir Walter Scott found "fault" with Austen for her coupling of that "once powerful divinity, Cupid" with "calculating prudence." He suggests that it is the novelist's responsibility—and Austen's—to "lend their aid" in writing about "Romantic feelings" that will, in transforming the lover into a kind of chivalric knight and the lady into an ideal paragon of femininity, "softe[n], grac[e], and amen[d] the human [male] mind" (235–236). The troubled Scott understood that Emma was more than "just" another novel with a fantasy marriage plot.

Austen's use of this riddle, with its attendant allusions to prostitution and syphilis, does indeed invoke Cupid with "calculating prudence," but in a different way than Scott meant: she exposes the patriarchal/ heterosexual world of conventional courtship as a dangerous, violent, and even life-threatening arena for both men and women. In the riddle, Garrick calls Cupid "a hoodwink'd boy," and that cynical suggestion that this "once powerful divinity" fools others because he himself is blind and deceived resembles the perspective that animates *Emma*, in which the matchmaking heroine so often misses the mark, both about others and herself. The novel ridicules a system that exploits women whose husbands infect them, children who are raped for a "cure," and the diseased, since these "cures," often administered by quacks, were dangerous and, for obvious reasons, rarely successful. These links between a "proper" novel and a riddle associated with the Hell-Fire Club break down the gap between the Kittys and Fannys of the *New Foundling Hospital for Wit* and the women of *Emma*, all of whom—at least at one level of signification—are themselves chimneys. That is, their function is to remain fixed in place, designed to heat, to pleasure, and to heal others.[14] No wonder Mr. Woodhouse worries about Emma marrying; no wonder Emma, the novel's own Cupid, thinks matchmaking a better option than marriage.

Because of the riddle's subject matter, Austen's interlacings question attitudes toward the fallen woman and her seducer. Her inclusion of "Kitty" parallels the oxymoronic attitudes toward written material about prostitutes. Ellis describes how Fordyce and others regarded the genre of the novel as a contaminating influence for young female readers, that in fact "reading certain novels is equivalent to being a prostitute" (165). Earlier in the eighteenth century, the Magdalen Hospital published a poem by Sterne, though only two years later the

Reverend Dodd, minister at the institution, "wrote a verse attack on the licentiousness of *Tristram Shandy*, hypocritically arguing that it was improper"; further, the Magdalen Hospital supported itself in part through the publication of narratives of seduction and redemption, narratives that the "corrupting" novels in fact resemble (Ellis 177–178). In *Emma*, the riddle offers a humorous juxtaposition to the "proper" environment of Highbury; it parallels the buying and selling— the prostitution—of genteel girls with fallen ones; it examines the sentimentalization of the prostitute; and it exposes the fallacy in conjoining seduction or rape with the mere reading of such narratives.

The riddle also illuminates Miss Woodhouse's seduction of Harriet, who has just the sort of beauty "which Emma particularly admired. She was short, plump and fair, with a fine bloom, blue eyes, light hair, regular features, and a look of great sweetness" (23). So engrossed is Emma in appreciating Miss Smith's loveliness, "so busy in admiring those soft blue eyes, in talking and listening, and forming all those schemes in the in-betweens, that the evening flew away at a very unusual rate" (24). In a milder way than the riddle's narrator, yet still in a manner that has a sexual intonation, Harriet satisfies Emma's needs since the younger girl is "one whom she could summon at any time to a walk" and therefore is "a valuable addition to her privileges" (26). In the riddle, "Each day some willing victim bleeds, / To satisfy my strange desires" (15–16). In the novel, Harriet indeed becomes a "willing victim" to Emma's desires, to Elton's contempt, and, later, to the gypsies' sadism: "such an invitation for attack could not be resisted" (333).

The presence of "Kitty a fair, but frozen maid" offers another context for Emma's reactions to Harriet's illegitimacy: she was "the natural daughter of somebody. Somebody had placed her, several years back, at Mrs. Goddard's school, and somebody had lately raised her from the condition of scholar to that of parlour-boarder" (22–23). Though Emma fantasizes throughout the novel that Harriet is the daughter of a gentleman, it turns out to be otherwise:

> Harriet's parentage became known. She proved to be the daughter of a tradesman, rich enough to afford her the comfortable maintenance which had ever been her's, and decent enough to have always wished for concealment.—Such was the blood of gentility which Emma had formerly been so ready to vouch for!—It was likely to be as untainted, perhaps, as the blood of many a gentleman: but what a connexion had she been preparing for Mr. Knightley—or for the Churchills—or even for Mr. Elton!—The stain of illegitimacy, unbleached by nobility or wealth, would have been a stain indeed. (481–482)

That *Emma*'s readers learn the class status of Harriet's father, but not of her mother, suggests that the latter's rank is inconsequential. Emma's twisted logic here betrays a value system based on class affiliation, rather than on any recognizable moral code, religious or otherwise. The word "untainted" introduces images of disease and contagion, and Emma suggests that although it is possible that the tradesman's blood is "clean," she convinces herself that a gentleman's would be immaculate. Thus she implies that Harriet may be contaminated with something other than the embarrassing fact of having had a father "decent" enough to support her but indecent enough to have seduced and then abandoned both mother and daughter. The novel subverts Emma's reliance on rank as an indicator of purity since she herself apes the gentleman's role of seducer and poisoner of poor women and innocent wives, and thereby "taints" Harriet, contaminating her with ambition. Further, with all her talk of taint and blood, she inadvertently underscores how the gentlemen's blood was "perhaps" purer, not because of their birth, but because they had the knowledge of avoidance strategies and the money for remedies, which were more expensive than those for other illnesses. Buchan's *Observations Concerning the Prevention and Cure of the Venereal Disease* (1796) was, as Trumbach points out, written for gentlemen, who were inoculated in all kinds of ways from infection, including avoiding street prostitution, seeking out "approved whores," and soliciting "virgins and girls newly on the town" (205).

"CATHARINE, OR THE BOWER": "THE SEXED FEMALE BODY"

Catharine, or The Bower, part of Austen's Juvenilia, provides a powerful companion piece for the reading of *Emma* that I have offered thus far. This early fragment explores female sexuality in ways that suggest that she engaged these problems at the outset of her work as a writer and that her interest persisted throughout her career. Garrick's riddle points to the cause and effect relationship among discourses of sexuality: philosophies of women's sexual repression, extreme standards of female innocence and ignorance coupled with fear of female passion, libertine seductions, and male visits to prostitutes. "Kitty" discloses that either the narrator incurs venereal disease because his frozen maid sends him and his passion into a prostitute's lair or that the frozen Kitty, fountainhead of the narrator's disease, is now a dead Kitty. Dramatizing how belief in female iniquity makes female ignorance imperative, *Catharine, or The Bower* in turn emphasizes the way in which female repression distorts a girl's "natural frankness" (*Vindication* 28) by making her vulnerable to seduction and by inspiring the libertine to seek prostitutes. When and if venereal disease ensues, it leads in turn to hagiography of and destruction of innocence (through the rape of the virgin). In this unfinished novel, a woman, Catharine's Aunt Percival, rather than the riddle's dissolute male narrator, insists on female purity and punishment for infractions against this dictate. Austen's Catharine—or Kitty, as she is nicknamed—is a lively, artless young orphan with a "warm" imagination (193) raised by a pathological maiden aunt. Kitty's strong attachment to her companions, the Miss Wynnes, and their consummation of friendship in the building of and retired conversations in a "fine shady Bower" (193) reveal her sensibility. The novel heats up when the Stanley family arrives, and their son, Edward, plays at courting Kitty, muddling her brain with expectations and disappointments. This unfinished novel, like the riddle, examines sexual sanctions and codes of innocence and perversion.

Kitty—a fair, but not a frozen maid—enjoys Edward's risque jokes. Having convinced her to "admit [him] without any chaperone into [her] carriage," Stanley then wants her to enter the ballroom with him as a couple in order to "be the whole talk of the Country" (219). Alluding to sex and the loss of virginity, he implies that because Kitty has already "offend[ed] against Decorum" (by spending time alone with him in her carriage) she cannot offend "the *first time* again," by walking into the room with him (219, Austen's emphasis). Attracted to his humor and apparently receptive to this allusion to the loss of virginity, Kitty "finds him 'very ridiculous,'" and while "laughing," she replies, "but I am afraid your arguments divert me too much to convince me" (219). In the end, such play takes a nasty turn when he compels her to arrive with him, "forcibly seizing her arm within his, overpower[ing] her voice with the rapidity of his own"; then, Kitty, "half angry and half laughing, was obliged to go with him up stairs, and could even with difficulty prevail on him to relinquish her hand before they entered the room" (220). In "seizing her arm," Edward Stanley's actions resemble Elton's when he seizes Emma's hand, demands her attention, and "actually mak[es] violent love to her" (129).

Mrs. Percival's disturbed obsession with her niece's chastity emerges when she describes Kitty to Edward Stanley's father in terms that are at once grotesque and incoherent in relation to her niece's actual behavior, but also logical in the context of the culture's obsessive regulation of female sexuality. She defines Kitty as

> one of the most impudent girls that ever existed. [Her intimacies with
> young men are abominable, and it is all the same to her who it is, no
> one comes amiss to her.] I assure you Sir, that I have seen her sit and
> laugh and whisper with a young man whom she has not seen above half
> a dozen times. Her behavior indeed is scandalous, and therefore I beg
> you will send your son away immediately, or everything will be at sixes
> and sevens. (228)[15]

Though the story makes the playful and unreserved young girl's
innocence incontrovertible, in her Aunt's speeches, Kitty already has
fallen, has already "abandoned" herself to behavior that threatens to
"overthrow the establishment of the kingdom" (232), an argument
that decrees that the State owns the female body. In needing to read
Kitty as an outlaw, Mrs. Percival locates her niece's vice in her sexuality, in ways oddly similar to accusations made about revolutionary
French feminists after 1793: as Peter Brooks points out, whether they
were "political women, scribbling women, debauched women:
they all come together as examples of 'the sex' out of control"
("Melodrama" 13, 14).[16] The text, however, never censures Kitty's
easy frankness and, in fact, champions it, by critiquing Mrs. Percival in
ways similar to Wollstonecraft's commentary on the conduct-book
writer, Dr. Gregory, who

> recommends dissimulation, and advises an innocent girl to give the lie
> to her feelings, and not dance with spirit, when gaiety of heart would
> make her feel eloquent without making her gestures immodest. In the
> name of truth and common sense, why should not one woman
> acknowledge that she can take more exercise than another? . . .; and
> why, to damp innocent vivacity, is she darkly to be told that men will
> draw conclusions which she little thinks of?—Let the libertine draw
> what inference he pleases; but, I hope, that no sensible mother will
> restrain the natural frankness of youth by instilling some indecent
> cautions. (*Vindication* 28)

It is just such indecent cautions that Mrs. Pervical instills in Kitty, as
she strives to "damp innocent vivacity." Austen revised *Catharine* in
1808, when, as A. Walton Litz shows, she changed the aunt's name
from Mrs. Peterson to Mrs. Percival: she wrote to Cassandra that "We
have got a new Physician, a Dr. Percival, the son of a famous
Dr. Percival of Manchester, who wrote moral tales for Edward to give
to me" ("Jane Austen: The Juvenilia" 4). Austen's association

between this conduct book writer and a woman who interprets artless playfulness as a rancid display of sexual excess reveals her mordant opinion of such "moral" tales. A year later (1809), writing to her sister that she did "not like the Evangelicals," Austen changed Mrs. Pervical's recommendation for Catherine's reading from Archbishop Secker's *Lectures on the Catechism of the Church of England* (1769) to Hannah More's *Coelebs in Search of a Wife* (1809).[17] As Claudia Johnson points out, "Austen's revision is so telling because it demonstrably links Mrs. Percival with . . . Hannah More . . . [and thereby] certainly shows how little faith Austen had in the ideology of Tory conservatism to which many Austenian scholars believe she subscribed" ("Kingdom" 53). In Austen's story, then, the conservative Tory position on expected manners finds form in Aunt Percival, a character who embodies a pathological terror of sexuality and normal erotic desire since she opposes any kind of intimacy whatsoever, even honest flirtation. In this sense, she resembles Maria Edgeworth's Mrs. Smith, who refuses to teach her granddaughter to write since she believes that the only outcome of such knowledge would be love letters and ruin (*Belinda* 360). Mrs. Percival's extreme accusations and threats ineluctably draw the reader to a psychoanalytic point of view that "impudent," "abominable," and "scandalous" fantasies mesmerize *her*, not Kitty, and that the elder woman's overheated imagination projects these incriminations onto Kitty's "remarkably open and unreserved . . . disposition" (196). Displacing these desires and fantasies on to Kitty's bower—a delicate and sensuous image of "infantine Labors" (193), deep female friendships, and libidinous desires—she threatens to destroy the outdoor room. For Kitty, under constant surveillance, the bower represents a winsome retreat that "possessed such a charm over her senses, as constantly to tranquillize her mind and quiet her spirits," a place which Kitty believed "alone could restore her to herself" (193).

Mrs. Percival's fear of the bower, which the novel describes in picturesque terms, arises from political and cultural ideologies about governing the female body. In harmony with her allegiance with Hannah More, Mrs. Percival's threats to destroy Kitty's bower parallel the Tory reaction to Richard Payne Knight's picturesque theories: conservatives labeled him a Jacobin for using revolutionary metaphors in *The Landscape* (1794).[18] This poem offers an early ecological plea for protecting nature from the "sacrilegious waste" Knight identified with improvers like Capability Brown and Humphry Repton, whom he accused of encouraging an ostentatious display of wealth that required sacrificing a native wildness. As I discussed in the chapter on

Mansfield Park, Knight's pleas for emancipating nature in landscape design became controversial when he linked such emancipation to appeals for individual freedom. One specific Anti-Jacobin response, from Anna Seward, exposes how Mrs. Percival's aversion to Kitty's picturesque bower presages larger political controversies about the management of landscape and women.

> Mr. Knight would have nature as well as man indulged in that uncurbed and wild luxuriance, which must soon render our landscape-island rank, weedy, damp and unwholesome as the incultivate [*sic*] savannas of America . . . . Save me, good Heaven, from living in tangled forests, and amongst men who are unchecked by those guardian laws, which bind the various orders of society in one common interest. (Seward IV, 10–11)

Here, as in Austen's text, the conservative Tory fears the "uncurbed and wild luxuriance," the "damp and unwholesome" environment of less cultivated nature, which functions as a metonym for the ungoverned female body. The only physical contact in the novel does occur in this bower, but only because Edward, to bait the elder Aunt whom he observes watching them suspiciously, "seize[s]" Kitty's hand and "presse[s] it passionately to his lips" (231). After lecturing Kitty about this incident for some time, Mrs. Percival becomes convinced that lingering in the "damp and unwholesome bower" (Seward) in the evening has perhaps made her irrecoverably ill:

> I begin to feel very chill already. I must have caught a dreadful cold by this time—I am sure of being lain-up all the winter after it. . . . This is July. . . . Very likely I may not be tolerable again before May. I must and will have that arbour pulled down—it will be the death of me; who knows now, but what I may never recover—Such things *have* happened My particular friend Miss Sarah Hutchinson's death was occasioned by nothing more—She staid out late one Evening in April, and got wet through for it rained very hard, and never changed her Cloathes when she came home—It is unknown how many people have died in consequence of catching Cold! I do not believe there is a disorder in the World except the Smallpox which does not spring from it. (233–234)

The aunt's threats to demolish the sylvan retreat parallel her attempts to destroy Kitty's warm, passionate attachments, which the aunt thinks indicate a wild sexuality, one that she associates with disease. In claiming that all "disorders in the World except the Smallpox" spring from cold, wet conditions, she triggers associations to venereal disease in her category and to its slang name when she excludes Small*pox* from her list (emphasis added). In representing the bower as a female body, the site of illicit behavior, and as the source of all disease, Aunt Percival, perhaps unconsciously, associates the shady spot with current medical theories that the "sexed female body was a diseased body," and that sexual illness in men arose from damp, unclean, promiscuous conditions extant in a woman's body, arising from suspect, though "*natural secretions*" (Spongberg 38, 33).[19]

Mrs. Percival's attitudes about London repeat the same fears that she harbors toward the bower. She could never let her niece visit the metropolis, "the hothouse of vice," since Kitty was "inclined to give way to, and indulge in, vicious inclinations, and therefore was the last girl in the world to be trusted in London, as she would be totally unable to withstand temptation" (239). Clara Tuite interprets Mrs. Percival's threat to destroy the bower as a metaphor for "displaced defloration" by the maiden aunt who plays the role of "the sexually frustrated schoolteacher who inflicts the loss of innocence through cruel punishment" (49).[20] To be sure, this aunt, in her fear that Kitty's cravings include both hetero- and homosexual passion, reveals her own fantasies, finding letters between young women almost as dangerous and abhorrent as the kiss Stanley presses on Kitty's hand.

Posited between her paranoid aunt and Stanley's manipulating coquetry, Kitty's pleasure in dancing, sitting in her bower, flirting with Stanley, whispering to young men, and enjoying all her senses and sensuous reactions appears wholesome and refreshing. Kitty remains appealing even when she weaves a sentimental fiction of Stanley's love, whom she imagines suffering from his passion for her and who, she fantasizes, "is sacrificed to the vanity of his father" (238). The story presents a compelling critique of the way ideology pathologizes women's feelings by projecting onto their sexuality an unmanageable, luxuriant, and licentious character.

FRANK'S JOKES AND EMMA'S HOYDEN TRICKS

The riddle introduces the subject of prostitution and radicalism into the novel; so, too, does Frank Churchill's notorious trip to London "merely to have his hair cut" (205). His interest in grooming appears harmless to a modern audience, but the characters' shock and amusement draw attention to his act:

> There was certainly no harm in his travelling sixteen miles twice over on
> such an errand; but there was an air of foppery and nonsense in it which

[Emma] could not approve. It did not accord with the rationality of plan, the moderation in expense, or even the unselfish warmth of heart which she had believed herself to discern in him yesterday. Vanity, extravagance, love of change, restlessness of temper, which must be doing something, good or bad; heedlessness as to the pleasure of his father and Mrs. Weston, indifference as to how his conduct might appear in general; he became liable to all these charges. His father only called him a coxcomb, and thought it a very good story; but that Mrs. Weston did not like it, was clear enough, by her passing it over as quickly as possible, and making no other comment than that "all young people would have their little whims." (205)

The slang definition for "get[ting] one's hair cut" was to visit a woman,[21] a meaning Frank's father (who feels it is "a very good story") may have in mind, given that he calls him a "coxcomb"— a vain, self-conceited fellow (Grose 1811). Frank, in fact, goes to London to buy a piano for his secret fiancée, Jane Fairfax, so in a broad way Mr. Weston correctly fingers how his son exploits the hair cut as a cover story for romance of one kind or another. Mrs. Weston's "passing it over as quickly as possible" reinforces this reading insofar as it gives his trip to London an aura of taboo and scandal, which she would rather avoid. Because Frank has emotionally seduced Jane and promised marriage only in secret, the narrative links his behavior to rakish extravagance, and thus to the speaker in Garrick's riddle, who "each day" exploits a new "victim." And like the speaker, Frank does victimize Jane time and again by publicly humiliating her, all the while encouraging Emma to believe that Miss Fairfax has carried on an illicit love affair with her best friend's husband, Mr. Dixon. For example, Frank has told Jane that Emma suspects her of this love affair, so when he wants to play "puzzles" with Emma, he spells out "Dixon" with letters of the alphabet. Frank mortifies her when he "directly handed over the word to Miss Fairfax, and with a particular degree of sedate civility entreated her to study it": "blush[ing] more deeply than he had ever perceived her . . ., [Jane] pushed away the letters even with an angry spirit . . ." (348–349). As Knightley concludes, "disingenuousness and double-dealing seemed to meet [Frank] at every turn" (348).

Emma's own judgments about his expedition to the barber illustrate another association with haircuts and hairdressers: France and its revolution. France was the fashion capital of Europe, and whether the French were advocating the superficial with their pomading and powdering of the hair or representing radical beliefs in cropping it off, the English were suspicious, if also fascinated. As Dan Herzog points out in "The Trouble with Hairdressers," "English observers paid fretful attention to rapidly changing French hair styles, to shaggy sans culotte hair and well-pomaded muscadin hair, trying desperately to discern the deep meaning and vicissitudes of the Revolution by deciphering the language of hair" (24). Emma's suspicion that Frank loves change and has a restless temper couples him with the French, an association already manifest in his first name. Further, because hairdressers could make the "apprentice boy" indistinguishable from "his grace" (John Lovett, "Hairdresser," 1793, qtd. in Herzog 37); because some stayed open on Sundays; and because their clients tended to chat freely with them, hairdressers came to be associated with greater equality among the ranks of society and with political talk: all problematic and all linked to radicalism since in the "aftermath of the French Revolution, political discussion had unsavory ties to atheism" (Herzog 33). Frank has affianced himself to a woman not his "equal"—one he cannot marry until his wealth- and rank-obsessed Aunt dies. Further, because Frank is an ambivalent signifier of class hierarchy (his rich aunt and uncle adopted him while his less wealthy father still lives), he functions as a reminder, in some senses revolutionary, that birth is not destiny. Nor will birth or straitened circumstances be destiny for Jane Fairfax either, since the novel ends with their marriage.

CONCLUSION

In 1813, shortly before Austen began writing *Emma*, she critiqued Mary Brunton's Jacobin novel, *Self-Control*, as "an excellently-meant, elegantly-written Work, without anything of Nature or Probability in it" (234). *Emma*, by contrast, turns an unflinching gaze at "nature" and demonstrates the probable ways in which ideologies did affect women in her culture. Austen's manipulation of Garrick's riddle and her plaiting of it into both the main narrative as well as the subplots of the novel reveal the insistent way the patriarchal system fixes the female body. One could argue that Mr. Woodhouse, petrified of physical activity and connected with disease both through hypochondria and through his associations with the riddle, has himself "diseased" Emma by so dislodging her from normal physical activity that a solitary half-mile walk to visit Mrs. Weston is "not pleasant" (26). Disenfranchised from her body, she displaces it on to Harriet and Jane, contriving courtships and fantasizing seductions. Thus, like the riddle's narrator, she manipulates others in order to achieve her own satisfaction and "health." As I have argued throughout, Austen celebrates physical activity and exposes the negative effects of stagnation.

Describing the al-fresco strawberry party at Donwell Abbey, Austen integrates theories of landscape aesthetics and examples of sexual humor to reinforce how gender constructions and landscape descriptions remain subject to political, historical, and economic conditions. When the party walks through the Abbey gardens, we are told that

> It was hot; and after walking some time over the gardens in a scattered, dispersed way, scarcely any three together, they insensibly followed one another to the delicious shade of a broad short avenue of limes, which stretching beyond the garden at an equal distance from the river, seemed the finish of the pleasure grounds.—It led to nothing; nothing but a view at the end over a low stone wall with high pillars, which seemed intended, in their erection, to give the appearance of an approach to the house, which never had been there. (360)

The passage revels in the physical details of the heat, the delicious shade, and the languorous wandering through the landscape, which itself sensuously "stretch[es]" toward a site unconstrained by labor: the house that was never built, the "high pillars" left as a roving signifier of what?—of ease?—of loss?—of indecision?—of imagination unfulfilled? In an aesthetic that envisions the worker at rest and in a book in which intellectual laborers desert their toil (Emma, Knightley recounts, never finishes anything), and where the only signs of closure are marriages (themselves signs of process), the gestures of abandoned physical labor point to a kind of voluptuary lassitude.

The picturesque, in opposition both theoretically and practically to landscape improvement, triumphs here in that upgrades to this property have been aborted, just like Emma's attempts at human improvements. Thus a freer and wilder manipulation of the natural, though one still constructed, triumphs over a more invasive organization of raw nature, one that would have lauded the artificial and vain parade of "show" (Knight, *The Landscape*). The high pillars leading to "nothing but a view" stand in opposition to the fashion for showcasing the owner's wealth by emphasizing his property at the environment's expense, placing or reorienting the house, for example, at the top of a rise, unmediated or unmodulated by trees or shrubbery: in Knight's words, "if in solitary pride it stand, / 'Tis but a lump, encumbering land, / A load of inert matter, cold and dead, / The excrescence of the lawns that round it spread" (221–224). When Knight, arguing that the improver demands that ". . . in your grand approach / Magnificence requires some sacrifice:— / As you advance unto the palace gate, / Each object should announce the owner's state" (*Landscape* 159–162), he refers specifically to one of Repton's "expedients for viewing the extent of property," which was to place "the family arms upon the neighbouring mile-stones" (12, 159n.).

Mansfield Park emphasizes Repton's focus on the owner's assets when Rushworth, discussing his friend's estate, exclaims that "The approach now is one of the finest things in the country" (53).

As in *Mansfield Park*, in which an ambition for landscape and human improvement signifies exploitation and in which Sir Thomas sets his progressive sights on Fanny, Emma also wants to make Harriet one of the "finest things in the country." "*She* would notice [Harriet]; she would improve her; she would detach her from her bad acquaintance, and introduce her into good society; she would form her opinions and her manners" (23–24), but Emma's plans, like the "low stone wall with high pillars, which seemed intended, in their erection, to give the appearance of an approach to the house, which never had been there," gesture only toward the Harriet that Emma, as imperial architect, wanted to build, but never constructed. The avenue, long associated in British culture with French absolutism, leads, breathtakingly, to "nothing; nothing but a view." Austen's irony here illuminates how a view is everything: opinion, insight, judgment, expanse. Rather than being "nothing," the view occupies the border between the body and mind: seeing, walking, thinking, imagining. In this, as in all the novels, imagination takes on a palpable physicality as illusions become embodied in stone-like "realities." But because "nothing" can also mean "noting," as in Shakespeare's *Much Ado About Nothing*, the line implies Austen's self-referential acknowledgment of how a view leads to the physical act of writing and thus to the idea of Emma herself as a novelist, creating courtships (like Austen does) in Highbury's miniature world. Further, the bawdy meaning of "nothing" suggests that for Emma, the "view" of Donwell Abbey leads to erotic fulfillment through her alliance with Knightley. The novel reveals that Emma marries happily and that her husband leaves his house to move into her own. Austen sets in context, however, how little power Emma has, when she explains that the heroine's "landed property . . . was inconsiderable, being but a sort of notch in the Donwell Abbey estate" (136). That detail questions whether in this match and in this society, Emma is anything more than a "notch"— slang for female genitalia, a definition Rachel Brownstein offered during her Keynote Address, "England's *Emma*," at The Annual General Meeting of the Jane Austen Society of North America in 1999.[22] Austen takes a sober look at courtship when she articulates through bawdy humor Emma's "lack": her lack of inheritance in land, lack of power, and lack of agency, despite the novel's insistence in its opening words that she is "handsome, clever, and rich" (5).[23]

The heroine savors Knightley's house as "just what it ought to be, and it looked what it was—and Emma felt an increasing respect for it, as the residence of a family of such true gentility, untainted in blood and understanding" (358). Austen's taste for the rambling picturesque might coincide with Emma's, but Emma's unreflecting point of view diverges from the author's: it does not follow that just because Donwell Abbey is for the heroine "just what it ought to be, and it looked what it was" Austen herself views it as "natural." I personally would agree with Emma that Donwell Abbey's "low and sheltered" situation and "its ample gardens stretching down to meadows washed by a stream" (358) are attractive and appealing, but doubt seriously that Austen gazes at such a scene without realizing its ideological implications. Every one of Austen's novels challenges assumptions such as "it was just what it ought to be, and it looked what it was": Marianne, Catherine Morland, Elizabeth Bennet, Emma, Anne Elliot—all struggle with the very fact that things are not what they ought to be and never look exactly like what they are.

CHAPTER 6

"UNBECOMING CONJUNCTIONS":
COMIC MOURNING AND THE FEMALE
GAZE IN *PERSUASION*

*Personal size and mental sorrow have certainly no necessary
proportions. A large bulky figure has as good a right to be in deep
affliction, as the most graceful set of limbs in the world. But, fair or
not fair, there are* unbecoming conjunctions, *which reason will
patronize in vain,—which taste cannot tolerate,—which ridicule
will seize.*

—68, emphasis added

Austen's unbecoming conjunctions—the odd, uncomfortable
juxtapositions she includes in all the novels—multiply and problema-
tize meanings by rendering each half of the conjunction absurd or
indeterminate at the same time; by thus emphasizing context and
point of view, they destabilize any ready access to firm judgments and
tidy truths. In all the novels, they provide a wry humor, but nowhere
so much as in *Persuasion*, in which, linked to mourning, they offset
the "autumnal" tone often attached to this narrative and instead
expose the paradoxical nature of grief: sometimes it is moving, sometimes comical, sometimes erotic, sometimes ridiculous, sometimes all
of those simultaneously. When the novel mentions that Dick
Musgrove, whose death before his twentieth year has earned him the
appellation "poor Richard," had "been nothing better than a thick-
headed, unfeeling, unprofitable Dick Musgrove, who had never done
any thing to entitle himself to more than the abbreviation of his name,

living or dead" (51), Austen introduces how subjective taste determines the integrity and veracity of bereavement. Dick was "scarcely at all regretted, when the intelligence of his death abroad had worked its way to Uppercross" (50–51). This sentence, which presents his death as the best part of his life, the most intelligent and hardworking point of his existence, provides a striking example of the large issue Austen addresses: what role does aesthetic appeal play in how and about whom one repines? When Dick's mother emits "large fat sighings" over his death, the novel asks if the mourner's tastefulness renders what has been lost valuable? In asking such a question, the text renders resolutions unstable, for it shifts the focus from accepting loss and striving to restore an object to an emphasis on the precariousness and subjectivity that loss engenders; here painful regret becomes subject to aesthetics and to the inability to resuscitate what is missing. To explore dejection, Austen employs various kinds of humor, from her signature use of physical ribaldry to her "decent" laughter, especially in surprising situations, such as her witty, disturbing, and thought-provoking juxtapositions between the low bawdy and Anne's lofty sorrow, and between the valorous Captain Wentworth and his disastrous tactical decisions on domestic, as opposed to foreign and military grounds. In forming unbecoming conjunctions between naval battles and erotic ones; between mutinies at sea and at home; in aligning "good" friends and "bad"; in juxtaposing "under-hung" and "well-hung" suitors; and in comically undercutting both the hero and heroine, *Persuasion* defies the truism that the lamenting body occupies a serious and sacred space, cordoned off from critique, eroticism, and humor.

ANNE AND MRS. MUSGROVE: THE THIN AND THE BULKY

When the novel opens, Anne has been grieving for most of her life, first for her mother, and then for the end of her engagement to Frederick Wentworth, whose return to her world after eight years' absence further intensifies and agitates her fervent emotions. Anne's anguish takes the form of self-recrimination, as she reproaches and reviles herself for having broken their engagement. To invoke Kristeva, Anne's loss "pulverizes [her] identity" ("Pain of Sorrow" 148). Wentworth nourishes these feelings of self-reproach and self-revulsion that manifest themselves in her sense of physical deterioration, one that leads her to believe that she deserves his contempt. Wentworth comments that Anne's appearance was "so altered he should not have known [her] again" (60). When told about this comment, the heroine reacts to his opinion by "fully submitt[ing], in silent, deep mortification. . . . [T]he years which had destroyed her youth and bloom had only given him a more glowing, manly, open look . . ." (60–61). By submitting to his opinion of her in "silent, deep mortification," she submits to her own "*morte*"—her own death.

Bewailing the lost becomes an aesthetic exercise when Anne builds upon Wentworth's comment that time has "altered" her: she imaginatively transforms her face into a ruin and Wentworth into the picturesque viewer who looks with nostalgia for the past in the rubble of the present landscape: "*Once* she felt that he was looking at herself—observing her altered features, perhaps, trying to trace in them the ruins of the face which had once charmed him . . ." (72). Robyn Warhol argues that "at no point in the novel does Anne take an unmediated look at her own body; her consciousness registers her appearance only through what others tell her about how she looks" (23). No one, of course, can register his appearance in an unmediated fashion, but Anne's filtering gaze reveals an unbecoming conjunction. Theatrically sketching herself as a ruin provides an unexpected result—though altered, she has become something worthy of the gaze, a touristic site suitable for a visit, an almost sublime object of *memento mori* that nevertheless provides aesthetic pleasure, her body functioning as a barometer of pain. Further, her wretchedness provides an opportunity to excite the senses when she provides music for dancing at Uppercross. Frederick asks his partner if Miss Elliot "never danced." Replying that Anne "has quite given up dancing. She had rather play. She is never tired of playing" (72), Louisa inadvertently introduces an ironic fusion between pleasure and woe in this image of Anne as a woman in grief—her eyes filling with tears—who "never tire[s] of playing."

This juxtaposition of misery and festivity—a despondent woman who entertains others without rest—uses comedy to examine the relationship between taste and sorrow and to test the reality of the "truth" of pain. In this party scene, in which Anne aches for lost love, Austen places her moving requiem for Wentworth in conjunction with Mrs. Musgrove's "large fat sighings" (68) for her dead son, the "unprofitable" Dick Musgrove (50). By setting these two sad figures side by side (once together on the same couch), Austen uses the sturdy physicality of bodies and their proximity to shift remorselessly back and forth between empathy for Anne and dismissal of Mrs. Musgrove. In an infamous proclamation, which I quoted at the beginning of this chapter, the narrator ruminates that "A large bulky figure has as good a right to be in deep affliction, as the most graceful set of limbs in the world. But, fair or not fair, there are unbecoming conjunctions, which reason will patronize in vain,—which taste cannot tolerate,—which ridicule will seize (68). Large bulky figures have "the right" to grieve, but the aesthetic judgment here suggests that such a body should not grieve. Other characters (Sir Walter, Elizabeth, Lady Russell, William Elliot) "cannot tolerate" unbecoming conjunctions arising from age or rank and so disgruntle readers; as this passage reveals, however, the novel itself focuses on the subject of physical appearance, even in the cordoned off, sacred state of mourning, in which everyone should be above reproach. Austen thereby broaches dangerous, because sacrilegious, territory in designating bereavement as an aesthetic event that is independent from or incongruent with the pathetic, such as is found in mid- to later-eighteenth-century paintings and the theories of Shaftesbury and Hutcheson (Paulson, *Breaking* 229).

The bulky Mrs. Musgrove looks preposterous grieving, and, to her family, Anne's grief looks ridiculous because it has aged her before her time. Without question, one sympathizes with Anne and disagrees with her relations' judgments of her, yet if Mrs. Musgrove's "large fat sighings" (68) depict her heartache as humorous (because tasteless), why don't Anne's musings on the "ruins" of her face appear absurd? In other words, if Mrs. Musgrove contaminates the sanctity of Anne's losses and puts her melancholia in serious danger of looking ridiculous, so should Anne's own regret, rendered meaningful in the novel, elevate Mrs. Musgrove's. In turn, if Mrs. Musgrove's monody is risible, perhaps Anne's is as well. Significantly, when Mrs. Musgrove begins to cry for this "worthless" son, it is Wentworth who comforts the mother, sitting down, notably enough, between them on the couch. The three of them form a visual tableau that introduces a series of further unbecoming conjunctions between Anne and Mrs. Musgrove and also between the "unfeeling," though now dead, sailor and the brave Captain, who, in contrast, is worth grieving for. Richard Payne Knight makes the observation that the ridiculous "seems indeed to be always lying in wait on the extreme verge of the sublime and pathetic; . . . the damp of a single low word or incongruous circumstance is sufficient to sink into meanness and ridicule the most lofty imagery, or pathetic effusion expressed otherwise in the most dignified and appropriate terms . . ." (*Analytical Inquiry* 422). Knight's comments reinforce Austen's point that subjectivity influences the aesthetics of mourning, rendering them unpredictable for both griever and observer.

More widows and widowers appear in *Persuasion* than in all of Austen's novels: out of eighteen adult characters, six have dead spouses, including Benwick, whose fiancée died; perhaps Anne should be included as well, given that she has immolated herself after having lost her chance at marriage to Frederick.[1] Such an emphasis allows Austen to explore one common form of loss in the nineteenth century, and to probe how the "quality" of their sorrow arises from subjective determinations: in particular, the question of how long grief should last or how it should be expressed. For example, Lady Russell avows that Mr. Elliot's sepulchral rituals have gone on quite long enough and, hoping to see Anne married to him, she begins "to calculate the number of weeks that would free him from all the remaining restraints of widowhood, and leave him at liberty to exert his most open powers of pleasing" (159). In contrast, the Harvilles feel that Benwick has not mourned quite long enough. Even before the miniature of him that had been intended for his now-dead first fiancée, Fanny, is "properly set," Captain Benwick is already engaged again and so will give the portrait to his new bride, Louisa Musgrove. In *Psychosocial Spaces*, Steven Gores argues that one can "trace the rise of the voyeuristic power of the miniature's owner to a compensating decline in the power of the sitter. Thus, although the portrait miniature originates as a representation of a particular individual, it is drained of direct reference to that individual and becomes instead a sign of the owner's taste in beauty and control over the erotic. In this way, the sitter is rendered virtually anonymous to all but the owner . . ." (152). I disagree with this idea in general terms but also in specific reference to how the miniature portrait functions in *Persuasion*. Austen presents an inversion of this power relationship when she highlights how easily exchangeable a bride is and how effortlessly Benwick transfers his image to various owners, rendering them "virtually anonymous." As both the sitter and the owner, he commands both the fate of his body and the representation of it. In another way of calling attention to the subjectivity of mourning, Austen also elides the varying functions of the portrait miniature as an object symbolizing personal loss and erotic value, insofar as the portrait, meant for one wedding, becomes associated with death, only then to be recycled for another bride. The miniature most certainly does not have the same impact on Benwick that Godwin describes in his *Essay on Sepulchres*: "I cannot love my friend, without loving his person. It is in this way that every thing which practically has been associated with my friend, acquires a value from that consideration; his ring, his watch, his books, and his habitation. The value of these as having been his, is not merely fictitious; they have an empire over my mind . . ." (22–23). For Benwick's disappointed friend, Harville (also the brother of the dead fiancée), this all happens too fast: "Poor Fanny! She would not have forgotten him so soon!" (232). Giving a present to one woman that was intended for another and interpreting the period of mourning for a dead wife in terms of certain conventional "restraints," as Lady Russell does, represent further unbecoming conjunctions that imply that neither man was or will be quite the loving husband any woman might want.

Austen directs questions about unbecoming acts of mourning to Anne herself, as the novel ponders whether the heroine's lamentation is ridiculous or at least has been nurtured for a ridiculously long time. On the walk to Winthrop, an event ripely caricaturizing both eros and thanatos, Anne bears pain from watching the lovers play at loving, and receives "*pleasure* . . . from the view of the last smiles of the year upon the tawny leaves and withered hedges, and from repeating to herself some few of the thousand poetical descriptions extant of autumn, that season of peculiar and inexhaustible influence on the mind of taste and tenderness . . ." (84). This bathetic reference to "the last smiles of the year" and to the fact that there are a "thousand poetical descriptions" of autumn ironically transform Anne's reverie and depression into an aesthetic construct by placing her afflictions within the context of the multitude—she joins another of the thousands who have associated their own loss with this season. Laughing at the other walkers, sympathizing with Anne, but also smiling at her hackneyed description of an autumn day influence our emotional response to this scene as Anne courageously, though perhaps misguidedly, attempts to detach herself from complete absorption in pain as she "occupied her mind as much as possible in such like musings and quotations . . ." (84).

As the contemplative figure in this picturesque landscape, Anne's presence here, as in Wentworth's eyes earlier, becomes a *memento mori*. She banishes herself and lets others banish her into the "distance": on this walk, her "object was, not to be in the way of any body, and where the narrow paths across the fields made many separations necessary, to keep with her brother and sister" (84). In a compressed way, this visual tableau turns to both past and present, future and foreground, middle ground and background as it recalls her decision to terminate her engagement and acquiesce to her family's desires: literally "to keep with her brother and sister"— thereby becoming a kind of autumnal object for elegy and, with her family, to die out. Austen thus offers a series of small deaths and little reincarnations as the scene sways back and forth between meaning and banality, sorrow and comedy.

Mrs. Smith and Mrs. Clay: The Ill and the Freckled

A subtle instance of a conjunction wherein one event's implications spread unchecked like a nasty virus to the other half involves the unbecoming pairing of the two widows, Mrs. Clay and Mrs. Smith, who Anne herself couples intimately. When she disgusts her father by visiting "A widow Mrs. Smith, lodging in Westgate-buildings!— A poor widow, barely able to live, between thirty and forty—a mere Mrs. Smith, an every day Mrs. Smith, of all people and all names in the world, to be the chosen friend of Miss Anne Elliot. . . . Mrs. Smith, such a name!" (158), Anne silently leaves it "to himself to recollect that Mrs. Smith was not the only widow in Bath between thirty and forty, with little to live on, and no sirname of dignity" (158). Since Anne's father has no intention of doing so, the burden of yoking Mrs. Smith and Mrs. Clay falls to the reader. Such a link provides two obvious conclusions: it demonstrates the poor, crippled, yet dignified Mrs. Smith's superiority to the poor, sycophantic Mrs. Clay, and it highlights how a flattering widow has captivated the self-absorbed Sir Walter.

Besides these obvious conclusions, what might the juxtaposition of two widows divulge? Early on, Austen foreshadows much of what circumstances later reveal about Mrs. Clay's villainy. When Mr. Shepherd tries to persuade Sir Elliot that he should rent Kellynch Hall to one of the "rich Navy Officers" (17), home now after the Treaty of Paris, Mrs. Penelope Clay supports her father's point when she exclaims that she has "*known* a good deal of the profession; and besides their liberality, they are so neat and careful in all their ways!" (18, emphasis added). In giving these words of "fine naval fervour" (167) to Mrs. Clay, Austen makes a ribald joke at the character's expense in order to reveal that she poses a serious threat to the family: not just intermarriage with a low adulator, but the contaminating presence of London morals, though nobody knows this until the novel's conclusion.[2] In a letter to *The Times Literary Supplement* in 1983, Nora Crook points out that Mrs. Clay's frequent use of Gowland's lotion, ostensibly applied to control her freckles, and "to be had . . . of every Vender in the United Kingdom,"[3] was also utilized to treat venereal disease since it contained mercury. And although it is unlikely that the future Sir William Elliot, heir to Kellynch Hall, would take a syphilitic bride, Austen does associate this character with the *demimonde* early in the novel, foreshadowing her eventual end, "established under [Mr. Elliot's] protection in London" (250), a living situation that establishes her as a paid inamorata. The novel offers some pungent details about Penelope's emotional and physical persuasions—her "abilities," "affections," "cunning," "wheedl[ing]," and "caress[ing]"—that will induce Mr. Elliot to marry her. To be sure, by the end, the novel has oiled the path for assuming that she has enjoyed "a good deal" of male company (that noble profession notwithstanding) and that her comment about the Navy's liberality implies that they pay well in all kinds of respects and that their ability to be "neat and careful in all their ways" puns on their ability to avoid venereal disease.[4] Thus, whether she has "known a good deal of the Navy," by the end of the novel, she has most certainly "known" William Elliot.

Will "taste tolerate" any link between Mrs. Clay, a woman whose future career lies in high-class prostitution, and Mrs. Smith, an invalid whom Anne feels has an "elasticity of mind, [a] disposition to be comforted, [a] power of turning readily from evil to good, and of finding employment which carried her out of herself, which was from Nature alone" (154)? Taste may not tolerate any such connection, but the novel, nevertheless, suggests one, for Mrs. Smith is willing, like Mrs. Clay, to victimize the Elliot family. How "double a game" (250) they both play becomes clear when it emerges that Mrs. Smith's fortune in the West Indies, recoverable if Mr. Elliot would take the time, is necessary to her, and thus so is her alliance with Anne, whom she envisions as the future Lady Elliot.[5] When she thinks that Anne wavers from marriage with Mr. Elliot because "it is a thing of course among us, that every man is refused—till he offers," she pleads his case: "But why should you be cruel? Let me plead for my—present friend I cannot call him—but my former friend. Where can you look for a more suitable match? Where could you expect a more gentle-manlike, agreeable man? Let me recommend Mr. Elliot" (196). Mrs. Smith's worldliness here, her brash premise that Anne spor-tively plays a conduct-book inspired game such as the one Collins imagines for Elizabeth, her cynical determination that no other man so "agreeable" could ever be found, and her triumphant illumination that Anne's only deterrent to marriage is that Mr. Elliot's wife has not been dead long enough ("Oh! If these are your only objections") all culminate in the rosy but self-mystifying contention that Anne's "peace will not be shipwrecked as [hers] has been" (196).

Once she discovers that Anne will not marry Elliot, her arch cosmopolitanism rapidly shifts to a melodramatic declaration of his villainy as she, in a speech that sounds like a parody of sensibility's war against knavery, describes the man she said was "suitable" for Anne. He is

a man without heart or conscience; a designing, wary, cold-blooded being, who thinks only of himself; who, for his own interest or ease, would be guilty of any cruelty, or any treachery, that could be perpetrated without risk of his general character. . . . Those whom he has been the chief cause of leading into ruin, he can neglect and desert without the smallest compunction. He is totally beyond the reach of any sentiment of justice or compassion. Oh! he is black at heart, hollow and black! (199)

To be sure, although she remains one of Mr. and Mrs. Wentworth's best friends, Mrs. Smith proves (to turn her own words about Elliot against her) to be a "designing, wary . . . being, who thinks only of [herself]" (199). In answer to Anne's surprise that having known how "hollow" Elliot was, her friend could "hav[e] spoken of him so favourably" (211) and been so enthusiastic about a possible marriage between Anne and Elliot, Mrs. Smith replies,

My dear, . . . there was nothing else to be done. I considered your marrying him as certain, though he might not yet have made the offer, and I could no more speak the truth of him, than if he had been your husband. My heart bled for you, as I talked of happiness. And yet, he is sensible, he is agreeable, and with such a woman as you, it was not absolutely hopeless. He was very unkind to his first wife. They were wretched together. But she was too ignorant and giddy for respect, and he had never loved her. I was willing to hope that you must fare better. (211)

This constitutes a remarkably specious act of self-defense, complete with her pretended empathy ("my heart bled for you") and her justification of Elliot's unkindness (a man she has described as "totally beyond the reach of any sentiment of justice or compassion") at the expense of another woman, his first wife, who, her words imply, "deserved" such treatment because she was unrespectable and unloved. Her remark that Elliot "is sensible, he is agreeable," recalls the nonsensical language in the Juvenilia, in which Austen parodies the gap between word and meaning in the fashionable world. What can it mean to be "sensible" and "agreeable" if one is "cold-blooded" and "unkind"? Mrs. Smith's sophistries here echo both Mrs. Clay's readiness to marry either of the Elliot men, depending on who bids the highest, and Elliot's easy willingness to transfer his affections from Anne to Mrs. Clay. When Mrs. Smith rationalizes to Anne, "My dear, . . . there was nothing else to be done," she parrots Elliot's refusal to help Mrs. Smith recover her property in the West Indies: "Mr. Elliot would do nothing . . ." (211, 210). The widow, who had led an expensive and dissipated life, "think[s] differently now; time and sickness, and sorrow, have given [her] other notions" (201); however, her behavior introduces a new worry: are her rules of conduct any stricter now than they were when she lived for "enjoyment" (201)? In this unbecoming conjunction, Mrs. Smith apes the bawd and Mrs. Clay the prostitute. The novel's penultimate paragraph explains that Wentworth has recovered Mrs. Smith's property in the West Indies, and in doing so, has "fully requited the services which she had rendered, or ever meant to render, to his wife" (252). In that phrase, "or ever meant to render," Austen punctuates the ambiguity of the nature of those "services": were they the true stories she revealed to Anne about Elliot or were they the kindness Mrs. Smith "meant" to render when she thought Anne and Elliot were engaged, but was unable to do so "because there was nothing else to be done" (211)?

CAPTAIN WENTWORTH AND MR. ELLIOT: THE WELL-HUNG AND THE UNDER-HUNG

In this novel, those who experience "the torment of trying for more" (21), as Mrs. Clay suggests, in any way whatsoever—either through work or emotional connection or suffering—are doomed to register such effects on their face, are indeed unable to "hold the blessings of health and a good appearance to the utmost" (21). Anne is faded, Mary has a "red nose" (142), all sailors' complexions are "mahogany" (20), and Sir Walter observes that while walking the streets of Bath, "one handsome face would be followed by thirty, or five and thirty frights" (141). No other Austen novel focuses so exclusively on faces and bodies: freckles, wrinkles, furrows, blooming and blushing cheeks, fine military figures, and handicaps such as sandy hair or unfortunate jawlines.

Sir Walter, an archetypal dandy, invests in "women's" interests: vanity and physical desirability. "Once, as he had stood in a shop in Bond-street, he had counted eight-seven women go by, one after another, without there being a tolerable face among them" (141–142). Sequestered in a warm shop, surrounded by the pristine and timeless materials of consumption, he gazes through the glass to those out in the sharp "frosty morning" (142). As Sir Walter assesses the sexual appeal of both women and men and registers his own desirability in the faces of others, Austen conjoins images of death and polymorphous eroticism in this Baudelairian moment turned to hectic comedy:

> "[T]here certainly were a dreadful multitude of ugly women in Bath; and as for the men! they were infinitely worse. Such scare-crows as the streets were full of! It was evident how little the women were used to the sight of any thing tolerable, by the effect which a man of decent appearance produced. He had never walked any where arm in arm with Colonel Wallis, (who was a fine military figure, though sandy-haired) without observing that every woman's eye was upon him; every woman's eye was sure to be upon Colonel Wallis." Modest Sir Walter! He was not allowed to escape, however. His daughter and Mrs. Clay united in hinting that Colonel Wallis's companion might have as good a figure as Colonel Wallis, and certainly was not sandy-haired. (142)

The passage allows for the existence of the female gaze, as "every woman's eye" ogles Colonel Wallis and Sir Walter, or at least allows for the latter's psychic inability to function without that appreciative look, even if he has only imagined it. Austen's repeated use of the term "tolerable" places beauty or lack of it within the category of the only bearable, of experiences at the perimeters of survival, and predicates meaningful existence on youthful aesthetic magnetism. The use of the word "scare-crow" recalls that in the nineteenth century, the fashion for a higher body fat content arose from the persistence and threat of famine, and that the unattractive eighty-seven women and numerous men who swarm by Sir Walter's gaze come to seem like the dead multitudes passing before Dante's eyes in the *Inferno*. Sexual appeal, and its inevitable link to fertility, exist here to deny the threat of death.

Hogarth's *Morning*, from *The Four Times of the Day* (1738), which makes an important appearance in *Tom Jones*, a novel Austen read, provides a possible frame for this episode (figure 6.1). In the print, an older woman crosses Covent Garden Square to attend St. Paul's. Her low-cut gown, three-quarter sleeves, and dancing hair ribbon seem absurd in the frosty early morning and suggest that she attends prayers to make a male conquest: in the later words of Dr. Fordyce: "never, perhaps, does a fine woman strike more deeply, than when, composed into pious recollection, . . . she assumes, without knowing it, superiour dignity and new graces . . ." (qtd. in Wollstonecraft 94). On her way into the church she passes prostitutes being violated on the street and

Figure 6.1   William Hogarth, *The Four Times of the Day: Morning* (1738). Courtesy: Upton House, The National Trust Photo Library.

drunken revelers leaving Tom King's Coffee House. Her skimpy dress links her to the prostitutes, and her little page, with his left hand thrust into his coat jacket, mirrors the rake thrusting his left hand into the prostitute's bodice; the common effort of securing the means to be "warm"—sex and money—connects all four intimately. The older woman replicates the "frights" Sir Walter sees while on his walk, but also duplicates him, an aging man obsessed with a youthful, sexually appealing appearance, and links his eyeing, flirting, and appraising of both women and men to the market in human flesh the print strikingly depicts.

Sir Walter's fears about the connections between age, invisibility, and the fertile continuance of his family bloodline colors his appraisal of Elliot's appearance: he extols "his very gentlemanlike appearance, his air of elegance and fashion, his good shaped face, his sensible eye," but, at the same time, "must lament his being very much under-hung, a defect which time seemed to have increased" (141). Here the presence of William's defect—his projecting lower jaw—doubles as a reference to his sexual appeal, which correlates to his inadequacy in perpetuating a thriving Elliot line. In this sense, Austen inverts any correlation between sexual virility and social class, a point I will develop below with regard to Captain Wentworth. In the *The Political Unconscious*, in a discussion of *La Vieille Fille*, Fredric Jameson argues that

> The function of the sexual comedy is essentially to direct our reading attention toward the relationship between sexual potency and class affiliation. Our assumption that it is the former which is the object of this particular game of narrative hide-and-seek is in fact the blind or sub-terfuge behind which the otherwise banal and empirical facts of social status and political prehistory are transformed into the fundamental categories in terms of which the narrative is interpreted. (163)

Austen uses what Jameson calls the "bonus of pleasure" in her sexual allusion in order to critique class, in particular the aristocracy. She participates in this joke insofar as the novel associates Sir Walter, Elizabeth, and William with the sick and ailing "scarecrows" of that dying and corrupted class.

In a later scene, Austen revisits this theme in unforgettable fashion when Anne, traveling with Lady Russell in Bath, sees Wentworth across the street. Now on the verge of reconciliation with him, Anne anxiously wonders how her guardian will react to him; but Lady Russell does not acknowledge that she has seen him and focuses on a different topic.

> At last, Lady Russell drew back her head.—Now, how would she speak of him? "You will wonder," said she, "what has been fixing my eye so long; but I was looking after some window-curtains, which Lady Alicia and Mrs. Frankland were telling me of last night. They described the drawing-room window-curtains of one of the houses on this side of the way, and this part of the street, as being the handsomest and best hung of any in Bath, but could not recollect the

exact number, and I have been trying to find out which it could be; but I confess I can see no curtains hereabouts that answer their description." (179)

This event functions as a displacement of Lady Russell's earlier rejection of Wentworth—his poverty prevented her from seeing his intrinsic worth; here again, she cannot see him because she fixes her eyes on the literal materials (curtains)—those that are the handsomest and best hung of any curtains in Bath—which function as a metonymy for her fixation on material wealth. It is also possible that she may have seen Wentworth, and instead chooses to focus on the curtains, covering up her reactions as a window curtain covers the means of viewing and being viewed: "Anne sighed and blushed and smiled, in pity and disdain, either at her friend or herself" (179).

An instance of heterodox wit, the curtains—"the handsomest and best hung in all of Bath"—metonymically evoke Wentworth's body. "Best hung" implies well-hung, which as early as 1667, the OED explains, was used to mean "decorated with rich hangings or tapestry, suspended or attached so as to hang well—that is a window-sash" as well as from 1611 to mean "furnished with large pendent organs; a man who has large genitals." Austen's use of this term corresponds to Freud's notion of the joke as a "displacement of the psychical emphasis on to a topic other than the opening one"; "it depends not on words but on the train of thought" (Jokes 51, 52). Displacement occurs on two levels in this scene: first, although we initially attend, like Lady Russell, to the curtains, a train of association leads next to thinking about Wentworth's body: in particular, his sexualized body. Second, a feminist point of view discloses the limitations of Freud's comic theories. Austen's joke here disturbs our rigid expectations of the direction one might assume her humor should take. "Getting" the joke reveals an unexpected view of her humor's full range and also of the way in which ideological blinders interfere with following that "train of thought."[6]

This joke reveals the possible influence of Sterne's Tristram Shandy (1760–1767), one of Austen's favorite novels and one that Park Honan explains "she knew intimately and that offered some of the most valuable models of narrative tactics she found" (120). The earlier novel offers a sustained play on both the slang term and its connection to windows when Sterne describes Tristram's inadvertent circumcision: "Susannah did not consider that nothing was well hung in our family,—so slap came the sash down like lightening upon us . . ." (Tristram Shandy 264). In the "who sees who" passage from

Persuasion that I quoted above, Austen desacralizes social constructions when she, a proper lady, candidly gestures toward the pleasures a woman can take in canvassing the male body, a banquet Austen also allows other characters to enjoy. In *Sense and Sensibility*, when Willoughby enters Barton cottage carrying Marianne, "the eyes of both [Elinor and Mrs. Dashwood] were fixed on him with . . . a secret admiration which . . . sprung from his appearance" (42). Austen's joke about Wentworth's body, as well as the vigilance paid to men's figures throughout her novels, makes sense from another point of view: early nineteenth-century male fashion, as Anne Hollander points out, "laid most stress on sexual attraction. Calf- or ankle-length pantaloons, close-fitting as tights . . . [were] usually very light in color and worn with shiny black boots"; the high, dark waistcoats, "cut away horizontally across the front with tails behind, . . . very much increased the visual importance of the male body from knee to the waist, with particular emphasis on the genital region" (*Seeing* 225–226). Further, "naval and military uniform during this same period was admirably suited to the rather sexually empathic display of men's bodies. . . . Between the gleaming short-waisted coat . . . and the glittering boots was a soft, creamy expanse of pale, tight-fitting doeskin" (*Seeing* 228).

More than Wentworth's creamy doeskin leads Anne to "thoroughly comprehend the sort of fascination he must possess over Lady Russell's mind, the difficulty it must be for her to withdraw her eyes, the astonishment she must be feeling that eight or nine years should have passed over him, and in foreign climes and in active service too, without robbing him of one personal grace!" (179). Anne's gaze, as Robyn Warhol argues, provides a "sourc[e] of unprecedented power for the heroine" (27); however, I have to disagree when she contends that "the heroine's one blunder of perception occurs in a scene [just quoted] where she herself is too absorbed in watching another woman's gaze to understand what is happening" (31). Instead, it seems to me that Anne here sees vividly and acutely from her own point of view; her "blunder" occurs in assuming that Wentworth possesses a "sort of fascination" for the widow, that Lady Russell will *delight* in gazing at the Captain's erotic charms, when in fact the opposite is so. The widow earlier objected to more than Wentworth's middling indigence, eschewing his sexual ardor and masculine confidence for Mr. Elliot's less virile attractions:

> full of life and ardour, [Wentworth] knew that he should soon have a
> ship, and soon be on a station that would lead to every thing he wanted.

He had always been lucky; he knew he should be so still.—Such confidence, powerful in its own warmth, and bewitching in the wit which often expressed it, must have been enough for Anne; but Lady Russell saw it very differently.—His sanguine temper, and fearlessness of mind, operated very differently on her. She saw in it but an aggravation of the evil. It only added a dangerous character to himself. He was brilliant, he was headstrong.—Lady Russell had little taste for wit; and of any thing approaching to imprudence a horror. She deprecated the connexion in every light. (27)

Here, as in the joke about being "well hung," Wentworth's body becomes the inscripted site of his physical passion and power—he is sanguine, which means optimistic but also full of blood—a man who desires his "ship" (gendered female) and the "station" that would lead to fulfillment.[7] Further, from a historical perspective, Austen links Wentworth (and the Navy in general) to a conception of physical and moral sinew that was, as Tim Fulford argues, a "myth of national character" dependent on "chivalric virtues . . . such as patriotism, self-reliance, courage, paternalism, and, above all, attentiveness to duty" ("Romanticizing" 163, 162). In particular, Wentworth's masculine prowess differentiates him from the feminizing inherent in aristocratic and colonial life that Sir Walter and Mr. William Elliot personify. Anne believes Lady Russell should be "astonished" that time—and even time passed in "foreign climes"—has not divested him of "one personal grace" (179). Finally, his ambition links him, as Fulford notes, to the "middle-class backlash" against "aristocratic immorality," a backlash that led to a "redefinition of the social and political order [that] relocated chivalric ideals from the aristocracy to the gentry and to the growing professional classes" (170–171).

Austen integrates the riddle in *Emma*, the "tumbling" in *Sense and Sensibility*, and the "making" in *Mansfield Park* into their respective novels; this is true, as well, for the "joke" about the well-hung Wentworth and the under-hung Mr. Elliot. Peter Brooks points out how "narratives in which a body becomes a central preoccupation can be especially revelatory of the effort to bring the body into the linguistic realm because they repeatedly tell the story of a body's entrance into meaning" (8). The narrative about the body, in this case, Wentworth's, "imprints it as a sign"—here the "sign" of masculinity and desire (Brooks 8). Austen's joke highlights the point where Wentworth's physicality becomes the site of Lady's Russell's resistance and Anne's subsequent loss and rekindled desire. As Lady Russell's fear and ideologies are all wittily condensed into the symbol of the handsomest and best-hung curtains in all of Bath, it is no wonder that she cannot "find what she is looking for," although Anne has found what suits her perfectly. Significantly, even though the male body "is the norm, [it] is veiled from inquiry, taken as the agent and not the object of knowing; the gaze is 'phallic,' its object is not" (Brooks 15). Here Austen inverts the power relations of courtship that Sir Walter had earlier established (warm and god-like, looking through a window judging women's appearances) as Anne pictures Wentworth's physique. Pivoting the norm, Austen turns the male body into the object of knowing. This is especially important in *Persuasion* where "to get the first look" at someone enables a character to exert tremendous power over another and to establish his or her own self-protection. As Anne says, "the part which provoked her most, was that in all this waste of foresight and caution, she should have lost the right moment for seeing whether he saw them" (179). In describing Wentworth's magnetism—his ardor, sanguine nature, brilliance, and wit—Austen links sexual energy to humor while also delineating the "bewitching" qualities of her own prose (27). Unlike Lady Russell, Austen embraces the delights of intoxicating wit and the wittily erotic.

TURNING HEADS AND BROKEN HEADS

In *Persuasion*, war provides Austen with some of her funniest unbecoming conjunctions as she dramatizes battles, mutinies, and injuries on the home front in a comic, miniature manner.[8] Intensifying feelings, the pressures of war tend to relax social rituals: celebrating with the Harvilles at Lyme, Anne delights in how Wentworth's presence introduces a "bewitching charm in a degree of hospitality so uncommon, so unlike the usual style of give-and-take invitations, and dinners of formality and display" (98). Austen also uses war imagery to flesh out representations of amorous love. Talking to Anne in a platonic, but nevertheless emotionally charged tone about gender and feelings, Harville, smiling, says he is in "very good anchorage . . ., well supplied, and want[s] for nothing" (234). In the next, decidedly unplatonic moment, Wentworth gives Anne a letter "with eyes of glowing *entreaty* (236, emphasis added); and then French politics are internalized, when "the revolution which one instant had made in Anne, was almost beyond expression" (237). Later Wentworth's jealousy is "vanquished" (241): under Anne's "irresistible governance" he "seized a sheet of paper, and poured out his feelings" to her (241). Once "free from the horror and remorse attending the first few days of Louisa's accident," he realizes that the community considers them engaged; responding like a prisoner of war, "he feels himself, though alive, not at liberty" (242); frustrated "to be waiting so long in inaction" (243), the Captain of a man-of-war is rendered passive by domestic entanglements.

The novel suggests that war also unsettles and makes supple rigid expectations of gender roles. When Anne feels she has been "stationed quite long enough" at Uppercross, the novel enforces her role there as an officer in command of a particularly disorderly crew (63). Admiral Croft asserts that if it were wartime, Frederick would have decided between Louisa and Henrietta "long ago" (92) and thereby implies that peace threatens to unman the British male. Wentworth needs, in his brother-in-law's words, to "spread a little more canvas, and bring us home one of these young ladies to Kellynch" (92). Charles Musgrove, a bit skeptical of Captain Benwick's rather delicate air, nevertheless asserts that the sailor has "fought as well as read" and that he is "a brave fellow"; his example of Benwick's valor, however, comically undercuts the compliment when he explains that the two of them "had a famous set-to at rat-hunting all the morning, in my father's great barns; and he played his part so well, that I have liked him the better ever since" (219). That women can become masculine, or, put another way, can assert their reason in times of war emerges in Mrs. Croft's assertion that women "may be as comfortable on board, as in the best house in England" and that women are "rational creatures" and not all "fine ladies" (69–70). Courting several women at a time, the Captain wages an eroticized battle on the home front that diminishes his stature. When the young people walk to Winthrop, Anne sees Wentworth and Louisa in the hedgerow, "making their way back, along the rough, wild sort of channel, down the centre" (87). Here in difficult "waters," the Captain navigates the aptly named Louisa—a parodic French monarch, who proclaims, "When I have made up my mind, I have made it."

Unbecoming conjunctions abound: the great Captain, reduced to navigating a miniature French "ship" down a hedgerow, in turn places Anne in an absurd position, for while the couple converses, Anne, sitting on a bench, "feared to move, lest she should be seen. While she remained, a bush of low rambling holly protected her . . ." (88). Anne, close to the earth, pressed near and shielded by the hedgerow, blends into the landscape as if she were a plant or an animal, camou-flaged into invisibility. Martial and erotic imagery coincide to offer a mock battle in which sides are drawn and terms decided: failure arises from a "yielding and indecisive . . . character," and triumph, absurdly enough, is associated with a firm, unpunctured "hazel-nut" (88). And in a moment of private indulgence, he flatters Louisa while thinking about Anne, as he makes an inadvertently comic analogy: " 'let those who would be happy be firm. . . . . To exemplify,—a beautiful glossy nut, which, blessed with original strength, has outlived the storms of autumn. Not a puncture, not a weak spot any where . . .' " (88). Yet, while empathizing with Anne, the novel also places her in a ridiculous situation, when the pontificating Wentworth, however obliquely, contrasts Anne to a nut, limning her as the less attractive of the two. In the aesthetics of mourning, this comparison offers another example of an "unbecoming conjunction, which reason will patronize in vain,—which taste cannot tolerate,—which ridicule will seize" (68). By aestheticizing these bereavements, Austen acknowledges war's domestic impact while also providing distance from the scene, for as they stand surrounded by the hedgerows that effaced the "originally" picturesque landscape, Louisa and Wentworth reiterate the loss of that pre-enclosed land by discussing the horrors of mutability.[9] Their travels down the channel allude to the changes in the countryside that the war in part had necessitated. A new round of landscape enclosures, achieved through the planting of hedgerows, helped finance the Napoleonic wars; thus the English sailor and the French monarch proceed down the backbone, as it were, of the barriers cultivated to enclose the land. Land enclosures thus symbolize Anne's own deprivations—losing Wentworth and her youth—while reinforcing the domestic consequences of foreign wars.

As I argued in my analysis of their travels to Winthrop, Austen subjects mourning to aesthetic criteria. In the episode at Lyme, she describes loss and longing by rendering the environs of the city in lush and sensuous terms, only later to have them provide the backdrop for another humorous parody of erotic sedition.

> The scenes in its neighbourhood, Charmouth, with its high grounds and extensive sweeps of country, and still more its sweet retired bay, backed by dark cliffs, where fragments of low rock among the sands make it the happiest spot for watching the flow of the tide, for sitting in unwearied contemplation;—the woody varieties of the cheerful village of Up Lyme, and, above all, Pinny, with its green chasms between romantic rocks, where the scattered forest trees and orchards of luxuriant growth declare that many a generation must have passed away since the first partial falling of the cliff prepared the ground for such a state. (95–96)

The passage moves rhythmically between outer, extensive views and inward, retired bays, between high grounds and low rock, between cheerful extroversion and contemplative introversion. The exuberant, voluptuous beauty of the scene, with its "green chasms between romantic rocks, where the scattered forest trees and orchards of luxuriant growth," arises from the passing of time, an idea that contradicts Sir Walter's association of vitality with youth, and with regular and predictable forms of beauty. Yet, even (or perhaps because of it) this death-in-life landscape becomes the setting for a comic mutiny.

Anne may turn heads in Lyme, but Louisa breaks hers. Wentworth, mourning for Anne, displaces his sexual energy onto Miss Musgrove, whose intoxicated steeplechase after him leads to her erotic "death," the consequence of wanting to be "jumped" again and again. Though by no means a joke, Louisa's fall, her near death, her serious concussion, and her consequent change of personality are rendered with salty wit. Elizabeth Bennet uses her own physical prowess and volition to jump over stiles on her walk to Netherfield; Louisa, though, "in all their walks" demands that Wentworth do the work: "he had had to jump her from the stiles; the sensation was delightful to her" (109). Since "all their walks" include the ones at Uppercross as well as Lyme, Wentworth has offered Louisa two months worth of "delightful" physical activity. And once a day is not enough: "instantly, to shew her enjoyment, [Louisa] ran up the steps to be jumped down again." Jumping "ship," Louisa mutinies against her Captain even though "he advised her against it, thought the jar too great; but no, he reasoned and talked in vain; she smiled and said, 'I am determined I will:' he put out his hands; she was too precipitate by half a second, she fell on the pavement on the Lower Cobb, and was taken up lifeless!" (109).

From the seventeenth century on, the term "to jump" referred to sexual intercourse. Shakespeare, for example, uses the expression to mean "To coit athletically and vigorously with (a woman)" (Partridge, *Bawdy* 129). In *The Winter's Tale*, a servant explains that a peddler "has the prettiest love-songs for maids; so without bawdry, which is strange; with such delicate burthens of dildos and fadings, 'jump her and thump her' " (IV.iv.193–195). In *Persuasion*, being "jumped," falling on one's head, and dying provide a network of allusions that all singly and polyphonically refer to sexual activity, the loss of virginity (she has lost her maidenhead), and orgasm. Gordon Williams records that the 1793 edition of Shakespeare's plays gives an erotic reading of "head": when Falstaff has "his poll clawed like a parrot" (*2 Henry IV*, II.iv.281) by "the whore seated on his lap, [it] represents a recognized amatory caress, . . . probably borrowed from 'the French, to whom we were indebted for most of our artificial gratifications' " (153–154 Steevens, qtd. in Williams).[10]

I am suggesting that Austen acknowledges Louisa's enthusiastic sexual desires and finds the bawdy allusion funny, not that the author implies that this jumping substitutes for any real hanky-panky between Wentworth and Louisa. Miss Musgrove's enjoyment of such physical sensations almost leads to her physical death and in some literal way does kill her vitality and high spirits, but the event's comic tone and the later treatment of Louisa's recovery from concussion, undermines the notion that Austen draws a stern lesson from her ardent, though imprudent, physicality and the "sad catastrophe" (126) of her subsequent injury.

Admiral Croft reinforces the conjunction of comedy, violence, sensuality, and sorrow explicit in this episode when he puns that Louisa's jumping and fall announce "a new sort of way this, for a young fellow to be making love, by breaking his mistress's head! . . . This is breaking a head and giving a plaister truly!" (126–127). Here, the Admiral refers to an old pun still current in the nineteenth century: to be hurt in the head signified to be cuckolded.[11] Austen thus finds humor in all the pain from lost love that the novel records: in "jumping" Louisa for two months, Wentworth has also been deceiving the suffering Anne, since he still loves her; Anne herself had earlier been disloyal to Wentworth by obeying her family; and Louisa "cuckolds" Wentworth when she transfers her affections to Benwick during her recovery. Breaking her head, or losing her maidenhead, becomes another joke here (what a way to make love by hurting her). In his reference to "giving a 'plaister,' " the Admiral uses, according to Patricia Meyers Spacks, "a proverbial expression, meaning that someone both gives and remedies an injury" (*Persuasion* 83, n1.). Here this expression works as a low witticism insofar as pleasure follows pain in coitus with a virgin. Understanding the meaning of a correlating expression— "plaister of warm guts"—further clarifies the Admiral's *double entendre:* the phrase, current between the seventeenth and mid-nineteenth century referred to "one warm belly clapped to another; a receipt frequently prescribed for different disorders" (Grose 1811), one common "disorder" being a man's need for a woman.[12]

Louisa's psychophysical reactions to her fall—her "head . . . was exceedingly weak, and her nerves susceptible to the highest extreme of tenderness" (129)—lead her to a state of hypersensitivity in which she wants quiet and can no longer process information at the same speed as she could before her fall. These side effects demonstrate that Austen knows the clinically correct symptoms arising from a blow to the head. Head injuries, although common, were, as Alan Richardson explains, "a politically loaded topic" since they revealed "the tense co-existence, in Austen's day, of two diametrically opposed yet equally credible notions of mind–body relations, one . . . dualist[,] . . . the other open to a materialist interpretation" (99, 101). Austen nevertheless renders Louisa's "new" personality and her new choice for a husband as rather absurd and thereby laughable.[13] How interesting then, in an unbecoming conjunction, when Anne, having just read Wentworth's declaration of love, suffers briefly from the same symptoms:

> Every moment . . . brought fresh agitation. . . . The absolute necessity of seeming like herself produced then an immediate struggle; but after a while she could do no more. She began not to understand a word they said, and was obliged to plead indisposition and excuse herself. . . . Would they only have gone away, and left her in the quiet possession of that room, it would have been her cure; but to have them all standing or waiting around her was distracting, and in desperation, she said she would go home. (238)

Austen connects the power of love with that of a head injury, uncannily emphasizing and undermining both through the words of the foolish Mrs. Musgrove, "who thought only of one sort of illness," [and] "could part with [Anne] cheerfully" only after "having assured herself, with some anxiety that Anne had not, at any time lately, slipped down, and got a blow on her head" (238).

"Tastelessly" conjoining a traumatizing fall and falling in love has the significant effect of emphasizing the heroine's somatic reactions and demonstrates how her body records her emotions. Austen takes a feminist stance when she reanimates Anne's and (to a lesser extent) Wentworth's bodies throughout the course of *Persuasion*. She makes buoyant what Teresa de Lauretis calls the "dynamic" at the "heart of subjectivity: a fluid interacting in constant motion . . . open to alteration by self-analyzing practice" (110, qtd. in Alcoff). Grief had turned Anne's body, in Cixous's words, "into the uncanny stranger on display—the ailing or dead figure, which so often turns out to be the nasty companion, the cause and location of inhibitions. Censor the body and you censor breath and speech at the same time" ("Laugh" 312). Once home from Lyme, Anne reflects on the "[s]cenes [which] had passed in Uppercross, which made it precious. It stood the record of many sensations of pain, once severe, but now softened; and of some instances of relenting feeling, some breathings of friendship and reconciliation, which could never be looked for again, and which could never cease to be dear" (123). In this Wordsworthian "spot of time,"

Anne understands through her body, through the "sensations of pain"; she knows friendship through its "breathings," as she embodies an abstraction in a life force—breath—that frees her physically and psychologically. In describing Laurence Sterne's writing, Anna Laetitia Barbauld contends that "[i]t is the peculiar characteristic of the author, that he affects the heart, not by long drawn tales of distress, but by light electric touches which thrill the nerves of the reader who possesses a correspondent sensibility of frame" (*Works*, III, 134, qtd. in Van Sant 94). Van Sant says of this passage that "[i]t would be impossible for Barbauld to separate the physiological from the psychological effects of language" (94). This melding of the physiological and psychological is precisely what characterizes the language in *Persuasion*.

Though the process of liberating their breath and speech starts when they are at Lyme, it accelerates when Anne and Wentworth converse before the concert in the Octagon Room begins. Entering the building, Wentworth "was preparing only to bow and pass on, but her gentle 'How do you do?' brought him out of the straight line to stand near her, and make enquiries in return, in spite of the formidable father and sister in the back ground" (181). Her speech curves the "straight line"—the inflexible, the unforgiving direction—he pursues. Because her back is to her family, she "knew nothing of their looks" (181), and beyond their censoring gaze, the one that had driven Anne and Wentworth apart, she summons her breath, her speech, and her body, an act which conjures his own physical response, "a little smile, a little glow" (181). In turn, his passionate declaration that "a man does not recover from such a devotion of the heart to such a woman!—He ought not—he does not" (183), decants Anne's body into the open: her cheeks had already begun to "redde[n]"; now she enters a state of sensuous hyperawareness: "Anne, who, in spite of [Wentworth's] agitated voice . . . and in spite of all the various noises of the room, the almost ceaseless slam of the door, and ceaseless buzz of persons walking through, had distinguished every word, was struck, gratified, confused, and beginning to breathe very quick, and feel an hundred things in a moment" (183).

CONCLUSION

Austen's multiple iteration of the courtship plot has drawn criticism from feminist critics who interpret her as endorsing only one possible outcome for her heroines: marriage. Her novels do end in marriage; however, the way that Austen demonstrates a shift of power from

Wentworth to Anne suggests a strong assertion that the basis of a happy marriage arises from the affirmation of a woman's physicality and mind—her body-consciousness. When Mrs. Croft discusses the interference of parents in their children's engagement (thus reminding Anne of her own melancholy past), the heroine feels "a nervous thrill all over her, and at the same moment that her eyes instinctively glanced towards the distant table, Captain Wentworth's pen ceased to move, his head was raised, pausing, listening, and he turned round the next instant to give a look—one quick, conscious look at her" (231). Here the pair exists in a euphonic moment of physical and mental synchronicity when Wentworth's "pen ceased to move." Later, when Anne claims to Harville that because men go to war, they cannot have tender feelings since "it would be too hard indeed" (233), Wentworth overhears her empathetic comment, causing him to disturb the conversation with the sound of his "pen ha[ving] fallen down" (233). These emotional and kinetic exchanges are full of yearning, yet poised perfectly at the torqued instant just before Anne and Frederick return full circle to their former intimacy.

These brief minutes, nevertheless, also momentarily unman the sailor no longer at war. The ceasing and the falling of the pen signal the Captain's loss of the physical prowess that made him rich and powerful. In doing so, Austen empowers her heroine. Thus, when Tony Tanner states that he is "not concerned with possible phallic interpretations of 'the pen': literalness is quite powerful enough here" (241), he overlooks the level of subversion at which Austen works. The phallic significance functions as part of a network of sexual allusions that supports the critique Tanner offers: "Wentworth at this critical moment has, however inadvertently, dropped (let go of, lost his grip on) that instrument which is at once a tool and a symbol of men's dominance over women: the means by which they rule women's destinies, literally *write* (through inscription, prescription, proscription) their lives" (241). At this intimate instant, Austen opens wide all of these ramifications of the "pen" and she does so in a way that engages body / bawdy humor; in Cixous's words, which I quoted above, she "break[s] up the 'truth' with laughter" ("Medusa" 316), that is, the truth that men have, to requote Tanner, written women's lives. As Captain Harville argues, there is a "true analogy between our bodily frames and our mental" (233). He uses this point to assert that men, therefore, have the strongest feelings because they have the toughest bodies; Austen, however, neutralizes his gender bias by reinvigorating Anne's health and vitality. Now physically stronger,[14] Anne's breath and speech also strengthen: while "apparently occupied in admiring a fine display of green-house plants, . . . she said—I have been thinking over the past, . . . and I must believe that I was right, . . . that I was perfectly right . . . in submitting to [Lady Russell]" (246). The Navy captain capitulates: "I shut my eyes, and would not understand you, or do you justice" (247). After writing his letter to Anne, he "placed it before [her] with eyes of glowing entreaty" (236); now, here, in the final "battle" of the novel as they canvas their past, he admits to her that he was wrong, and figuratively signs the marital peace "treaty" that exonerates her from error, embraces her with affection, and allows them to marry on a foundation that her conscientious decisions—and not his lingering resentment—have built.

CONCLUSION

Laughter is a vital factor in laying down that prerequisite for fear-lessness without which it would be impossible to approach the world realistically.[1]

A*usten's Unbecoming Conjunctions: Subversive Laughter, Embodied History* highlights Austen's interest in the body, popular culture, material history, and subversive linguistic play. The unbecoming conjunctions between her spontaneous delight in absurdity and her social criticism reveal that the humor in all her novels frequently provides an outlet for her hostility toward ideologies that dominate women. Her humor, that is, can be purposely aggressive or "tendentious." Freud asserts that "to the human psyche all renunciation is exceedingly difficult, and so we find that tendentious jokes provide a means of undoing the renunciation and retrieving what was lost" (*Jokes* 101). Joking, thus, "circumvents" censorship—the obstacle that stands in the way of satisfaction—by disguising "lustful or hostile" instincts and then satisfying those instincts in a way that society permits. In Freud's opinion, "women's incapacity to tolerate undisguised sexuality, an incapacity correspondingly increased with a rise in the educational and social level" provides the impediment (*Jokes* 101). He illustrates the limits of applying male-oriented critiques to women's humor, especially for Austen's bawdy humor. Her transgressive comedy isolates such biased ideology and maneuvers its borders through a humor that voices unacceptable expressions about sexuality and gender politics.

All of Austen's works show how rules for female behavior take form in the body and, in giving them a mass, make palpable what is often invisible. Her work manifests how "[t]he body is at once the most solid, the most elusive, illusory, concrete, metaphorical, ever present and ever distant thing—a site, an instrument, an environment, a singularity and a multiplicity" (Turner 8). By incorporating tiny, often trivial domestic items such as miniature portraits, quilled baskets, and amber crosses to show how her society couples marriage and money, her novels reveal how the self interacts with and depends on material environments. In this book, I have worked to imitate Austen's miniaturizing by showing how small details, such as riddles and locks of hair, open up her texts to larger worlds as they elucidate historical moments. To be sure, the miniature, like Austen's work in general, has been associated with the reminiscent, the domestic, and the unpolluted; however, I have examined in her ivory surfaces a historical, "physical," and disquietingly funny Jane Austen, one whose incorporation of humor and fleshly sundries provides her with the opportunity to examine in dazzling ways the performance and construction of the "natural"—constructions of the body, gender, landscape, identity, courtship, and love.

Bawdy allusions to getting one's hair cut, perilous carriage rides, well-hung curtains and gigs, tumbling and spraining ankles, rears and vices, mending pens, and frozen maids are simultaneously outrageous and funny, but they are also deeply wed to protests against patriarchal privilege, and they address contemporary historical notions of masculine and feminine identities. Austen denounces the unequal ratio between male freedom and female constraint, a ratio founded on men's entitlement. Laughing at the insufficiency and poverty of values such privilege represents, Austen renders doctrines, in the moment of laughter, instances of nonbeing, momentarily nullifying the power of ideology. But sometimes, too, her jokes appear just for the sake of diversion. Like the person who crashes witlessly into a lamppost, Mr. Woodhouse and other comic figures in these novels are funny.[2] Nor does she, in the end, spare herself, for she acknowledges the irony of the fact that, though fully aware of the dark side of courtship (think Willoughby, think Collins, think Mrs. Percival), she also joins the roster of Cupids who raise these "flames" in her devising of the courtship plot itself.

I have been engaged here in the work of recovery. To be sure, language—including the language of material objects—evolves, and the effects of that evolution include confusion and loss of meaning. On the one hand, this means that when a student reads that Emma, shut up in a carriage with Elton, finds the clergyman "making violent love to her," he or she must be instructed that, no, Jane Austen, in this example at least, did not mean *that*. But much else in Austen's lexicon has also altered, and in the other direction, and the full range of nuance available to her and her first readers can be better appreciated with a serious effort to recover linguistic registers now lost. Samuel Johnson points precisely to the nature of the problem in his edition of *Hamlet*. Claudius refers to Polonius's secret burial as a ceremony done in "hugger-mugger," and Johnson, in a note, points out that all the modern editions that he has consulted remove the original phrase and replace that Elizabethan coinage with a more transparent "in private." He then laments,

> That the words now replaced [that is, "hugger-mugger"] are better, I do not undertake to prove; it is sufficient that they are Shakespeare's: if phraseology is to be changed as words grow uncouth by disuse, or gross by vulgarity, the history of every language will be lost; we shall no longer have the words of any author; and, as these alterations will be often unskillfully made, we shall in time have very little of his meaning. (996)

The bowdlerizing of her letters aside, no editor has, of course, replaced Austen's words. Problematically, however, words that are familiar to modern readers do not necessarily signify just what they might think, and so Austen's meanings, like Shakespeare's, have often been lost.

Austen integrates into all her fiction pleasurable and unabashed inscriptions of a subjectivity that is fully embodied, an embodiment that is at the foundation of her art, and not something incidental or anomalous. W. H. Auden wrote that "Beside her Joyce seems innocent as grass."[3] Austen's comedies of the flesh may sometimes shock, but they shock because she wanted them to, as she exposes a multitude of worlds, some of them unsavory indeed, within the well-known worlds of courtship and marriage. By laughing, and while laughing, she does after all really mean *that*.

NOTES

INTRODUCTION: DID JANE AUSTEN
REALLY MEAN *THAT*?

1. *The Novels of Jane Austen*, edited by R. W. Chapman. Further references from Austen's novels are to this edition and are included in the text.
2. Claudia Johnson forged a new direction for Austen studies in *Jane Austen: Women, Politics, and the Novel*. I am deeply indebted to her work as well as to that of William H. Galperin, *The Historical Austen*, Deidre Shauna Lynch, *The Economy of Character: Novels, Market Culture, and the Business of Inner Meaning*, and Mary Ann O'Farrell, *Telling Complexions: The Nineteenth-Century English Novel and the Blush*. That said, different concerns do shape my project. O'Farrell and I share a central focus on the body in Austen, though we tend to move in dissimilar directions about the kind of somatic work this novelist performs; while O'Farrell commits herself to an understanding of the blush as an expression of pleasure, she also analyzes it in subtle Foucauldian terms as a regulatory device. Lynch's book places Austen at the capstone of her ambitious study of the relationship between the novel's development and economic change; in this context, she demonstrates how the kind of "characters" associated with the novel (individuals with depth) emerge as a way for people to accommodate themselves to a new and commercialized world. I share with her an interest in the play between surface and depth in characters, and my focus on material objects opens an avenue, I hope, for further exploration of how Austen uses things to foster a sense of inwardness for the characters in her fiction. Another valuable book on Austen, by Clara Tuite, discusses Austen as a Romantic writer and, therefore, focuses on issues like canon-formation and her present-day reception; I share her conviction that Austen lives during the Romantic era, but also participates in this era's concerns, and my study explores several ways to place her in that tradition. Galperin's work, the most recent, investigates, as I do, social history and the history of aesthetics.
3. Regina Barreca, culling the work of many feminist interpreters of comedy, argues that female wit is radical insofar as the one making jokes is a woman. More "revolutionary," "anarchic," and "apocalyptic" than men's humor, women's wit depends on "disunity and disharmony" in its aim to destroy, not renew "established patterns" (16, 18, 19, 22).

Eileen Gillooly, on the other hand, argues that women's comedy forges a bond between humorist and victim. Instead of a Hobbesian "sudden glory" at another's misfortune, she claims that women's humor exists in a kind of expanse like the one D. W. Winnicot describes: a transitional space of creative play where "Law is suspended, anxiety kept at bay, and desire is safely mediated" (27–28).

4. Notable exceptions include Alice Chandler's important article, " 'A Pair of Fine Eyes,' " and Claudia L. Johnson's "What Became of Jane Austen? *Mansfield Park*." Less extended discussions appear in Edward Neill, Grant I. Holly, Jan Fergus, Robert Polhemus, and Alison G. Sulloway.

5. A. J. Dezallier d'Argenville (1712) explains that this word stems from the French term "Claire-voie, or an Ah, Ah." According to the *OED*, the derivation is from the "ha!" of surprise.

6. For the purposes of this study, I have chosen to use an edition from 1776, assuming that if the family owned this manual they might have received or purchased it around the date of Mr. and Mrs. Austen's marriage (1764).

7. Hamilton's *Family Female Physician* of 1793 is the first American edition.

8. The many dictionaries and glossaries that I consulted when researching the bawdy double meanings in circulation during Austen's time include those of Farmer and Henley, Grose, Thomas Hamilton Haddington, Henke, the indispensable Eric Partridge, and the *OED*. In his *Jane Austen's English*, K. C. Phillipps does not treat bawdiness; he does discuss what he calls "the vulgar," but his concerns there are matters of class and grammatical correctness.

9. Ballaster sees Austen's *Lady Susan* (ca. 1793) as "a paradigm of the fate of the woman writer of early amatory fiction in a newly moralistic order" (210). Austen's bawdy humor, however, suggests that if *Lady Susan* represents such a paradigm, then Austen herself did not continue to feel as confined as Ballaster indicates.

10. See *Parodies of the Romantic Age* for the entire poem (I, 92) and for Graeme Stones's note on the Shakespearian allusion (I, 302, n. 39).

11. Many thanks to my colleague, the classicist Professor Peter Knox, for this translation.

12. Christian Huygens (1629–1695) was a Dutch mathematician, astronomer, and physicist.

13. The footnote explains that the Parabola is the "curve described by projectiles of all sorts, as bombs, shuttlecocks, & c" (Ver. 107, in *Parodies* 177).

14. These are aptronyms, a word coined by Franklin P. Adams for a name that is suited to its owner. <http://www.m-w.com/lighter/name/aptronym.htm>.

15. The "Old Woman" is identified as Mrs. Priscilla Nevil in July 1798. It is unclear whether the autobiography provided is authentic, as Edward W. R. Pitcher points out (263).

16. As Graeme Stones points out in *Parodies of the Romantic Age*, "Pitt's disinterest in women had long been a source of innuendo" (I, 299, n. 21).

17. Deidre Lynch, in *The Economy of Character*, discusses a related phenomenon, the popularity of novels in the eighteenth century, such as *The Adventures of a Guinea*, which take a piece of money as their point of view character; see 94–102.

18. As Leslie Adelson argues in *Making Bodies, Making History*, "embodiment," which is "crucial to any feminist enterprise," denotes a process of "making and doing the work of bodies—of becoming a body in a social space" (xiii).

19. Another example of this bawdy meaning of "tail" comes from Garrick, who tells the following story: "Some sailors, and their ladies were playing at what are my thoughts like? A lady . . . asked 'why do you say that Admiral Keppell is like a shrimp?' 'Because . . . I knew that his *head* is good for nothing, and your sister there says, that his *tail* is not worth a straw' " (*Garrick's Jests* 88).

20. For example, see John Halperin's biography of Austen, where he characterizes the narrator's comments about Dick and Mrs. Musgrove as "gratuitously harsh, shockingly cruel and malicious" (305).

21. For Higonnet's use of the term "metissage" see Françoise Lionnet.

1 BEJEWELING THE CLANDESTINE BODY/BAWDY: THE MINIATURE SPACES OF *SENSE AND SENSIBILITY*

1. "On Genuine Wit." *The Lady's Monthly Museum* (May 1807): 216–217. David Nokes shows that Austen was aware of this new journal since "her mother had lately subscribed to [it]." In fact, as he suggests, the title of this novel could have arisen from the magazine's inclusion of the "bold headline," "Sense and Sensibility" (174).

2. Women were often paid for painting in miniature and working and setting hair. And though men usually employed and managed women, these were two professions where women could have their own businesses (Bury 41).

3. Seals were made for women, but they were associated with men for the obvious reason that they were used to seal letters, but also because ornate jewelry for men had almost gone out of style after 1789. Thus, their accessories might consist of pins set with jewels that fastened shirts or colorful seals, sometimes worn in bunches (see Clare Phillips 62).

4. The pun between the words heir and hair was still current in the mid-nineteenth century. See, e.g. the parody of Lord Lytton's "The Rightful Heir," entitled, *The Frightful Hair; or, Who shot the Dog?* An Original Travestie on Lord Lytton's "The Rightful Heir." (Both play and parody were written and produced in 1868.) The heir, Vyvian,

cries out "Wreckcliffe before we dine, if you've a pair / Of scissors, you may trim my Frightful Hair" (41).

5. Alison Sulloway argues that "the oblique contrast between Marianne, a genuinely tender if foolish and solipsistic virgin of seventeen, and Pope's painted Belinda, who knows all the arts of avoiding actual seduction while enjoying its preludes, cannot be accidental. Belinda's "two locks, which graceful hung behind," did so, "to the Destruction of Mankind," whereas Marianne's "long lock," which "tumbled down her back," did so only to her own near destruction (Sulloway 45).

6. In my opinion, Austen treats the discourses of sense and sensibility with great subtlety and does not favor one over the over. Critics on this issue have argued that Austen critiques sensibility (Butler, *Romantics* 104 and Dussinger 96); endorses it (Neill 32 and Brodey 114); and/or that readers have misunderstood her subtle treatment of what only seems to be her didactic binary between sense and sensibility (Waldron 66 and Seeber 223, 228).

7. Here, Sheumaker is writing about hair jewelry in the mid-nineteenth-century United States.

8. See e.g., Fielding's *Tom Jones* where Sophia Western keeps her money in her "little gilt pocket book" (447), and Scott's *Redgauntlet* where Darcy Lattimer keeps his silver in his pocket book (35, 177, 182).

9. Juliet McMaster notes this gender inversion: when Willoughby reflects Marianne's preferences in books and music, his "taste is only reflective, as a woman's desire is meant to be. Austen has reversed the stereotype again[.] . . . He becomes Marianne's echo and duplicate" (181).

10. See the "Panomimical Drama," *Obi; or, Three-Fingered Jack* for another contemporary example of this ancient association of hair with magic. The Advertisement includes a description of "The Science of Obi," which creates a spell "for the purpose of bewitching People, or cursing them by lingering illness, . . . made of Grave Dirt, Hair, Teeth of Sharks, and other Animals . . ." (Arnold 4); in the play's finale, the soloist explains that the Obi bag contains "Tom cat foot[,] pig tail, duck beak" (*Slavery* 5:213).

11. Although figure 1.6 is a mourning ring—see information around the rim ("Died 12 Sep.: 1791")—this detailed photograph shows how the hair was plaited, or braided, and how difficult it would be to determine whose hair it was. For another example of a ring with plaited hair, see the ring in figure 1.2.

12. Analyzing the ring as the "primary analogue to the letter-as-artefact . . . which . . . prefigures the subsequent failure of correspondence within the novel," Nicola Watson writes that "in being capable of sustaining more than one reading, the ring signals its inauthenticity, an inauthenticity made possible by its status as artefact . . ." (87).

13. Compare this nineteenth-century longing for the authentic hair to the recent work of the artist Jordan Baseman, who celebrates the

anonymity that arises from the hair he orders from wholesale suppliers (Malbert 116).

14. In 1803, the painter Albin Roberts Burt advertised "Miniatures on Ivory for 3, 5, and 10 Guineas each" (qtd. in Coombs 98).

15. Publications instructed a lady on how to design her own jewelry or decide on a pattern she liked. See William Halford and Charles Young, Manufacturing Jewellers, *The Jewellers' Book of Patterns in Hair Work.* (1864) and William Martin, *The Hair Worker's Manual* (1852).

16. This basket, like Robert Ferrars's toothpick case, has no useful purpose. As James Thompson says of the toothpick case, it "serves as an ostentatious example of emulative spending, a product that has no imaginable function beyond the lavish display of wealth.... During this early stage of incipient commodification, Austen recognizes ... that 'fantastic form of a relation between things' as an encroachment of exchange over use value ..." (37).

17. That Lucy is expected to work filigree by candlelight, something even Lady Middleton acknowledges is hard on the eyes, and that this work is linked to the labor of courtship, provides an excellent example of James Thompson's observation that "in this period young women seem to have had to endure the duties, responsibilities, and blame of courtship, without much of the benefits. We can draw a general analogy between women working toward marriage and the laboring classes. The latter may eventually have benefited from the industrial and capitalist revolutions, but nevertheless, in the period when patriarchy was disintegrating, so was the sense of moral responsibility, and with the loss of responsibility went all the patronizing institutions of patriarchy. As a consequence ... between 1790 and 1820 ... for the laboring classes, conditions became much worse before they became better.... Austen focuses on this period in which the working conditions, as it were, declined for young women engaged in the work of courtship" (148).

18. Claudia Johnson discusses how "[t]he most striking thing about the tales of the two Elizas is their insistent redundancy. One Eliza would have sufficed as far as the immediate narrative purpose is concerned, which is to discredit Willoughby with a prior attachment. But the presence of two unfortunate heroines points to crimes beyond Willoughby's doing, and their common name opens the sinister possibility that plights such as theirs proliferate throughout the kingdom" (*Jane Austen* 57). And D. A. Miller asserts that the many cases of mistaken identities in the novel suggest that "It is as though events were asserting an interchangeability that threatened to obtain among the three men and between the two sisters" (67).

19. As Erin Mackie notes, in the eighteenth century "The new ideal masculine character is a domesticated man who ... is by no means a beau or a pretty fellow" (192).

20. In contrast, Susan Morgan asserts that "though Willoughby does come right out of the tradition of villainous seducer, that is exactly not

the point of his relations with Marianne. Willoughby betrays Marianne, but not sexually" (45).

21. Edward Neill alludes here to Balibar and Macherey's discussion of the novel (Neill 42).

22. See Mary Evans who argues that "The semi-fantastical figure of Willoughby who emerges out of the woods to rescue Marianne is a figure who eventually reveals himself to have been created by Marianne's dreams and romantic aspirations . . ." (*Jane Austen* 40); Mary Lascelles rightly contends that Marianne "has built out of her favourite books an illusionary world which will not hold actual people. There is room in it for the simulacrum of Willoughby which her love has created" (65).

23. I agree with Jocelyn Harris in "Burden of the Male Past" that this scene sounds Miltonic: she interprets Marianne's "fall" in the context of "Austen's cal[m] and confiden[t] appropria[tion] [of] Milton's . . . *Paradise Lost*"; however, I disagree that Willoughby plays "the parts of both Satan and Adam" (89).

24. In contrast, Juliet McMaster points out that Marianne's sloppy dressing renders her "conventional" in the tradition of the "careless desolation of the melancholy lover" (126).

25. Contrast this to Maaja A. Stewart, who contends that "Colonel Brandon's vision of his cousin Eliza . . . absolves her of moral responsibility for her own actions" (79). I agree with Poovey that Eliza's story "begins and ends in her infidelity to Brandon; only as an extension of this does her infidelity to her husband matter, only as the origin of his pain does Eliza's unhappiness figure. The weakness of this woman—of her sexual abandon—are 'natural,' according to Brandon" (96). Important here is Galperin's convincing argument that Brandon "micromanage[s] the progress of the characters in his sway" and that includes withholding information that "expose[s] Marianne to almost certain risk" (117, 116).

26. Contrast my reading to Mary Evans's, who finds Eliza culpable: Willoughby's statement, she argues, offers evidence of Austen's feminism, in that it "reveals [her] perception of sexual behavior as a construct in which woman are far from the passive victims of male desire" (*Jane Austen* 84), and to Susan Morgan's, who exonerates Willoughby, arguing that "we are not finally allowed to think of Willoughby as a seducer. We cannot categorize him as a villain or a hero, just as a badly educated young man with a certain charm" (45).

27. Partridge says this meaning appears in the mid-nineteenth century, but the play suggests an earlier origin. For example, the play contains several references to "meat" and "flesh" in a sexual context, and Mercutio, the deliverer of the Queen Mab speech, is responsible for several of them: see II.iv.131–136, where he speaks of "An old hare hoar" is "very good meat in lent / But a hare that is hoar / Is too much for a score, / When it hoars ere it be spent." Also see

II.iv.37–44, where Mercutio describes Romeo thus: "Without his roe, like a dried herring: O flesh, flesh, how art thou fishified! Now is he for the numbers that Petrarch flowed in. Laura, to his lady, was but a kitchen-wench—marry, she had a better love to be-rhyme her; Dido a dowdy; Cleopatra a gipsy; Helen and Hero hildings and harlots; Thisbe a grey eye or so, but not to the purpose." The joke here is "roe" as "sperm"—and Mercutio thinks Romeo still loves "Ro-saline," who has unmanned him with love. Thanks to Katherine Eggert for help in the glossing of sweetmeat.

28. Mary Lascelles points out that "the good-humoured worldling, Mrs. Jennings, [has a] crude raillery [that] comes at length to seem almost like frank common sense set over against Marianne's excessive sensitiveness and reticence" (158).

29. Contrast this to Claudia Johnson's observation that "Charlotte, to [her husband's] perpetual annoyance, is too vacuous to feel [the] sting" of his "abuse" (*Jane Austen* 54). I argue here for volition on Charlotte's part and collusion between the husband and wife.

30. Trumpener is here quoting Stella Gibbons's *Cold Comfort Farm* (20).

2   THE ANXIETIES AND "FELICITIES OF RAPID MOTION": ANIMATED IDEOLOGY IN *PRIDE AND PREJUDICE*

1. John Wiltshire argues that we "glimpse, in the violence of [Mrs. Bennet's] emotions, in the volubility of her discourse, in the unnuanced, coarse vibrations of her presence, a great deal of . . . sexual energy" (183).

2. Nokes points out that Austen "found some amusement in all the scandalous stories surrounding [Lord] Nelson's relationship with Lady Hamilton" (295). See also the discussion of Emma Hamilton's "attitudes" in relation to Austen in Honan (163–164).

3. For a different interpretation of this scene, see O'Farrell, who focuses on what she calls the "erotics of embarrassment," and sees a kind of pleasure in Elizabeth's "mortification" (21–22).

4. This phrase comes from Austen's *Lesley Castle*, in a scene in which Margaret describes her sister-in-law, who had so "openly violated the conjugal Duties" by eloping with "Danvers & dishonour" (110). Nokes says that the "prospect of marriage had clearly brought Cassandra none of those gloomy apprehensions of domestic dullness and 'conjugal duties' that Eliza so dreaded" (164).

5. Perry may be correct that sexual disgust was an eighteenth-century invention, but Austen's novels provide evidence that the female characters experience this phenomenon. In *Sense and Sensibility*, Marianne exhibits disgust for Brandon, and Elinor physical repulsion for Robert Ferrars while she watches him pick out a toothpick case; in

Mansfield Park, Fanny Price reacts to Crawford and Maria Bertram to her husband with revulsion.

6. Contrast my reading to Julia Prewitt Brown's point that in *Pride and Prejudice*, "we have only the disembodied voices of wife and husband clashing in an empty space" (66).

7. For the association between the pen and penis, see Judith Mueller, who discusses *The Case of Impotency, As Debated in England*; this was the "best-selling 1719 reprint of the early seventeenth-century trial in which the Lady Frances Howard sued her husband, the Earl of Essex, for divorce on the grounds of impotence. There, the Lord Chamberlain speculates, 'That, perhaps, the Father's Sin' (the older Earl had been beheaded as a traitor) 'was punish'd upon the Son: [and] That it was Truth, that the Earl had no Ink in his Pen' " (Mueller 87).

8. Austen's use of the name "Strephon" recalls a popular song, "The Shepherdess *Lerinda's* Complaint," by Walter Overbury: Lerinda complains that Strephon is dull until she is "kind" to him, then "Such strange alteration as will her confute, / That *Strephon's* transported, that *Strephon's* transported / That *Strephon's* transported and grown more acute" (VI 85). This song is reprinted in *Wit and Mirth: or Pills to Purge Melancholy*, a facsimile reproduction of the 1876 reprint of the original edition of 1719–1720. Thus, though the song is from an earlier era, its reprinting history suggests that these songs remained popular for over 150 years.

9. Once bribed, Mrs. Younge reveals Wickham's and Lydia's address, which the novel never discloses.

10. Hazlitt uses this phrase in *The Spirit of the Age* (1825): "From the sublime to the ridiculous [in *Don Juan*] there is but one step. You laugh and are surprised that any one should turn round and *travestie* himself" (241).

11. For an excellent reading of the interrelated issues of Lydia, embarrassment (or its lack), and sexuality, see O'Farrell, who discusses how "the text that engenders embarrassment offers and teaches as a pleasure indulgence in mortification's textually modulated pain" (20).

12. Harriette was a mistress to Lord Craven, the patron of Tom Fowle, Cassandra Austen's fiancé. Whether Austen had met Harriette Wilson is unclear; Tom Fowle's cousin, Eliza Fowle, did and told her about it: Eliza "found [Lord Craven's] manners very pleasing indeed.—The little flaw of having a Mistress now living at Ashdown Park, seems to be the only unpleasing circumstance about him" (Le Faye 71).

13. Austen may be making an ironic joke when she names the shy Miss Darcy after the cosmopolitan Georgiana Cavendish, Duchess of Devonshire. See Stephen Derry, "Two Georgianas: The Duchess of Devonshire and Jane Austen's Miss Darcy."

14. This passage occurs in a section that addresses whether a man can tell if a woman is a virgin; this example gives the woman the benefit of the doubt.

15. Eliza de Feuillide took the lead role. Nokes points out that "Eliza loved [the character of] the lascivious officer, Colonel Britton, who lusted after a nunnery full of 'soft, plump, tender, melting, wishing, nay, willing girls' " (95).

16. Here Lamont refers to Austen's famous letter of May 12, 1801, in which she records having seen an adulteress (actually her cousin) at a party (Le Faye 85).

17. February 4, 1813. This is the famous letter (quoted in its entirety at the end of this chapter) in which Austen describes *Pride and Prejudice* as "light & bright & sparkling" (203).

18. My point differs somewhat from Mary Poovey's suggestion that the strategy of doubling allowed women writers the "opportunity not only to dramatize the negative counterparts of the heroine's perfect qualities but also play at different roles, to explore . . . direct actions forbidden to the more proper lady" (43). She suggests that, in Austen, "apparent polarities" give way to "myriads of possible combinations, each understood in terms of costs and benefits, sacrifices and opportunities" (44).

19. Contrast this to Galperin, who (without using the word) discusses a kind of doubling between Elizabeth and Lydia (representatives of individual expression) and Darcy and Lady Catherine (aristocrats, and upholders of a conservative order). For Galperin, these parallel characters frustrate the attempt to find a stable ideology in the novel, since each pair contains a representative who makes their ideology look good, and one who makes it look bad (*Historical* 136).

20. On seeing Lydia as a decoy see, e.g., Claudia Johnson, *Jane Austen*, 76.

21. For a slightly different point, see Mary Poovey: "Jane Austen unintentionally echoes the values of individualism when she assigns to individual women the task of correcting the moral wrongs of an entire class if not of society as a whole. However, her heroines's limited accomplishments and the fairytale quality of her novels' conclusions suggests that Austen senses, at some level, the futility of this 'solution' " (28).

22. Susan Staves's research on pin money explains why a woman's use of her independent resources was politically fraught insofar as laws controlled what a wife could do with them. She quotes Samuel Richardson who complains in Johnson's *Rambler* (97) about pin money, which "makes a wife independent, and destroys love, by putting it out of a man's power to lay any obligation upon her, that might engage gratitude, and kindle affection" (2:158). See Staves's *Married Women's Separate Property in England, 1660–1833* (159). Elizabeth remains both independent and affectionate.

23. Waldron makes the excellent point that this letter reveals how the novel is "primarily an experiment in new possibilities in fiction rather than the vehicle for any moral or didactic purpose" (60).

24. See Joseph Litvak who argues that Austen's "fits of disgust" also refer to her repugnance at the novel's conformity to the ideological expectations of heteronormative romance: "For if the novel functions discreetly and thus all the more efficaciously as a kind of conduct book, the good manners and good taste it works to implant operate in the service of a eugenic teleology of *good breeding*: that is, of the marriage plot, whereby the traditional novel idealizes heterosexuality and its reproduction" (22).

3   FASHIONING THE BODY: CROSS-DRESSING, DRESSING, UNDRESSING, AND DRESSAGE IN *NORTHANGER ABBEY*

1. Bermingham bases this interpretation in part on a passage from *Northanger Abbey* that satirizes the high moral tone often used in denouncing interest in fashion: "Dress is at all times a frivolous distinction, and excessive solicitude about it often destroys its own aim. Catherine knew all this very well; her great aunt had read her a lecture on the subject only the Christmas before . . ." (*NA* 73). Austen treats this philippic ironically.

2. In this long passage, of which I am only quoting one line, Austen's satirical tone mimics that of the didactic "Old Woman," whose "column" appeared in many issues of the *Lady's Monthly Museum*. In March 1799, e.g., in "On subject of female dress," she contends that "Men, whose approbation females court, are less dazzled by splendour than they are charmed by consistency. She who affects more than her situation permits, will never be the object of their sincere regard" (212).

3. Blaise Cendrars wrote this poem for the fashion designer Sonia Dellauay (Wilson, *Defining Dress* 3, quoting Jennifer Craik).

4. This essay was published in March 1800, at a point when Austen could still have been working on *Northanger Abbey*, since it was not sold until 1803.

5. For example, see Mary Waldron (Henry "has . . . problems of his own" (28)) and Claudia Johnson (*Jane Austen* 37). Harry Shaw argues against the idea that Tilney is "a perfectly centered, enviably efficient bearer of a male discourse of power" (152).

6. Elfenbein notes that "Although the eighteenth-century theorists who wrote about genius never intended to limn the homosexual character, the image that they created would replace the religious image of the sodomite and would provide an image of the homosexual for late nineteenth-century sexology. In the late eighteenth and early nineteenth centuries, the link between genius and homosexuality was never as sharp as it later became. Instead, late eighteenth-century images like the man of feeling, the antidomestic genius, and the feminized creator provided alternatives to the conventional images of the

heterosexual husband, father, and lover. As such, they always teetered on the brink of associations with effeminate sodomy, although these associations rarely, if ever, became explicit" (34–35).

7. See Elfenbein's discussion of how writers often associated genius with "originality and sublimity" (28). Elfenbein quotes Jackson and Wordsworth.

8. In *Vested Interests*, Garber differentiates between those who use cross-dressing as "an instrumental strategy rather than an erotic pleasure and play space" (70). The former, she argues, are unconvincing because "they rewrite the story of the transvestic subject as a cultural symptom . . . [and because] the consequent reinscription of 'male' and 'female' . . . reaffirms the patriarchal binary and ignores what is staring us in the face: the existence of the transvestite, the figure that disrupts" (70). In terms of Henry's poses, see Howard Babb, who points out that "Henry's . . . artificial manner ought to warn Catherine that she is entering a world of 'assumed' poses and affected responses" (qtd. in Burlin 92), and Diane Hoeveler, who sees Henry as a "female ventriloquiz[er]. . . . If she can haggle over muslin by the yard, so can he" (126).

9. Here I would disagree with Alisa Solomon's thesis that "If men dressed as women often *parody* gender, women dressed as men, on the other hand, tend to *perform* gender—that is, they can reveal the extent to which gender, as Judith Butler suggests, is a 'regulatory fiction'— and thus it often takes very little for women to be designated as cross-dressers (Butler 1990: 141)" (145–146). Henry in fact reveals how gender is a regulatory fiction.

10. This is from an article discussing *Belle Reprieve*, the 1991 Split Britches–Bloops collaboration based loosely on *A Streetcar Named Desire*.

11. Joseph Litvak argues that "Henry's interest in Gothic fiction looks forward to the appropriative hipness of a certain opportunistic style of 'male feminism.' Impressing his interlocutors with the arresting . . . image of his 'hair standing on end the whole time,' [he reads *Udolpho*] he stages his petrification (or castration) in the paradoxical, apotropaic mode of erection. Indeed, Henry disarmingly, that is, aggressively, installs himself in the space of novelized 'femininity,' all the better to engage in a menacing display of cultural capital as phallic privilege" (*Strange Gourmets* 52).

12. Margaret Thornton coined this term "to label the invisible man who is the assumed subject of western legal and political discourses" (Brook 97).

13. See his discussion of the broadside, *The Woman Hater's Lamentation* (51–53). Erin Mackie also discusses this issue of gender identity in terms of *The Tatler* and *The Spectator*.

14. The Paul referred to is the biblical Paul of I Corinthians 6.9–21.

15. Here Flügel, drawing on psychoanalytic theory, compares neurotic symptoms, specifically blushing, to "the same tendencies as those

which find expression in clothes. Thus the attacks of psychological blushing . . . are, on the one hand, exaggerations of the normal symptoms of shame, but, on the other hand, as psycho-analytic examination has demonstrated, at the same time involuntarily draw attention to the sufferer and thus gratify his unconscious exhibitionism" (21).

16. Here I would disagree with Marilyn Butler, who collapses the turban and the color purple into one object, seeing the turban as purple: it is important to see the distinction made between the hat and the color since Isabella has used these items separately to mirror each potential marriage partner ("The Purple Turban" 6).

17. See Rousseau's *Emile* (356–357).

18. Also crediting the importance of the laundry and laundry list Catherine discovers, Diane Hoeveler argues that "they are the visible residue of women's lost and unpaid labor for the family. The domesticities, rather than reassuring Catherine, should have horrified her" (131). Litvak also finds significance in the dirty linen: "Just as the most charming young man in the world gets linked, through his servant, with the 'washing-bills' Catherine misidentifies in her Gothic wishfulness, and hence with dirty linen, so Henry threatens to reveal the nauseating versatility of the body in charm" (*Strange Gourmets* 54).

19. Litvak argues that Austen needs "some other, less visibly contradictory, more discreetly upscale literary paradigm through which to chart her heroine's progress," than the "gold-digging, social-climbing Isabella Thorpe" (39).

4   MAKING AND IMPROVING: FALLEN WOMEN, MASQUERADES, AND EROTIC HUMOR IN *MANSFIELD PARK*

1. Contrast my reading to Brian Southam's: "while Edmund finds Mary's joke indecorous and tasteless, at worst, offensive, he detects nothing gross, nothing wholly outrageous. . . . So, although both Edmund and Fanny catch a lurking indelicacy in Mary's language, neither reacts as if some unspeakable indecency has struck their ears" (*Navy* 185).

2. John Skinner points out Mary's comment about the "*address* of a Frenchwoman," seeing it as a case of "semantic slippage" and noting that "the two relevant senses of the word in question are recorded by the *OED* as having occurred well before 1814" (141, n. 22), but he does not discuss the rest of Mary's speech, which contains the references to "dying" that I mention. Although John Skinner does not list the precise definitions he is referring to here, two possibilities that illustrate his and my meanings in the *OED* are first, number 10, under "noun" and second, the definition in the "Additions Series 1997": "[II.][8.] e. *trans.* To pay one's addresses to (a woman); to

woo, court. Cf. ADDRESS *v.* 8 c. *arch.*" Significantly, one of the examples the *OED* gives is from *Mansfield Park* itself: "You may live eighteen years longer without being addressed by a man of half Mr. Crawford's estate, or a tenth part of his merits" (318).

3. For an extended discussion of the erotics of riding in *Mansfield Park*, see Johnson, "What Became of Jane Austen" (59–70).

4. Neill also points out that marriage to Crawford would also "promote" Fanny (76).

5. Shakespeare sets a clear precedent for using the word "make" in the way I believe Austen employs it. In *Shakespeare's Bawdy*, Partridge collects the following definitions of make or made: to "make a monster" means "to cuckold"; to "make defeat of virginity" means "to persuade a virgin to yield her virginity before marriage"; to "make love": "to indulge in sexual caresses and intercourse (fr. Faire l'amour)"; to "make one's heaven in a lady's lap": to " 'womanize' or to devote myself to love-making"; to "make the diseases": "to form— or to infect with—venereal disease"; and finally " 'making": "effectual copulation regarded as an act of creation—in short, procreation. 'There was good sport at his making, and the whoreson must be acknowledged,' *Lear*, I, i. 23–24" (Partridge 143–144).

6. The word "homosocial," defined as "social bonds between persons of the same sex," is, according to Sedgewick, a "neologism, obviously formed by analogy with 'homosexual,' and just as obviously meant to be distinguished from 'homosexual.' " Because most societies are unable to allow an "unbroke[n] . . . continuum between homosocial and homosexual" interaction, male bonding usually requires "intense homophobia, fear and hatred of homosexuality" (1).

7. Peter Knox-Shaw argues that when Austen alludes in chapter 16 (156) to Barrow's edition of Lord Macartney's embassy to China, she links Fanny's refusal to act in *Lovers' Vows* and to marry Crawford to Macartney's perseverance in Peking.

8. Bradford Mudge explores this scandal in terms of the stories prostitutes themselves narrate (237–242) and Tim Fulford, in "Romanticizing the Empire," argues that Austen's *Persuasion* works to counteract such corruption by presenting a navy that "redefines gentility in terms of professional activity and discipline" (189).

9. *The Sporting Magazine* reads "bad characters" for "loose characters" (April 1795, 41). This date is earlier than the actual scandal's, but even by 1784, the Duke's advisors felt he "hunted and drank too much and delighted in boorish horseplay"; by 1794, he had suffered humiliating defeats abroad and "there was a growing conviction at Westminster that the inexperience of the royal commander-in chief contributed to allied disasters" (Palmer 64, 69).

10. Fanny was the name of Austen's favorite niece, and Fanny Price is the heroine of Crabbe's *Parish Register* (1807), who is almost seduced by a libertine.

11. Though amber was more popular in Turkey and China than in Europe (Williamson 177), William follows a popular trend here, since all kinds of objects, such as sewing implements, toothpicks, and patch boxes were made of amber during the eighteenth century (Fraquet 47).

12. Philip James Hartmann theorized in "*Succini Prussici Historia Physica et Civilis*" (1677)—a tract that Robert Hooke wrote a series of discourses on and delivered to the Royal Society in 1692—that amber was petrified vegetable juice (qtd. in Williamson 109–111).

13. It was named amber because it was confused with ambergris, a morbid substance expelled from the intestines of Sperm whales (*OED*). Amber, an organic substance, is a fossilized resin from evergreens that grew millions of years ago.

14. See Rule 1, from "Provisional Rules. Concerning the duration of Life and the Form of Death" (n.p.).

15. As a cross, this ornament would have spiritual connotations for the religious Fanny, though Austen does not emphasize those; further, given that amber is a fossil, questions arise as to Austen's thoughts about the geological debates that fossils were inspiring in the early nineteenth century, debates that had serious religious ramifications. As Anne D. Wallace argues, "nothing advanced the deepening of time more rapidly during [the Romantic] period than the study of fossils . . . . The threat was not just the possibility of a self-generating materialist cosmos, but that the very methods by which we recognized that possibility might fail us, that the confident empirical claim of traceable causation might prove as false as David Hume had warned" (87).

16. R. W. Chapman points out in his notes to the novel that "Miss Austen may have remembered that Mr. Gilpin . . . had quoted these lines" (542). See Gilpin's *Observations on the Western Parts of England, relative chiefly to Picturesque Beauty*, 1798, 40.

17. See Malcolm Andrews, Ann Bermingham, Stephen Copley and Peter Garside, Tim Fulford, Alan Liu, and Sidney Robinson, as well as my own examinations of this topic, especially "Liberty, Connection, and Tyranny," and the introduction (coauthored with Gary Harrison) to the recent special issue of *European Romantic Review* devoted to the picturesque, "Variations on the Picturesque: Authority, Play, and Practice."

18. Contrast my argument to Alistair Duckworth's in *The Improvement of the Estate*: "The context of the paper war, however, is only a partial explanation of Jane Austen's intentions in *Mansfield Park*, and to the degree that it suggests that her distaste for Repton was merely aesthetic, implying a preference for the more naturalistic styles of Price and Knight, it can be misleading. . . . Austen commonly treats an enthusiasm for this style with some irony in her fiction . . ." (41–42). Galperin devotes his second chapter, "The Picturesque, the Real and the Consumption of Jane Austen," largely to a discussion of that topic. As he notes (252, n. 5) our readings of the relationship between the novelist and this popular

aesthetic are "altogether different," as he is most concerned with what he calls her "unease" with these ideas (*Historical* 8).

19. As I have discussed in "Liberty, Connection, and Tyranny: the Novels of Jane Austen and the Aesthetic Movement of the Picturesque," Repton transformed Stoneleigh much to the family's dismay. Repton's *Red Book for Stoneleigh* (1809) shows that he altered the course of the river, bringing it nearer the south end of the house and sought to preserve an island Leigh wanted removed. The family disapproved of these changes. Leigh and Repton's correspondence reveals strong differences of opinion over these improvements and suggests that his transformation caused direct conflict (see Aslet 1937).

20. R. F. Brissenden connects Mary with the Portsmouth parlor as well; although he feels that such a parallel "may not have been consciously intended by the author, . . . it evidences, if nothing else, the intensity with which Jane Austen's imagination is working at this point" (158).

21. The finger bowl has been associated with hygiene throughout history: the Aztec ruler, Montezuma, had several "beautiful and clean women hold his finger bowl, gourds and towels to wash his mouth and hands" (Flor), and Catholic priests routinely use finger bowls during the mass.

22. See Addison's letter to *The Guardian*, September 7, 1713, reprinted in Stephens, *The Guardian* (502).

5   "Praying to Cupid for a Cure": Venereal Disease, Prostitution, and the Marriage Market in *Emma*

1. This is the last line of the riddle, entitled "Kitty, a Fair but Frozen Maid," which I cite in its entirety at the beginning of the chapter.

2. The riddle as transcribed here can be found in *The Poetical Works of David Garrick*, vol. 2 (507). The reader will note some textual variants in the stanza Austen transcribes. It was also republished in other compendiums of riddles and conundrums, with further revisions; e.g., *Riddles, Charades, and Conundrums, the greater part of which have never been published* (London, 1822) does not reproduce the third stanza and substitutes "forward" or "thoughtless" for "frozen" (73, Riddle #134).

3. I cannot determine whether Austen found "Kitty" in *The New Foundling Hospital for Wit*, and as I have pointed out in the previous endnote, it was reprinted in other publications; however, her allusion to a riddle that was originally identified with "slander, scandal, and satire" makes its association with Mr. Woodhouse's youthful adventures even funnier, as I will analyze in the course of the chapter.

4. The author of the poem is identified by his initials: KGL.

5. For a Lacanian analysis of the sexual riddles in *Emma*, see Grant I. Holly's article, "*Emma*grammatology." For more on the erotics of

Emma and Harriet's relationship, see Susan M. Korba's article, " 'Improper and Dangerous Distinctions.' "

6. For a good example of the slang meaning of "kiss" see *I know my own heart: The Diaries of Anne Lister, 1791–1840* (95).

7. Trumbach describes how "Men certainly had oral and anal intercourse with males [to avoid disease] as late as the first decade of the eighteenth century. As the century wore on, however, the new role of the molly made anal intercourse with either a male or a female very controversial" (202).

8. The Lock Hospital, which exclusively treated venereal disease, especially child victims who had been infected in the way the riddle describes, tried to educate the public about this widely held fallacy in a well-publicized campaign. The line "some willing victim bleeds" is tragically wrong insofar as these children were the victims of violent rapes. Garrick was also a major sponsor of the Lock Hospital. See Linda E. Merians, "The London Lock Hospital and the Lock Asylum for Women" (129–145).

9. Having consulted many of these *Elegant Extracts* from the first decade of the nineteenth century, I was unable to find either the riddle or any bawdy humor whatsoever, though Garrick, himself, is a well-represented author.

10. Alan Bewell creates a different but fascinating context for Mr. Woodhouse's food peculiarities in his discussion of British diet in the late eighteenth and nineteenth centuries; it was thought that one way to prevent disease, in particular the frightening new maladies from the colonies, was to eat locally: the produce of one's own farm or estate, such as those apples that Mr. Knightley gives to the Bates. Bewell also sees a possible connection between Mr. Woodhouse's strict diet and the miserliness of the monarch, George III (132, 135–145).

11. On the libidinous connotations of the chimney, see Mr. Higgins's *The Loves of the Triangles*, discussed in the Introduction.

> Lo! Where the chimney's sooty tube ascends,
> The fair TROCHAIS from the corner bends!
> Her coal-black eyes upturn'd, incessant mark
> The eddying smoke, quick flame, and volant spark; (ll. 45–48)

Higgins's footnote glosses Trochais as "[t]he Nymph of the Wheel" (*Parodies* 171), and both the poem and the falsely learned note, while using geometry to satirize Darwin's botany, take on an unmistakeably sexual coloration, partly because the subject matter is generation (of the universe, in fact), but also because of the inevitable connections that chimneys seem to have provoked at this time.

12. After a prolonged struggle with her relatives, Lady Caroline Keppel ultimately married her Robin Adair, an Irish surgeon who became Surgeon-General to George III (Scholes 884).

13. In his description of the sweeps' May Day festival, Hone draws from (and acknowledges) Lamb's essay. *The Every-day Book* is, in fact,

dedicated to Lamb. The latter offers a further connection between chimney sweeps and the clergy. Describing another of their ritual celebrations, held during St. Bartholomew's Fair, Lamb notes that their toasts include one to the King and another to "the Cloth," another common metonym for the clergy (260).

14. My thanks to Claudia Johnson for this suggestion.

15. The *OED* defines this phrase: "six and seven, sixes and sevens, etc., originally denoting the hazard of one's whole fortune, or carelessness as to the consequences of one's actions, and in later use the creation or existence of, or neglect to remove, confusion, discover, or disagreement. The original form of the phrase, *to set on six and seven*, is based on the language of dicing, and is probably a fanciful alteration of *to set on cinque and sice*, these being the two highest numbers. . . . [T]he plurals *sixes and sevens . . .* became the standard form in the eighteenth century."

16. Giving visceral examples of sexual crimes attributed to powerful women, who were often termed "monsters," Brooks explains how "in the generalised need to read crimes as bodily, where women were on trial there seemed to be a specific need to place criminality squarely on their sexuality" (14, 13). He does not discuss Austen.

17. See Austen's letters from October 7, 1808 and from January 24, 1809. Litz does not examine the implications of naming Mrs. Percival after Thomas Percival.

18. *Catharine* is dated 1792; however Austen did reread and revise the Juvenilia throughout her lifetime. Thus, even though *The Landscape* first appeared in 1794, it is possible that responses to the poem influenced Austen's later revisions of this material.

19. The term *"natural secretions"* comes from Dr. Burder's "On Syphiloid Diseases," *Medico-Chirurgical Journal*, Vol. I, No. 6 (1818) (248, emphasis added).

20. Tuite's discussion of the Juvenilia is excellent; however, I cannot agree with her that *Catharine, or The Bower* is a "burlesque pedagogical closet drama" (53) or a "farce" (32).

21. Partridge dates this slang definition as later in the nineteenth century (*Slang* 366), though the multiple associations with hair dressers that I examine suggest that the usage was in play much earlier than he has determined.

22. Brownstein pointed out that Mary Shelley used this slang term in a letter to Jane Williams (1822). Eric Partridge dates the usage of this term from the late eighteenth century. *A Dictionary of Slang and Unconventional English.* Also see *The Classical Dictionary of the Vulgar Tongue.*

23. This phrase, "much ado about nothing," is used also to refer to men; in an example of eighteenth-century humor, e.g., David Garrick's *Jests* include the following: "Lord D——has an ugly trick of thrusting his hand in, and groping his breeches," said Lady Gros——r to Lady

D——by. "Phoo, says she, don't you know he is always *making much ado about nothing?*" (58, Garrick's emphasis).

6 "UNBECOMING CONJUNCTIONS": COMIC MOURNING AND THE FEMALE GAZE IN *PERSUASION*

1. Other critics who have discussed widowhood in the novel include Julia Prewitt Brown, Wiltshire, Duckworth, and Mooneyham.
2. Not every use of the word "known" would suggest a sexual connotation, but I hope it will become clear that Mrs. Clay's does.
3. This is from the advertisement for "Gowland's Lotion Improved," a poem of rhyming couplets extolling its efficacy for healing "pimples and freckles . . . and scrophula" (qtd. in *The So-Called Age of Elegance*).
4. This statement can be read ironically since at least "in the second half of the eighteenth century it was common for 20% to 40% of British sailors to be venereally infected" (Trumbach 201). Between 1765 and 1795, 20 seamen out of 109 were venereally infected on the Tamar (Dening 384), the ship on which Charles Austen served as Second Lieutenant for three weeks in 1798.
5. Most readers find Mrs. Smith an exemplary individual; Galperin, as I do, finds her to be "a manipulative and mendacious person" (*Historical* 232–233).
6. Compare O'Farrell, 33–34, who argues that Lady Russell's comment reveals her embarrassment.
7. In her discussion of Austen's allusions to Robert Burton's *Anatomy of Melancholy*, Juliet McMaster points out that "the person of sanguine temperament whose blood predominates over the other humours of his body, is most likely to fall victim to the love disease," and Elton, she points out has, in Austen's words, a "sanguine state of mind" (112, 122; *Emma* 131).
8. My thanks to Mary Favret, who put me on the track toward this line of thought.
9. In his biography of Austen, John Halperin relates how in writing *Mansfield Park*, Austen had Cassandra inquire into whether there were many hedgerows in Northamptonshire. Halperin says that "Whether or not a particular geographical area had hedgerows during the period from, roughly, 1750–1850, depended on how vigorously Enclosure was being administered there—thus, the novel's question: she wanted to get it right. The answer from Cassandra was no, and she abandoned in *Mansfield Park* any thought of using the device, picked up later in *Persuasion*, of eavesdropping through hedgerows" . . . (212).
10. See Alan Richardson, for his reading of Louisa's love of "jumping," and his extended discussion of her fall throughout his chapter on

Austen (103–104). He reinforces the sense of a unity of mind and body in his analysis, though he is less concerned than I am with the sexual dynamics of this episode.

11. Such a pun occurs in Shakespeare's *The Merry Wives of Windsor* and *Troilus and Cressida*. A "head-mark" allowed one to recognize a cuckold by his horns; "low: mid-C 18–20 ob. punning in the SE sense" (Partridge).

12. I analyze this episode within the context of popular culture so as to offer a "historicist dimension," to use John Wiltshire's words. See *Jane Austen*, 196.

13. Richardson's provides an extensive, useful historical context for my reading of the "physical" Austen and specifically for this chapter on *Persuasion*. See his chapter, "Minds, brains, and the subject of *Persuasion*."

14. Contrast my argument to Wiltshire's, who says that "it is through language, not nervous gestures or looks, that the truth is revealed. . . . The presence of the body is in fact reduced to a metaphor . . ." (*Jane Austen* 192).

CONCLUSION

1. *The Dialogic Imagination: Four Essays by M. M. Bakhtin* (23). Quoted in *Parodies of the Romantic Age*. General Introduction (xviii).

2. For a longer discussion of the pleasure one can receive from watching such mishaps, see "The Laughter of Being," *Bataille: A Critical Reader* (156).

3. From his "Letter to Lord Byron," part I, in W. H. Auden and Louis MacNeice, *Letters from Iceland* (1937).

Bibliography

Adamson, Joseph and Hilary Clark, ed. *Scenes of Shame: Psychoanalysis, Shame, and Writing*. New York: State University of New York Press, 1999.

Addison, Joseph. "Letter to *The Guardian*. 7 Sept. 1713." *The Guardian*. Ed. John Calhoun Stephens. Lexington: University Press of Kentucky, 1982. 501–504.

"Address." Def. 10 and Def. 8e from the "Additions Series 1997." *Oxford English Dictionary*. 2nd ed. 1989.

Adelson, Leslie. *Making Bodies, Making History: Feminism and German Identity*. Omaha: University of Nebraska Press, 1993.

Alcoff, Linda. "Cultural Feminism Versus Post-Structuralism: The Identity Crisis in Feminist Theory." *Culture/Power/History: A Reader in Contemporary Social Theory*. Ed. Nicholas B. Dirks, Geoff Eley, and Sherry B. Ortner. Princeton: Princeton University Press, 1994. 96–122.

Alexander, Sally. "Women, Class and Sexual Differences in the 1830s and 1840s: Some Reflections on the Writing of a Feminist History." *Culture/Power/History: A Reader in Contemporary Social Theory*. Ed. Nicholas B. Dirks, Geoff Eley, and Sherry B. Ortner. Princeton: Princeton University Press, 1994. 269–296. Originally published in *History Workshop Journal* 17 (Spring 1984): 125–149.

Alighieri, Dante. *The Divine Comedy*. Trans. C. H. Sisson. Chicago: Regnery, 1981.

Allen, Dennis W. "No Love for Lydia: The Fate of Desire in *Pride and Prejudice*." *Texas Studies in Literature and Language* 27.4 (1985): 425–443.

Andrews, Malcolm. *The Search for the Picturesque*. Stanford: Stanford University Press, 1989.

Aristotle's Compleat Master-Piece, in Three Parts, Displaying the Secrets of Nature in the Generation of Man. 31st ed. London: The Booksellers, 1776.

Aslet, Clive. "Stoneleigh Abbey, Warwickshire." *Country Life*. Part I: 1844–1848 (December 13, 1984), and Part II: 1934–1937 (December 20, 1984).

Auden, W. H. "Letter to Lord Byron (W. H. A.), Part I." Ed. W. H. Auden and Louis MacNeice, *Letters from Iceland*. New York: Random House, 1937. 21.

Austen, Henry. *Biographical Notice of the Author*. 1817. *The Novels of Jane Austen: Northanger Abbey and Persuasion*. 1923. Ed. R. W. Chapman. 3rd ed. Vol. V. Oxford: Oxford University Press, 1988.

Austen, Jane. *Emma*. Introduction by Joseph Jacobs and Illustrations by Chris Hammard. London: George Allen, 1898.

——. *Jane Austen's Letters*. Ed. Deirdre Le Faye. Oxford: Oxford University Press, 1995.

——. *Jane Austen's Letters to Her Sister Cassandra and Others*. Ed. R. W. Chapman. Oxford: Clarendon, 1932.

——. *Minor Works*. Vol. 6. Ed. R. W. Chapman. Rev. B. C. Southam. Oxford: Oxford University Press, 1988.

——. *The Novels of Jane Austen*. 1923. Ed. R. W. Chapman. 3rd ed. 6 vols. Oxford: Oxford University Press, 1988.

——. *Sanditon*. *Minor Works*. Vol. 6. Ed. R. W. Chapman. Rev. B. C. Southam. Oxford: Oxford University Press, 1988.

Austen-Leigh, James Edward. *A Memoir of Jane Austen, by her nephew J. E. Austen-Leigh*. 1870. Oxford: Clarendon, 1967.

Austen-Leigh, William and Richard Arthur Austen-Leigh. Revised and enlarged by Deirdre Le Faye. *Jane Austen: A Family Record*. New York: Barnes and Noble. Published in association with The British Library, 1989, 1996.

Áywyós. *Hints on Etiquette and the Usages of Society with a Glance at Bad Habits*. 1834. London: Turnstile, 1946.

Bachelard, Gaston. *The Poetics of Space*. Trans. Maria Jolas. New York: Orion, 1964.

Bacon, Francis. *History of Life and Death. Sylva sylvarum, or, A natural history: in ten centuries: whereunto is newly added the History naturall and experimentall of life and death, or, Of the prolongation of life / both written by Francis Lo. Verulam, Viscount St. Alban; published after the authors death by William Rawley. Hereunto is now added an alphabetical table of the principall things contained in the ten centuries*. London: William Lee, 1658.

Baetjer, Katharine, Michael Rosenthal et al. *Glorious Nature: British Landscape Painting 1750–1850*. New York: Hudson Hills, 1993.

Ballaster, Ros. *Seductive Forms: Women's Amatory Fiction from 1684–1740*. Oxford: Clarendon, 1992.

Ballaster, Ros, Margaret Beetham, Elizabeth Frazer, and Sandra Hebron. *Women's Worlds: Ideology, Femininity, and the Women's Magazine*. London: Macmillan, 1991.

Barclay, James. *A Complete and Universal English Dictionary*. Davies and Booth: Leeds, 1800.

Barreca, Regina. *Untamed and Unabashed: Essays on Women and Humor in British Literature*. Detroit: Wayne State University Press, 1994.

——, ed. *Last Laughs: Perspectives on Women and Comedy*. New York: Gordon and Breach, 1988.

Barringer, Tim. *Reading the Pre-Raphaelites*. New Haven: Yale University Press, 1998.

Bataille, Georges. *On Nietzsche*. New York: Paragon House, 1992.

Beerbohm, Max, Sir. *Letters to Reggie Turner*. Ed. Rupert Hart-Davis. London: Hart-Davis, 1964.

Beeton, Mrs. *Beeton's Book of Household Management.* 1869. London: S. O. Beeton, 1880.

Benjamin, Walter. *Arcades Project.* Trans. Howard Eiland and Kevin McLaughlin. Ed. Rolf Tiedemann. Cambridge, MA: Belknap Press of Harvard University Press, 1999.

Benstock, Shari and Suzanne Ferriss. *On Fashion.* New Brunswick: Rutgers University Press, 1994.

Bergeron, David M. *King James & Letters of Homoerotic Desire.* Iowa City: University of Iowa Press, 1999.

Bermingham, Ann. *Landscape and Ideology: The English Rustic Tradition, 1740–1860.* Berkeley: The University of California Press, 1986.

———. "The Picturesque and Ready-to-wear Femininity." *The Politics of the Picturesque.* Ed. Stephen Copley and Peter Garside. Cambridge: Cambridge University Press, 1994. 81–119.

Bewell, Alan. *Romanticism and Colonial Disease.* Baltimore and London: The Johns Hopkins University Press, 1999.

Bilger, Audrey. "Goblin Laughter: Violent Comedy and the Condition of Women in Frances Burney and Jane Austen." *Women's Studies* 24 (1995): 323–340.

———. *Laughing Feminism: Subversive Comedy in Frances Burney, Maria Edgeworth, and Jane Austen.* Detroit: Wayne State University Press, 1998. 16.

Blau, Herbert. *Nothing in Itself: Complexions of Fashion.* Bloomington: Indiana University Press, 1999.

Borch-Jacobsen, Mikkel. "The Laughter of Being." *Bataille: A Critical Reader.* Ed. Fred Botting and Scott Wilson. Oxford: Blackwell, 1998. 146–166.

Boswell, James. *Boswell's Life of Johnson. Together with Boswell's Journal of a Tour to the Hebrides and Johnson's Diary of a Journey into North Wales.* Ed. George Birkbeck Hill. Rev. by L. F. Powell. Vol. IV. Oxford: Clarendon, 1934–1950.

Brett, Gerard. *Dinner is Served: A Study in Manners.* Hamden, Conn: Archon Books, 1969.

Breward, Christopher. *The Culture of Fashion: A New History of Fashionable Dress.* Manchester: Manchester University Press, 1995.

Brissenden, R. F. "*Mansfield Park*: Freedom and the Family." *Jane Austen: Bicentenary Essays.* Ed. John Halperin. Cambridge: Cambridge University Press, 1975. 156–171.

Brodey, Inger Sigrun. "Adventures of a Female Werther: Jane Austen's Revision of Sensibility." *Philosophy and Literature* 23.1 (1999): 110–126.

Brook, Barbara. *Feminist Perspectives on the Body.* London and New York: Longman, 1999.

Brooks, Peter. *Body Work: Objects of Desire in Modern Narrative.* Cambridge, MA: Harvard University Press, 1993.

———. "Melodrama, Body, Revolution." *Melodrama: Stage, Picture, Screen.* Ed. Jacky Bratton, Jim Cook, and Christine Gledhill. London: British Film Institute, 1994. 11–24.

Brown, Julia Prewitt. *Jane Austen's Novels: Social Change and Literary Form.* Cambridge, MA: Harvard University Press, 1979.

Browne, Ray B., ed. *Objects of Special Devotion: Fetishism in Popular Culture.* Bowling Green, OH: Bowling Green University Press, 1982. 89–106.

Brownlow, Timothy. *John Clare and Picturesque Landscape.* Oxford: Clarendon, 1983.

Brownstein, Rachel. "England's *Emma.*" Keynote Address. *The Annual General Meeting of the Jane Austen Society of North America.* Colorado Springs, CO. October 9, 1999.

Brunton, Mary. *Self-Control.* Introduction by Sara Maitland. 1810/11. London and New York: Pandora, 1986.

Buchan, William. *Domestic Medicine: or, a Treatise on the Prevention and Cure of Diseases by Regimen and Simple Medicines.* 16th ed. London: A. Strahan, T. Cadell and W. Daries, 1798.

———. *Observations Concerning the Prevention and Cure of Venereal Diseases.* London, 1796. Reprint GRS: New York, 1985.

Buck, Anne. "The Costume of Jane Austen and her Characters." *The So-Called Age of Elegance. Costume: 1785–1820.* Proceedings of the Fourth Annual Conference of the Costume Society, 1970. London: Published for the Society, 1971. 36–45.

Bullough, Vern L. *Cross Dressing, Sex, Gender and Others.* Philadelphia: University of Pennsylvania Press, 1993.

Burder. "On Syphiloid Diseases." *Medico-Chirurgical Journal* 1.6 (1818): 248.

Burlin, Katrin Ristkok. "'The pen of the contriver': the four feathers of Northanger Abbey." *Jane Austen: Bicentenary Essays.* Ed. John Halperin. London and Melbourne: Cambridge University Press, 1975. 89–111.

Burnand, Francis Cowley. *The Frightful Hair; or, Who shot the Dog? An Original Travestie on Lord Lytton's "The Rightful Heir."* London: Phillips, 1868.

Bury, Shirley. *An Introduction to Sentimental Jewellery. Victoria and Albert Museum Introductions to the Decorative Arts.* Owings Mills, MD: Stemmer House; London: Victoria and Albert, 1985.

Butler, Judith. *Gender Trouble: Feminism and the Subversion of Identity.* New York: Routledge, 1999.

Butler, Marilyn. *Jane Austen and the War of Ideas.* Oxford: Clarendon, 1975.

———. "The Purple Turban and the Flowering Aloe Tree: Signs of Distinction in the Early-Nineteenth-Century Novel." *Modern Language Quarterly* 58.4 (December 1997): 475–495.

———. *Romantics, Rebels and Reactionaries: English Literature and its Background 1760–1830.* Oxford: Oxford University Press, 1981.

———. "Simplicity." Rev. of *Jane Austen: A Life,* by David Nokes, and *Jane Austen: A Life,* by Claire Tomalin. *London Review of Books* 20.5 (March 5, 1998): 3, 5–6.

Buzard, James. *The Beaten Track: European Tourism, Literature, and the Ways to Culture, 1800–1918.* Oxford: Clarendon, 1993.

Byrde, Penelope. *Jane Austen Fashion.* Middlesex: CTD Printers Ltd., 1998.

Canning, Kathleen. "The Body as Method? Reflections on the Place of the Body in Gender History." *Gender and History: Retrospect and Prospect.* 1999. Ed. Leonore Davidoff, Keith McClelland, and Eleni Varikas. Malden, MA and Oxford, UK: Blackwell, 2000.

Carson, James. "Narrative Cross-Dressing and the Critique of Authorship in the Novels of Richardson." *Writing the Female Voice: Essays on Epistolary Literature.* Ed. Elizabeth Goldsmith. Boston: Northeastern University Press, 1989. 95–113.

Castellano, Gabriela. *Laughter, War and Feminism: Elements of Carnival in Three of Jane Austen's Novels.* New York: Peter Lang, 1994.

Castle, Terry. *The Female Thermometer: Eighteenth-Century Culture and the Invention of the Uncanny.* Oxford: Oxford University Press, 1995.

Cendrars, Blaise. *Complete Poems.* Trans. Ron Padgett. Berkeley: University of California Press, 1992.

———. "The Simultaneous Dress." Qtd. in *Defining Dress: Dress as Object, Meaning and Identity.* Ed. Amy de la Haye and Elizabeth Wilson. Manchester: Manchester University Press; New York: St. Martin's, 1999. 2.

Centlivre, Susanna. *The Wonder; A Woman Keeps a Secret! A Comedy.* New York: D. Longworth, 1812.

Chandler, Alice. "A Pair of Fine Eyes: Jane Austen's Treatment of Sex." *Studies in the Novel* 7.1 (1975): 88–103.

"Changes in French Fashions." *The Ladies Monthly Museum, or Polite Repository of Amusement and Instruction: Being an assemblage of whatever can tend to please the Fancy, interest the Mind, or exalt the Character of The British Fair. By a Society of Ladies.* From the French of M. Pouce. 1789. (March 1800): 305–308.

Chapman, R. W. "Notes." *The Novels of Jane Austen and Minor Works* 1923. Ed. R. W. Chapman. 3rd ed. 6 vols. Oxford: Oxford University Press, 1988.

Churchill, Charles. *The Poetical Works of Charles Churchill.* Ed. Douglas Grant. Oxford: Clarendon, 1956.

Cixous, Hélène. "The Laugh of the Medusa." *Critical Theory since 1965.* Ed. Hazard Adams and Leroy Searle. Tallahassee: Florida State University Press, 1986. 309–320.

Cixous, Hélène and Catherine Clément. *The Newly Born Woman.* Trans. Betsy Wing. Minneapolis: University of Minnesota Press, 1986.

Clark, Fiona. *Hats.* London: B.T. Batsford; New York: Drama Book Publishers, 1982.

Clark, Robert, ed. *Sense and Sensibility and Pride and Prejudice.* New York: St. Martin's, 1994.

Clarkson, Thomas. *The History of the Rise, Progress, and Accomplishment of the Abolition of the African Slave-Trade by the British Parliament.* 2 vols. London: Longman & Co., 1808.

Cleland, John. *Memoirs of a Woman of Pleasure.* Ed. Peter Sabor. Oxford: Oxford University Press, 1995.

Clifford, Derek. *A History of Garden Design*. New York: Frederick A. Praeger, 1963.

Clinton, Catherine. Rev. of *Titters*. *Cultural Correspondence: Sex Roles and Humor* 9 (Spring 1979): 30.

Clinton, Kate. "Making Light." *Trivia* 1 (1981): 37–42.

Clueless. Dir. and Screenplay by Amy Heckerling. Paramount, 1995.

Coffin, Sarah, and Bodo, Hofstetter. *Portrait Miniatures in Enamel*. London: Philip Wilson Publishers, 2000.

Cohen, Ed. "Legislating the Norm: From Sodomy to Gross Indecency." *Displacing Homophobia: Gay Male Perspectives in Literature and Culture*. Ed. Ronald R. Butters, John M. Clum, and Michael Moon, 169–205. Durham, NC: Duke University Press, 1989. 181–217.

Conner, Susan P. "The Pox in Eighteenth-Century France." *The Secret Malady: Venereal Disease in Eighteenth-Century Britain and France*. Ed. Linda Merians. Lexington: University Press of Kentucky, 1996. 15–33.

Coombs, Katherine. *The Portrait Miniature in England*. London: Victoria and Albert Publications, 1998.

Copley, Stephen, and Peter Garside, ed. *The Politics of the Picturesque: Literature, Landscape and Aesthetics since 1770*. Cambridge: Cambridge University Press, 1994.

Cox, Jeffrey N. *Poetry and Politics in the Cockney School: Keats, Shelley, Hunt and their Circle*. Cambridge: Cambridge University Press, 1998.

Crabbe, George. *The Complete Poetical Works*. Ed. Norma Dalrymple-Champneys and Arthur Pollard. 3 vols. Oxford: Clarendon Press, 1988.

Craft-Fairchild, Catherine. "Cross-Dressing and the Novel: Women Warriors and Domestic Femininity." *Eighteenth-Century Fiction* 10.2 (January 1998): 171–202.

Cromie, Robert, ed. *1811 Dictionary of the Vulgar Tongue, Unabridged*. Chicago: Follet, 1971.

Crook, Nora. "Letter." *Times Literary Supplement* (October 7, 1983).

Crossley, Anthony. *Dressage: The Seats, Aids and Exercises*. London: Penguin, 1988.

Culler, Jonathan. *Framing the Sign: Criticism and its Institutions. Oklahoma Project for Discourse and Theory*. Vol. III. Norman and London: University of Oklahoma Press, 1988.

Darwin, Erasmus. *The Loves of the Plants*. 1789. First published as *Botanic garden*, part two. Ed. Jonathan Wordsworth. Oxford and New York: Woodstock Books, 1991.

Davies, J. M. Q. "*Emma* as Charade and the Education of the Reader." *New Casebooks: Emma*. Ed. David Monaghan. New York: St. Martin's, 1992. 77–88.

De Courtais, Georgine. *Women's Headdress and Hairstyles in England from AD 600 to the Present Day*. London: B.T. Batsford, 1973.

de la Haye and Elizabeth Wilson, ed. *Defining Dress: Dress as Object, Meaning and Identity*. Manchester and New York: Manchester University Press, 1999.

Dean, Tim. "Transsexual Identification, Gender Performance Theory, and the Politics of the Real." *Literature and Psychology* 39.4 (1993): 1–25.

Deleuze, Gilles. "Plato and the Simulacrum." Trans. Rosalind Krauss. *October* (Winter 1983), 27: 44–56.

Dening, Greg. *Mr. Bligh's Bad Language: Passion, Power and Theatre on The Bounty.* Cambridge: Cambridge University Press, 1992.

Deresiewicz, William. "Community and Cognition in *Pride and Prejudice.*" *ELH* 64 (1997): 503–535.

Derry, Stephen. "Jane Austen's Use of *Measure for Measure* in *Sense and Sensibility.*" *Persuasions* 15 (1993): 37–41.

———. "Two Georgianas: the Duchess of Devonshire and Jane Austen's Miss Darcy." *Persuasions* 11 (1989): 15–16.

Dewdney, George. *Pattern Book of Souvenirs in Hair, and List of Prices.* London: Crosland & Co., 1851.

Dézallier d'Argenville, Antoine-Joseph. *The theory and practice of gardening: wherein is fully handled all that relates to fine gardens, commonly called pleasure-gardens, as parterres, groves, bowling-greens &c. ... / by John James ; together with remarks and general rules in all that concerns the art of gardening; done from the French original, printed at Paris, anno 1709.* Trans. John James. London: G. James, 1712.

Dibdin, Thomas. "The Tight Little Island." *The British Taft.* London: 1797.

Directions and Instructions to Enable Ladies to Prepare and Work their own Materials. Illustrated with Designs and Diagrams. Brighton, 1852.

Douglas, Aileen. *Uneasy Sensations: Smolett and the Body.* Chicago: University of Chicago Press, 1995.

Douglas, Mary. *Purity and Danger: An Analysis of Concepts of Pollution and Taboo.* London: Routledge & Kegan Paul, 1966.

Duckworth, Alistair. *The Improvement of the Estate: A Study of Jane Austen's Novels.* Baltimore: Johns Hopkins University Press, 1971.

———. " 'Spillikins, paper ships, riddles, conundrums, and cards': games in Jane Austen's life and fiction." *Jane Austen: Bicentenary Essays.* Ed. John Halperin. Cambridge: Cambridge University Press, 1975. 279–297.

Dunlap, Barbara. "The Problem of Syphilitic Children in 18th-Century France and England." *The Secret Malady: Venereal Disease in Eighteenth-Century Britain and France.* Kentucky: University Press of Kentucky, 1996. 114–145.

D'Urfey, Thomas. *Wit and Mirth: or Pills to Purge Melancholy.* 6 vols. Reprint of the 1876 edition (reprint of the original edition of 1719–1720). New York: Folklore Library Publishers, 1959.

Dussinger, John A. *In the Pride of the Moment.* Columbus: Ohio State University Press, 1990.

———. "Madness and Lust in the Age of Sensibility." *Sensibility in Transformation: Creative Resistance to Sentiment from the Augustans to the Romantics. Essays in Honor of Jean H. Hagstrum.* Ed. Sydny McMillen Conger. Assoc. University Press, 1990. 85–102.

Eagleton, Terry. *The Idea of Culture*. Oxford, UK and Malden, MA: Blackwell, 2000.

Easton, Celia. "*Sense and Sensibility* and the Joke of Substitution." *Journal of Narrative Technique* 23.2 (1993): 114–126.

Edelman, Lee. *Homeographesis: Essays in Gay Literary and Cultural Theory*. New York and London: Routledge, 1994.

Edgeworth, Maria. *Belinda*. Ed. Kathryn J. Kirkpatrick. Oxford: Oxford University Press, 1994.

Eger, Elizabeth, and Charlotte Grant et al., ed. *Women, Writing, and the Public Sphere, 1700–1830*. Cambridge: Cambridge University Press, 2001.

Egger, Gerhart. *Generations of Jewelry from the 15th through the 20th Century*. Photos by Helga Schmidt-Glassner. West Chester, PA: Schiffer, 1984.

Elfenbein, Andrew. *Romantic Genius: The Prehistory of a Homosexual Role*. New York: Columbia University Press, 1999.

Ellis, Markman. *The Poetics of Sensibility: Race, Gender and Commerce in the Sentimental Novel*. Cambridge: Cambridge University Press, 1996.

Elegant Extracts. Ed. S. Hamilton Weybridge and C. Robinson. London: J. Johnson, 1809.

Emck, Katy. "Female Transvestism and Male Self-Fashioning in *As You Like It* and *La vida es sueno*." *Reading the Renaissance: Culture, Poetics, and Drama*. Ed. Jonathan Hart. New York: Garland, 1996.

"Epigrammata Bacchanalia." *The Spirit of the Public Journals for 1797. Being an Impartial Selection of the Most Exquisite Essays and Jeux D'Esprits, Principally Prose, That Appear in the Newspapers and Other Publications*. Vol. 1. 3rd ed. London, 1802. 1–17.

Epstein, Julia. *Altered Conditions: Disease, Medicine, and Storytelling*. New York: Routledge, 1995.

Evans, Mary. *Jane Austen and the State*. London and New York: Tavistock Publications, 1987.

Exhibition of Portrait Miniatures. Vol. xxiii. London, Burlington Fine Arts Club: 1889.

Farmer, John, ed. *Slang and its Analogues Past and Present*. New York: Kraus Reprints, 1950.

Farmer, John S. and Henley, W. F., eds. *Slang and Its Analogues Past and Present*. 7 vols. Rpt. New York: Kraus Reprints, 1965.

Favret, Mary. "Flogging: The Anti-Slavery Movement Writes Pornography." *Romanticism and Gender*. Ed. Anne Janowitz. Essays and Studies 1998 for the English Association. Cambridge: D.S. Brewer, 1998. 19–43.

Fawcett, John. *Obi; or, Three-Finger'd Jack*. 1800. Ed. Jeffrey N. Cox. *Slavery, Abolition, and Emancipation*. Gen. Ed. Peter Kitson and Debbie Lee. 8 vols. London: Pickering and Chatto, 1999.

"Female Novelists." *New Monthly Review*. xcv. May 1852. 17–23.

Fergus, Jan S. "Sex and Social Life in Jane Austen's Novels." *Jane Austen in a Social Context*. Ed. David Monaghan. Totowa, NJ: Barnes and Noble, 1981.

Ferguson, Moira. "*Mansfield Park*: Slavery, Colonialism, and Gender." *Critical Essays on Jane Austen*." Ed. Laura Mooneyham White. New York: G. K. Hall; London: Prentice Hall, 1998. 103–120.

Fielding, Henry. *Amelia*. Ed. Martin C. Battestin. Middletown, CT: Wesleyan University Press, 1984.

——. *The History of Tom Jones, A Foundling*. Ed. John Bender and Simon Stern. Oxford: Oxford University Press, 1996.

——. *Joseph Andrews / Shamela*. 1741 and 1742. London: Penguin, 1999.

Fishman, Jenn. "Performing Identities: Female Cross-Dressing in She Ventures and He Wins Restoration." *Studies in English Literary Culture, 1660–1700*. 20.1 (Spring 1996): 36–51.

Flieger, Jerry Aline. *The Purloined Punchline: Freud's Comic Theory and the Postmodern Text*. Baltimore Johns Hopkins, 1991.

Fleming, Laurence, and Alan Gore. *The English Garden*. London: Michael Joseph, 1979.

Flor, D. J. "History of the Mexican Table." *La Avenida*. September 27, 2002. <http://www.igroupsonline.com/laavenida/table.htm>.

Flügel, J. C. *The Psychology of Clothes*. London: Hogarth Press, 1930. Rpt. 1940.

Folsom, Maria McClintock, ed. *Approaches to Teaching Austen's* Pride and Prejudice. New York: Modern Language Association (MLA), 1993.

Fraiman, Susan. "Jane Austen and Edward Said: Gender, Culture, and Imperialism." *Janeites: Austen's Disciples and Devotees*. Ed. Deidre Lynch. Princeton: Princeton University Press, 2000. 206–223.

Fraquet, Helen. *Amber*. London and Boston: Butterworths, 1987.

"Frederick Augustus, Duke of York and Albany." *Dictionary of National Biography*. Ed. Sir Leslie Stephens and Sir Sydney Lee. 1917. Vol. 7. Oxford: Oxford University Press, 1973. 673–675.

Freud, Sigmund. *The Complete Psychological Works of Sigmund Freud*. Trans. James Strachey. Vol. XIV. London: Hogarth Press and the Institute of Psycho-Analysis, 1957.

——. *Jokes and their Relation to the Unconscious*. London: Hogarth Press, 1905.

Frow, John. "Tourism and the Semiotics of Nostalgia." *October* 57 (Summer 1991): 123–151.

Frushell, Richard C., ed. *The Plays of Susanna Centlivre*. New York and London: Garland, 1982.

Fulford, Tim. *Landscape, Liberty and Authority: Poetry, Criticism and Politics From Thomson to Wordsworth*. Cambridge: Cambridge University Press, 1996.

——. "Romanticizing the Empire: The Naval Heroes of Southey, Coleridge, Austen, and Marryat." *MLQ* 60.2 (1999): 161–196.

Fuseli, Henri. *The Nightmare*. Frankfurt: Goethe Museum, 1790–1791.

Gagnier, Regina. "Between Women: A Cross-Class Analysis of Status and Anarchic Humor." *Last Laughs: Perspectives on Women and Comedy*. Ed. Regina Barreca. New York: Gordon and Breach, 1988. 135–148.

Gaines, Jane and Charlotte Herzog, ed. *Fabrications: Costume and the Female Body*. New York: Routledge, 1990.

Gallagher, Catherine. *Nobody's Story: The Vanishing Acts of Women Writers in the Marketplace, 1670–1820*. Berkeley: University of California Press, 1994.

Gallery of Fashion. With plates by Heideloff and Ackermann. London: W. Bulmer and Co., 1790–1805.

Galperin, William H. *The Historical Austen.* Philadelphia: University of Pennsylvania Press, 2003.

Garber, Marjorie. *Vested Interests: Cross-dressing and Cultural Anxiety.* New York: Routledge, 1997.

Gard, Roger. *Jane Austen's Novels: The Art of Clarity.* New Haven: Yale University Press, 1992.

Garrick, David. *The Poetical Works of David Garrick.* 1968. Vol. II. New York and London: Benjamin Blom, 1975. 507.

Garrick's Jests; or, Genius in High Glee. Containing all the Jokes of the Wits of the Present Age. London, [?1790].

Gilbert, Sandra M. and Susan Gubar. *The Madwoman in the Attic: The Woman Writer and the Nineteenth-Century Literary Imagination.* New Haven: Yale University Press, 1979.

Gill, Pat. *Interpreting Ladies: Women, Wit, and Morality in the Restoration Comedy of Manners.* Athens: University of Georgia Press, 1994.

Gillooly, Eileen. *Smile of Discontent: Humor, Gender, and Nineteenth-Century British Fiction.* Chicago: University of Chicago Press, 1999.

Gilpin, William. *Observations on the Western Parts of England, relative chiefly to Picturesque Beauty.* London: T. Cadell Jun. And W. Davies, Strand, 1798.

Gilpin, William. *Three Essays: On Picturesque Beauty; on Picturesque Travel; and on Sketching Landscape: To Which is Added a Poem, on Landscape Painting.* 2nd ed. London: R. Blamire, 1794.

Gilroy, Amanda and Wil Verhoeven. "Introduction: The Romantic-Era Novel: A Special Issue." *Novel: A Forum on Fiction* 34.2 (Spring 2001): 147–162.

Girard, Rene. *Deceit, Desire and the Novel: The Self and Other in Literary Structure.* Trans. Yvonne Freccero. Baltimore: Johns Hopkins University Press, 1961.

Girouard, Mark. *Life in the English Country House.* New York: Penguin, 1980.

Godwin, William. *Essay on Sepulchres, or, A Proposal for Erecting some Memorial of the Illustrious Dead in all Ages, On the spot where their remains have been interred.* New York: M. and W. Ward, 1809.

Gordon, Paul. *The Critical Double: Figurative Meaning in Aesthetic Discourse.* Tuscaloosa and London: University of Alabama Press, 1995.

Gores, Steven J. *Psychosocial Spaces: Verbal and Visual Readings of British Culture, 1750–1820.* Detroit: Wayne State University Press, 2000.

Gould, Gerald L. "The Gate Scene at Sotherton in *Mansfield Park.*" *Literature and Psychology* 20.2 (1970): 75–78.

Gray, Erik. "Severed Hair from Donne to Pope." *Essays in Criticism* 47.3 (1997): 220–239.

Grose, Francis. *A Classical Dictionary of the Vulgar Tongue.* London: S. Hooper, 1785.

——. *A Classical Dictionary of the Vulgar Tongue*. 2nd ed. London: S. Hooper, 1788.

——. *A Dictionary of Buckish Slang, University Wit, and Pickpocket Eloquence. Compiled originally by Captain Grose and now considerably altered and enlarged, with the modern changes and improvements, by a member of the Whip Club*. London, 1811.

Grosz, Elizabeth. *Volatile Bodies: Toward a Corporeal Feminism*. Bloomington and Indianapolis: Indiana University Press, 1994.

——. "Inscriptions and Body Maps: Representation and the Corporal." *Feminine/Masculine/Representation*. Ed. Terry Threadgold and Anne Cranny-Francis. Austin: Harry Ransom Humanities Research Center, 1990.

Gunn, Daniel. "In the Vicinity of Winthrop: Ideological Rhetoric in *Persuasion*." *Nineteenth-Century Literature* 41 (1987): 403–418.

Haddington, Thomas Hamilton [6th Earl of Harrington]. *Select Poems on Several Occasions*. London, 1730.

Halford, William and Charles Young. *Manufacturing Jewellers: The Jewellers' Book of Patterns in Hair Work. Containing A great Variety of Copper Plate Engravings of Devices and Patterns in Hair; suitable for Mourning Jewellery, Brooches, Rings, Guards, Alberts, Necklets, Bracelets, Miniatures, Studs, Links, Earrings, &c., &c., &c.* London, 1864.

Halperin, John, ed. *Jane Austen: Bicentenary Essays*. Cambridge: Cambridge University Press, 1975.

——. *The Life of Jane Austen*. Baltimore: Johns Hopkins University Press, 1984.

Hamilton, Alexander. *The Family Female Physician, or a Treatise on the Management of Female Complaints, and of children in Early Infancy*. Worcester, MA: Isiah Thomas, 1793.

Hammonds, E. "Text for Exhibition of Hogarth's Work." *Haley & Steele*. London: Tate Gallery, 1971. <http://www.haleysteele.com/hogarth/toc.html>.

Handler, Richard and Daniel Segal. *Jane Austen and the Fiction of Culture: An Essay on the Narration of Social Realities*. Tucson: University of Arizona Press, 1990.

Hares-Stryker, Carolyn, ed. *An Anthology of Pre-Raphælite Writings*. Washington Square, NY: New York University Press, 1997.

Harris, Jocelyn. "Jane Austen and the Burden of the (Male) Past: The Case Reexamined." *Jane Austen and Discourses of Feminism*. Ed. Devoney Looser. New York: St. Martin's, 1995. 87–100.

——. *Jane Austen's Art of Memory*. Cambridge: Cambridge University Press, 1989.

Harrison, Gary and Jill Heydt-Stevenson. "Variations on the Picturesque: Authority, Play and Practice." Special Topics Issue on the Picturesque. Ed. Harrison and Heydt-Stevenson. *European Romantic Review* 13.1 (March 2002): 3–10.

Hazlitt, William. *Lectures on the English Poets*. Everyman's Library. New York: Dutton, 1967.

Hazlitt, William. *Liber Amoris, or, The New Pygmalion.* 1823. Oxford: Woodstock Books, 1992.

Henderson, Mae, ed. *Borders, Boundaries, and Frames: Cultural Criticism and Cultural Studies.* New York: Routledge, 1995.

Henderson, Tony. *Disorderly Women in Eighteenth-century London: Prostitution and Control in the Metropolis, 1730–1830.* London: Longman, 1999.

Henke, James. *Gutter Life and Language in the Early "Street" Literature of England: A Glossary of Terms and Topics Chiefly of the Sixteenth and Seventeenth Centuries.* West Cornwell, CT: Locust Hill Press, 1988.

Herzog, Dan. "The Trouble with Hairdressers." *Representations* 53 (Winter 1996): 21–43.

Heydt-Stevenson, Jill. "Liberty, Connection, and Tyranny: The Novels of Jane Austen and the Aesthetic Movement of the Picturesque." *Lessons of Romanticism.* Ed. Thomas Pfau and Robert F. Gleckner. Durham: Duke University Press, 1998.

———. "The Pleasures of Simulacra: Rethinking the Picturesque in Coleridge's Notebooks and 'The Picture, or the Lover's Resolution.' " *Nineteenth Century Prose* 29.2 (Fall 2002): 23–52.

———. " 'Unbecoming Conjunctions': Mourning the Loss of Landscape and Love." *Eighteenth-Century Fiction* 8.1 (October 1995): 51–71.

———. "Slipping into the Ha-Ha": Bawdy Humor and Body Politics in Jane Austen's Novels." *Nineteenth-Century Literature* 55.3 (December 2000): 309–339.

Higgins, Mr. "Loves of the Triangles." *The Spirit of the Public Journals for 1798. Being an Impartial Selection of the Most Exquisite Essays and Jeux D'Esprits, Principally Prose, That Appear in the Newspapers and Other Publications.* (Originally published by *The Anti-Jacobin,* or the *Weekly Examiner.*) London, 1805.

"The High-prized Pin-Box." Henke, James, *Gutter Life and Language in the Early "Street" Literature of England: A Glossary of Terms and Topics Chiefly of the Sixteenth and Seventeenth Centuries.* West Cornwall, CT: Locust Hill Press, 1988.

Higonnet, Margaret R. "Academic Anorexia? Some Gendered Questions about Comparative Literature." *Comparative Literature* 49 (Summer 1997): 267–274.

———. "Comparative Literature on the Feminist Edge." *Comparative Literature in the Age of Multiculturalism.* Ed. Charles Bernheimer. Baltimore: John Hopkins University Press, 1995. 155–164.

Hill, Constance. *Jane Austen, Her Homes and Her Friends.* London: John Lane, 1904.

Hill, Draper. *Fashionable Contrasts: Caricatures by James Gilray.* London: Phaidon Press, 1966.

Hitchcock, Tim. *English Sexualities, 1700–1800.* Social History in Perspective. New York: St. Martin's, 1997.

Hobbes, Thomas. *The English Works of Thomas Hobbes*. Ed. Sir William Molesworth. 11 vols. Vol. 4. London: John Bohn, 1839–1845.

Hoeveler, Diane Long. "Vindicating *Northanger Abbey*: Mary Wollstonecraft, Jane Austen, and Gothic Feminism." *Jane Austen and Discourses of Feminism*. Ed. Devoney Looser. New York: St. Martin's, 1995. 117–135.

Hollander, Anne. *Seeing Through Clothes*. New York: The Viking Press, 1978.

———. *Sex and Suits*. New York: Knopf, 1994.

Holly, Grant I. "*Emma*grammatology." *Studies in Eighteenth-Century Culture* 19 (1989): 39–51.

Holme, Charles, ed. *The Gardens of England in the Northern Counties*. 1911. London: Offices of the Studio, 1961.

Holquist, Michael, ed. *The Dialogic Imagination: Four Essays by M. M. Bakhtin*. Austin: University of Texas Press, 1981.

Honan, Park. *Jane Austen: Her Life*. New York: Fawcett Columbine, 1987.

Hone, William. *The Every-day book and Table book; or, Everlasting calendar of popular amusements, sports, pastimes, ceremonies, manners, customs, and events, incident to each of the three hundred and sixty-five days, in past and present times; forming a complete history of the year, months, and seasons, and a perpetual key to the almanac . . . for daily use and diversion. By William Hone. With four hundred and thirty-six engravings*. 1825–1828. Vol. I. London: T. Tegg, 1841.

Hoskins, W. G. *The Making of the English Landscape*. 1955. London: Hodder and Stoughton, 1988.

Howard, Jacqueline. *Reading Gothic Fiction: A Bakhtinian Approach*. Oxford: Clarendon, 1994.

Howard, Jean E. "Cross-Dressing, the Theater, and Gender Struggle in Early-Modern England." *Crossing the Stage: Controversies on Cross-Dressing*. Ed. Lesley Ferris. London and New York: Routledge, 1993. 20–46.

Howard, Tom. *Austen Country*. New York: Smithmark, 1995.

Hubback, J. H. and Edith C. Hubback. *Jane Austen's Sailor Brothers: Being the Adventures of Sir Francis Austen, G.C.B., Admiral of the Fleet and Rear-Admiral Charles Austen*. 1906. Westport, Connecticut: Meckler, 1986.

"The Humours of the Card-Table." *The Lady's Magazine*. London: Dean and Munday, July, 1789.

Humphrey, Mary Jane. "Mrs. Palmer and Her Laughter." *Persuasions* 13 (1991): 13–15.

Hunt, John Dixon. *Gardens and the Picturesque: Studies in the History of Landscape Architecture*. Cambridge, MA: MIT Press, 1992.

Hunt, John Dixon and Peter Willis, ed. *The Genius of the Place: The English Landscape Garden 1620–1820*. 1975. Cambridge, MA: MIT Press, 1990.

Hunt, Leigh. *The Feast of the Poets, with notes and other pieces in verse by the Editor of the Examiner*. New York: Van Winkle and Wiley, 1814.

———. "Pocket Books and Keepsakes." *The Keepsake*. London: Hurst, Chance & Co., 1828.

Hunt, Lynn. "Freedom of Dress in Revolutionary France." *From the Royal to the Republican Body: Incorporating the Political in Seventeenth- and Eighteenth-Century France.* Ed. Sara E. Melzer and Kathryn Norberg. Berkeley: University of California Press, 1998. 224–249.

Inchbald, Elizabeth. *Lovers' Vows. A Play in Five Acts.* Repr. in Claudia L. Johnson, ed. *Mansfield Park.* New York: Norton, 1998.

Jackson, William. "Whether Genius be born, or acquired." *The Four Ages; Together with Essays on Various Subjects.* London: Cadell and Davies, 1798. 185–198.

Jackson-Stops, Gervase, Gordon J. Schochet et al., ed. *The Fashioning and Functioning of the British Country House.* Vol. 25. *Studies in the History of Art.* London: University Press of New England, 1989.

Jacox, Francis. "Female Novelists." *The New Monthly Magazine and Humorist* 95 (1852): 22.

James, Henry. *The Question of Our Speech. The Lesson of Balzac. Two Lectures.* 1905. Folcroft, PA: Folcroft Press, 1969.

Jameson, Frederick. *The Political Unconscious: Narrative as a Socially Symbolic Act.* Ithaca: Cornell University Press, 1981.

Janowitz, Anne. *England's Ruins: Poetic Purpose and the National Landscape.* Cambridge, MA: Basil Blackwell, 1990.

Jenkins, Elizabeth. *Jane Austen: A Biography.* London: Victor Gollancz, 1968.

Johnson, Claudia L. "Austen Cults and Cultures." *The Cambridge Companion to Jane Austen.* Ed. Edward Copeland and Juliet McMaster. Cambridge: Cambridge University Press, 1997. 211–226.

———. *Equivocal Beings: Politics, Gender, and Sentimentality in the 1790s Wollstonecraft, Radcliffe, Burney, Austen.* Chicago: University of Chicago Press, 1995.

———. *Jane Austen: Women, Politics, and the Novel.* Chicago and London: University of Chicago Press, 1988.

———. " 'Not at All What a Man Should Be!': Remaking English Manhood in *Emma.*" *Critical Essays On Jane Austen.* Ed. Laura Mooneyham White. New York: G. K. Hall, 1998. 146–159.

———. "The Divine Miss Jane: Jane Austen, Janeites, and the Discipline of Novel Studies." *Janeites: Austen's Disciples and Devotees.* Ed. Deidre Lynch. Princeton: Princeton University Press, 2000. 25–55.

———. " 'The Kingdom at Sixes and Sevens': Politics and the Juvenilia." *Jane Austen's Beginnings: The Juvenilia and Lady Susan.* Ed. J. David Grey. UMI Research Press. Ann Arbor, MI: University Microfilms, 1989. 45–58.

———. "What Became of Jane Austen? *Mansfield Park.*" *Persuasions* 17 (December 16, 1995): 59–70.

Johnson, Samuel. "The History of Misella Debauched by her Relation" and "Misella's Description of the Life of a Prostitute." *The Rambler.* Vol. 5. 170–171. *The Yale Edition of the Works of Samuel Johnson.* Ed. W. J Bate and Albrecht B. Strauss. New Haven: Yale University Press, 1969. 135–145.

————. "To Miss ___, on her giving the Author a Gold and Silk Net-work Purse of her weaving." *Elegant Extracts*. Ed. S. Hamilton Weybridge and C. Robinson. London, 1809.

————. *The Rambler*. Vol. 5. *The Yale Edition of the Works of Samuel Johnson*. Ed. W. J. Bate and Albrecht B. Strauss. New Haven: Yale University Press, 1969.

Jones, Margery Hargest. *Songs of Scotland: 36 Favourite Songs for Voice and Piano*. London: Boosey and Hawkins, 1992.

Kelly, Gary. "Religion and Politics." *The Cambridge Companion to Jane Austen*. Cambridge: Cambridge University Press, 1997.

Keppel, Lady Caroline. "Robin Adair." *Songs of Scotland*. Ed. Margery Hargest Jones. London: Boosey & Hawkes, 1992.

Kipling, Rudyard. *Debits and Credits*. New York: Doubleday, Page & Co., 1926.

Kirkham, Margaret. "Feminist Irony and The Priceless Heroine of *Mansfield Park*." *Jane Austen: New Perspectives*. Ed. Janet Todd. Vol. 3 of *Women and Literature, New Series*. New York: Holmes and Meier, 1983. 231–247.

————. *Jane Austen, Feminism and Fiction*. Sussex: Harvester, 1983.

Knight, Richard Payne. *An Analytical Inquiry into the Principles of Taste*. London: Luke Hansard and Sons, 1805.

————. *The Landscape*. London: Bulmer and Co., 1795.

Knox-Shaw, Peter. "Fanny Price Refuses to Kowtow." *The Review of English Studies* 47 (May 1996): 212–217.

Kolb, Gwin J. *Samuel Johnson: Rasselas and Other Tales*. New Haven: Yale University Press, 1990.

Kolodny, Annette. "Dancing through the Minefield: Some Observations on the Theory, Practice, and Politics of a Feminist Literary Criticism." *Critical Theory since 1965*. Ed. Hazard Adams and Leroy Searle. Tallahassee: Florida State University Press, 1986. 499–512. First published in *Feminist Studies* (Spring 1980): 1–25.

Korba, Susan M. " 'Improper and Dangerous Distinctions': Female Relationships and Erotic Domination in *Emma*." *Studies in the Novel* 29.2 (1997): 139–163.

Kristeva, Julia. "The Pain of Sorrow in the Modern World: The Works of Marguerite Duras." *PMLA* 102 (March 1987): 138–151.

————. *Powers of Horror: An Essay on Abjection*. New York: Columbia University Press, 1982.

The Lady's Magazine. Dean and Munday. London, 1770–1832.

The Lady's Monthly Museum, or Polite Repository of Amusement and Instruction: Being an assemblage of whatever can tend to please the Fancy, interest the Mind, or exalt the Character of The British Fair. By a Society of Ladies. London, 1798–1807.

Lamb, Charles. *Elia*. London: Taylor and Hessey, 1823. Repr. Oxford: Woodstock Books, 1991.

Lamb, Mary. "On Needle-Work." *Mary Lamb*. Ed. Alexandra Gilchrist, London: W. H. Allen, 1883, 186–194.

Lamont, Claire. " 'Let other pens dwell on guilt and misery': Adultery in Jane Austen." *Scarlet Letters: Fictions of Adultery from Antiquity to the 1990s.* Ed. Nicholas White and Naomi Segal. New York: St. Martin's, 1997. 70–81.

Landry, Donna. *The Invention of the Countryside: Hunting, Walking and Ecology in English Literature, 1671–1831.* New York: Palgrave, 2001.

Laqueur, Thomas. *Making Sex: Body and Gender from the Greeks to Freud.* Cambridge, MA and London: Harvard University Press, 1990.

La Rochefoucauld, François. *Mélanges sur l'Angleterre.(A Frenchman's year in Suffolk: French impressions of Suffolk life in 1784.)* Trans. and ed. Norman Scarfe. Wolfeboro: Boydell, 1988.

Lascelles, Mary. *Jane Austen and Her Art.* 1939. Oxford: Oxford University Press; London: Humphrey Milford, 1941.

Le Faye, Deirdre, ed. *Jane Austen's Letters.* 3rd ed. Oxford and New York: Oxford University Press, 1995.

Lefkovitz, Lori Hope, ed. *Textual Bodies: Changing Boundaries of Literary Representation.* SUNY Series: *The Body in Culture, History, and Religion.* Albany: State University of New York Press, 1997.

Leigh, Dale and Simon Ryan, ed. *The Body in the Library.* Amsterdam and Atlanta: Rodopi, 1998.

Leighton, Angela. "Sense and Silences." *New Casebooks: Sense and Sensibility and Pride and Prejudice.* Ed. Robert Clark. New York: St. Martin's, 1994. 53–66.

Lew, Joseph. "That Abominable Traffic: *Mansfield Park* and The Dynamics of Slavery". *History, Gender, and Eighteenth-Century Literature.* Ed. Beth Fowkes Tobin. Athens: University of Georgia Press, 1994. 271–300.

Lewis, Helen Block. "Shame and the Narcissistic Personality." *Many Faces.* Ed. Nathanson. 93–132.

Lewis, Matthew. "Giles Jollup the Knave and Sally Green, a Romance." *The Spirit of the Public Journals for 1797. Being an Impartial Selection of the Most Exquisite Essays and Jeux D'Esprits, Principally Prose, That Appear in the Newspapers and Other Publications.* 3rd ed. Vol. 1. London, 1802.

Lewis, Matthew G. *The Monk, a Romance.* London: Oxford University Press, 1973.

Lewis, W. S. et al., ed. *The Yale Edition of Horace Walpole's Correspondence.* Vol. XIX. New Haven: Yale University Press, 1955.

Lionnet, Francois. *Autobiographical Voices: Race, Gender, Self-Portraiture.* Ithaca: Cornell University Press, 1989.

Lister, Anne. *No Priest But Love: Excerpts from the Diaries of Anne Lister, 1824–1826.* New York: New York University Press, 1992.

Little, Judy. *Comedy and the Woman Writer: Woolf, Spark, and Feminism.* Lincoln: University of Nebraska Press, 1983.

Litvak, Joseph. *Caught in the Act: Theatricality in the Nineteenth-Century English Novel.* Berkeley: University of California Press, 1992.

———. *Strange Gourmets: Sophistication, Theory, and the Novel.* Durham: Duke University Press, 1997.

Litz, A. Walton. "Jane Austen: The Juvenilia." *Jane Austen's Beginnings: the Juvenilia and Lady Susan.* Ed. J. David Grey. Ann Arbor, MI: UMI Research Press. 1989. 1–6.

Liu, Alan. *Wordsworth: The Sense of History.* Stanford: Stanford University Press, 1989.

Lloyd, Christopher and Vanessa, Remington. *Masterpieces in Little: Portrait Miniatures from the Collection of Her Majesty Queen Elizabeth II.* London: Boydell, 1996.

Lodge, David. *Changing Places: A Tale of Two Campuses.* Harmondsworth: Penguin, 1978.

Looser, Devoney, ed. *Jane Austen and the Discourses of Feminism.* New York: St. Martin's, 1995.

Loudon, J. C. *The Landscape Gardening and Landscape Architecture of the Late Humphrey Repton, being his entire works on these subjects.* London, 1840.

Luthi, Anne Louise. *Sentimental Jewellery.* Haverfordwest: CIT Printing, 1998.

Lynch, Deidre. *The Economy of Character: Novels, Market Culture, and the Business of Inner Meaning.* Chicago: Chicago University Press, 1998.

———, ed. *Janeites: Austen's Disciples and Devotees.* Princeton: Princeton University Press, 2000.

Lyttelton, George. "Advice to a Lady." *A Collection of Poems. By Several Hands. In Three Volumes.* 3 vols. London: R. Dodsley, 1748.

Lyttle, Bethany. "Quilling Valentines." Photographs by Gentl and Hyers. *Martha Stewart Living* (February 2002): 142–147.

Lytton, Edward Bulwer, Baron. *The Dramatic Works of Edward Bulwer Lytton (Lord Lytton).* New York: P. F. Collier, 1875.

MacCannell, Dean. *The Tourist: A New Theory of the Leisure Class.* Berkeley: University of California Press, 1976.

MacDonagh, Oliver. *Jane Austen: Real and Imagined Worlds.* New Haven: Yale University Press, 1991.

Mackie, Erin. *Market à la Mode: Fashion, Commodity, and Gender in* The Tatler *and* The Spectator. Baltimore and London: Johns Hopkins University Press, 1997.

Maccubbin, Robert Purks, ed. *'Tis Nature's Fault: Unauthorized Sexuality during the Enlightenment.* Cambridge: Cambridge University Press, 1985.

Maeder, Edward, ed. *An Elegant Art: Fashion & Fantasy in the Eighteenth Century, Los Angeles County Museum of Art Collection of Costumes and Textiles.* Los Angeles: Los Angeles County Museum of Art; New York: H. N. Abrams, 1983.

Malbert, Roger. "Fetish and Form in Contemporary Art." *Fetishism: Visualising Power and Desire.* Ed. Anthony Shelton. London: The South Bank Centre and The Royal Pavilion, Art Gallery and Museums, Brighton, Great Britain, in assoc. with Lund Humphries Publishers, 1995. 89–124.

Martin, William. *The Hair Worker's Manual, Being A Treatise on Hair Working, Containing Direction and Instructions to Enable Ladies to*

Prepare and Work their own Materials. Illustrated with Designs and Diagrams. Brighton, 1852.

McAllister, Marie. "John Burrows and the Vegetable Wars." *The Secret Malady: Venereal Disease in Eighteenth-Century Britain and France.* Ed. Linda E. Merians. Lexington: University Press of Kentucky, 1996. 85–102.

McKendrick, Neil. "Introduction: The Birth of a Consumer Society." *The Birth of a Consumer Society: The Commercialization of Eighteenth-Century England.* Ed. Neil McKendrick, John Brewer, and J. H. Plumb. Bloomington: Indiana University Press, 1982.

McMaster, Juliet. *Jane Austen the Novelist: Essays Past and Present.* New York: St. Martin's, 1996.

McMaster, Juliet and Bruce Stovel, ed. *Jane Austen's Business: Her World and Her Profession.* New York: St. Martin's, 1996.

Meinig, D. W., ed. *The Interpretation of Ordinary Landscapes: Geographical Essays by J. B. Jackson, Peirce F. Lewis, David Lowenthal, D. W. Meinig, Marwyn S. Samuels, David E. Sopher, Yi-Fu Tuan.* Oxford: Oxford University Press, 1979.

Melmoth. "Defence of Riddles: in a letter to a Lady." *Elegant Extracts: Being a Copious Selection of Instructive, Moral and Entertaining Passages, from the Most Eminent British Poets.* 10 vols. Vol. 5. London: John Sharpe, 1810. 265–268.

Mennell, Stephen. *All Manners of Food: Eating and Taste in England and France from the Middle Ages to the Present.* Chicago: University of Illinois Press, 1996.

Merians, Linda. "The London Lock Hospital and the Lock Asylum for Women." *The Secret Malady: Venereal Disease in Eighteenth-Century Britain and France.* Ed. Linda Merians. Lexington: University Press of Kentucky, ca. 1996. 128–145.

Merrill, Lisa. "Feminist Humor: Rebellious and Self-Affirming." *Last Laughs: Perspectives in Women and Comedy.* Ed. Regina Barreca. New York and London: Gordon and Breach, 1988. 271–280.

Miller, D. A. *Narrative and its Discontents: Problems of Closure in the Traditional Novel.* Princeton: Princeton University Press, 1981.

Miller, Pamela A. "Hair Jewelry as Fetish." *Objects of Special Devotion: Fetishism in Popular Culture.* Ed. Ray Browne. Bowling Green, OH: Bowling Green University Press, 1982. 89–106.

Miller, William Ian. *Humiliation: And Other Essays on Honor, Social Discomfort, and Violence.* Ithaca and London: Cornell University Press, 1993.

Milton, John. *Paradise Lost.* Ed. Alastair Fowler. New York: Longman, 1998.

Monaghan, David. *Jane Austen: Structure and Social Vision.* London: Macmillan, 1980.

———, ed. *Emma.* New York: St. Martin's Press, 1992.

———, ed. *Jane Austen in a Social Context.* Totowa, NJ: Barnes and Noble, 1981.

Mooneyham, Laura G. *Romance, Language, and Education in Jane Austen's Novels.* Basingstoke: Macmillan, 1988.

More, Hannah. *Coelebs in Search of a Wife*. 2 vols. London: T. Cadell & W. Davies, 1808.

Morgan, Susan. *Sisters in Time: Imagining Gender in 19th-Century British Fiction*. New York and Oxford: Oxford University Press, 1989.

Mowbray, John, *The Female Physician, Containing all the Diseases incident to that Sex, in Virgins, Wives, and Widows; Together With their Causes and Symptoms, their Degrees of Danger, and respective Methods of Prevention and Cure*. London: Stephen Austen, 1730.

Mudge, Bradford. *The Whore's Story: Women, Pornography, and the British Novel, 1684–1830*. Oxford: Oxford University Press, 1985.

Mueller, Judith C. "Fallen Men: Representations of Male Impotence in Britain." *Studies in Eighteenth-Century Culture* 28. Ed. Julie Candler Hayes and Timothy Erwin. Baltimore and London: Johns Hopkins University Press, 1999. 85–102.

Murray, Douglas. "Gazing and Avoiding the Gaze." *Jane Austen's Business: Her World and Her Profession*. Ed. Juliet McMaster and Bruce Stoval. New York: Macmillan, 1996.

Neill, Edward. *The Politics of Jane Austen*. New York: St. Martin's, 1999.

New Foundling Hospital for Wit. Being a Collection of Curious Pieces in Verse and Prose, by Sir C. Hanbury Williams, Earl of Chesterfield, Earl of Delawarr, Earl of Hardwicke, Earl of Carlisle, Lords Lyttelton, Harvey, Capel, Lady M. W. Montague, T. Potter, C. Townshend, J. S. Hall, J. Wiles, D. Garrick, B. Thornton, G. Colman, R. Lloyd. Part 4. London, 1771.

Newman, Karen. "Can This Marriage Be Saved: Jane Austen makes sense of an ending." *ELH* 50.3 (Fall 1983): 693–710.

Newton, Judith Lowder. *Women, Power, and Subversion: Social Strategies in British Fiction, 1778–1860*. Athens: University of Georgia Press, 1981.

Nichol, Donald W. "Slander, Scandal and Satire." *TLS: The Times Literary Supplement* (January 28, 2000): 14–15.

Nicolson, Nigel. "Not Fanny Price, more Mary Crawford." Rev. of *Jane Austen: A Life*, by David Nokes, and *Jane Austen: A Life*, by Claire Tomalin. *The Spectator* (September 27, 1997): 41–42.

Nietzsche, Friedrich. *Thus Spake Zarathustra*. Trans. Thomas Common. Carlton House: New York, n.d.

———. *The Will to Power*. Trans. Walter Kaufmann and R. J. Hollingdale. New York: Random House, 1967.

Nokes, David. *Jane Austen: A Life*. New York: Farrar, Straus and Giroux, 1997.

Norton, Rictor. *Mother Clap's Molly House: The Gay Subculture in England, 1700–1830*. London: GMP; East Haven, CT: In Book, 1992.

Nussbaum, Felicity. "One Part of Womankind: Prostitution and Sexual Geography." Memoirs of a Woman of Pleasure. *Differences: A Journal of Feminist Cultural Studies* 7.2 (1995): 16–39.

O'Farrell, Mary Ann. *Telling Complexions: The Nineteenth-Century English Novel and the Blush*. Durham: Duke University Press, 1997.

"Ode to Fashion." *The Ladies Monthly Museum, or Polite Repository of Amusement and Instruction: Being an assemblage of whatever can tend to please the Fancy, interest the Mind, or exalt the Character of The British Fair. By a Society of Ladies.* From the French of M. Pouce. 1789. (March 1800): 177.

"On a Pincushion." *New Foundling Hospital for Wit. Being a Collection of Curious Pieces in Verse and Prose,* by Sir C. Hanbury Williams, Earl of Chesterfield, Earl of Delawarr, Earl of Hardwicke, Earl of Carlisle, Lords Lyttelton, Harvey, Capel, Lady M. W. Montague, T. Potter, C. Townshend, J. S. Hall, J. Wiles, D. Garrick, B. Thornton, G. Colman, R. Lloyd. Part 4. London, 1771.

"On Puns and Other Substitutions for Wit." *Elegant Extracts: Being a Copious Selection of Instructive, Moral and Entertaining Passages, from the most Eminent British Poets.* 10 vols. Vol. 5. London: John Sharpe. 268–272.

"Orgies of Bacchus." *The Spirit of the Public Journals. Being an Impartial Selection of the Most Exquisite Essays and Jeux D'Esprits, Principally Prose, That Appear in the Newspapers and Other Publications.* 3rd ed. Vol. 1. London, 1802. 261–284.

Owenson, Sydney. *Wild Irish Girl.* Oxford: Oxford University Press, 1999.

Palmer, Alan. *Crowned Cousins: The Anglo-German Royal Connection.* London: Weidenfeld and Nicolson, 1985.

Parker, Todd C. *Sexing the Text: The Rhetoric of Sexual Difference in British Literature, 1700–1750.* New York: State University of New York Press, 2000.

Partridge, Eric. *Shakespeare's Bawdy: A Literary and Psychological Essay and a Comprehensive Glossary.* 1947. London: Routledge & Kegan Paul, 1968.

———. *A Dictionary of Slang and Unconventional English.* 7th ed. New York: Macmillan, 1970.

Paulson, Ronald. *The Art of Hogarth.* London: Phaidon, 1975.

———. *The Beautiful, Novel, and Strange: Aesthetics and Heterodoxy.* Baltimore: Johns Hopkins University Press, 1996.

———. *Breaking and Remaking: Aesthetic Practice in England, 1700–1820.* New Brunswick: Rutgers University Press, 1989.

———. *Hogarth: His Life, Art, and Times.* New Haven and London: Yale University Press, 1971.

Peakman, Julie. *Mighty Lewd Books: The Development of Pornography in Eighteenth-Century England.* Houndmills, Basingstoke, Hampshire: Palgrave Macmillan, 2003.

Perkins, Moreland. *Reshaping the Sexes in Sense and Sensibility.* Charlottesville: University Press of Virginia, 1998.

Perkins, Pam. "A Subdued Gaiety: The Comedy of *Mansfield Park.*" *Nineteenth-Century Literature* 48.1 (June 1993): 1–25.

Perry, Ruth. "Sleeping with Mr. Collins." *Persuasions* 22 (2000): 119–135.

Phelan, Peggy. "Crisscrossing Cultures." *Crossing the Stage: Controversies on Cross-Dressing.* Ed. Lesley Ferris. London and New York: Routledge, 1993. 155–170.

Phillips, Clare. *Jewels and Jewelry*. Photos by Ian Thomas. New York: Watson-Guptill Publications, 2000.

Phillipps, K. C. *Jane Austen's English*. London: Andre Deutch, 1990.

Pigott, Charles D. *A political dictionary: explaining the true meaning of words. Illustrated and exemplified in the lives, morals, character and conduct of the following most illustrious personages among many others. The King, Queen, Prince of Wales. . . .* New York: Thomas Greenleaf, 1796.

Pietz, William. "The Problem of the Fetish, I." *RES* 9 (Spring 1985): 5–17.

———. "The Problem of the Fetish, II: The Origin of the Fetish." *RES* 13 (Spring 1987): 23–45.

———. "The Problem of the Fetish, IIIa: Bosman's Guinea and the Enlightenment Theory of Fetishism." *RES* 16 (Autumn 1998): 106–123.

Pitcher, Edward W. R. *The Lady's Monthly Museum First Series: 1798–1806*. An Annotated Index of Signatures and Ascriptions. Studies in British and American Magazines. Vol. 2. Lewiston, NY: The Edwin Mellen Press, 2000.

Pliny, The Elder. *Natural History*. Trans. H. Rakham. Cambridge, MA: Harvard University Press, 1963.

Pointon, Marcia. *Hanging the Head: Portraiture and Social Formation in Eighteenth-Century England*. New Haven: Yale University Press, 1993.

———. "Materializing Mourning: Hair, Jewelry and the Body." *Material Memories: Design and Evocation*. Ed. Marius Kwint, Christopher Breward, and Jeremy Aynsley. Oxford, England: Berg Publishers, 1999. 39–57.

———. "Wearing Memory: Mourning, Jewellery, and the Body." *Trauer tragen—Trauer zeigen: Inszenierungen der Geschlecter*. Ed. Gisela Ecker. Munich: William Fink Verlag, 1999. 65–81.

Polhemus, Robert M. *Erotic Faith: Being in Love from Jane Austen to D. H. Lawrence*. Chicago: University of Chicago Press, 1990.

Poovey, Mary. "Ideological Contradictions and the Consolations of Form (1)." *New Casebooks: Sense and Sensibility and Pride and Prejudice*. Ed. Robert Clark. New York: St. Martin's, 1994. 83–100.

———. *The Proper Lady and the Woman Writer: Ideology as Style in the works of Mary Wollstonecraft, Mary Shelley, and Jane Austen*. Chicago: University of Chicago Press, 1984.

Pope, Alexander. *Poetry and Prose of Alexander Pope*. Boston: Houghton Mifflin, 1969.

Poplawski, Paul. *A Jane Austen Encyclopedia*. Westport, CT: Greenwood Press, 1998.

Porter, Roy. "The Literature of Sexual Advice before 1800." *Sexual Knowledge, Sexual Science: The History of Attitudes to Sexuality*. Ed. Roy Porter and Mikuláš Teich. Cambridge: Cambridge University Press, 1994. 134–157.

———. "Mixed Feelings: The Enlightenment and Sexuality." Ed. Paul-Gabriel Bouce. *Sexuality in Eighteenth-Century Britain*. Totowa, NJ: Manchester University Press, 1982. 1–27.

———. " 'The Secrets of Generation Display'd': *Aristotle's Master-piece* in Eighteenth-Century England." *'Tis Nature's Fault': Unauthorized*

Sexuality during the Enlightenment. Ed. Robert Purks Maccubbin. Cambridge: Cambridge University Press, 1987. 1–21.

Potter, Humphry Tristram. *A New Dictionary of all the Cant and Flash languages, Both Ancient and Modern*. London: B. Crosby, 1797.

Preziosi, Donald, ed. *The Art of Art History: A Critical Anthology*. Oxford: Oxford University Press, 1998.

Price, Uvedale. *An Essay on the Picturesque, As Compared with the Sublime and Beautiful; and, on the Use of Studying Pictures, for the purpose of Improving Real Landscape*. 1794. 3 vols. London: Hereford, 1810.

Puzzlewell, Peter. *A Choice Collection of Riddles, Charades, Rebusses, Etc. Chiefly Original*. London: E. Newberry, 1794.

Radcliffe, Ann. *Mysteries of Udolpho*. Ed. Jacqueline Howard. London: Penguin, 2001.

Rees, A. *The Cyclopedia of Arts, Sciences and Literature*. Vol. XXIV. London: Longman, 1819.

Ribeiro, Aileen. *The Gallery of Fashion*. Princeton: Princeton University Press, 2000.

Rice, Patty C. *Amber: The Golden Gem of the Ages*. 1980. New York: The Koscuiszko Foundation, 1993.

Richardson, Alan. *British Romanticism and the Science of the Mind*. Cambridge: Cambridge University Press, 2001.

Richardson, Samuel. *Clarissa, or The History of a Young Lady*. Ed. Angus Ross. Harmondsworth: Penguin, 1985.

———. *The History of Sir Charles Grandison*. Ed. Thomas Archer. London: Routledge, 1924.

———. *Pamela, or Virtue Rewarded*. Ed. Peter Sabor. Harmondsworth: Penguin, 1980.

Riddles, Charades, and Conundrums, the greater part of which have never been published. With a preface on the antiquity of riddles. London, 1822.

Roberts, David. *The Ladies: Female Patronage of Restoration Drama*. Oxford: Clarendon, 1989.

Roberts, Warren. *Jane Austen and the French Revolution*. 1979. London and Atlantic Highlands, NJ: Athlone, 1995.

Robinson, Lillian S. "Treason our Text: Feminist Challenges to the Literary Canon." *Critical Theory Since 1965*. Ed. Hazard Adams and Leroy Searle. Tallahassee: Florida State University Press, 1986. 572–582. Originally appeared in *Tulsa Studies in Women's Literature* 2 (1983): 83–98.

Robinson, Mary. "Lesbia and her Lover." *The Wild Wreath*. London: Printed for Richard Phillips, 1804. 151–152.

Robinson, Sidney K. *Inquiry into the Picturesque*. Chicago: University of Chicago Press, 1991.

Roe, Sue, ed. *Women Reading Women's Writing*. New York: St. Martin's, 1987.

Roeder, Sharlene. "The Fall on High-church Down in Jane Austen's *Sense and Sensibility*." *Persuasions* 12 (1990): 60.

Rousseau, Jean-Jacques. *Emile*. Trans. Barbara Foxley. London: J.M. Dent and Son, 1955. 356–57.

Ross, Andrew. *Amber*. London: The Natural History Museum; Cambridge, MA: Harvard University Press, 1998.

Ruderman, Anne Crippen. *The Pleasures of Virtue: Political Thought in the Novels of Jane Austen*. Lanham, Md: Rowman and Littlefield, 1995.

Rudofsky, Bernard. *The Unfashionable Human Body*. Garden City, NY: Doubleday, 1971.

Rugoff, Ralph. "Homeopathic Strategies." *At the Threshold of the Visible: Minuscule and Small-Scale Art, 1964–1996*. Ed. Ralph Rugoff and Susan Stewart. New York: Independent Curators Incorporated, 1997. 11–17.

Rzepka, Charles. "The Feel of Not to Feel It." *PMLA* 116.5 (Oct. 2001): 1422–1431.

Said, Edward W. *Culture and Imperialism*. New York: Vintage Books, 1994.

Sales, Roger. *Jane Austen and Representations of Regency England*. London and New York: Routledge, 1994. 9–10.

———. "In Face of All the Servants: Spectators and Spies in Austen." *Janeites*. Ed. Deidre Lynch. Princeton: Princeton University, 2000. 188–205.

Satan's Harvest Home: or the Present State of Whorecraft, Adultery, Fornication, Procuring, Pimping, Sodomy, And the Game at Flatts. Collected from the Memoirs of an Intimate Comrade of the Hon. Jack S-n-r. London: J. Roberts, 1749.

Savigny, John. *Instructions at Large for Making and Repairing Pens*. London, 1786.

Scarry, Elaine. *The Body in Pain: The Making and Unmaking of the World*. New York: Oxford University Press, 1985.

Scholes, Percy A. *The Oxford Companion to Music*. 10th ed. London: Oxford University Press, 1970.

Scott, Sir Walter. *Redgauntlet*. Ed. Kathryn Sutherland. Oxford: Oxford University Press, 1998.

———. Rev. "*Emma*: a Novel." *On Novelists and Fiction*. Ed. Ioan Williams. London: Routledge, 1968.

Secker, Thomas. *Lectures on the Catechism of the Church of England*. 2 vols. London: J. & F. Rivington, 1769.

Sedgewick, Eve Kosofsky. *Between Men: English Literature and Male Homosocial Desire*. New York: Columbia University Press, 1985.

———. "Jane Austen and the Masturbating Girl." *Solitary Pleasures: The Historical, Literary, and Artistic Discourses of Autoeroticism*. Ed. Paula Bennet and Vernon Rosario II. New York: Routledge, 1995. 133–153.

Seeber, Barbara. "'I See Everything as You Desire Me to Do': The Scolding and Schooling of Marianne Dashwood." *Eighteenth-Century Fiction*. 11.2 (1999): 223–233.

Senelick, Laurence. "Boys and Girls Together: Subcultural Origins of Glamour Drag and Male Impersonation on the Nineteenth-Century Stage." *Crossing the Stage: Controversies on Cross-Dressing*. Ed. Lesley Ferris. London: Routledge, 1993. 80–95.

"Sent in a Snuff Box, to Lady S– L-." *Garrick's Jests; or, Genius in High Glee. Containing all the Jests of the Wits of the Present Age*. London, 1790 [?].

Seward, Anna. "Anna Seward to J. Johnson, Esq." *Letters of Anna Seward, 1784–1807.* 6 vols. Edinburgh, 1811.

Shakespeare, William. *Henry IV, Part II. The Complete Works of Shakespeare.* 1951. Ed. Hardin Craig and David Bevington. Glenview, IL: Scott Foresman, 1973.

———. *Merchant of Venice. The Complete Works of Shakespeare.* 1951. Ed. Hardin Craig and David Bevington. Glenview, IL: Scott Foresman, 1973.

———. *The Merry Wives of Windsor. The Complete Works of Shakespeare. 1951.* Ed. Hardin Craig and David Bevington. Glenview, IL: Scott Foresman, 1973.

———. *Much Ado About Nothing. The Complete Works of Shakespeare.* 1951. Ed. Hardin Craig and David Bevington. Glenview, IL: Scott Foresman, 1973.

———. *The plays of William Shakespeare; with the corrections and illustrations of various commentators, to which are added notes by Samuel Johnson and George Steevens, with an appendix.* 1773. Ed. George Steevens and Issac Reed. London: Longman, 1793.

———. *Romeo and Juliet. The Complete Works of Shakespeare.* 1951. Ed. Hardin Craig and David Bevington. Glenview, IL: Scott Foresman, 1973.

———. *Troilus and Cressida. The Complete Works of Shakespeare.* 1951. Ed. Hardin Craig and David Bevington. Glenview, IL: Scott Foresman, 1973.

Shaw, Harry E. *Narrating Reality: Austen, Scott, Eliot.* Ithaca: Cornell University Press, 1999.

Shaw, Peggy and Weaver, Lois. *Belle Reprieve.* New York: La Mama Theater, 1991.

Shelton, Anthony. "Introduction." *Fetishism: Visualising Power and Desire.* Ed. Anthony Shelton. London: The South Bank Centre and The Royal Pavilion, Art Gallery and Museums, Brighton in Assoc. with Lund Humphries Publishers, 1995.

Shenstone, William. "The School-Mistress, a poem in imitation of Spenser." London, 1742.

Sherbo, Arthur, ed. *Johnson on Shakespeare.* 2 vols. New York and London: Yale University Press, 1968.

Sheumaker, Helen. " 'This Lock You See': Nineteenth-Century Hair Work as the Commodified Self." *Fashion Theory* 1.4 (December 1997): 421–446.

Shields, Carol. "Jane Austen's Images of the Body: No Fingers, No Toes." *Persuasions* 13 (1991): 132–137.

Silverman, Debra. "Making a Spectacle: Or, Is There Female Drag?" *Critical Matrix: The Princeton Journal of Women, Gender, and Culture* 7.2 (1993): 69–89.

Silverman, Kaja. "Fragments of a Fashionable Discourse." *On Fashion.* Ed. Shari Benstock and Suzanne Ferriss. New Brunswick: Rutgers University Press, 1994. 183–196.

Simond, Louis. *Journal of a tour and residence in Great Britain during the years 1810 and 1811: with remarks on the country, its arts, literature, and politics, and on the manners and customs of its inhabitants / by a French traveller.* New York: T. & W. Mercein, 1815.

Simons, Judy, ed. *Mansfield Park and Persuasion.* New Casebooks. London: Macmillan, 1997.

Skinner, John. "Exploring Space: The Constellations of *Mansfield Park.*" *Eighteenth-Century Fiction* 4.2 (January 1992): 125–148.

Smith, Johanna M. " 'I Am a Gentleman's Daughter': A Marxist-Feminist Reading of *Pride and Prejudice.*" *Approaches to Teaching Austen's* Pride and Prejudice. Ed. Marcia McClintock Folsom. New York: Modern Language Association (MLA), 1993. 67–73.

Smith, Willard. *The Nature of Comedy.* Boston: R. G. Badger, 1930.

"A Soldier's Wife." "Select Scraps of Wit and Humour." *The Entertaining Magazine, or Polite Repository of Elegant Amusement.* London: Harrison & Co, 1803. 135.

Solomon, Alisa. "It's Never Too Late to Switch: Crossing Toward Power." *Crossing the Stage: Controversies on Cross-dressing.* Ed. Lesley Ferris. London: Routledge, 1993. 144–154.

Southam, B. C. *Jane Austen: The Critical Heritage 1870–1940.* London: Routledge & Kegan Paul; New York: Barnes and Noble, 1968.

———. *Jane Austen and the Navy.* London: Hambleton and London, 2000.

———. *Jane Austen's "Sir Charles Grandison."* Oxford: Clarendon, 1980.

———., ed. *Critical Essays on Jane Austen.* New York: Barnes and Noble, 1968.

Spacks, Patricia Meyer. "Austen's Laughter." *Last Laughs: Perspectives on Women and Comedy.* Ed. Regina Barreca. New York: Gordon and Breach, 1988. 71–85.

———, ed. *Persuasion.* London and New York: Norton, 1995.

Speight, Alexanna. *The Lock of Hair: Its History, Ancient and Modern, Natural and Artistic; with the Art of Working in Hair. Illustrated by Numerous Designs.* London, 1871.

The Spirit of the Public Journals for 1797. Being an Impartial Selection of the Most Exquisite Essays and Jeux D'Esprits, Principally Prose, That Appear in the Newspapers and Other Publications. 3rd ed. Vol. 1. London, 1802.

The Spirit of the Public Journals for 1799. Being an Impartial Selection of the Most Exquisite Essays and Jeux D'Esprits, Principally Prose, That Appear in the Newspapers and Other Publications. Vol. 3. London, 1805.

Spongeberg, Mary. *Feminizing Venereal Disease: The Body of the Prostitute in 19th-Century Medical Discourse.* New York: New York University Press, 1997.

The Sporting Magazine; or Monthly Calendar of the Transactions of The Turf, The Chace, And every other Diversion Interesting to The Man of Pleasure and Enterprize. London: Rogerson and Tuxford, April 1795.

Stallybrass, Peter and Allon White. *The Poetics of Transgression.* Ithaca: Cornell University Press, 1986.

Starobinski, Jean et al. *Revolution in Fashion: European Clothing, 1715–1815.* New York: Abbeville, 1989.

Staves, Susan. *Married Women's Separate Property in England, 1660–1833.* Cambridge MA: Harvard University Press, 1990.

———. "Comedy of Attempted Rape." *History, Gender, and Eighteenth-Century Literature.* Ed. Beth Fowkes Tobin. Athens: Georgia University Press, 1994.

Stead, Jennifer. *Food and Cooking in Eighteenth-Century Britain.* Birmingham: English Heritage, 1985.

Steevens, George, ed. *Twenty of the Plays of Shakespeare, being the whole number printed in Quarto during his life-time, or before the Restoration; collated where there were different copies, and publish'd from the originals by G. Steevens.* 4 vols. London: J. & R. Tonson, 1766.

Steevens, George and Issac Reed, ed. *The Plays of William Shakespeare.* 4th ed. 15 vols. London: Longman, 1793.

Sterne, Laurence. A *Sentimental Journey Through France and Italy, by Mr. Yorick; to Which are Added "The Journal to Eliza" and "A Political Romance."* Ed. Ian Jack. New York: Oxford University Press, 1968.

———. *Tristram Shandy.* Ed. Howard Anderson. New York: Norton, 1980.

Stewart, Maaja A. *Domestic Realities and Imperial Fictions: Jane Austen's Novels in Eighteenth-Century Context.* Athens: University of Georgia Press, 1993.

Stewart, Mary Margaret. " 'And blights with plagues the Marriage hearse': Syphilis and Wives." *The Secret Malady: Venereal Disease in Eighteenth-Century Britain and France.* Ed. Linda Merians. Lexington: University Press of Kentucky, 1996. 103–113.

Stewart, Susan. *On Longing: Narratives of the Miniature, the Gigantic, the Souvenir, the Collection.* Durham: Duke University Press, 1993.

Stoller, Robert J. *Sex and Gender: On the Development of Masculinity and Femininity.* London: Hogarth Press, 1968.

Stone, Lawrence. *The Family, Sex and Marriage in England: 1500–1800.* New York: Harper & Row, 1979.

Stones, Graeme, *Parodies of the Romantic Age.* Vol. I. *The Anti-Jacobin.* London: Pickering & Chatto, 1999.

Strachan, John and Graeme Stones. *Parodies of the Romantic Age.* Vol I. "General Introduction." London: Pickering & Chatto: 1999.

Sulivan, Richard Joseph. *A View of Nature, in Letters To a Traveller Among the Alps. With Reflections on Atheistical Philosophy now Exemplified in France.* 6 vols. Vol. II. London, 1794.

Sulloway, Alison G. *Jane Austen and the Province of Womanhood.* Philadelphia: University of Pennsylvania Press, 1989.

Swabey, Marie Collins. *Comic Laughter: A Philosophical Essay.* New Haven: Yale University Press, 1961.

Tanner, Tony. *Jane Austen.* Cambridge, MA: Harvard University Press, 1986.

Thomson, E. P. "The Moral Economy of the English Crowd in the Eighteenth Century." *Past and Present* 50 (1971): 96–136.

Thompson, James. *Between Self and World: The Novels of Jane Austen.* University Park and London: Pennsylvania State University Press, 1988.

Todd, Janet, ed. *Jane Austen: New Perspectives.* Vol. 3. *Women and Literature, New Series.* New York: Holmes and Meier, 1983.

Tomalin, Claire. *Jane Austen: A Life.* New York: Knopf, 1998.

Tompkins, Joanne. "Dressing Up/Dressing Down: Cultural Transvestism in Post-Colonial Drama." *Post-Colonial Drama: Theory, Practice, Politics.* London and New York: Routledge, 1996.

Troost, Linda and Sayre Greenfield, ed. *Jane Austen in Hollywood.* Lexington: University Press of Kentucky, 1998.

Trumbach, Randolph. *Sex and the Gender Revolution.* Vol. I. Chicago: University of Chicago Press, 1998.

Trumpener, Katie. *Bardic Nationalism. The Romantic Novel and the British Empire.* Princeton: Princeton University Press, 1997.

———. "The Virago Jane Austen." *Janeites.* Ed. Deidre Lynch. Princeton and Oxford: Princeton University Press, 2000. 140–165.

Tucker, George Holbert. *Jane Austen, The Woman: Some Biographical Insights.* New York: St. Martin's, 1994.

Tuite, Clara. *Romantic Austen.* Cambridge: Cambridge University Press, 2002.

Turner, Bryan S. *The Body and Society: Explorations in Social Theory.* Oxford and New York: Basil Blackwell, 1984.

Van Sant, Ann Jessie. *Eighteenth-Century Sensibility: The Senses in Social Context.* Cambridge: Cambridge University Press, 1993.

Van Sickle Johnson, Judy. "The Bodily Frame: Learning Romance in *Persuasion.*" *Nineteenth-Century Fiction* 38 (June 1983): 43–61.

Vickery, Amanda. *The Gentleman's Daughter: Women's Lives in Georgian England.* New Haven: Yale University Press, 1998.

Vinken, Barbara. "Transvesty-Travesty: Fashion and Gender." *Fashion Theory* 3.1 (1999): 33–50.

Visser, Margaret. *The Rituals of Dinner: The Origins, Evolution, Eccentricities, and Meaning of Table Manners.* New York: Grove Weidenfeld, 1991.

Waldron, Mary. *Jane Austen and the Fiction of Her Time.* Cambridge and New York: Cambridge University Press, 1999.

Walker, Richard. *Miniatures: A Selection of Miniatures in the Ashmolean Museum.* Oxford: Ashmolean Museum, 1997.

Wallace, Anne. D. "Picturesque Fossils, Sublime Geology? The Crisis of Authority in Charlotte Smith's *Beachy Head.*" "Variations on the Picturesque." Ed. Gary Harrison and Jill Heydt-Stevenson. *European Romantic Review* 13.1 (March 2002): 77–93.

Walpole, Horace. "Chapter V: Painters in Enamel and Miniature, Statuaries, and Medallions, in the Reign of George II." *Anecdotes of Painting in England; Collected by the late Mr. George Vertue.* 3rd ed. Vol. III. London: Ward, Lock, & Co., 1879.

Warhol, Robyn. "The Look, The Body, and the Heroine of *Persuasion*: A Feminist-Narratological View of Jane Austen" *Ambiguous Discourse: Feminist Narratology & British Women Writers.* Ed. Kathy Mezei. Chapel Hill and London: University of North Carolina Press, 1996. 21–39.

Warner, Marina. "Bush Natural." *Parkett* 27 (1991): 6–11.

Warwick, Alexandra and Dani Cavallaro, ed. *Fashioning the Frame: Boundaries, Dress and the Body.* Oxford: Berg Publishers, 1998.

Watson, Nicola J. *Revolution and the Form of the British Novel, 1790–1825: Intercepted Letters, Interrupted Seductions.* Oxford: Clarendon, 1994.

Weldon, Fay. *Letters on First Reading Jane Austen.* London: Michael Joseph, 1984.

West, Gilbert. "Epigram VIIII On Mrs. Penelope." *A Collection of Poems. By Several Hands. In Three Volumes.* Ed. George Lyttelton, 3 vols. London: R. Dodsley, 1748.

Whatley, Richard. "Review of *Northanger Abbey* and *Persuasion.*" *Quarterly Review* 24 (1821): 352–376; rpt. B. C. Southam, ed. *Jane Austen: The Critical Heritage.* Vol. 1. London: Routledge & Kegan Paul, 1968. 87–105.

Whitbread, Helena, ed. *I Know My Own Heart: The Diaries of Anne Lister (1791–1840).* London: Virago Press, 1988.

White, Laura Mooneyham. "Jane Austen and the Marriage Plot: Questions of Persistence." *Jane Austen and Discourses of Feminism.* Ed. Devoney Looser. New York: St. Martin's, 1995. 71–86.

Williams, Gordon. *A Glossary of Shakespeare's Sexual Language.* London and Atlantic Highlands, NJ: Athlone, 1997.

Williams, Ioan, ed. *Sir Walter Scott on Novelists and Fiction.* London, Routledge, 1968.

Williams, Raymond. *The Country and the City.* New York: Oxford University Press, 1973.

Williams, Tennessee. *A Streetcar Named Desire.* New York: New Directions, 1947.

Williamson, George C. *The Book of Amber.* London: Ernest Benn Limited, 1932.

Wilmot, John [Earl of Rochester]. *The Dictionary of Love: In which is contained the Explanation of most of the Terms used in that Language.* London: R. Griffiths, 1753.

Wilson, Anne C. *Food and Drink in Britain: From the Stone Age to Recent Times.* London: Constable and Company, 1973.

———., ed. *The Appetite and the Eye: Visual Aspects of Food and its Presentation Within their Historic Context.* Edinburgh: Edinburgh University Press, 1991.

Wilson, Elizabeth. *Adorned in Dreams: Fashion and Modernity.* Berkeley: University of California Press, 1985.

Wilson, Francesca M., ed. *Strange Island: Britain through Foreign Eyes, 1395–1940.* London: Longmans, Green and Co., 1955.

Wilson, Harriette. *The Memoirs of Harriette Wilson: Written by Herself.* 1825. 2 vols. London: Privately printed for the Navarre Society Limited, 1924.

Wilson, Philip. "Exposing the Secret Disease: Recognizing and Treating Syphilis in Daniel Turner's London." *The Secret Malady: Venereal Disease in Eighteenth-Century Britain and France.* Ed. Linda Merians. Lexington: University Press of Kentucky, 1996. 68–84.

Wilt, Judith. "The Laughter of Maidens, the Cackle of Matriarchs: Notes on the Collision Between Humor and Feminism." *Gender and the Literary Voice.* Ed. Janet Todd. New York: Holmes and Meier, 1980. 173–196.

The Whore's Rhetorick: Calculated to the Meridian of London and Conformed to the Rules of Art. In Two Dialogues. London, 1683; New York: I. Obolensky, 1961.

Wiltshire, John. *Jane Austen and the Body: "The Picture of Health."* Cambridge: Cambridge University Press, 1992.

———. "Mrs. Bennet's Least Favorite Daughter." *Persuasions* 23 (2001): 179–187.

Wollstonecraft, Mary. *A Vindication of the Rights of Woman.* Ed. Carol H. Poston. 2nd ed. New York: W. W. Norton & Co., 1988.

"The Woman-Hater's Lamentation," 1707. Ed. Rictor Norton. *Homosexuality in Eighteenth-Century England: A Sourcebook.* <http://www.infopt.demon.co.uk/hater.htm>.

Wordsworth, Jonathan. Introduction. *The Loves of the Plants.* By Erasmus Darwin. Oxford and New York: Woodstock Books, 1991.

Wordsworth, William. "Essay, Supplementary to the Preface [of 1815]." *Romantic Critical Essays.* Ed. David Bromwich. Cambridge: Cambridge University Press, 1987: 29–51.

Wyatt, John. *Wordsworth's Poems of Travel, 1819–1842: "Such Sweet Wayfaring."* New York: St. Martin's, 1999.

Yarwood, Doreen. *Fashion in the Western World: 1500–1990.* New York: Drama Book Publishers, 1992.

Yeazell, Ruth Bernard. *Fictions of Modesty: Women and Courtship in the English Novel.* Chicago: University of Chicago Press, 1991.

Žižek, Slavoj. *The Plague of Fantasies.* London and New York: Verso, 1997.

———. *Tarrying with the Negative: Kant, Hegel, and the Critique of Ideology.* Durham: Duke University Press, 1993.

INDEX

CPSIA information can be obtained at www.ICGtesting.com
Printed in the USA
BVOW071022020712

294156BV00002B/7/P